Lethal Measures

"Goldberg enlivens [*Lethal Measures*] with his formidable knowledge of forensic investigation, creating a graphic but believable foundation for his tale." —*Publishers Weekly*

"Acutely observant . . . a believable thriller with one humdinger of a tension-filled finale." —*Booklist*

"Exciting and intellectually interesting . . . an absorbing tale." —*Library Journal*

"A gripping tale that sails along on the wings of Joanna's Holmesian genius for gory and relentless deductive detail." —*Kirkus Reviews*

"Anyone who enjoys a Patricia Cornwell tale will gain much pleasure from *Lethal Measures*. The medical thriller stars a forensic pathologist with a great sense of self-deprecating humor and that makes her more likable and gentler than Scarpetta. The fast-paced story line has touches of romance that provide a solid counterpoint to the rising tension. . . . Besides the characters seeming real, Memorial Hospital feels like a genuine place and that adds to the believability of the tale. After this story, readers will quickly search for other novels by Leonard Goldberg." —*Midwest Book Review*

Deadly Exposure

"Goldberg has created another exciting story."   —*Booklist*

"A sharply written, edge-of-the-seat thriller."
    —*New York Times* bestselling author Michael Palmer

"Rushes along at a brisk clip."   —*Chicago Tribune*

"A riveting biological thriller . . . a nonstop thrill ride of medical suspense."   —*Lincoln Journal Star* (NE)

"Goldberg mines his considerable knowledge to create a story that will terrify his audience. This is the stuff of nightmares."   —*Library Journal*

Deadly Harvest

"Diabolical . . . a first-rate medical thriller."
    —*Virginian Pilot*

"Excellent . . . a tangled web of a case. . . . Goldberg has the anatomy of ingenious murders down pat."
    —*Kirkus Reviews*

"A page-turner with ample plot twists, medical realism, believable dialogue, and characters who command our sympathies."   —*Charleston Post and Courier*

"Thanks to his clear style and storytelling ability, this is another bell ringer for Goldberg, who, teaching and practicing physician that he is, appends to his yarn a note pointing out how desperate the real organ-transplant situation currently is."   —*Booklist*

continued . . .

FEVER CELL

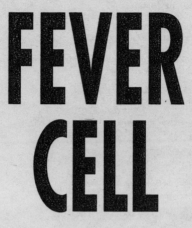

Leonard Goldberg

A SIGNET BOOK

SIGNET
Published by New American Library, a division of
Penguin Group (USA) Inc., 375 Hudson Street,
New York, New York 10014, U.S.A.
Penguin Books Ltd, 80 Strand,
London WC2R 0RL, England
Penguin Books Australia Ltd, 250 Camberwell Road,
Camberwell, Victoria 3124, Australia
Penguin Books Canada Ltd, 10 Alcorn Avenue,
Toronto, Ontario, Canada M4V 3B2
Penguin Books (N.Z.) Ltd, Cnr Rosedale and Airborne Roads,
Albany, Auckland 1310, New Zealand

Penguin Books Ltd, Registered Offices:
80 Strand, London WC2R 0RL, England

First published by Signet, an imprint of New American Library,
a division of Penguin Group (USA) Inc.

First Printing, December 2003
10 9 8 7 6 5 4 3 2 1

In memory of I. M. and our radio days

ACKNOWLEDGMENTS

Special thanks to Jane Jordan Browne, extraordinary agent and friend, who has guided me so well along the literary path.

"Now I have become Death, the destroyer of worlds."
—*Bhagavad Gita*

"Those who appease the crocodile will simply be eaten last."
—Winston Churchill

1

Mojave Desert
California

There was a full moon that April night, with hundreds of twinkling stars. The ghostly light illuminated the long rows of parked passenger jets. From his perch on the motorized lift, Ahmed Hassan could see the names painted on the fuselages: TransContinental, World, National. All of the planes' windows and engines were covered with tape to prevent the desert sand from seeping in. A graveyard for old commercial jets, Hassan thought. Most would be converted into scrap metal, but the six newer 747 jumbo jets lined up side by side would fly again. And soon.

From somewhere in the darkness Hassan heard a clanking noise and was instantly on guard. He peered out into the night and tried to pick up any signs of movement, but saw only the giant shadows cast by the planes. Sweat broke out on his forehead as he envisioned what would happen to them if they were caught. They would be executed, or at the least spend the rest of their lives in prison. Hassan slowly started down the steps of the motorized lift. His friend, Khalil Mahmoud, would have to fend for himself.

The clanking came again, but this time Hassan breathed a sigh of relief. The sound originated from deep within the 747 jet, where his friend was busily working away, performing a task that would guarantee them both a place in paradise. And a life of comfort while they were on earth as well. Each would receive a stipend of $50,000 annually, and if they died as martyrs the payments would go to their families. They would have enough money to buy homes near the Mediterranean, where flowers would grow and cool night breezes would come in from the sea.

Once more Hassan heard the clanking, exaggerated by the stillness of the night. Although no one else was around, the noise still bothered him. Maybe the airlines had hired somebody to check on their planes periodically. Or maybe the manager of the storage facility would decide to make one of his rare late-night visits. A thousand maybes, any of which could cost him his life.

Hassan leaned against the closed door of the 747 and gazed out at the commercial jets stored at the desert facility. All were there as the result of the economic downturn brought on by the events of 9/11. A great day, Hassan thought, his mind picturing the twin towers collapsing into a giant heap of rubble. Over and over he had read the lists of those killed, looking for those with Jewish names. There were some, but not nearly enough. Maybe they would have better luck this time.

The thousands of New Yorkers killed by the suicide bombers didn't bother Hassan in the least. It didn't begin to even the score. After all, how many Muslims were murdered by the Christian Crusaders when they tried to conquer the Arab world? And how many Muslims were slaughtered when the Ottoman empire was crushed by the Western powers? And how many Muslims had been cut down by Israeli guns? How many Muslims were blown to bits by American bombs in Iraq and Afghanistan? Add them all up and the answer would be millions. As far as Hassan was concerned, what happened in New York was just the start of a payback.

Because their planes were flying at only one-third capacity, the airlines in America were forced to cut back their schedules drastically. The grounded 727s and 737s were sent to the desert, where they would be stored and later scrapped. But the newer 747s were treated differently. Immediately upon landing, the jumbo jets had been "pickled," with their fuel and oil drained, and their engines and windows taped over.

That had occurred almost a year ago. That was when Hassan was sent from Seattle to southern California with instructions to apply for a job as a security guard at the Mojave facility. The previous guard had died suddenly and unexpectedly. The Holy Land League had seen to that. Two years earlier, in their infinite wisdom, they had also planted his friend Khalil at the large Boeing plant in Seattle, where he worked on jumbo jets. The two men had roomed together while waiting for their orders.

They were to bide their time and fit in. Although both were devout Muslims, they shaved their mustaches, ate pork, drank alcohol, and visited topless bars. In ethnically diverse Seattle and southern California, the men did not stand out. They had friends and lovers, they went to ball games, their coworkers liked them.

Then the American economy picked up. People began flying again, and the airlines needed their 747s for the growing demand. A day earlier Hassan had learned that the six jumbo jets were to be serviced and fueled and ready to fly within a week. He immediately notified the Holy Land League, and they ordered Mahmoud to take an emergency leave of absence from Boeing—with the excuse that his father had suffered a massive heart attack.

Hassan checked his watch. It was late, much later than he had realized. Another forty minutes and it would be dawn. They were running out of time. He nervously wiped the sweat from his forehead and neck with his sleeve, trying not to panic. Sometimes the guard on morning duty came early, just as the sun was rising. And although Mahmoud was now working on the last 747, they still had many things to do. The door of the plane had to be retaped shut and the motorized lift moved back to its original position in the shed a half mile away. And Mahmoud had to leave the facility so Hassan could lock the front gate and write up his morning report.

The problem was, Mahmoud wasn't even close to finishing up his work on the final 747. Hassan looked down at the small box containing the six slender cylinders, each the size of a large cigar. According to Mahmoud, the cylinders contained a gas that would instantly put all the passengers to sleep, except for those who took an antidote before boarding. The cylinders would be inserted into special devices that would slowly disperse the gas throughout the plane. The devices had small, telescoped antennae that allowed them to be activated by remote control.

Hassan held up one of the cylinders and studied it against the moonlight. There was some lettering in English on the side, but he couldn't make it out. As he brought the cylinder down, it slipped from his hand and fell to the ground below. Hassan prayed to Allah that it hadn't broken, and hurried down the steps of the lift. Using a small flashlight, he searched the area until he found the cylinder.

Allah had not answered his prayer. The cylinder was shattered, its powdery white contents spilled out. Hassan knelt down and closely examined the cylinder and its white powder to see if there were any way it could all be put back together. There wasn't. The cylinder was smashed into tiny bits.

Suddenly Hassan remembered the potent effect of the powder and jerked his head away. He took several deep breaths of the desert air, and, feeling no ill effects, he made a deep groove in the ground with his heel. He pushed the cylinder in and covered it with sand.

He heard the door of the 747 opening and hurried back to the top of the lift.

"Is there trouble?" Mahmoud asked, coughing loudly as phlegm rattled in his throat.

"It is nothing," Hassan said nervously, catching his breath. "I thought I heard a sound. But it was nothing."

Mahmoud carefully studied the ground below, not trusting his accomplice. "You are sure?"

"It was nothing," Hassan said again, then quickly changed the subject. "Why are you making so much noise within the plane?"

"Several panels were put on incorrectly," Mahmoud explained. "I had to pry them off."

"But no one will see what you have done. Right?"

"No one will see." Mahmoud wondered again why the Holy Land League would use an inexperienced man like Hassan for such an important mission. Perhaps because he was so expendable. "Give me the last of the cylinders."

Hassan passed the box over, keeping his hands as steady as he could.

Mahmoud gazed down at the contents, then brought his head up quickly. "There are only five cylinders here. One is missing."

Hassan feigned surprise. "That cannot be."

"See for yourself."

After a careful count, Hassan said, "Maybe there were only five in this box."

"Maybe," Mahmoud said, not believing it for a second. He considered the possibility that Hassan had stolen the missing cylinder. "These tubes can cause death if not used properly. They have no value on the open market."

"Do you believe that somebody stole one?"

"It is possible," Mahmoud replied, turning toward the plane door. "Five will have to do."

Hassan waited for the door to close, then smiled to himself. He had always been a good liar, even when he was a little boy. Lying had gotten him out of trouble a thousand times before. And it had worked again. He could tell that from Mahmoud's expression.

Hassan shrugged his shoulders. So what if one cylinder was missing? Mahmoud himself had said that six cylinders were more than enough to put all the passengers to sleep. And when the passengers were asleep, the guerrilla fighters on board who had received the antidote would take over the planes. They hadn't told him what would happen after that. All he knew was that thousands upon thousands of Americans would die.

The plane door opened and Mahmoud stepped out onto the lift.

"Done," he said matter-of-factly.

Mahmoud had coffee and doughnuts for breakfast, then bought a newspaper to read on the plane trip to Paris. He walked out into the main corridor of the overseas terminal at Los Angeles International Airport, which was now filling up with passengers for the early-morning flights. Mahmoud felt more comfortable in the overseas terminal, where everybody wasn't so white. There were Asians and Africans and Hispanics and a sprinkling of Arabs. Mahmoud was just another foreigner among them. Even the woman who inspected his carry-on luggage didn't give him a second look, despite his clearly Arabic features. Had he been in a domestic terminal, they would have gone over him with a fine-tooth comb. And, of course, found nothing. His weapons of mass destruction had been left behind in America.

Mahmoud glanced at his watch. It was 8:25, an hour and a half before boarding. He double-checked his ticket and his passport with its false identification. When he reached Paris he would visit with his family, then pick up another false passport and travel to Athens, where he would await further orders from the Holy Land League.

He pondered whether or not he should tell his superiors about the missing cylinder. They would want details that he couldn't supply, and that could cause trouble. Better to say nothing, he decided. Because soon he would be the only one aware that a cylinder was missing. Mahmoud knew that Hassan was a doomed man, a recruit needed for only one mission. Now he was a loose thread that needed to be taken care of. Within hours, the Holy Land League would send assassins to kill Hassan and bury his body in a place where it would never be found. If Hassan had the cylinder, it would be buried with him.

Mahmoud began to cough vigorously, bringing up copious amounts of sputum. He went to a nearby trash can and expectorated into it. People passing by gave him disgusted looks. Mahmoud ignored them, now wondering if he should take yet another antibiotic pill. He decided to wait because too much of the Cipro could upset his stomach. And that was the last thing he wanted to happen on his plane trip to Paris. He coughed again, harder this time, and again brought up sputum and spat it into the trash can.

Mahmoud felt the urge to urinate and headed for the nearest men's room. As he entered, he didn't notice the two men in cleaning uniforms just behind him. They put down a

CLOSED FOR CLEANING sign, then pushed their mops and buckets into the men's room.

Mahmoud stood next to another man at a urinal who was finishing up. He paid no attention as the man washed his hands and left. Shaking the last drops of urine from his penis, Mahmoud turned and saw the two cleaning men with Middle Eastern features. Egyptian or Libyan, he guessed. Then he saw their eyes and knew he was a dead man. He started to bolt, but his feet barely moved. They, too, knew his fate was sealed.

The taller of the two assassins thrust a long, thin knife into Mahmoud's chest just below the sternum. Then he expertly pushed the blade up at an angle and ripped open the left ventricular wall of Mahmoud's heart. Mahmoud jerked away from the knife in a violent spasm, then crumpled to the floor. He lay there gasping, picturing his wife and two sons, whom he would never see again.

The tall assassin placed his foot on Mahmoud's chest and pushed up and down, as if he were performing a strange form of CPR. What he was really doing was pumping the blood out of Mahmoud's heart and helping him bleed to death. When he was finished, they quickly dragged the body inside a stall. Moments later they closed the door and set about mopping the tiles clean.

2

Cody Wallace, the manager of the Mojave Motel, groaned when he saw the two Arabs coming through the front door. He didn't like foreigners in general, but Arabs were the worst. They broke fixtures, stained the carpets, and stopped up the plumbing on a regular basis. And they stank.

"Yes, sir," Wallace greeted them. "Can I help you?"

The taller of the assassins said, "We are looking for our friend, Ahmed Hassan. Which room is he in?"

"He was in eight," Wallace answered. "But he checked out this morning."

"Do you know where he went?"

Wallace shrugged. "All he said was that they fired him from his job at the airplane storage place."

The assassin's senses were suddenly heightened. He wondered if someone had discovered that the jumbo jets had been tampered with. "The firing will be bad news to his family. You see, he was sending money back to them regularly."

"Well, he was plenty upset about losing his job, I can tell you that," Wallace went on. "They accused him of playing around with one of those motorized lifts they use out there. He said that was a lie. Swore to it on his mother's grave."

The idiot, the tall assassin was thinking. Not only had Hassan blundered, but he was talking about it to anyone who would listen. "It is important that we find him. His father has become gravely ill."

Wallace shrugged again. "Wish I could help."

"Perhaps we could look in his room," the assassin suggested. "Maybe he left something behind which will tell us where he is."

Wallace thought for a moment, then nodded. "I don't see any harm in that."

The manager led the way out. The day was bright and hot, with the sun beating down on the single row of units that made up the motel. Each unit had a rusty air conditioner in its window.

The manager opened the door to unit eight and entered. The room was littered with empty pizza cartons and crushed soda cans. A small television set with a bent antenna was atop a dresser, and next to it was a stack of Arabic magazines. The bed was unmade, the sheets stained with faded brown spots.

The shorter of the assassins quickly searched the dresser and night table, then the floor underneath the bed. He found nothing. Next he flipped through the magazines and looked under the television set. Again nothing. Finally he went to the wall closet, where a suit and several shirts were hanging. He came back holding a pack of cigarettes with a book of matches tucked under the cellophane wrapping. He handed the pack to the tall assassin.

The tall assassin studied the matchbook cover, which contained an advertisement for a place called Rosa's. "What is Rosa's?"

"It's a Mexican restaurant a couple of blocks down from here," Wallace said. "The food is pretty good."

"Did Hassan go there?"

Wallace nodded. "I saw him there a few times with that Mexican girl he dates."

"Do you know her name?"

"Nope."

"Think!" the assassin urged, and produced a twenty-dollar bill.

Wallace grabbed the bill. "I don't know her name, but I know who does."

"Who?"

"Rosa, the woman who owns the restaurant."

The lunch crowd at Rosa's had thinned out to a young couple drinking margaritas at a corner table. They paid no attention to the two assassins who walked over to a small bar, where an attractive, plump woman with long black hair was going through a stack of receipts.

She looked up at the newcomers and said, "I'm sorry, gentlemen, we are closed until six."

"Are you Rosa?" the tall assassin asked.

"Yes."

"Perhaps you can help us," the man said, sighing wearily for effect. "We are trying to find our cousin Ahmed, whose father has become gravely ill back home. We inquired at the motel where he stays, but he is no longer there. The manager told us that he frequently comes here with his girlfriend."

"Did you say Ahmed?"

"Yes."

Rosa stacked the receipts into a neat pile, then said, "I don't know anyone named Ahmed."

"Please, it is important," the assassin implored, wondering if the fat pig would remember Ahmed if there were a knife at her throat. "He comes in often with his Mexican girlfriend. According to the motel manager, you know his girlfriend."

Rosa furrowed her brow, concentrating, then slowly nodded. "Oh, you must mean Maria."

"Ah, Maria," the assassin repeated.

"I didn't know her friend's name," Rosa apologized. "I have so many customers, you see."

"Of course." The assassin waved away the apology. "Perhaps Maria could help us find Ahmed."

"I'm certain she could."

"How can we get in touch with her?"

"That I do not know."

The assassin took a deep breath and tried to control his anger. "But she is your friend."

Rosa shook her head. "I know her only as a customer. I have never seen her outside the restaurant."

"Could you tell us her last name?"

"Rodriguez, I think," Rosa said hesitantly. "Yes, Maria Rodriguez."

"Do you know where she works?"

Rosa stared up at the ceiling, as if the answer were written there. "I think she works as a housekeeper, but I don't know where."

"Is there any way we could find out?"

"You could ask her," Rosa said. "She comes in every Saturday night at six for our special."

"We will return then."

As the assassins walked out, Rosa called after them, "Would you like me to reserve a table for you?"

The assassins left without answering.

3

Rupert Anderson began writing a multimillion-dollar check. Without looking up he asked, "Should I make it out to Los Angeles Memorial Hospital?"

"That will be fine," replied Simon Murdock, the dean of the medical center.

"Should I say that it's for a forensic DNA laboratory?"

"If you wish."

Murdock leaned back in his swivel chair and watched, thinking that Anderson wrote a check for millions the way most people would write one for ten dollars. But then, when a man was a billionaire, a few million here or there really didn't matter. And the man had billions, with most of his wealth centered around aviation and the metal industry. He was listed among the top hundred wealthiest people in America. Murdock gazed over at the morning sun streaming through the window in his office and wondered if Anderson would accept a seat on the board of directors at Memorial.

"Here you are," Anderson said, and slid the check across the desk.

As Murdock glanced down at the check, his eyes suddenly widened. The amount written was $2,500,000. Momentarily taken aback, Murdock cleared his throat and asked, "Is there another project you would like the additional funds directed to?"

"Two million is to be used to establish the Glen Anderson Forensic DNA Laboratory in memory of my son," Anderson said softly. "The final half million is to fund a faculty position for someone who is an expert in DNA analysis. The endowed position should be named after my late wife, Grace."

"You are most generous, Mr. Anderson," Murdock said. "And again, please accept our condolences on the passing of your wife and son."

"Yes, yes." Anderson nodded briskly, uncomfortable with sympathy. "I'll of course want a voice in who is selected to fill the endowed position."

"You will be consulted every step of the way," Murdock assured him.

"And I'll want veto power," Anderson demanded.

Murdock hadn't expected this. "Oh?"

"That way I can be certain that no one from the Middle East is appointed to the position," Anderson went on. "If that were to happen, my wife would turn over in her grave."

"Surely, Mr. Anderson, you realize that there are some very fine Americans whose ancestors came from the Middle East. It's really not fair—"

Anderson held up his hand, cutting Murdock off. "I'll tell you what's not fair. It's not fair that a bunch of those bastards flew commercial jets into the World Trade Center and killed three thousand Americans. It's not fair that my youngest son was on the eighty-second floor and died with all the others. And it's not fair that my wife decided life wasn't worth living when she learned of our boy's death. And now they're buried side by side and I get to visit them every day and cry as I read their headstones. That, Dr. Murdock, is what's not fair."

The check was still on the desk, but Anderson held his hand firmly atop it. "Now I want your answer. Yes or no?"

Murdock thought quickly. He wasn't about to let those millions slip away. "Suppose we appoint Joanna Blalock the first Grace Anderson Professor of Forensic Pathology?"

"Good!" Anderson agreed. "And what do you propose doing with the money currently being used for Dr. Blalock's salary?"

"We'll appoint a new faculty member with expertise in DNA analysis."

"And that new staff member will not be from the Middle East," Anderson countered.

Murdock steepled his fingers and gazed over them at Rupert Anderson. The billionaire was a big, barrel-chested man in his mid-sixties, with a squared-off jaw and a shock of white hair. The expression on Anderson's face told Murdock that his mind was made up and couldn't be changed. Two and a half million dollars, Murdock was thinking, and it was about to fly out the window. But he couldn't discriminate against Arabs or anyone else. Federal law prohibited it, and Murdock wasn't going to take any chances, not with Memorial receiving over two hundred million dollars a year in grants from the National Institutes of Health.

"Well?" Anderson broke into Murdock's thoughts.

"I cannot give you any guarantees."

Anderson pulled the check back to the edge of the desk and started to pick it up.

"However," Murdock went on quickly, "I could obtain a list of qualified candidates from Dr. Blalock and then narrow the names down to three. Then you and I would choose the best candidate. And if Dr. Blalock agreed, that person would be offered the position."

"So you're saying that you and I will make the final choice?"

Murdock nodded ever so slightly. "From Dr. Blalock's list."

Anderson pushed the check back across the desk. "We'll want a recognized expert on DNA."

"Of course."

"Someone who's older and distinguished."

Murdock hesitated. "I would prefer someone in their thirties or early forties."

"Why?"

"Younger faculty tend to live longer and work harder," Murdock explained. "The older ones are inclined to rest on their laurels."

Anderson considered the suggestion. "Kind of like middle management, eh?"

"Exactly."

"I see your point," Anderson said agreeably. "But we should find someone who has already made important discoveries in the field of DNA. You know, a researcher who has already published . . ."

Murdock appeared to be listening attentively, but he could see the intercom button on his phone flashing. His secretary knew how important his meeting with Anderson was, so the call had to be urgent. Still, he tried to ignore the flashing button.

"I mean, if we could get someone who is bright and aggressive," Anderson was saying, "that person could establish an internationally renowned DNA section within a few years."

"There is no way to predict how long it will take," Murdock cautioned.

"Oh, I know that," Anderson said. "But I'm certain that in medicine, like aviation, there's a fast track and a slow track. I'm interested in the fastest track."

There was a brief knock on the door and Murdock's secretary walked in. "I'm sorry to disturb you, Dr. Murdock, but you have a call from Washington. They need to talk with you now."

Murdock kept his expression even, but he knew that calls from Washington usually meant big trouble. He rose quickly and shook Anderson's hand. "I'm afraid you'll have to excuse me."

"Of course."

"Could I invite you to lunch next week at the faculty club?" Murdock asked, watching the flashing phone button in his peripheral vision. "I'd like very much to have more of your input on this matter."

"I'd be delighted."

"My secretary will make the arrangements."

The secretary came over and handed Murdock a note, then ushered Rupert Anderson out, closing the door behind them.

Murdock read the note. The call was from William Kitt, the director of the FBI's counterterrorism unit. He reached for the phone.

"Simon Murdock here."

"Dr. Murdock, please hold for the director," a female voice said.

Murdock waited, wondering what the call was about and hoping that it wasn't going to involve Memorial with terrorists again. The last time it happened a laboratory was blown up and two people were killed.

"Dr. Murdock, this is William Kitt at the FBI. I believe we've spoken before."

"Indeed we have."

"Another matter has come up which I hope you'll be able to help us with."

"Of course." Murdock reached for a pen and legal pad.

"If you're taking notes, please destroy them after this conversation. Understood?"

"Understood."

"Dr. Murdock, we would like the forensics department at Memorial to perform an autopsy for us. The body is listed as John Doe and has already been transported from the county morgue to your department of pathology. One of our operatives accompanied the body, with instructions to transfer it to Dr. Joanna Blalock and no one else. Dr. Blalock was told only that she would shortly receive instructions regarding an imminent autopsy. We would like Dr. Blalock to perform the autopsy as soon as possible, preferably this morning. All findings and reports are to be given to Det. Lt. Jake Sinclair from the Los Angeles Police Department. He will act as liaison between Memorial and our office."

"Should records of the autopsy be kept on file here?" Murdock asked.

"No," Kitt said firmly. "And we will arrange to have the remains picked up after the autopsy is completed."

"I'm certain Dr. Blalock would like some background information here," Murdock probed gently.

"That will be supplied by Lieutenant Sinclair," Kitt told him. "Suffice it to say, this conversation is highly confidential, and I trust you will keep it that way."

"By all means."

"And, of course, you will be reimbursed for all expenses incurred."

"We have contingency funds to cover costs such as this."

"The FBI thanks you for your assistance."

The phone went dead.

Murdock pushed the intercom button and spoke to his secretary. "Find Dr. Blalock for me."

"Do you want her in your office?"

"Just find her."

Murdock looked down at his legal pad and the few notes he'd scribbled. He tore off the top sheet and passed it through a shredding machine, then began pacing the floor in his office. He hated the idea of Memorial's becoming involved in terrorism again. And it wouldn't matter whether the autopsy was being done on a terrorist or a victim. Either way Memorial could be put at risk. Terrorists didn't like clues of any kind left behind. Memorial had found that out the hard way several years ago, when the dead victims of a terrorist bomb were being studied at the hospital. The terrorists learned about it and blew up a forensics laboratory, killing a policeman in the process. They also murdered a patient who was a potential witness.

Murdock went back to the intercom on his desk and pushed the button. "Well?"

"They're still trying to track down Dr. Blalock."

Murdock started pacing again, glancing out the window at the towering research institutes that surrounded the hospital. Even they weren't immune to terrorism. A year ago a renowned Israeli physician who had done pioneering work in the treatment of ovarian cancer was invited to lecture at the Cancer Research Institute. Someone started a rumor that he had experimented on Palestinian women—which was untrue. But the story spread and some Arab groups protested. A bomb threat was received a day before the lecture. The program went on, but only under heavy security.

The door to the office opened and the secretary stuck her head inside. "Dr. Blalock is in the autopsy room."

"Tell her to stay put," Murdock said, and hurried out.

Murdock took the elevator to the B level and strode down the corridor, still thinking about terrorists and the possible risks they posed for Memorial. He considered asking the police to guard the forensic facilities around the clock, but that would only draw the attention of others. And besides, they had had police guards the last time. Maybe the autopsy could be done in secret. In and out. Fast. With no records kept.

Murdock went through a set of double doors with a sign that read, POSITIVELY NO ADMITTANCE EXCEPT FOR AUTHORIZED PERSONNEL. A secretary talking on the phone looked up and, seeing the dean of the medical center, returned to her conversation. Murdock pushed through another set of swinging doors and entered the autopsy room.

He quickly scanned the brightly lighted area with its eight stainless steel tables, all holding corpses in various stages of dissection. As pathologists worked on the bodies, they spoke into overhead microphones. Their voices filled the air with a low-pitched, continuous hum. Murdock stood on his tiptoes and gazed over at the row of X-ray view boxes mounted on the far wall. Joanna Blalock was pointing out some findings to a small group of residents.

Murdock walked around the periphery of the room, glancing down at the corpses, which always seemed so unreal to him. With their chests split wide open and their thoracic cavities emptied, they looked more like plastic mannequins than humans. He came to the wall that housed the individual refrigerated units where the corpses awaiting dissection were kept. He wondered which one held the FBI's John Doe.

Murdock leaned against the cool wall and waited for Joanna to finish her teaching session. She was pointing to a chest film that had radiopaque particles scattered throughout it. Probably metallic fragments, Murdock guessed.

"Maybe it was an explosion," one of the residents ventured. "You know, like a boiler blowing up."

"Think again," Joanna coaxed.

The resident moved in closer, his nose almost touching the X ray. "It's not an explosion, huh?"

"I didn't say that."

Murdock studied Joanna's profile as she spoke, thinking that she had changed so little in the twelve years she'd been at Memorial. Although she was now forty-two, she could easily pass for being in her mid-thirties. She had soft patrician features, with sandy blond hair that was severely pulled back and held in place by a simple barrette. Her youthful appearance seemed perennial.

When he first interviewed her for the position of forensic pathologist at Memorial, he couldn't believe that someone so young and pretty could be so bright. He thought her letters of recommendation from Johns Hopkins had exaggerated her talents. But they hadn't. She had a quick, penetrating mind that was geared to solve difficult problems. In short order, she established a forensics laboratory at Memorial that was considered among the best in America. She was frequently called in as a consultant for high-profile cases, usually by the LAPD and sometimes by the FBI. Murdock disliked her outside work because he felt it took her away from Memorial too often. He also felt that Joanna was using Memorial's facilities to enrich herself. Her standard fee was $5,000 a case. These arrangements rubbed against Murdock's grain and, at times in the past, he had considered having Joanna replaced with someone who would toe the line and be less independent. But that was not possible now. Joanna Blalock was too valuable to Memorial.

Had it not been for Joanna, Rupert Anderson would have never given millions of dollars to Memorial. Murdock sighed softly as he thought about the pain Anderson must have felt when he lost his son. Murdock knew that pain, for he, too, had lost a son years ago to an overdose of heroin. But at least Murdock had been able to bury his son quickly and bring some closure. Rupert Anderson's sadness had dragged on and on because he couldn't recover his adopted son's remains. Finally, after the last debris from the World Trade Center disaster had been cleared, there were still hundreds of body parts that could not be identified. The authorities obtained toothbrushes and combs and brushes belonging to Anderson's son in an effort to obtain skin or hair or mucous-membrane cells that could provide a source of DNA to match up with the unidentified remains in New York. No such material was found in young Anderson's things.

Joanna was called in and thoroughly investigated the son's life. She learned that he was a member of an athletic club in downtown Los Angeles. But she was told it had already been checked. Joanna went to the club and searched the locker again. In the bottom behind a pair of tennis shoes, she found a used disposable razor. It contained traces of blood and skin. A DNA match was made and the young man's remains were buried next to his mother's. A week later Joanna Blalock received a check for $10,000. She returned the check with a note expressing her condolences. Murdock wondered if he would have returned the check.

"What brings you down here, Simon?" Joanna asked, walking over to him.

"Business," Murdock said, lowering his voice so no one could eavesdrop. "We have to do someone a favor."

"Who?"

"The FBI," Murdock told her. "They want you to do an autopsy on a John Doe from the county morgue ASAP."

Joanna looked over at a corpse on a nearby stainless-steel table. At his feet was a large plastic bag containing his clothes and shoes. "So that's what the mysterious body is all about."

Murdock followed her line of vision and briefly studied the corpse of a thin, balding man with dark, Arabic features. *A terrorist,* Murdock thought sourly, *a goddamn terrorist.*

"The FBI wants everything done confidentially," he said. "Perhaps you could do the autopsy in the special room where contaminated cases are done."

Joanna considered the suggestion and then shook her head. "That always attracts the curious. It would probably be better to do him out in the open and make believe he's just another case."

"What about the dictation on your findings?" Murdock inquired quietly. "We should avoid the general steno pool."

Joanna nodded. "I won't use the overhead microphone. I'll speak into a Dictaphone in my pocket and have my secretary type it. Then I'll destroy the tape."

"Don't make any copies," Murdock instructed her. "And give the original to your Lieutenant Sinclair."

Joanna smiled awkwardly at the phrase *your Lieutenant Sinclair.* She and Jake Sinclair had been lovers off and on for over ten years and had lived together for the past two. But their relationship was over now. It was finished, done. "So Jake is working this case with the FBI?"

"He is their liaison with the LAPD."

"Which explains his message that he is on his way over now."

"Those people don't waste any time, do they?"

The sound of an electric saw cutting through bone filled the air. It was a high-pitched squeal, like a dentist's drill. They waited for the noise to stop.

Joanna's mind went back to Jake and the fight they'd had. Jake hadn't shown up at a dinner party Joanna had held for a dozen guests. There were to be fourteen in all, but they ended up with *thirteen* because Jake wasn't there. He had forgotten. He was tired. He was this; he was that. But most of all he was inconsiderate. And that was Jake's big flaw. That caused all of their fights. And the last fight had been the worst, with yelling and screaming and Jake stomping out of her condominium at midnight. That was a month ago. They hadn't spoken since.

Joanna glanced over at Simon Murdock, who had always disapproved of her relationship with Jake. He considered the homicide detective to be far below her station in life, and he was particularly unhappy when he learned they were living together. Murdock came from the old school and believed couples should marry and then live together—forever. Joanna studied Murdock's chiseled features and snow-white hair. Maybe he was right, she thought. Maybe the old way was better.

The noise of the electric saw stopped abruptly, then started again. It seemed even louder now and more high-pitched.

Joanna stared down at the floor, still thinking about Jake and their failed relationship. It wasn't all Jake's fault. Some of the blame was hers as well. Like Jake, she put her profession first, and everything else was placed on the back burner. Her whole life seemed to revolve around crime. Even with Jake it was mostly crime and criminals. And although the high-profile cases were fascinating and paid well, it didn't leave her time for anything else. Her social life was virtually nonexistent, and the life she did have seemed to be repeating itself over and over again. She was in a rut and she had to get out of it. Breaking up with Jake was a start. Limiting the amount of work she did outside of Memorial was the next move. She was going to free up more time and start traveling and enjoying life, and maybe find somebody interesting to talk to and date and perhaps even marry. And that person wasn't going to be Jake.

Goodness knew Jake was handsome enough, and far more interesting than most people thought. He wasn't just some dumb cop. He could be witty and charming and a great lover, but their relationship wasn't going anywhere. And then there was Jake's past. He couldn't put aside the memory of Elena, a beautiful flight attendant from Greece whom he married and two years later divorced. He was haunted by her tragic death in a car accident outside Athens, believing she would be alive today if they had stayed married. The past was always there for Jake, pulling him back to a world he should have left behind long ago. Maybe that was Jake's real flaw.

The noise of the electric saw whined down, then stopped altogether.

Joanna looked up and pushed the picture of Jake from her mind. She glanced up at the wall clock: 11:25. She was already an hour behind schedule.

"Dr. Blalock," a resident called over, "we've got to run to Dr. McKay's slide review session."

"I'll catch up with you later," Joanna called back.

The resident took one final look at the unusual chest film. "Are you sure the metal fragments in this guy's chest aren't from a boiler or a stove explosion?"

"Do you see any large wounds or scars on his thorax?"

"Not really."

"Then he wasn't around a big explosion."

The resident scratched at the back of his neck. "So what was the source of the metal fragments?"

"It could be a lot of things," Joanna said vaguely. "We'll talk about it later."

Murdock watched the residents file out, then brought his eyes over to the X rays on the wall. He moved in for a closer look. "Are these films from our John Doe?"

"Yes. They came over with the body."

"And you really have no idea where the small metal fragments in his chest came from?"

Joanna ignored the question. "What do we know about this man?"

"Absolutely nothing, except that the autopsy was requested by the FBI's counterterrorism unit."

Murdock gazed down at the nude corpse and studied its facial features. "He looks like an Arab."

"That would be my guess."

"Any idea where he came from?"

"A very rough neighborhood, I'd say."

"Based on what?"

"His X rays."

A young secretary hurried over to Joanna. "There's a Lieutenant Sinclair here to see you."

"Send him back."

Murdock waited for the secretary to leave, then turned to Joanna. "Should I ask the lieutenant for police protection while we're involved with this business?"

Joanna shook her head. "That would only attract more attention. And besides, police guards around the clock didn't help last time."

Murdock rubbed his chin nervously. "Let's just get this damn autopsy over with quickly and arrange things so that it would appear that Mr. John Doe was never here."

The swinging doors opened and the secretary entered with Jake Sinclair a step behind her. She pointed to the rear of the autopsy room, where Joanna was standing.

Jake made his way over. He walked softly for a big man and almost seemed to glide. His footsteps produced no sound.

"Lieutenant," Murdock said formally, nodding but not bothering to shake hands. "I hope we can conclude this matter as quickly as possible."

"That's my plan," Jake said, not liking the arrogant physician, not even a little.

"I'll be on my way then," Murdock told him. "If you require anything at my end, let me know."

As Murdock walked away, Jake turned to Joanna. "How have you been?"

"Fine," Joanna said neutrally. She took a deep breath and lowered her voice. "I want you to pick up your things. I want everything of yours cleared out."

Jake nodded. "First chance I get."

"By this weekend," Joanna insisted.

"I'll call before I come."

That'll be a first, Joanna started to say, but she held her tongue. "Let's get to the business at hand. What's so special about this John Doe?"

"A lot," Jake said, taking her arm and guiding her to a corner of the room, well out of earshot from the other pathologists. Still, he kept his voice barely above a whisper. "This guy was a bunch of people rolled up into one."

"How do you mean?"

"Let's start at the beginning," Jake said, taking out his notepad. "Three days ago the victim was found dead in a men's room in the overseas terminal at LAX. He was sitting upright on a toilet in a closed stall. There was a stab wound in the upper abdomen. He had no wallet, no passport, no ticket. The investigating officer thought it was assault and robbery. The victim was listed as John Doe and taken to the county morgue."

"Was there any blood on the floor?"

"Not a drop. And there wasn't much on him either."

Jake turned to a new page in his notepad. "Anyhow, when the guy arrives at the morgue, they take his clothes off and one of the attendants notices something funny in the shoulders of the victim's coat. In each shoulder pad is a passport with a crisp thousand-dollar bill in it. The French passport says his name is Ziad Nazar, which turns out to be a phony. Ziad Nazar was an Algerian businessman who died in an accident outside Paris four years ago. The second passport was Greek and belonged to Jibril Badawi. That one was phony, too. Nice, huh?"

Joanna walked over to the corpse and studied the stab wound in the upper abdomen just below the sternum. It was small, no more than an inch across, with smooth edges that were covered with dried blood. "So what brought the FBI in?"

"We sent the victim's fingerprints to Interpol in Paris. They matched them with a real nasty character named Khalil Mahmoud, who's a terrorist on their most-wanted list."

Joanna went over to the X rays on the wall and examined the chest film at length. She ignored the metallic fragments scattered within the thoracic cavity and paid particular attention to the left lung field, which was densely clouded over. It contained virtually no air. "What was this guy's specialty?"

"Oh, he was a jack-of-all-trades. He firebombed a Jewish delicatessen in Paris, tried to place explosives on an El-Al plane in Rome, and helped set up the murder of a CIA agent in Athens. And the list goes on and on."

Now Joanna was examining the corpse's facial features. "Do they know where he's from?"

Jake shrugged. "They're not sure. But he usually works with the most radical Arab fringe groups. You know, the ones nobody knows very much about."

"And nobody can control," Joanna added.

"That too," Jake said, and moved in closer. "Tell me what you think so far."

"He's a terrorist who was killed by an expert assassin."

"How do you figure that?"

"The murder weapon was a knife with a long, slender blade," Joanna explained. "That's why the abdominal wound is so small and bled so little externally. The assassin knew what he was doing, too. He pushed the knife up under the sternum and through the diaphragm, then ripped open the heart." She pointed to the chest film. "That's why the left side of his chest is so opaque. It's filled up with blood."

"He died quick, huh?"

Joanna nodded. "Within a minute or two."

Jake touched the chest X ray with his index finger. "What are these little white spots?"

"Metallic fragments that probably came from a hollow-nosed bullet," Joanna told him. "This fellow kept very bad company."

They stopped their conversation as an orderly pushing a gurney approached. He went to a refrigerated wall unit and began extracting the body of a teenage girl killed in a motorcycle accident. She hadn't worn a helmet. The top of her head was shaved off down to the brain.

Jake glanced at the gruesome sight, then returned to his notepad and looked for details he might have left out.

Out of the corner of her eye, Joanna was watching Jake. She was trying not to, but her eyes kept drifting over to him. He was a big man, well over six feet tall, with broad shoulders and rugged good looks. His hair was thick and swept back over his ears. In the bright light of the autopsy room, the gray flecks scattered throughout his hair seemed to sparkle. But it was his eyes that got to her. They were blue-gray, deep-set, and at times peered right into her soul. Joanna forced herself to look away. *It's over,* she reminded herself. *It's over.*

The gurney moved away, carrying the dead teenager to a waiting stainless-steel table.

"So," Jake said, continuing their conversation, "we've got a big-time terrorist who was killed on his way out of America. And the FBI doesn't think he was here on vacation."

"Terrorists," Joanna grumbled, thinking that no place was safe from them. They were everywhere—here, Israel, Europe—just waiting to strike. And there was no good way to stop them. "Who do they think killed him?"

"Probably his own people," Jake answered. "They were the only ones who knew he was here."

Joanna squinted an eye. "Why would they kill one of their own?"

"To make sure he doesn't talk," Jake answered. "The FBI says they do that when they have something big planned. The fewer people who know, the less chance that it will leak out."

"Do they have any idea what this terrorist event is going to be?"

"Not even a clue."

"Christ!" Joanna muttered under her breath. She looked down at the terrorist's hands. His palms were uncallused, his fingernails long and filthy with dirt caked under them. Joanna wondered how many people those hands had killed.

"And that's where you come in," Jake went on. "The FBI wants you to tell them where the terrorist was in America and what he was planning to do there."

"How am I supposed to do that?" Joanna asked. "I'm not a magician."

"Well, you'd better become one fast," Jake said, turning to leave. "Otherwise a lot of people are going to get hurt."

"Don't forget to pick up your things," she reminded him.

Jake was stung by the coldness in her voice. He tried to think of something to say that might smooth things over between them, but nothing came to mind. *Better to say nothing,* he told himself, *than to say the wrong thing.* He didn't want to start another fight. He finally said, "I'll see you around."

Joanna watched Jake walk away, knowing that he would

look back from the door and give her one of his wonderful smiles. And he would expect her to smile back. *Forget that,* she thought. It wasn't going to happen. She had read somewhere that if you stayed away long enough from someone you were attracted to, the attraction faded. Joanna planned to stay away from Jake long enough. And then some. It was time to move on.

She slipped on a pair of latex gloves and turned her attention to the dead terrorist, Khalil Mahmoud.

4

The anthrax patient looked more dead than alive.

"What are his chances?" Joanna asked.

"Nil," said Mack Brown, the director of infectious diseases at Memorial. "If this is pulmonary anthrax, he's got no chance at all."

"Whoever thought that delivering the mail would be a dangerous job?"

The ventilator in the ICU switched on, expanding the patient's lungs and forcing oxygen into them. His chest moved up and down, but his skin color remained deeply cyanotic.

"Will antibiotics help at all?" Joanna asked.

Mack shook his head. "At this stage, all the antibiotics in the world won't save Benjamin Bell."

The ventilator clicked on again, forcing more oxygen into the patient's lungs. Mack Brown reached over and adjusted one of the dials. He was a tall, lanky Texan, middle-aged, with tousled auburn hair and a square jaw. He was named after the famous cowboy film star Johnnie Mack Brown.

"Are you certain he's got anthrax?" Joanna inquired.

"I'll tell you his story. Then you can tell me what you think."

Mack quickly summarized the patient's history. Benjamin Bell was a fifty-six-year-old postal worker from New Jersey who came to Los Angeles five days ago to visit his daughter. On the morning of his departure he felt like he had a cold, with fever, malaise, and a cough. He got better for a few days, then suddenly developed respiratory distress and cyanosis. He was admitted to Valley Lutheran Hospital with the diagnosis of pulmonary embolus. "The doctors figured that on the long plane ride the patient developed thrombophlebitis in his legs and later threw a big pulmonary embolus," Mack explained. "But all the tests for embolism were negative. Then someone noticed his chest film showed a widened mediastinum with pulmonary infiltrates. They quickly did a blood test for anthrax, which was reported to be weakly positive. That's when they rushed the patient over to Memorial."

"It sounds like anthrax," Joanna concluded.

"It sure does," Mack agreed. "Except we repeated the blood test for anthrax and it turned out negative."

"But it could still be anthrax."

"It could be," Mack said. "But you'd have to explain why he's the only case. Why weren't other coworkers infected? Inhalation anthrax doesn't occur as an isolated incident."

"Could he be the first case?"

"We don't think so," Mack replied. "The incubation period for inhalation anthrax is six days minimum. By now other postal workers at the New Jersey facility should have been affected."

"So you're saying it may not be anthrax?"

"I'm saying we've got to be double sure," Mack said cautiously. "If this case is proven to be anthrax, it'll set off a chain of events that will involve thousands of people and cost millions upon millions of dollars. We'll have to determine the source of the anthrax and whether it's bioterrorism or not. Hundreds of postal workers will have to be examined and have nasal swabs done, and most of those will go on Cipro or doxycycline for at least two months. And of course the postal facility will have to be shut down until it's shown to be free of anthrax. And on and on. And if a second case turns up, all hell will break loose."

The patient tried to cough, but the ventilator pushed oxygen into his lungs, cutting the cough short.

"So you can see how important an accurate diagnosis of anthrax is," Mack continued. "And we have to know as soon as possible. That's where you come in. This patient will be dead within seventy-two hours. I'll notify you when he expires so you can do a stat autopsy."

Joanna sighed wearily. "Another stat autopsy."

Mack's eyebrows went up. "You've got another case of suspected anthrax?"

"No, no," Joanna said quickly. "It's an unexplained case of murder."

Mack brought his mind back to the upcoming postmortem examination on Benjamin Bell. "When you perform the autopsy, you should do it in that special room down in pathology."

"Right."

"Use standard barrier isolation precautions," Mack instructed. "There's no need for high-efficiency particulate air-filter masks, or any other measures for airborne protection. But be real careful. And if you think you've been exposed to anthrax in any way, let me know and I'll put you on prophylactic antibiotics."

Joanna gave Mack a long look. "But there's never been a case of human-to-human transmission of this disease. Right?"

"Correct," Mack told her. "But then again, we've never had to deal with such a high grade of anthrax before."

"What do you mean, high grade?"

"The anthrax bacteria in the last outbreak back east was finely ground and very light, so that it would stay suspended in the air for a long time. That way it could infect a whole bunch of people. What I'm saying is that particular anthrax was made by a professional to be used as a biological weapon."

"Christ," Joanna muttered. "So it had to be made by terrorists?"

"Of course," Mack said matter-of-factly. "There's no other explanation. All of the consultants who were called in, including me, agreed on that."

"Did you tell that to the FBI?"

"Damn right we did," Mack said. "But I'm not sure they listened. Those federal boys hear what they want to hear."

"But why does the FBI keep insisting that the anthrax outbreak was caused by some disgruntled laboratory worker?"

Mack shrugged. "Beats me. But this wasn't some pissed-off technician sneaking a little anthrax out of the lab. This stuff was made in a very sophisticated facility that cost really big bucks to run."

"Are you saying that it was government-sponsored terrorism?"

"Had to be," Mack said firmly. "Anyhow, that's why you have to be doubly careful doing that autopsy. You don't want to be the first case of human-to-human transmission of anthrax."

"Amen!" Joanna said, thinking that she'd use a high-efficiency mask, just to be on the safe side.

Mack held the door open for Joanna as they left the isolation unit in the ICU. "The world is really getting screwed up, isn't it?"

"And it's becoming worse by the day."

"You can't even mail a goddamn letter without getting sick."

Joanna nodded slowly. "Mack, do you ever think about moving back to your ranch in south Texas, doing a little private practice, and saying the hell with all this craziness?"

"All the time," Mack said seriously. "All the time."

5

Det. Sgt. Lou Farelli gazed around the interior of the huge mosque. It had a very high, domed ceiling and white walls that were covered in places with Arabic inscriptions. A gentle breeze was coming from somewhere, but it was still uncomfortably warm in the mosque.

Farelli pulled at his collar with an index finger and turned to Jake Sinclair. "I feel like I'm in another world."

"That's because you are," Jake said.

They were standing in the reception area of the King Faisal Mosque, waiting for the imam to appear. People of all colors and ages were streaming by: white, black, brown, old, young. Most were males dressed in Western apparel, although some wore typical Muslim attire. The few women had on dresses that concealed their arms and legs. All had their heads covered with scarves.

"How many times a day do these people pray?" Farelli asked.

"Five, if they're religious."

Farelli pulled at his collar again. "I don't figure our terrorist to be a regular churchgoer."

"You never know," Jake told him. "Some of the worst terrorists are religious fanatics."

"Yeah," Farelli said, nodding. "Like that asshole Osama bin Laden."

A young secretary walked over to them. She was wearing a long white dress and a white scarf over her head. Her skin, even without makeup, was flawless. "The imam will be with you shortly," she said. "Would you care to sit?"

"We're fine," Jake said, thinking that even the religious liked pretty secretaries.

They watched the secretary move through the crowd, her gait more of a float than a walk. The men in the reception area made a conscious effort not to stare at her beauty. Some succeeded; most didn't.

"How do you want to handle the chief rabbi?" Farelli asked in a low voice.

"Nice and easy," Jake answered. "Like it's no big thing."

"They're going to be suspicious."

"Well, we can't help that."

Jake knew the Arab community in America was closely knit. Most had a fear of outsiders in general and law enforcement in particular. Whenever there was an act of terror, they felt they were always the ones unjustly singled out and presumed guilty. Thus, getting information from them was difficult. They didn't want to be involved or even noticed. They only wanted to be left alone.

But, Jake thought, the fact of the matter was that most terrorists were Arabs. And big-time terrorist events, according to the FBI, just didn't happen on a whim. Terrorists didn't simply come over and commit acts of terror. They needed a network to help them. They required supplies and equipment and intelligence and cash and accomplices and safe houses and on and on. And mosques were the largest gathering places for Arabs in America. There was a distinct possibility that someone in some southern California mosque had seen or had contact with Khalil Mahmoud. But finding that individual would be hard, and getting him to talk even harder.

"I'm sorry to have kept you waiting," the imam said, walking over to them. He was a tall man in his early sixties, with a heavily grayed beard and sharp features. "I am Mohammed Malik. How can I help you?"

Jake flashed his shield.

The imam studied it briefly, then sighed wearily. "Not again."

"What happened before?"

"A Jewish day school across the park was vandalized. Somebody sprayed the walls with swastikas and signs that read 'Free Palestine.' And we were considered the only suspects, because we were Arab Americans." The imam sighed deeply again. "I believe that's called racial profiling, Lieutenant."

It's also called good police work, Jake was thinking, but said nothing.

"We were investigated not once, not twice, but three times," the imam went on. "And each time they asked us the same questions."

Jake shrugged. "Maybe they found some new evidence that required them to reexamine things."

"Or maybe they were trying to determine if we would answer the same questions the same way every time."

"That too."

Jake reached into his pocket and took out a touched-up photograph of Khalil Mahmoud. The terrorist looked as if he were still alive. Jake showed the photo to the imam. "Have you ever seen this man?"

The imam carefully examined the photograph. "What has he done?"

"He got himself killed at LAX," Jake replied. "We think

it was a burglary, since all of his belongings were missing. No ticket, no passport, no wallet, no ID."

"So he is the victim?"

"So it would seem," Jake said.

"Does the LAPD always go to this much trouble to identify a victim?" the imam asked suspiciously.

"Only if we want to apprehend the person who killed him."

The imam smiled thinly, then looked back at the photograph. "I have never seen this man before."

Jake turned to Farelli. "You got any questions for the imam?"

Farelli nodded and took out his notepad. "Sir," he began respectfully, "does the mosque here sponsor any social events for men?"

"That is not our role," the imam said stonily.

"What about athletic events, like soccer matches?"

"Again, that is not our role."

Farelli furrowed his forehead, as if deep in thought. "What about Bible— Check that. What about Koran-study classes?"

"We have those," the imam said, warming to the subject. "But your victim was not in attendance."

"What about other religious activities that might attract a visitor?"

The imam stroked his beard, thinking hard.

Jake smiled inwardly at how much at ease the imam was with Farelli. That was partly because of the seemingly innocuous questions on religion. But it also had to do with Farelli's nonthreatening appearance. Farelli was short and stocky, with a round face and a quick grin. People thought he looked like an Italian waiter in a neighborhood restaurant. But Jake knew that Farelli was tough as nails. He was the man you wanted on your side in a fight.

"We have our equivalent of a Sunday school," the imam said finally. "But strangers are usually not present."

Farelli closed his notepad.

Jake asked, "Who usually greets visitors to your mosque?"

"My secretary," the imam replied.

"May we talk with her?"

The imam hesitated for just a fraction of a moment, and then said, "If you wish."

The detectives followed the imam back toward the main entrance to the mosque, then turned into a small reception office. The pretty secretary dressed in white was seated behind a desk. She rose immediately as the men entered.

"Rawan," the imam said, "the detectives would like to ask you some questions."

"Of course," she said in a soft, delicate voice.

Jake handed her the photograph of the terrorist. "Have you ever seen this man?"

The secretary glanced briefly at the photograph, saying, "No."

Jake gave her an appraising stare, as if weighing whether she was telling the truth. "Are you sure?"

The secretary studied the photo again, harder this time.

Jake gazed around the plain white office. There were no pictures or decorations or plants. On the wall behind the desk was a bulletin board with notices and announcements pinned to it.

"I have never seen him," the secretary said firmly.

"If you do, please give us a call." Jake took the photograph back and gave her his card. "Thanks for your time."

They walked out into a warm, overcast day. The sun was barely visible through the clouds, the air heavy with humidity.

Farelli asked, "Do you think he was telling the truth?"

"Not about those meetings, he wasn't," Jake said. "On the bulletin board in that office I saw a notice for some type of Muslim association thing."

"Shit!" Farelli groused. "We ought to go back in there and nail him."

Jake waved away the idea. "He'd just say it wasn't associated with the mosque."

"I think he's holding back."

"Could be," Jake said, nodding. "Maybe we should take a closer look at the old imam. I want you to check out that vandalism case and find out why the cops came back three times. Something must have attracted their attention."

"Gotcha." Farelli jotted down a reminder in his notepad. "And it's probably not worthwhile to ask them to put the terrorist's picture on the bulletin board. It'd stay there all of five minutes."

"And we don't want too many people seeing the photograph anyhow," Jake thought aloud. "The last thing we need is to tip off the terrorist group that we're trying to ID one of their pals."

Farelli nodded. "That could drive them into deep cover."

"Oh, it could do something a lot worse."

"Like what?"

"Like make them speed up their timetable," Jake said darkly.

Haj Ragoub picked up his twin daughters from the private school they attended in Pasadena and drove them to their home ten minutes away. He watched them run across the expansive lawn to the waiting arms of their mother. They waved to him and blew kisses. He did the same, then headed for his electronics store in Glendale.

As Ragoub drove by his comfortable home on a tree-lined street, he was reminded how pleasant America could

be, with its spaciousness and genial people, and how much
freedom he enjoyed with his green card that gave him the
same rights as every citizen, except for voting. Yes, he liked
America, but he hated its foreign policy that gave the go-
ahead to bomb Iraq and Afghanistan mercilessly, slaughter-
ing too many to count. And he particularly hated the policy
that gave Israel guns and F-16 jets and Apache helicopters,
which were used to kill Palestinians and steal their land and
rob them of their dignity. All this to give the Jews a homeland in the Middle East, where they didn't belong in the first
place.

Ragoub turned onto Brand Boulevard, a busy thorough-
fare in downtown Glendale. He went past a row of sky-
scrapers, some going up forty stories or more. Not even half
the height of the World Trade Center buildings, Ragoub calculated in his mind. He remembered the jubilation he had
felt when the nineteen martyrs flew the giant jets into the
towers and destroyed them. *Nineteen of our bravest brought
America to a standstill and cost their economy a half trillion
dollars.*

Ragoub drove down an alley and pulled into a parking
space at the rear of his large electronics store. He entered
through a side door and was delighted to see how good business was. Customers were everywhere, the salesclerks trying desperately to keep up. The store had just received a big
shipment of personal computers and television sets, and now
Ragoub wished he had ordered more. The store manager, a
Pakistani named Shariff, waved happily. Ragoub waved
back as he ascended the stairs leading to the second floor.

At the top of the steps, Ragoub stopped and briefly studied himself in a wall mirror. He was a short, heavyset man,
olive-complected, with deep-set, dark eyes and a receding
hairline. And he was putting on too much weight as a result
of his calorie-rich American diet. But those pounds would

come off when he returned permanently to his home on the
Mediterranean. He was sure of that.

Ragoub sucked in his paunch and walked by unopened
crates and boxes of electronic goods that were stacked to the
ceiling. At the rear was his private office, which was always
kept locked. Only Ragoub had the keys. He entered and,
after punching in a code to deactivate the alarm system, re-
locked the door.

He found a message on his answering machine. It was
from his friend Joe, who was feeling better and would definitely meet him for lunch at *one* o'clock. *One* o'clock sharp.

Ragoub erased the coded message and then hurried over
to the door to make certain it was locked. He came back to
his desk and punched numbers into a handheld remote control. A wall panel opened, exposing a giant television screen.
He pushed another button and moments later a picture appeared on the screen. It showed a soccer match taking place
in England. Liverpool was playing Manchester United.

Ragoub quickly entered a string of numbers into the remote control. This activated the system, which would locate
the position of the six 747s that Khalil and Hassan had
worked on. Each plane had a device that transmitted a signal to the global positioning satellite, which then relayed the
exact locations of the planes back to the giant screen in
Ragoub's office.

The big screen abruptly went blank, then turned deep
blue. A white outline of the United States appeared. In
southern California, five white dots were bunched together
and flashing simultaneously. They were all stationary. A single, blinking dot was over Nevada and moving slowly eastward.

One of the jumbo jets from the Mojave storage facility
was back in service and in the air.

6

Joanna dimmed the lights in the forensics laboratory and projected the first slide onto a large screen. It showed the palms of the terrorist's hands.

"The skin of his palms is fairly smooth," Joanna commented. "No calluses or scars or anything else to indicate heavy labor."

"So?" Jake asked.

"So you'll see why that may be important in a minute." Joanna punched a button on the projector and another slide came onto the screen. It showed the terrorist's fingernails, which were chipped and filthy, with dirt caked beneath them. "His bad hygiene was good for us."

"What'd you find under those nails?"

"This."

The next slide illustrated what appeared to be tiny bits of threads and multicolored fragments of a material with a shiny surface. In some places the material seemed to coat the threads.

"The threads are pieces of copper wiring," Joanna went on. "And the solid material is plastic. Our terrorist wasn't doing any heavy work, but he was playing around with electrical circuitry."

"Are we talking about detonators?"

"Could be," Joanna said thoughtfully. "But our preliminary analysis shows no TNT or C-four."

"I'll still bet it's a detonator," Jake said, more to himself than Joanna. "What else did you find?"

"A lot of dirt that contained a large amount of organic material."

"Like topsoil?"

"Like rich topsoil anywhere," Joanna told him. "We're trying to determine where it came from, but our chances of success here are small."

"So we don't know where this guy was prior to his death?"

"I didn't say that."

The final slide showed the terrorist's shoes, which were made of worn leather and covered with fine red dust.

Jake asked, "Is that clay?"

Joanna shook her head. "The grains measure one to one and a half millimeters in diameter, which is too large for clay. This is sand, which has a very high percentage of silica and very small amounts of organic material. It would be classified as an aridisol."

"What the hell does that mean?"

"It's from the desert."

Jake's eyes narrowed. "Are we talking about Arab deserts?"

After a pause, Joanna said, "I don't think so. His shirt has laundry marks on its collar, and it's cleaner than he is. This suggests he was in America long enough to get his shirt laundered, so most of that desert sand on his shoes—if it did come from Arabia—would have worn off by now. In addition, I found some rich soil caked onto the soles of his shoes, and this was covered with a fine layer of desert sand. So my best guess is that he came to America, date undetermined, stepped in some topsoil, then went to the desert just before he was killed."

"Any idea which desert?"

Joanna nodded. "We obtained sand samples from Arizona, New Mexico, and the Mojave Desert and compared it to the sand on the terrorist's shoes. The best match came from the Mojave Desert."

Jake nodded back. "And since the Mojave Desert is only an hour away from Los Angeles, that would explain why the desert sand didn't have a chance to wear off his shoes."

"That's how I see it."

Jake switched on the lights and began pacing the floor. "What's out in the Mojave Desert that might attract a terrorist?"

"Hoover Dam," Joanna ventured.

Jake considered the possibility, then shook his head. "Too big. They'd need an atomic bomb for that."

"Las Vegas?"

"Not important enough," Jake said. "These bastards are looking for ways to cripple us."

"What about Edwards Air Force Base?" Joanna suggested. "You know, where they land the space shuttle."

"Possible," Jake said after a moment's thought. "But that place is heavily guarded. They'd have a hell of a time getting to that shuttle."

"Unless they had somebody on the inside."

"Yeah," Jake said sourly. "Those bastards could have planted a guy in there. I'd better run that by the FBI."

"You can also tell the FBI that the terrorist was sick at the time of his assassination," Joanna added.

"With what?"

"Moderately severe bronchitis."

"Well, it wasn't bad enough to stop him from flying."

"He may have been improving," Joanna continued on. "We found a high level of the antibiotic Cipro in his blood."

Jake mulled over the new information carefully. "Does the high level of Cipro indicate he took it recently?"

"Within hours of his death."

"And you need a prescription to get this antibiotic. Right?"

"Right."

"Then why didn't we find a bottle of pills on him?"

"I'd guess the assassins took it," Joanna surmised. "A prescription would have had his name and other identifying features on it."

Jake exhaled wearily. "These guys were really careful."

"And they were very good with a knife too." Joanna reached for her slides and placed them in a large manila envelope, then handed it to Jake. "My typed report on the terrorist is in here as well. You can tell the FBI to pick up his clothes and remains anytime today. As far as Memorial is concerned, this John Doe never existed."

Jake hesitated uncomfortably and searched for the right words. "You, ah, you want to have dinner this weekend?"

"I want you to clear your things out of my condominium this weekend," Joanna said straightforwardly.

"There's no way we can talk this through, huh?"

"The talking is over, Jake."

Jake took a deep breath, again searching for words. "Look, I know I screwed up. I know I was wrong. I—"

"It's not a matter of right or wrong," she cut him off. "It's just not working. I'm tired of fighting and arguing over why you didn't do this or why I didn't do that. But I could still live with that. What I can't live with is the fact that we're standing still. Year after year nothing in our relationship changes, nothing happens. We just stay in the same place."

"Are you talking about a commitment?"

"I hate that word," Joanna said, raising her voice. "It sounds like something you have to do in order to keep a relationship going."

"What the hell do you want?" Jake snapped.

"I want you to leave," Joanna told him calmly. "And I want to get on with my life. I want some of my life to be away from corpses and murder. I want a real family, I guess."

"So it's your biological clock we're talking about?"

"It's my goddamn life clock," Joanna countered angrily. "I'm forty-two, which means my life is half over. Next thing you know it'll be sixty percent over, then eighty percent. And you'll still be coming and going, Jake. Because that's what you do. Come and go."

Jake stared at her, thinking she was so damn gorgeous, even when she was angry. "Do you want to think this over for a little while?"

"I already have."

"If I leave, I won't come back."

"Just make sure you call before you come over for your things."

Jake headed for the door, then angrily spun around. "You always talk about commitments, but you've never made one, have you? You wait for the other person to do it."

"What the hell are you talking about?"

"I'm talking about the fact that you're beautiful and bright and sexy. And yet you've never been married."

"But you have. Right?"

"Damn right!"

"And it lasted all of two years," Joanna went on. "And do you know why it lasted only two years? Because you kept coming and going, and never thinking about the other person."

"Bullshit!"

Joanna turned away, saying, "Make sure you call before you come over this weekend."

7

"I think I've got the flu." Ahmed Hassan shivered.

"You look real sick," Maria Rodriguez said, concerned.

Hassan pulled the blanket up to his chin as another chill swept through his body. He had never felt this bad, never in all his life. The chills and fever had come on suddenly an hour ago, and now his head hurt so much he could barely stand it. His whole body seemed to ache.

"Could you draw down the shade?" Hassan requested weakly. "The sunlight bothers my eyes."

Maria sat on the edge of the bed and touched Hassan's sweaty, hot brow. "Maybe I should get the doctor."

"No," Hassan said at once.

"He won't mind." Maria walked over to the window and lowered the shade. "He has helped my friends before without charging. Let me get him."

"No," Hassan said, and turned his back on her.

They were in a small guesthouse at the rear of a retired doctor's home, where Maria worked as a maid. The doctor was dying of prostate cancer and rarely left the house, but he still received drug samples from the pharmaceutical companies and would occasionally treat the people who worked for him and their friends. He was a gruff old man, but he was always kind and generous to Maria. And he never interfered with her social life. He knew she brought her boyfriends back to the cottage and never complained. Once he even treated Carlos from Tijuana for tonsillitis.

Maria sighed to herself, thinking about Carlos, who had promised to marry her when he returned from Mexico. He never came back. She looked over at Hassan, who was now sweating profusely.

"Would you like some water?" Maria asked.

Hassan shook his head as he tried to devise a way out of the predicament he was in. Not only was he sick, but he had screwed up the job that the Holy Land League had assigned him. The people at the storage facility had fired him because they discovered he had moved the motorized lift. They thought he had just been joyriding to pass the time. But suppose they investigated later and found that the 747s had been tampered with? Just suppose? Then the planes would be grounded and the great attack would never occur. And more important, his employers would send the police to look for him. And if they caught him, he would spend the rest of his life in prison.

His fever started to climb again as Hassan tried to think through his problem. Maybe he should make a run for it. Get out of America. Yes, that might be best. But first he would have to contact the Holy Land League.

"Let me get the doctor," Maria urged.

"No," Hassan said with finality. "I will be fine."

Then the chills returned. Hassan shook so hard his teeth chattered.

The two assassins sat at the bar at Rosa's and waited patiently. They talked enthusiastically about an upcoming soccer match, but every time the door to the restaurant opened, they quickly studied the newcomers.

It was just after seven, and all the tables were occupied. The only vacant seats were two stools at the bar. The air was filled with the sounds of gaiety and laughter. A flamenco guitarist was playing from his chair in the corner.

The taller assassin glanced up at the wall clock and then over to Rosa, who was pouring sangria into glasses at a nearby table.

"Do you think the fat whore was telling us the truth about Hassan?" he asked quietly.

His companion shrugged. "Why would she lie?"

"But Hassan and the girl were supposed to be here by now."

"Maybe they decided not to come."

"Maybe they were warned."

The taller assassin put a smile on his face and signaled Rosa over. With each step she took, her ponderous breasts bounced up and down. *Like a cow's,* the assassin thought.

"Yes?" Rosa asked pleasantly.

"Our friend seems to be late."

Rosa nodded. "And that is very unusual. If anything they arrive early, before the others."

"So you don't think he will come?"

Rosa gestured with her hands. "That I cannot say. But they are never late." She pointed to the bartender. "You can ask José. He makes special margaritas for Maria."

The assassin turned to the bartender. "What is so special about Maria's margaritas?"

"Very little salt," José said. "She does not like the salt."

"And you have made these drinks for her over a long period of time?"

"Two years or more."

"So you must know her?"

José hesitated a moment, then said, "We talk about our families in Mexico, about our jobs."

The assassin saw his opening. He saddened his face and told the bartender about the illness of Hassan's father and how sick he was and how important it was for Hassan to be located. "We thought we might see them here, but he has not shown up."

"The father is dying?" José asked sympathetically.

The assassin nodded. "And it is a son's duty to see his father before death takes him away."

The bartender nodded back solemnly. "A sacred duty."

"Maybe Maria could help us find Hassan."

"It is possible."

"Do you know where we can contact Maria?" the assassin probed.

The bartender shrugged. "I only see her here."

"Perhaps we could reach her at her work," the assassin coaxed. "What type of job does she have?"

"She is a housekeeper."

"Where?"

"That I do not know, señor," Jose said honestly. "All she told me was that she worked for a doctor."

The assassins paid their bill, leaving a generous tip, and hurried out of the restaurant.

8

"Why do you think this guy had anthrax?" Dr. Lori McKay asked.

"Because he was a postal worker who had respiratory distress and died quickly," Joanna replied, then pointed to the chest X ray on the view box. "And he also had widening of the mediastinum."

Lori briefly studied the X ray. The mediastinum, the thoracic area between the left and right lungs, was definitely widened, and there was no evidence of pneumonia. The findings were characteristic for pulmonary anthrax. "Do you believe he's got it?"

"Maybe."

Lori squinted an eye. "Is there some clue that says he might not have anthrax?"

"Maybe," Joanna said again. "If I were you, I'd carefully check his external features."

Joanna leaned back against the cool wall and took the weight off her feet. It was four o'clock and she was dead tired from a heavy Monday workload that had started at seven. That was when she received the phone call from Mack Brown, who informed her that the suspected case of anthrax was in extremis. The patient's progressive shortness of breath had worsened, and he had become deeply cyanotic. It took Benjamin Bell another six hours to die.

Lori McKay, an assistant professor of forensic pathology, was now examining the corpse's skin with a magnifying glass. She paid close attention to the faded tattoo on his forearm. "I don't find very much, except for the fact he's skinny," Lori said finally.

"Has he always been skinny?" Joanna asked.

"I'm not sure I can tell that from a postmortem examination."

"Sure you can," Joanna coaxed. "Feel the tattoo and the tissue beneath it."

Lori palpated the area and easily picked up the skin, which was so loose and wrinkled the tattoo was hard to discern. "He's lost a lot of subcutaneous fat, which means he's lost a lot of weight."

"Recently?"

Lori gazed over the corpse, now noting the sunken eyes and other signs of cachexia. "This kind of weight loss takes time."

"And what does that tell you about the possibility of anthrax?"

Lori sighed to herself, wondering if she'd ever get her brain to work half as well as Joanna's. "He supposedly had been sick for the past six days. It took him a lot longer than that to lose all this weight. He must have had some disease in addition to anthrax."

"Or some disease *other* than anthrax."

"There's one way to find out," Lori said, and reached for a scalpel.

They were standing in the special autopsy room where contaminated cases were done. Both women wore caps, gowns, masks, and goggles, although Joanna knew there was no scientific evidence to show that anthrax could be spread from patient to patient or patient to doctor. Still, Joanna thought again, she didn't want to be the first case.

Joanna stretched her legs and tried to get the weariness out of them. Again she glanced at the wall clock. Now it was 4:10 and she still had at least four hours of work waiting on her desk. There were phone calls to answer, letters to dictate, slides to review. And then there was Jake's stuff in her condominium, which he still hadn't picked up. *Damn it!* And he promised he would. But that was Jake. He came and went as he pleased. Well, let him find someone else to do that with.

"Here we go," Lori said, breaking into Joanna's thoughts. She grasped the cut edges of the sternum and pulled them apart, exposing the pink lung tissue. With care, she gradually teased open the space between the left and right lungs, then gazed down at the mediastinum. "I'll be damned!"

"What?" Joanna asked.

"Look!"

The mediastinum was filled with malignant tissue. Lymph nodes and lungs were so plastered together it was difficult to tell one from the other. And there were large areas of hemorrhage scattered throughout the tumor mass.

"I'll bet its bronchiogenic carcinoma," Joanna said.

Lori nodded. "That's why he had all that weight loss. He'd been sick for a long while."

Joanna pointed to the extensive hemorrhagic areas in the cancerous growth. "It was really the hemorrhaging that widened the mediastinum so much."

Lori nodded again. "Just like in pulmonary anthrax."

Joanna stripped off her gloves. "Would you mind finishing up here?"

"Not at all."

"And make sure you culture everything for anthrax, although I doubt you'll find it."

"Will do."

"I'll catch you later."

As Joanna turned to leave, Lori called after her. "By the way, some shoe company called in a report they said you wanted."

"What did they say?"

Lori knitted her brow, thinking back. "That the shoe was foreign made, but they didn't know where. And that the heel was manufactured by a company in America."

"Good," Joanna said, nodding to herself.

"What's that all about?"

"Just a project I'm working on," Joanna said evasively, and left the room.

Joanna wriggled out of her surgical gown and discarded it in a clothes bin, then hurried down a long corridor, heading for her office. Her stomach growled audibly, reminding Joanna that she had skipped lunch and breakfast too, except for a piece of fruit. And dinner would probably consist of a cold sandwich from the hospital cafeteria. She promised herself for the hundredth time that she was going to slow down and rearrange her schedule before a big myocardial infarction did it for her.

Joanna entered her office and waved to her secretary. "Get Mack Brown on the phone for me, please."

The secretary reached for the telephone. "You have a visitor in the forensics lab."

"Who?"

"Lieutenant Sinclair."

Joanna sighed wearily. "What does he want?"

"He didn't say."

Joanna walked through the front laboratory, removing her surgical cap and patting her hair in place. She had a sudden urge to stop in her office and check her makeup and brush her hair, but quickly decided not to. *To hell with it!* She wasn't going to primp for Jake Sinclair anymore.

Joanna opened a door and stepped into the forensics laboratory. Jake was sitting on a countertop with a cup of coffee in one hand and a cigarette in the other. He gave her one of his million-dollar smiles. And as always, she wondered how his teeth stayed so white despite their constant exposure to coffee and tobacco. *Why couldn't you be ugly, Jake Sinclair? It would make things so much easier.*

"I hope this visit is professional," Joanna said evenly.

"It is," Jake replied.

"Good." Joanna sat in a swivel chair and leaned back. "Before we get down to business, I've got a question."

"Fire away."

"Why didn't you pick up your things from my condo yesterday, like you promised?"

"I was going to," Jake said, crushing out his cigarette in an ashtray. "But I stopped by the Farellis' for a drink and lost track of time. It was their twentieth wedding anniversary."

"You should have mentioned their anniversary to me," Joanna said softly, as she thought about the Farellis and their children and their silly bloodhound, Sniff. "You should have mentioned it."

"I didn't know we were still talking—on a social level, I mean."

"Ah-huh," Joanna muttered, not believing him. Jake always had an excuse for his faults. She made a mental note to send the Farellis a belated anniversary card. "So what brings you to Memorial?"

"Two things," Jake said, all business now. "First, I'm going to fill you in on some new information about the dead terrorist we're tracking. Second, the FBI has a question they hope you can help them with."

The door to the laboratory opened, and the secretary stuck her head in. "Sorry to bother you, Dr. Blalock, but no one is answering the phone in Dr. Brown's office or lab. They may have left early."

"Have the hospital operator page him." Joanna waited for the door to close, then turned back to Jake. "So what's new about Khalil Mahmoud?"

"His shirt," Jake said, and lit another cigarette.

Joanna gave him a disapproving look. "You've got to stop smoking, Jake. You're killing yourself."

"I know," Jake said, inhaling deeply. "Anyhow, you remember the guy's shirt, right?"

Joanna nodded. "It was cheap, cotton and polyester, with a brand name we couldn't track down."

Jake took out his notepad and began thumbing through pages. "The brand name was Goodfit. According to the FBI, it was made in China and shipped to America unlabeled. The chain of discount stores that sells them puts in its own brand name. That's why you had trouble tracing it."

"Where is this chain of discount stores located?"

"In the Northwest," Jake answered. "Most of their stores are in Washington and Oregon."

Joanna slowly nodded. "So that's where our guy lived?"

"That's what the FBI thinks," Jake told her. "But there's no way to determine which store sold the shirt to the terrorist."

"And it's going to be impossible to track down the laundry marks on that shirt."

"So we're left with the entire Northwest, which is a big as hell area."

"What would attract a terrorist to the Northwest?" Joanna asked thoughtfully.

Jake shrugged. "A million different things. It has big ports and bridges and military installations and factories and dams and on and on."

"And the Space Needle in Seattle," Joanna added.

Jake growled under his breath. "Those bastards would love to take that down."

"It's like looking for an ant in the forest," Joanna said disconsolately.

"And until we know where he lived, we'll never find out what he was planning."

"It has to be something big," Joanna mused. "Otherwise they wouldn't have sent one of their most experienced terrorists."

"Oh, it's big, all right," Jake agreed. "And in order to prevent it, the FBI needs to know who, what, and when. They're working on the who and what. They need your help on the when."

Joanna looked at Jake quizzically. "How could I determine when they plan to do it?"

"The FBI is talking in general terms," Jake explained. "They'd like your best guess as to how long he was in this country."

"How will that help them decide when the event is scheduled to occur?"

"Their line of thinking goes this way," Jake went on. "Really big acts of terror require a lot of planning. We're talking months and months here. So if our terrorist was in America for only a few weeks, it was probably just to get things set up. If, on the other hand, he was here for months and months, chances are the entire operation is ready to go."

Joanna let the new information sink in, then said, "So if the terrorist lived here for a few weeks, the event will probably be months away, which gives the FBI time to uncover the plot."

Jake nodded gravely. "And if he lived here for months, the act of terror is going to happen real soon, like maybe tomorrow or next week. That may be why our terrorist was leaving America—to get the hell out just before the big event occurs."

Joanna rocked back in her swivel chair, going over all the bits of evidence at hand. "The laundry marks won't help here. They could have been made weeks or months apart."

"The FBI says that too."

Joanna was now concentrating on the terrorist's autopsy. None of the findings would set a timetable, as far as Mahmoud's recent past was concerned. The scarred bullet wound was very old, the stab wound very new. Her gaze drifted over to her desk and the phone report Lori had scribbled down, regarding the terrorist's shoes. A shiver ran through Joanna's body. "The FBI has no time."

"What!" Jake came off the countertop. "Are you sure?"

"It's a guess," Joanna admitted. "But it's a damn good one."

"Tell me about it." Jake extinguished his cigarette, then turned to a new page in his notepad and reached for a pen. "And go real slow."

Joanna read the handwritten note twice, making certain there were no discrepancies between Lori's spoken and written words. "The terrorist was wearing well-worn shoes that looked like they hadn't been polished in months. The heels on the shoes were worn down as well and would have to be replaced in the near future. The shoes were foreign made, with a style that suggested they were manufactured somewhere in Europe. The heels were definitely made in America."

Jake quickly put the pieces of the puzzle together. "So you figure he had those heels replaced at least once in America?"

Joanna nodded. "And since those American heels were well worn down, I think it's safe to assume that he was here for months."

"How many months?"

"If he wore those shoes every day and did the usual activities, I'd say it took approximately six months to wear those heels down that far."

"Son of a bitch," Jake growled.

"Of course, it's just a guess," she reminded him.

"Yeah, but it rings true." Jake jotted down the information and closed his notepad. "I'd better let the FBI know."

Joanna's stomach made a loud, rumbling noise. She smiled faintly. "I forgot lunch."

Jake studied her pretty face and soft features, resisting the urge to grab her and hold her close and tell her how much she meant to him.

Joanna stared back at him. "Is something wrong?"

Jake shook his head. "I was just wondering if you had time for a quick hamburger at Big Bob's."

Joanna tried to say no, but couldn't bring herself to do it. Big Bob's was their favorite place—or used to be—for delicious hamburgers served with French fries and onion rings. There was always a big bowl of catsup on the table, and the patrons ate everything with their hands. And the beer was always ice cold. She was about to say yes to the invitation. But it was going to be only hamburgers and beer, and nothing more. And afterward she'd remind Jake to pick up his things from her condominium. "Well, I—"

The door to the forensics laboratory opened and the secretary stepped in. "Dr. Blalock, I finally found Dr. Brown," she said. "He's on the loading dock behind the hospital waiting for a patient. If you need to see him, that's where he'll be."

Joanna got to her feet. "I'm on my way."

"And he said to tell you to wear a surgical mask."

Joanna reached into her desk drawer for a mask and a

pair of latex gloves. "I've got to run, Jake. If the FBI needs more information on the shoes, tell them to call me later."

"I'll try to pick up my things tonight."

"Good."

Joanna dashed out of the laboratory and down a long corridor that led to the freight elevator. Slipping on her latex gloves, she wondered what sort of patient Mack Brown was waiting for. Most patients—even those with serious infectious diseases—were usually admitted to the hospital via the ER. The fact that Mack was awaiting this case on an isolated loading dock indicated that the person had some grave, highly contagious illness. Joanna put on her surgical mask and tied it securely.

She stepped into the empty elevator and pushed the button for the first floor. As the elevator slowly ascended, her mind drifted back to the last time she was on the loading dock with Mack Brown. They were fully capped and gowned and wearing masks and goggles, awaiting the arrival of Joanna's younger sister, Kate, from Guatemala. Kate had contracted a deadly virus while on an archaeological dig and was being airlifted to Memorial's Viral Research Center for specialized care. The center was a self-contained unit that had been built in the basement of Memorial Hospital over twenty years ago and continually updated ever since. Its purpose was to serve as a backup for the United States Army Medical Research Institute for Infectious Diseases, the government's major viral research center. Like USAMRIID, the facility at Memorial studied some of the most virulent viruses known to man. It also had four isolation beds for patients infected with contagious lethal viruses.

Joanna shivered to herself, remembering how close Kate came to dying in one of those beds. The elevator jerked to a stop. Joanna retied her surgical mask as tightly as she could.

She got off the elevator and waved to Mack Brown, who was wearing a cap, mask, gloves, and gown.

"Where's your gown?" Mack yelled over.

"My secretary didn't mention a gown," Joanna yelled back.

Mack pointed to a table that held neat stacks of surgical attire. "Put one on and tuck the ends of the sleeves under your gloves."

Joanna wriggled into a surgical gown. "What have you got?"

"Possibly a false alarm."

"You're going to a lot of trouble for a false alarm," Joanna said, noticing that the entire loading dock was roped off. On the far side a nurse wearing protective gear was adjusting an IV pole attached to a sheet-covered gurney.

"Some retired doc in the Mojave Desert thinks he's got a case of Ebola fever," Mack told her, shaking his head in disbelief. "Ebola fever in the middle of the desert? Now, that's a first, isn't it?"

"Is the patient from Africa?" Joanna asked.

"Nope," Mack said. "And he's never visited there or been in contact with anyone who's been there recently."

"Then it's not Ebola."

"That's what I told the doctor," Mack went on, chuckling softly to himself. "So the old fart tells me, 'Great! I'll go inform the patient not to worry about his rash and chills and fever of a hundred and four.' "

"Does the patient have hemorrhages?"

"All over," Mack replied. "And according to the old doctor, they look exactly like the hemorrhagic rash of Ebola that he's seen in the medical journals."

"So it could be Ebola."

Mack shrugged. "A lot of diseases can present with fever

and a hemorrhagic rash. Like gram-negative sepsis and meningococcemia, just to name a couple."

"But it could still be Ebola."

"Anything is possible." Mack pulled down his surgical mask and breathed in the cool late-afternoon air. In the distance he could hear a siren. He pulled his mask up and turned back to Joanna. "What brings you to the low-rent district?"

"Your supposed case of pulmonary anthrax."

"And?"

"It ain't." Joanna told him about the bronchiogenic carcinoma that had invaded the mediastinum and caused hemorrhaging into it. "That's why the mediastinum was widened."

Mack nodded. "And that's why the blood test for anthrax, which was reported to be weakly positive elsewhere, was negative here. The first test must have been a false positive."

"And the reason he was so short of breath was that the tumor mass was pressing down on the large bronchi."

Mack sighed unhappily. "There used to be a time when a postman with a cough was thought to have a cold. Now our presumptive diagnosis is anthrax delivered by some goddamn terrorist."

The sound of the siren grew much louder. Mack gazed out to the rear of the lot behind Memorial, where a security guard was opening the gates for an approaching ambulance. "We have to make doubly sure that he doesn't have anthrax on top of his bronchiogenic carcinoma."

"I know," Joanna said. "Lori McKay will culture everything, looking for the anthrax organism. We'll also make slides of the lungs and search for the bug."

"And have her do gram stains on the patient's bronchial washings."

"We do that routinely in patients who die from pneumonia."

"If you find anything that resembles the anthrax microorganism, give me a buzz so I can check it," Mack requested. "And don't release the body or any organs until all the studies are completed."

"Do you think you'll want further tests?"

"No," Mack told her. "But if it's anthrax, we'll want to cremate everything to prevent further transmission."

"I checked his chart and he's Jewish," Joanna said. "I don't think they allow cremation."

"If it's anthrax, they may not have any choice."

The ambulance pulled up to the loading ramp and its rear door opened. A young black attendant jumped out. He was dressed in white, with a stethoscope around his neck. The ambulance driver came around and helped the black attendant pull a gurney out and extend its legs.

The gurney came up the ramp, the driver pushing, the attendant pulling. Mack and Joanna stepped in for a closer look.

"He's in bad shape," the attendant said. "Half the time he's talking out of his mind. He keeps yelling out for *nacbar* or something like that."

Mack lifted the sheet and peered down at the gurney. It held a young, dark-complected man with Middle Eastern features. His mouth was open, his eyes rolled back and staring into nothingness. A black, hemorrhagic rash over his chest and neck extended up to his mouth. Dark blood was caked around his lips and nostrils. Mack noted the small pustules scattered everywhere over the patient's trunk and face. Using a tongue blade, Mack separated the patient's lips and saw that the pustules extended onto the mucous membranes.

The patient suddenly dry heaved. Then he heaved again

and brought up a large amount of black vomitus that sprayed through the air. Everybody threw up their hands instinctively, trying to protect their faces. He retched once more, but only a little spittle came up.

Mack rapidly surveyed the medical personnel around the gurney. Everyone had bloody vomitus on them. The white uniforms of the ambulance driver and attendant were heavily stained with red and black blotches. They also had some on their faces. But he and Joanna and the nurse had gotten the worst of it. Their gowns were soaked with putrid gastric contents, as were their gloves and shoes. And Joanna had some of it on her forehead.

"Quick! Everybody into the elevator!" Mack ordered urgently. "Now!"

As the gurney was pushed into the freight elevator, Joanna asked, "What do you think he has, Mack?"

"A nasty virus."

Joanna's eyes widened. "Ebola?"

"No."

"What then?"

"I can't be sure," Mack said, aware that the others were listening in. But he was sure. He knew all about the virus—its history, characteristics, its devastating effect on mankind over the centuries. Where the hell did it come from? Mack asked himself. The virus was supposed to be extinct in nature, but here it was in the middle of Los Angeles.

As the elevator began to descend, Mack became aware of a peculiar taste in his mouth. After a few seconds he realized what it was. He was tasting the bloody, virus-laden vomitus that had landed on his mask and soaked into it. Terror flooded through him. In his mind's eye he could see the deadly smallpox virus entering his oral cavity and spreading to every part of his body.

The elevator jerked to a stop. As the door opened, Mack glanced around at the others, all heavily contaminated with the smallpox virus. He wondered if any of them would ever see the light of day again.

9

Jake and Lou Farelli were sitting in an unmarked car across the street from a small grocery store in West Hollywood. The store was run by a Pakistani who owned the building and rented the second floor to the Holy Land League. The lights on the second floor were on.

"So this league's a charity, huh?" Farelli asked.

"That's what they claim," Jake said. "But according to the FBI, the league is just a front that funnels money to terrorist groups in the Middle East."

"Why don't they nail those bastards and ship them out of here?"

"Because the FBI thinks this bunch will eventually lead them to the entire network."

"How big is this league?"

"They're in at least a dozen states."

"Shit."

The door to the second floor opened, and two teenagers with Middle Eastern features stepped onto the sidewalk. They were talking loudly, giggling at something. They went into the grocery store and moments later came out carrying cartons of soft drinks and large brown bags. Then they went back up the stairs.

Jake watched the two teenagers disappear. "It looks innocent enough, doesn't it?"

"Maybe they're just errand boys," Farelli suggested.

"Or maybe the league is just teaching them young." Jake reached for a handheld tape recorder and switched it on. "This tape was made by an FBI plant at one of the league's meetings. Listen to the crap they spew out."

There was a long run of static; then a male voice with a Middle Eastern accent came on.

"Yet another bomb was exploded in Jerusalem today, and eight Jews were killed."

There was loud applause, with yells of jubilation.

"And fifty more were badly wounded."

The applause came again, louder this time.

"And the brave young woman who martyred herself today will be welcomed in paradise."

"Kill the Jews! Kill the Jews!"

"And death to those who support them!"

Jake switched off the recorder. "And this tape wasn't made in Syria or Iraq or the West Bank. It was made right here in Los Angeles."

"Those assholes," Farelli growled. "Does the FBI know the names of the people on that tape?"

"They know one."

"Yeah? Who?"

"The imam's son."

Farelli's face went stone cold. "This guy really gets around, doesn't he?"

"Like how?"

"Like he's the reason the cops went back to the King Faisal Mosque three times to investigate the vandalism at that Jewish school."

"Give me the details."

Farelli told Jake about Yusef Malik, the only son of the

imam and a known Arab extremist. Now thirty years old, Yusef was a perennial student who moved from one college to the next in southern California, never graduating but always espousing radical Muslim causes. "Yusef Malik is a real sweetheart," Farelli concluded.

"And he's a player too," Jake added. "He likes women, booze, and nightclubs."

"So he's not such a good Muslim, after all."

"Maybe, maybe not," Jake said. "According to the terrorism experts, when these guys want to fit into our culture they can drink and raise hell, and it's not considered a sin by their religious leaders. You see, they're doing it for a noble cause."

"Kind of like a dispensation, huh?"

"I guess."

Jake settled back in his seat and studied the West Hollywood neighborhood, located just off Sunset Boulevard. The area had once been upscale and middle-class, with fashionable shops and expensive restaurants and apartment houses that everybody wanted to live in. But that had all changed now. Everything had turned seedy, with littered streets and drug dealers on every corner and prostitutes on every curb. Gangbangers rode past in their low-riding cars, music blasting, cruising up and down the boulevard looking for action. The crime rate was soaring, the tax base shriveling up. "This whole area is turning into a giant shithole," Jake commented.

"It used to be nice around here," Farelli reminisced. "You know, with coffeehouses and outdoor restaurants and everything. This is where I proposed to Angela."

"Man! That must have been a while ago."

"Twenty years," Farelli told him. "She was a nurse at Cedars-Sinai, working the three-to-eleven shift. We used to meet down here when she got off."

"Twenty years, huh?"

Farelli nodded. "This coming Thursday."

Jake glanced over at his partner, wondering why marriage seemed to suit some people so well and others not at all. "So that little party you gave on Sunday was just a warm-up?"

Farelli nodded again. "This Thursday I'm going to take her to a fancy restaurant and give her a nice piece of jewelry. If you want to, you can bring the doc over for a quick drink. I know Angela would love to see her."

Jake took a deep breath and exhaled noisily. "We've split up."

"Again?"

"Again," Jake replied. "She says it's just not working out. Whatever the hell that means."

"She's fantastic, Jake. You're not going to find another one like her."

"Tell me about it," Jake said quietly. "But I guess there's just been too many splits too many times."

"Whose fault was it this time?"

"Who the hell knows? Her fault, my fault, our fault. It doesn't really matter."

"Sure it matters," Farelli insisted. "If you want to patch it up, you've got to find out the cause."

"It's those goddamn demands," Jake groused.

"Hell, all women have demands," Farelli said authoritatively. "They come with the territory."

"I don't know how to handle this," Jake admitted. "I don't know what to do."

"Maybe you ought to marry her."

"You think so?"

Farelli smiled to himself. "Norman Mailer once said that in all relationships there comes a time when you either marry or move apart for good."

Jake looked at Farelli strangely. "You read Mailer?"

"Shit, no! My wife told me that twenty years ago, so I married her."

"Sounds like a demand to me."

"Like I said, all women have them."

The door leading up to the second floor of the building opened. Two young men walked out onto the sidewalk.

"Get down!" Jake said. He and Farelli slouched low in their seats.

The two young men stood under a bright streetlight, so Jake could easily make out their features. One man was short and pudgy, no more than twenty, with a scraggly beard. He was wearing a jogging outfit. The second man was tall and clean-shaven, in his early thirties, with broad shoulders and a strikingly handsome face. He could have been from the Middle East or from any country bordering the Mediterranean.

"The tall one is Yusef Malik," Jake whispered.

Farelli studied Yusef carefully, focusing in on his clothes. He wore designer jeans and a black leather jacket that appeared to be formfitting. If he was carrying a concealed weapon, Farelli couldn't spot it.

The two young men pecked each other's cheeks and bade each other farewell. Yusef walked over to a BMW convertible parked at the curb and climbed in.

"Going to school must pay real good," Farelli observed.

Jake waited for Yusef to drive away, then made a U-turn and followed him at a distance of half a block. Jake didn't know if Yusef was a professional who could spot a tail, so he played it safe, changing speed and lanes frequently. He wondered if Yusef was a real terrorist or just a rabble-rouser who liked to stir things up but not get his hands dirty. The FBI wasn't sure either, but they had Yusef Malik on their watch list. They knew he rubbed elbows with people who were suspected of having terrorist ties and often went to places frequented by these people. Jake was hoping Yusef would lead him to places where Khalil Mahmoud might have visited and been seen. It was a long shot.

Jake noticed Yusef glancing up at his rearview mirror and wondered if he had been spotted. Probably not, Jake decided, because Yusef was reaching up to adjust the rearview mirror. But to make sure, Jake pulled over and switched off his lights, all the while keeping Yusef Malik's car in view. After five seconds, Jake turned his headlights back on and continued his tail.

"You get his license number?" Jake asked.

"You bet," Farelli said. "I'll check it out later."

Yusef pulled over to the curb and walked up to the entrance of a large apartment complex. He stopped at the locked gate and spoke into the intercom system, paying no attention to the cars passing behind him.

Farelli adjusted the rearview mirror and kept Yusef in sight. "He's not going in."

Jake asked, "You figure he's picking somebody up?"

"That'd be my guess."

Jake made a U-turn at the next intersection, then turned off the car lights and parked across from the apartment complex, which had seen better days. Its outer wall was cracked and peeling and had rust stains from the metal bars that protected the ground-level windows. A sign next to the gate said there was a furnished one-bedroom apartment available and that there was a manager on the premises. Jake memorized the address, planning to return in the morning and see if the tenant list had any Arabic-sounding names.

The gate to the apartment complex opened, and a slender woman wearing jeans and a white turtleneck sweater stepped out. She and Yusef embraced and kissed on the lips, then walked to his convertible.

Jake started his car and drove by the complex, keeping one arm up to cover the side of his face. But he still got a good look at the woman climbing into the BMW convertible.

"Son of a bitch," Jake muttered under his breath.

"What?" Farelli asked.

"Guess who Yusef is playing kissy-face with?"

"I give up."

"Rawan, the imam's secretary at the mosque."

Farelli jerked his head around and glanced out the rear window, but they were too far away. "Are you sure?"

Jake nodded. "You don't forget that gorgeous face, with or without a scarf on top of it."

"And they're a pair too."

"That's for damn sure," Jake agreed, making a sudden U-turn and slowing down as the convertible pulled away from the curb. "That kiss wasn't just a hello. And I noticed that Yusef had his hand on her ass, too."

"She probably goes to all those kill-the-infidel meetings with him," Farelli said sourly. "Hell, she might even be a terrorist."

Jake shrugged. "Could be. But as a rule those Middle Eastern groups like men to do the dirty work."

"Except for when they strap explosives on a teenage girl and send her into some discotheque in Tel Aviv."

"Well, at least they haven't done that in America yet."

"Right," Farelli said bitterly. "All they've done here is fly commercial jets into buildings and kill thousands of innocent people."

Now they were on Sunset Boulevard. Traffic was heavy, so Jake closed the gap between his car and the BMW convertible. He stayed only three car lengths back. They drove by record stores and dress shops and seedy nightclubs where young people were lined up to get in. A black-and-white unit was putting cuffs on a drunk who could barely stand.

They came to a red light and stopped. Ahead, Jake watched Yusef lean over to Rawan and nibble on her ear. She laughed and threw her head back, her long black hair flowing in the night air. She was beautiful, Jake thought, wondering if Rawan was an innocent young woman who just happened to be attracted to a handsome extremist. Or maybe she was in it for the excitement that came with being a part of a radical cause. Either way, chances were she was going to get hurt.

The light changed to green. Traffic began to move. Yusef stayed in the right lane for another two blocks, then slowed and pulled up in front of a restaurant called Arabia. A large group of people were gathered on the sidewalk, laughing and yelling to one another. Some were carrying signs that were written in Arabic.

"What do you think?" Farelli asked.

"I think it's a gathering place for our Arab brethren."

They watched Yusef and Rawan being greeted enthusiastically by the sign carriers. A woman wearing Muslim garb came over to Rawan and exchanged kisses on the cheeks. Someone yelled out, "On to Jerusalem!"

The crowd applauded.

"Do you believe this shit?" Farelli grumbled.

Jake studied the crowd outside the restaurant. Most were middle-aged and appeared to be middle-class. Virtually all were dressed in Western attire, although some of the men wore Muslim skullcaps as well. Jake noted that the people approaching Yusef Malik paid particular deference to him. That type of respect came with power and money.

Jake glanced down at his watch. It was 9:30. "It's late and we're not going to get anything out of this crowd. We'll come back another time and see if anybody remembers Khalil Mahmoud."

As they drove away, a black Mercedes pulled up in front of the restaurant. The crowd shouted greetings to the new arrival as he climbed out of his car. Neither Jake nor Farelli saw Haj Ragoub warmly embrace Yusef Malik.

10

"Smallpox!" Joanna gasped.

"Smallpox," Mack reiterated. "From a skin lesion on our patient's face."

There was a stunned silence in the small conference room of the Viral Research Center. All eyes were on a projection screen that showed a picture of the smallpox virus magnified forty thousand times. It appeared to be white and biscuit-shaped, with a smooth surface.

"Son of a bitch!" the black ambulance attendant muttered. "We're all going to die."

"Maybe not." Mack switched off the projector and turned on the lights. He glanced around at the people sitting at the conference table: Joanna, the ambulance driver and attendant, and the nurse, Kathy Wells. All were trying to put on brave faces. "There is a smallpox vaccine and we have some on hand in the unit."

Everybody's expressions suddenly brightened. The ambulance driver and the attendant gave each other a high five.

"But even with the vaccine, we're not out of the woods yet," Mack cautioned. "Let me tell you why."

Everyone leaned forward, ears pricked, the smiles gone from their faces.

"The incubation period for smallpox—that is, the time between initial exposure to the virus and the onset of disease—is about fourteen days," Mack went on. "The vaccine usually gives full protection within ten days after vaccination."

Mack waited for the others to do the calculations in their heads.

"Hell, we're home free," the ambulance attendant blurted out. "We'll be protected before the disease has a chance to break out."

Mack nodded hesitantly. "That holds true if the vaccine we have on hand has full potency, and if this particular virus has a fourteen-day incubation period. Some of the smallpox viruses don't."

"What's the shortest incubation period ever reported?" Joanna asked at once.

"That depends on the dose and the virulence of the virus, and the immune status of the host," Mack replied. "But it can be as short as a few days."

"Shit," Joanna murmured under her breath.

Kathy Wells reached for the gold crucifix that hung from her necklace. She fingered it gently. "Can you tell if this virus is particularly virulent?"

Mack shrugged and decided to tell a half-truth. "Not based on a single case."

"So we'll just have to wait it out," Kathy concluded.

"It looks that way."

A hush fell over the room as each person considered his own mortality. The only audible sound was the monotonous ticking of a wall clock.

Joanna leaned back in her chair, thinking about the nightmare they were all living in. Mack must have known it was smallpox right from the start, Joanna thought. That was why he hurried them off the loading dock and down into the Viral

Research Center with such urgency. Everyone was ordered to take off all their clothes, which were promptly incinerated. Then, individually, they went through a small room bathed in deep-blue ultraviolet light. The light gave off no heat, but it destroyed any exposed viruses, smashing their genetic material and making them unable to replicate. And finally, each person entered a shower where a powerful spray of water washed away any vomitus or other contaminated materials. This was followed by a powerful blast of Enviro Chem, a disinfectant that killed viruses on contact. And all of that might not have been enough, Joanna thought miserably, trying to control her fear. They might still die, because all those procedures just removed surface viruses and not those in one's mouth or nostrils or any other body opening. The smallpox virus could be multiplying inside her body at this very moment.

She took a deep breath and strained to keep her voice even. "Mack, are you certain this is smallpox? Is the electron microscopic picture that definitive?"

"The EM picture is not diagnostic in that other pox viruses have a similar appearance," Mack told her. "But the patient's clinical features are characteristic for smallpox. To make double certain, we're doing a polymerase chain reaction test for the virus. But it'll be positive. There's no doubt he's got smallpox."

"Christ." Joanna groaned, then nervously wet her lips. "Do you have any idea where it came from?"

"That's the million-dollar question," Mack said. "According to the referring doctor, the patient dated the doctor's Mexican housekeeper quite a bit over the past several months. So our best guess is that he lives somewhere in the Mojave area."

Joanna looked at Mack oddly. "Doesn't he have an address?"

Mack shook his head. "No ID, no wallet. And both he and the Mexican housekeeper said his name was John Smith."

"John Smith, my ass!" the black ambulance attendant interjected. "That boy spoke with a real foreign accent, even when he was talking out of his head."

"And he doesn't look like a John Smith, either," Joanna added. "From his face and color, I'd guess he's Middle Eastern. Most likely Pakistani or Indian. Less likely Persian or Arab."

The others stiffened in their chairs on hearing the word *Arab*.

Mack studied the patient's face at length. "I think his features are too fine to be Arabic."

Joanna nodded. "And his deeper pigmentation suggests lower-class Indian or Pakistani."

Kathy Wells was still thinking about the word *Arab*. She slowly rubbed her crucifix between her fingers. "Do you think this is bioterrorism?"

Mack considered the idea briefly, then waved it away. "I doubt it. This is a single case out in the middle of nowhere. That doesn't sound like a bioterrorism attack. A more reasonable explanation is that he visited someplace in the Middle East and contracted it there."

Joanna asked, "Have there been any recent outbreaks of smallpox in that part of the world?"

"No," Mack had to admit. "The last reported case of smallpox was in Somalia in 1977."

"Maybe a visiting friend brought it over here," Joanna suggested.

"Then we'd be seeing a bunch of cases," Mack argued. "The visitor would have infected people at the airport and on the airplane. And, of course, the visitor would now be very sick with smallpox. Since none of that happened, I think John Smith is our ground-zero case in America."

Joanna nodded slowly. "So you think we'll be hearing about other cases somewhere in the Middle East soon?"

"That would be my best guess."

Joanna tapped her chin with a finger. "I don't like the fact that our patient is using an alias. That bothers me."

"Those foreigners do that all the time," the ambulance attendant informed her. "Most of them are illegal aliens, and if they give their real names, they know they'll get their butts shipped out of the country."

"But you can't be certain of that," Joanna countered.

"That would be my best guess," the ambulance attendant said, mimicking Mack's earlier response. "And I'll tell you why. His Mexican girlfriend out at the doctor's place told me her name was Maria Jones. Which, of course, it ain't because the old doctor told me her name was Maria Rodriguez. She's an illegal, just like him."

"The damn country is full of them," the ambulance driver commented.

"And getting worse every day," the attendant agreed wholeheartedly.

The driver and the attendant began telling stories about illegal immigrants who were sick and poor as dirt and couldn't speak a word of English. Yet they all wanted to be seen by American doctors and treated in American hospitals, which they had no way of paying for. The men from the ambulance service were convinced that was the main reason the health-care system in America was going to hell.

Mack blocked out their conversation and glanced up at the wall clock. It was eleven o'clock. He wondered why the Centers for Disease Control hadn't returned his phone call yet. *Goddamn it,* he fumed; the first case of smallpox in over a quarter of a century and the CDC was taking its time about getting back to him. Of course, he had spoken to the CDC operator and hadn't mentioned the word *smallpox,* and wouldn't until he talked with the doctor on call for the Epidemic Intelligence Service.

Mack thought back to the time he was an EIS officer at the CDC and had helped track down an outbreak of Lassa fever in the forests of Nigeria. He had written a paper on the disease and the virus that caused it, and it had made him famous in the field of virology. That all seemed like a lifetime ago now. He brought his mind back to the present and the terrible problem he faced. The terrible problem they *all* faced.

Mack put his hands on the conference table and pushed himself up. "Well, folks, we've got a lot of work to do. As far as tracking the smallpox virus, we'll leave that up to the people at the CDC, who are very good at it. We have a different order of business down here, and for better or for worse, you'll have to do exactly as I say. Our first priority is to get everybody vaccinated. If you have HIV or any immune deficiency, let me know now, because you can't be immunized against the virus without suffering terrible side effects."

Mack looked around the table to see if any hands went up. None did. "Good. Kathy Wells, our senior nurse, will do the vaccinations here and now. Then she'll show you to your quarters. We have four isolation units, one of which is currently occupied by our patient. Kathy and the two ambulance men will sleep in the vacant units. Dr. Blalock and I will stay in the on-call room at the rear of the facility."

"What about food?" The ambulance driver was a portly, middle-aged man with a red face and small spider veins on his cheeks. "Do we eat down here?"

"You'll do everything down here," Mack said firmly. "Meals will come to us on a dumbwaiter from the cafeteria

and be served on paper plates, which will later be incinerated."

"Do we get a menu?" the driver asked, and chuckled.

No one laughed with him.

"There will be some choices," Mack went on. "And
you'll eat three times a day—breakfast, lunch, and dinner.
The meals will be similar to the ones you usually eat, and
this will be important in keeping your body clock on schedule. You see, we have no windows down here, so you'll have
no way of knowing whether it's day or night."

The ambulance attendant asked, "How long will we have
to stay down here?"

"At least fourteen days," Mack answered.

A collective groan came from the group sitting at the conference table.

"If no one gets the disease within fourteen days after vaccination, then we're all safe," Mack explained, then continued on with his instructions. "While we're here, everybody
will work on a regular schedule. Dr. Blalock and I and Kathy
Wells will look after the patient. The men from the ambulance service will serve as aides."

"Wait a minute!" the beefy driver interrupted. "I don't
want to get too close to that guy with smallpox."

"You've already been too close," Mack said, giving the
man a hard stare. "But while you're around the patient, we'll
keep you well protected."

The driver squirmed in his seat, obviously unhappy with
the situation he was being placed in.

Mack gazed down at the two men from the ambulance
service. "Since we're going to be working together for a
while, we'd better know each other's names and what each
of us does."

Everyone quickly introduced themselves. The ambulance
driver's name was Charlie Cook, the black attendant's

Melvin Hughes. They served only as transport agents and had no clinical experience whatsoever.

"I would like each of you to write down a brief summary of your medical history," Mack requested. "We need to know what illnesses you have had, what medications you take, and what you're allergic to. This information will be critical if you become ill while in the unit."

Kathy Wells began handing out large index cards and ballpoint pens, telling everyone to print clearly and use more than one card if necessary. She was a pretty, petite woman, with short brown hair and doelike eyes. The ambulance men smiled at her as she spoke, and she smiled back. But her mind was elsewhere. She was wondering whether she should write down that she was two months pregnant.

Mack broke into her thoughts. "After you've collected the cards, you can start the vaccinations."

"In the left or right upper arm?" Kathy asked.

"Left."

Mack and Joanna walked out of the conference room and headed down a narrow corridor, then down another, wider corridor. They came to a metal door that was tightly sealed. It was marked with a sign that read:

CAUTION
PATIENT ISOLATION AREA
AUTHORIZED PERSONNEL ONLY
BEYOND THIS POINT

Mack pressed on a pedal on the floor and the door opened. They entered a small area with a large Plexiglas window that looked into four separate isolation units. Each unit had a single bed surrounded by sophisticated monitoring equipment. Only one of the beds was occupied.

Joanna glanced in at the patient. There was an IV running

into his arm, an oxygen cannula in his nose. He lay perfectly still, nude except for the sheet that came up to his knees. His body seemed to be covered with black blotches.

"Is that what they call the blackpox?" Joanna asked.

Mack nodded. "It's the most virulent form of smallpox known. The patients become very toxic and hemorrhage into their skin and mucous membranes. That's why the guy puked up blood."

"I've read that it's universally fatal."

"Without exception."

The patient began to move and turn in his bed. Side rails were in place to prevent the patient from falling to the floor.

"So," Joanna said softly, "we really are dead?"

"The cards are stacked against us," Mack conceded. "But with a little luck, we can still make it."

"You're hoping against hope," Joanna told him. "That vomitus we were sprayed with had to contain a fair amount of the smallpox virus."

"But we had on protective garb."

"Not enough," Joanna retorted.

"Time will tell."

"Save your false optimism for the others," Joanna said bluntly. "I want a straight answer from you. What are our chances of surviving this nightmare?"

Mack took a deep breath and exhaled noisily. "In all like-lihood, we're going to die down here."

Although Joanna had expected the worst, her face still lost color. *Thinking* you were going to die and *knowing* you were going to die were two different things. She swallowed hard. "Do we have any chance at all?"

Mack took another deep breath. "You wanted it straight. Here's straight. That guy's vomitus was loaded with tons of smallpox virus, and it got all over us—on our masks, our gowns, our shoes. Every goddamn where. And it soaked through. That means we were exposed to a huge dose of the virus, which will greatly shorten the disease's incubation period. We could be covered with those pox lesions in a matter of days."

"Jesus," Joanna moaned quietly. "And the vaccine could never protect us that rapidly."

Mack nodded gravely. "Now you understand what we're up against. And add to that the fact that we're dealing with a particularly virulent form of smallpox virus."

"Will we all get the blackpox?"

"Maybe. Maybe not," Mack said, his tone clinical now. "The same virus can affect different people differently. For example, pregnant women who are infected tend to get the blackpox much more frequently than others."

Joanna looked in on the smallpox patient. He was thrashing about more in his bed, his arms pushing out the side rails. "Who thought we'd ever see this damn disease again?"

"Nobody," Mack answered. "That's why we stopped vaccinating people over twenty years ago. There is virtually nobody in the world who is now protected against this virus."

"So this is the start of an epidemic?"

"More like a pandemic," Mack corrected her. "If you consider the way people travel now, this virus could spread to five continents in the blink of an eye."

"And kill millions."

"Make that hundreds of millions."

The patient in the isolation unit suddenly lashed out at the air, arms flailing and beating against the metal back of the bed. He quieted for a moment, then started thrashing about again, trying to climb over the side rails.

"He's got to be sedated," Mack said quickly. "Come on. I might need your help."

They hurried over to another tightly sealed metal door

with no lock or handle. Mack stepped on a floor pedal and the door opened into a small dressing area. They rapidly donned caps, gowns, goggles, shoe coverings, and specialized high-efficiency air-filter masks. Joanna's body temperature began to rise to the point of being uncomfortable, but she ignored it. Her goggles fogged up briefly, then cleared.

The door to the isolation unit opened and Joanna felt the pull of negative pressure ventilation, which ensured that contaminated air stayed in the unit and never leaked out. She followed Mack to the bedside and watched as he gently held the patient down and applied soft cotton restraints.

The patient was yelling out in a foreign language that Joanna didn't recognize. He kept repeating a word that sounded like *nacbar*.

"Do you understand English?" Joanna called out to him.

The patient stared up at her, his eyes glazed and not moving. His body was covered with black hemorrhages and the pustules of smallpox. It gave off the pungent, putrid odor of rotting flesh.

"Can you speak English?" Joanna asked loudly.

"Water! Water!" the patient cried out between parched, cracked lips.

Joanna reached for a square of gauze and soaked it with saline, then placed it on the patient's mouth to wet his lips.

The patient sucked greedily on it and swallowed, then shrieked out in pain. "Aaaah! Aaah! Aaaaaah!"

Joanna jumped back, startled, wondering if she'd done something wrong.

"He can't swallow," Mack explained. "The pustules you see on his skin are also present in the mucosal lining of his throat and lungs. So even a half swallow causes incredible agony." He injected Valium through the IV line and watched the patient slowly close his eyes. "Can you think of anything worse? Here you are dying of thirst and desperately wanting a sip of water. And when you swallow, it feels like someone set your throat on fire with kerosene."

"Are the lung lesions as bad as the ones in his throat?" Joanna asked.

Mack nodded. "And they exude pus and plasma and God knows what else, and the patient ends up drowning in his own fluids. It's gruesome to watch because you can't do a damn thing about it."

He took Joanna's arm and guided her to the door. "We'd better go get ourselves vaccinated."

Joanna glanced over her shoulder, thinking about the patient's pain and agony and the excruciating death that awaited him. It was a fate beyond horror.

Stepping out of the unit, Joanna said softly, "What an awful way to die."

It's the way we're all going to die, Mack started to say, but he held his tongue.

11

Dr. Elliot Durr heard the chirping of a cell phone. He was half asleep and his mind told him the phone was in another apartment. It couldn't be his because he always placed his phone on the night table in his bedroom. He ignored the chirping sound and tried to turn in bed, but his arm was pinned down by the buxom blonde he was sleeping with. Opening his eyes, he saw the face of the woman he'd picked up in the gym the night before. Her makeup was smeared, her hair a mess. And she was snoring. He wondered if he could extract his arm without waking her and sneak out of her apartment.

The cell phone in the living room chirped again.

Durr bolted up in bed, suddenly aware he wasn't in his apartment but hers. And his cell phone wasn't on the night table. *Oh, shit!* Nude, he jumped out of bed and dashed for the living room.

"What's wrong, honey?" the blonde called after him, sleepy-voiced.

Durr saw his pants and coat on the living room floor and pushed them aside to get to his cell phone. Quickly he pushed the talk button.

"Hello," he said, trying to clear the morning hoarseness from his voice. "This is Dr. Durr."

"Dr. Durr, this is the operator at the CDC," a pleasant female voice said. "Can you hold for the duty officer?"

Durr heard two clicks before the officer came on the line.

"Where the hell have you been, Durr?" he asked, skipping the amenities. "We've been trying to reach you for hours."

"My cell phone was accidentally switched off," Durr lied.

"Great!" the duty officer said sarcastically. "You're the EIS officer on call for all of America, and you've got your head up your ass."

"What have you got?" Durr asked impatiently.

"A call from Dr. Mack Brown in Los Angeles," the duty officer replied. "He asked for you specifically."

Durr cursed under his breath. "That guy is driving me crazy with his bullshit anthrax diagnoses."

"Anthrax?"

"Yeah, yeah." Durr leaned over for a cigarette, lit it, and coughed. "He called me a couple of days ago and told me about a patient with fever, respiratory distress, a widened mediastinum, and a positive blood test for anthrax. Then he called back later and told me a repeat blood test was negative, so the patient may not have anthrax after all. Now I guess he's changed his mind again."

"He didn't mention anthrax. He talked about some nasty ass virus."

"So it's a virus this time, huh?" Durr watched his blond bed partner walk by and prance into the kitchen. She was wearing a scanty silk robe. "Maybe we should have Marshall Wolinsky put the entire Virology Section on alert."

"As a matter of fact, Dr. Brown wanted to talk with the chief," the duty officer said. "He only agreed to speak with you after I informed him that Wolinsky was en route to Atlanta from Seattle and couldn't be reached."

Durr became alarmed. "He knew Wolinsky by name?"

"They're old buddies."

Durr puffed nervously on his cigarette. "Is Mack Brown somebody I should know?"

"Jesus Christ! You *are* new to this game, aren't you?" the duty officer said, then added a profanity before continuing. "J. Mack Brown was a principal member of the team that first described Lassa fever and tracked down its cause. And according to Wolinsky, Brown had a special name for the bug that caused the disease."

"What was that?"

"He called it some nasty ass virus."

Durr gulped. "You don't think he's got a case of Lassa fever in California, do you?"

"I don't know what he's got. But you'd better call him back damn quick and find out. Here's his number."

Durr wrote down the information and, taking a deep breath, started to punch in numbers. But then he changed his mind and placed the phone down. He wanted to clear his brain first. Maybe then he wouldn't sound like an idiot to J. Mack Brown.

Durr put on his underpants and went into the kitchen. The pretty blonde was standing by the refrigerator, sipping from a glass of orange juice. Outside it was a clear, bright morning in Atlanta. Sunlight was streaming in through a large window.

Durr stepped over to a dinette table and picked up a large carton of orange juice, then drank directly from it. It was ice-cold and tasted delicious going down.

The blond woman moved in next to him and rubbed up against his chest. "Last night was great, wasn't it?"

"Yeah," Durr said absently.

"Feel like going extra innings?" She chuckled, placing her hand inside his shorts.

Durr felt himself stir, but kept his mind focused. "I'd like to, but I've got a sick patient at the hospital."

"Real sick?" the blonde asked, withdrawing her hand. "Like emergency sick?"

"Like emergency sick."

Durr walked back into the living room, wishing he were in his office, where all his textbooks and manuals were. They would have come in handy if his conversation with Mack Brown went over his head, which it was likely to do. With his books nearby, Durr could have stalled for time and quickly retrieved the needed information on any given infectious disease. But he didn't have his goddamn books, and he was probably going to end up sounding like an idiot— which was the way he must have sounded when he spoke with Mack Brown earlier. A supercilious idiot.

Durr sighed deeply, knowing that his behavior was just a reflection of his own insecurity and lack of experience with exotic infectious diseases. Lack of experience, he scoffed at himself. Hell, he had virtually no experience. He had expected the CDC to transform him into a world-renowned specialist who would have job offers pouring in from the great academic centers of America. That was why he applied for the position of Epidemic Intelligence Service officer during his final year of an internal medicine residency at Stanford. Yet after ten months at the CDC he didn't feel a damn bit smarter than when he started. He had been assigned to the Department of Virology, Special Pathogen Branch, where all the action was supposed to be. The current AIDS epidemic and the episodic outbreaks of Ebola and other hemorrhagic viral diseases had catapulted virology onto the cutting edge of medical research. And Durr had thought he was going to be right in the center of it. Instead he ended up spending most of his time behind a desk doing biostatistics and reading about rare diseases he would never encounter.

"Is something wrong with your cell phone?" the blonde asked from the kitchen door.

"No," Durr said, coming out of his reverie. "I was just trying to remember something."

Durr began punching in Mack Brown's phone number in Los Angeles. He coughed loudly and cleared his throat.

Mack Brown answered on the second ring. "Yeah?"

"Dr. Brown?"

"Yeah."

"Hi. This is Elliot Durr at the CDC," Durr said, trying to put some warmth into his voice. "I'm sorry I didn't get back to you sooner, but my cell phone went on the fritz."

"It happens."

"Is this regarding your possible case of anthrax?"

"That turned out to be a mediastinal malignancy with a lot of hemorrhaging," Mack told him. "But that's not the purpose of my call."

There was a long pause before Mack continued. "Are you by yourself right now?"

Durr waved the blonde back into the kitchen, then said, "Yes, sir."

"Is anyone else on this line?"

"No, sir."

"Listen carefully to what I'm about to say and follow my instructions to the letter. You got that?"

"Yes, sir."

"What I'm about to tell you is for your ears only," Mack went on. "You're not to say a word to anybody. And I mean anybody. Understood?"

"Yes, sir." Durr reached for a cigarette and lit it, his hand shaking with excitement. *Christ!* he thought to himself. *This has to be something big.*

"Your duty officer told me that Marshall Wolinsky will be landing in Atlanta at nine A.M. You check with Wolinsky's office and find out what flight he's on; then go to the airport and meet him at the gate. So far so good?"

"Yes, sir."

"You take Wolinsky by the arm and guide him to a place where no one is within twenty feet. Then whisper to him that I called. And tell him that we have a bona fide case of small-pox in Los Angeles."

Durr's jaw dropped. It took him a few moments to ask, "Are you sure?"

"Son, I'm one of the few doctors in America who has actually seen cases of this goddamn disease. So when I tell you it's smallpox, it's smallpox."

"Holy shit! Holy shit!" Durr puffed on his cigarette and it caused him to cough so hard he began to hyperventilate.

"Gather yourself, son. You've got a lot of things to do. Are you at the CDC now?"

"No, sir. I'm on my way over."

"When you get there, sneak into the supply room and grab a handful of vials of smallpox vaccine. And make sure nobody sees you. Can you do that?"

"I think so."

"Good. Then go home, pack some carry-on luggage, and meet Wolinsky at the airport."

Durr knitted his brow, thinking. "Carry-on luggage for what?"

"For your trip to Los Angeles. You'll be accompanying Wolinsky."

It was the chance of a lifetime, Durr thought excitedly, his chance to be part of medical history. But his excitement flagged as he realized that Wolinsky would want senior people to work with him at the epicenter of an epidemic in the making. He'd need infectious-disease experts with years of experience, not a junior EIS officer who was barely out of his residency. Durr knew his chances of going to Los Angeles with Wolinsky were nil. "Sir, I should tell you that I've been at the CDC for less than a year. I'm really short on experience."

"When it comes to smallpox, everybody is short on experience."

"But I think Dr. Wolin—"

"Just do what I tell you," Mack cut him off. "Don't think, just do. And things will work out fine."

"Yes, sir," Durr said, his spirits soaring.

"Now get your ass in gear and keep your mouth shut."

Durr stood across from gate twenty-four on the A Concourse at Hartsfield International Airport, his carry-on luggage at his feet. He leaned against a wall and studied the crowds of people passing by. The concourse was packed with deeply tanned vacationers and well-dressed businessmen and happy college students on spring break. Everybody was staring up at a group of professional basketball players, all of whom appeared to be seven feet tall or more. Some kids ran over to them for autographs. One of the players picked up a tot with golden blond hair and hoisted her high in the air. The child giggled and the people watching laughed with her.

Elliot Durr's expression remained grim. Happy people, he thought, all living normal lives and looking forward to the future. And none aware that everything in their world was about to change. A catastrophe of immense proportions was waiting for them.

On the cab ride to the airport, Durr had quickly reviewed the extensive section on smallpox in the infectious-disease textbook he'd brought along. Everything about the disease was chilling. Smallpox was caused by a large DNA virus that was highly contagious and had a guaranteed kill rate of at least 30 percent. The more virulent strains caused death in 100 percent of victims. The suffering induced by the virus was terrifying. The patients were covered with painful pustules that made them feel as if their skin were on fire. And the lesions in their throats and lungs assured the victims of an agonizing death. In terms of viciousness and mortality, no other disease even came close. It had been estimated that in the twentieth century alone, smallpox had killed over 300 million people.

The PA system came on. The announcer said that National flight 1480 from Seattle would be deplaning at gate twenty-four.

Durr picked up his suitcase and strolled over to the gate. He knew that Marshall Wolinsky would be one of the first passengers off the plane, because Wolinsky always flew first-class. Wolinsky was a huge man, six feet four in height and weighing close to 250 pounds, with a bushy gray beard and thick eyebrows. His oversize body frame necessitated his sitting in a roomier first-class seat. For such a large man, Wolinsky had a surprisingly soft and kind demeanor. At the CDC he was known as "Gentle Ben."

An attractive flight attendant almost bumped into Durr. She smiled at his handsome face, focusing in on his deep blue eyes and wavy brown hair. Involuntarily she licked her lips, checking out his body, which was nicely muscled from his thrice-weekly workouts at the gym.

Durr smiled and said, "I'm sorry."

The stewardess was about to say something, but before she could do so, Durr walked past her.

The door at gate twenty-four was opening.

Marshall Wolinsky was the second passenger off the

plane. He saw Durr waiting for him and hurried over, his eyes glued on Durr's suitcase.

"I take it we've got a problem," Wolinsky said evenly.

"Big-time."

"Regarding?"

"A phone call from your friend, Dr. Mack Brown."

"And the message?"

"He said to whisper it to you only when no one was within twenty feet of us."

Wolinsky quickly glanced around the crowded concourse. There was barely standing room. People seemed to be taking up every square foot. He took Durr's arm and guided him down the wide corridor. "We'll go this way. The gates at the end of the concourse are usually vacant."

They walked as fast as possible, weaving their way around carts and wheelchairs and slow-moving passengers. People who saw Wolinsky coming moved out of his way.

"Good flight?" Durr asked, making conversation.

"Yes," Wolinsky said absently, thinking that most emergencies in his professional life seemed to occur when he was in the air and couldn't use his cell phone. That had been the case when there was an outbreak of Hantavirus in Arizona, and in the miniepidemic of hemorrhagic fever in Central America, and in the reappearance of Rift Valley fever in Africa. And each time there was someone from the CDC waiting for him when his plane landed. He wondered why Mack Brown had entrusted his message to Elliot Durr rather than someone more senior. And why were Durr's bags packed? What use would a junior EIS officer be?

As they went by gates with diminishing numbers, the crowds thinned noticeably. Wolinsky picked up the pace, eyeing Durr's suitcase, which the young EIS officer was pulling along on its wheels. Wolinsky could think of a dozen people he'd rather have with him to solve an outbreak of anything. Not that Durr wasn't bright, because he was. The young man was naturally gifted with good looks and a quick mind. And he used these features to glide by in life. He never really worked hard at anything, and because of this he would turn out good but never excellent results.

They came to gate two, which was vacant. The person closest to them was a black female clerk at a small newsstand twenty-five feet away.

"Okay," Wolinsky said, "what?"

"Smallpox," Durr told him straight out. "Mack Brown has a patient with bona fide smallpox."

Wolinsky's eyes bulged. His lips moved but took a moment to form a barely audible word. "Smallpox?"

"Smallpox."

Wolinsky collected himself and focused his mind on the problem. "How many cases?"

"One."

"There's no such thing as one case of smallpox," Wolinsky said. "There's only a first case, with more to come."

"Then he's looking at the first case."

Wolinsky went over to a large glass window and watched a Boeing 767 jet being pulled away from its slot. "Does anyone else know about this?"

"Not at the CDC," Durr answered. "Dr. Brown instructed me to tell no one except you."

"Good," Wolinsky said, still wondering why Mack Brown had entrusted Durr with the message. "Do you know Dr. Brown?"

"No, sir," Durr replied, then corrected himself. "Well, I really don't know him, but I spoke with Dr. Brown a few days ago about a possible case of anthrax, which turned out not to be."

Wolinsky nodded, now understanding why the junior EIS officer was at the airport with his bags packed. Mack wanted to make certain that the news of smallpox didn't leak out, and it would have if he had spoken to anyone else at the CDC. But a junior EIS officer like Durr would keep his mouth shut, particularly when he realized that he was going to be part of the investigating team. Had word gotten out, Durr would have been replaced by a more senior officer and thus lost his chance for fame and a place in medical history. Oh, yes, Durr would be as silent as a tomb. Mack knew that because he, too, had once been an EIS officer and had grabbed the ring of fame with his now-famous study of Lassa fever. He also knew that Durr could function as a legman while Wolinsky set up a command center.

Wolinsky finally asked, "Did he describe the case? Did he tell you anything about it?"

"No, sir."

"We've got to get out there," Wolinsky muttered, more to himself than to Durr.

"National has a flight to Los Angeles leaving at noon," Durr suggested, trying to be helpful.

Wolinsky shook his head. "We'll fly by private jet."

He reached for a cell phone and walked off, quickly punching in numbers. He made three separate calls, the final one lasting nearly ten minutes. When he came back to Durr, he took out a notepad and scribbled a note to himself. "It's smallpox," he reaffirmed.

"Yes, sir."

"Did you bring the vaccines with you?"

"Yes, sir."

Wolinsky grunted in approval. There was yet another important reason why Mack had Durr meet him at the airport with the smallpox vaccine in hand. That would save Wolinsky hours of valuable time. "And nobody saw you take the vials?"

"Nobody," Durr assured him.

"Our plane leaves in an hour," Wolinsky said, and stripped off his coat. "Let's vaccinate each other."

From her cash register the black clerk watched the two men roll up their sleeves and begin the injections. *Son of a bitch! Those white honkies are shooting up right here in the airport!* She thought about calling security but decided not to. Those addicts would be long gone by the time security got here. And besides, she'd have to fill out a report. The clerk shook her head, thinking the whole world was going to hell, then went back to reading her true-romance magazine.

12

Haj Ragoub was very pleased with the recent shipment of Japanese camcorders and television sets that he had bought at a bankruptcy auction. He had paid only ten cents on the dollar, but of course he had a fake invoice that stated he bought the merchandise at the usual wholesale price. He would make a very nice tax-free profit under the table. Then he would wire the money through Mexico to a Middle Eastern bank near his home on the Mediterranean.

Ragoub glanced up at the stacks of boxes on the second floor of his store, thinking how easy it was to make and steal money in America. If a man couldn't become a millionaire here, he was either lazy or a fool or both.

Ragoub heard a loud whistle coming from high on a ladder behind him. He looked up at the young Hispanic male there. The storeroom worker was pointing at the blinking red light above the door to Ragoub's office.

Ragoub hurried across the large open area and reached his office just as the light stopped flashing. His answering machine picked up the phone message.

"This is Joe. I thought I could come at four o'clock, but I can't. Maybe we can go to the movies another time."

Four, Ragoub thought, picking the coded word from the

message. He made sure the door to his office was locked, then went back to his desk and punched numbers into a remote control. As the wall panel opened, a large television screen came into view. He punched another set of numbers and waited for the picture to appear. It showed the Italian Open tennis tournament in Rome. Two women were playing in bright sunlight on a red clay court.

Ragoub pushed more buttons. The screen went blank, then turned a deep blue. A white outline of the United States appeared. Two white dots were bunched together and blinking simultaneously in southern California. Both were stationary and represented the planes still on the ground at the Mojave storage facility. Ragoub's gaze went to the four moving dots and followed their paths. Four planes were now in the air, heading eastward. Two were over New York. One was entering Illinois. A fourth was crossing over Alabama into Georgia.

Ragoub quickly reached for the phone and made four separate calls to agents back east. All were airport workers: two in New York, one in Chicago, one in Atlanta. They were told in coded messages that their designated planes were about to land.

Ragoub switched off the television set and closed the wall panel. Things were going more smoothly than he had anticipated. The only kink was the missing Ahmed Hassan. The stupid little shit had gotten himself fired, which he wasn't supposed to do. Stupid! *Stupid!* The half-Arab, half-Pakistani idiot had screwed up, and now he was running scared and hiding somewhere. But Hassan wasn't a pro, and it was just a matter of time before Ragoub's men found him.

Hassan's girlfriend was the key. She would lead the assassins to her boyfriend. Weak men always ran to their women when they got into trouble. And Hassan was a weak man. He would be found. Nevertheless, for now Hassan was a loose thread, and that bothered Ragoub. He wanted Hassan dead and buried in the desert before the big event occurred.

Ah! Ragoub thought happily, the big event. It would make 9/11 look like a traffic accident. Ragoub's only misgiving was that he'd have to give up his business and leave America prematurely. Given a few more years, he could have easily made another million. But he had enough for his family as it was.

The intercom on Ragoub's desk buzzed loudly.

He pushed the switch down. "Yes?"

"Mr. Ragoub," his Pakistani store manager said excitedly, "we are swamped with customers down here. I tell you, the entire shipment you just purchased will sell out so quickly. Perhaps you should order more."

"Perhaps we should increase the prices by ten percent."

"Most excellent." The manager chuckled. "But you will consider another order. Yes?"

"We'll see," Ragoub replied, but he knew the shipment that had just arrived would be the last one he would ever order in America. Why buy more merchandise when there would be no more customers? Dead people did not shop.

Ragoub switched off the intercom and placed the remote control back into the top drawer of his desk. He briefly eyed the plane tickets in the drawer, which he had bought for his wife and children. In another week they would leave to visit their grandmother's house, where they would enjoy the cool breezes of the Mediterranean and be well out of harm's way.

Ragoub would join them—but only after the big event.

13

Ahmed Hassan's condition was deteriorating. His breathing was becoming more labored, and he was having trouble clearing the secretions from his throat and lungs. He was strangling on his own fluids.

Joanna tried to clear the patient's airway with a suction tube, but got a scant return. "It's not helping much," she reported.

"Keep at it," Mack said as he adjusted the condom-catheter device that collected and recorded the patient's urine output. "Remember, that stuff is thick as glue."

Joanna inserted the tube deeper and managed to suck out a small glob of mucus. The patient's breathing improved, but not by much. He was moaning and uttering phrases in a language that sounded like Arabic. One of the words he kept repeating was *nacbar*.

An alarm bell went off.

Mack and Joanna quickly looked up at the panel of monitors above the bed. A red light was flashing. The patient's pulse appeared bizarre and erratic, then dropped to a flat line. Yet Hassan was still writhing and babbling on in Arabic. Mack glanced down at the patient's chest. A monitoring device had slipped off. Mack replaced it, then pushed a button to silence the alarm bell.

"By the way," he told her, "if this patient goes sour, we'll let him die. No heroics. Right?"

"Right." Joanna stepped back, but her eyes were still on the patient's face. It was covered with large, dark pustules that distorted his features and gave him a hideous appearance. He no longer looked human. "This is a nightmare."

"It could get worse," Mack said.

"What could be worse than a patient with smallpox?"

"Two patients with smallpox."

They walked out of the isolation unit and stripped off their protective gear. After undergoing a thorough decontamination procedure, they passed through metal doors that closed after them and walked down a long, well-lit corridor. The lights were turned on brightly during the day and dimmed at night, which was supposed to help the staff's body clocks stay on schedule despite the windowless environment.

They turned into another corridor and entered Mack's crowded office. Floor-to-ceiling bookcases and large metal files lined the walls. His desk was a mess, with papers and opened textbooks strewn over every square inch. In the far corner of the room was a small coffee machine.

Joanna slumped down wearily in a leather-covered director's chair and watched Mack pour coffee into plastic cups. Her eyes drifted over to a textbook on Mack's desk. It was opened to a chapter on smallpox. "You know, Mack, there are three of us now looking after a single patient with smallpox. And we can barely keep up. One more case would overwhelm us."

"Which gives you some idea of what the future holds," Mack said grimly as he handed her a steaming cup of coffee.

"How do you mean?"

"I mean this country is woefully unprepared to deal with a major outbreak of smallpox. We couldn't even begin to deal with it."

"Even with all the hospitals and medical facilities we have available in America?"

"Ha!" Mack forced a laugh. "Let me give you some real-world numbers. If a bioterrorist attack with smallpox were to occur in Washington, D.C., there would be only a hundred isolation beds in the entire metropolitan area that could handle smallpox patients. A hundred beds!" he repeated. "For a population of well over a million."

Joanna had to think about that, then said, "But there won't be a million cases of smallpox."

"There doesn't have to be," Mack explained. "Just a couple of hundred cases would paralyze the health care system. And remember, we're talking about a bioterrorist attack on the capital. There would be thousands and thousands of cases."

"But that shouldn't be a problem for us," Joanna countered back. "We only have one case here."

"So far." Mack sipped from his cup of coffee. "It's been estimated that each case of smallpox spreads the disease to at least ten others. In all likelihood our patient has transmitted the virus to you, me, Kathy, and the two ambulance men."

"But we're contained and sealed off from the world. Shouldn't that stop the spread?"

"You're forgetting about the other people who came in contact with this patient," Mack went on. "I'm talking about the old doctor who looked after him and his girlfriend who was sleeping with him. And then there are his coworkers and friends, and maybe family who were close to him and may develop the disease before we can track them down. The list goes on and on, and everybody on it is a potential carrier and spreader of the disease."

"What about mass vaccination?" Joanna asked.

"Is there enough vaccine to go around?" Mack challenged.

After a pause, Joanna shrugged.

"I think not," Mack informed her. "Not nearly enough for America, and certainly not enough for the rest of the world. And remember, in all likelihood we're going to be dealing with a pandemic here."

"Jesus," Joanna hissed softly under her breath.

"And even if we had adequate supplies of the vaccine, I doubt that we could ever stamp out the disease again," Mack said gloomily. "You see, there are millions and millions of people whom we can't vaccinate."

"Like who?" Joanna asked, taken aback.

"Like anyone with a compromised immune system," Mack replied. "You can't vaccinate people with HIV/AIDS, or cancer patients on chemotherapy, or organ-transplant recipients receiving immunosuppressive drugs. You vaccinate them with the virus and, rather than building up immunity, they'll come down with the full-blown disease. Since we can't vaccinate these patients, a fair number of them will get the disease and act as a natural reservoir for the smallpox virus."

Joanna swallowed nervously. "You could be talking about ten million people in America."

"And ten times that number worldwide."

"We'd better hope to God our patient hasn't spread his virus."

"Yeah," Mack said somberly, now thinking back to the meeting he'd attended in 1999. The Center for Civilian Biodefense Studies, a think tank at Johns Hopkins University, had organized a symposium on bioterrorism. On the second day of the meeting a role-playing exercise was held. It featured a terrorist group releasing the smallpox virus in a medium-sized American city. The single event caused wave after wave of smallpox outbreaks. The health system was quickly overwhelmed. Thousands upon thousands of people died. Then the disease spread worldwide. Despite the best efforts of medical experts, and despite mass vaccination programs, the disease could not be controlled. The failure to contain the initial cases of smallpox in a single American city led to a national epidemic and finally a global pandemic. It had been only an exercise, Mack reminded himself, but it still scared the shit out of everybody.

After a gentle knock on the door, Kathy Wells looked in. "Have you got a minute, Dr. Brown?"

"Sure." Mack glanced over at the nurse. Standing beside her was Charlie Cook, the ambulance driver. "What's up?"

"Charlie is claustrophobic," Kathy reported. "He can't tolerate being closed in down here."

"Give him ten milligrams of Paxil," Mack said.

Cook stepped forward. He was wearing a freshly laundered scrub suit. His heavily tattooed arms were folded across his chest. "I want out of here. And I want out *now*."

Mack got to his feet. "You're not going anywhere. You're going to stay down here with the rest of us."

"I'm getting out of here," Cook said, agitated. "And if I were you, Doc, I wouldn't get in my way."

Mack walked toward the ambulance driver. "Do you want to live?"

Cook unfolded his arms and let them drop to his sides. His hands were tightly clenched into fists. "I want to live. And I can do that in a hospital that's got windows."

"You'll never get out of here," Mack warned.

"Yeah?" Cook scoffed. "Who's going to stop me?"

"The policemen on the loading dock," Mack said. "If the

freight elevator opens and anyone steps out, they've got orders to shoot. Your body will come back down on the elevator and we'll put you away in the freezer until this is over."

Cook stared at Mack, wondering if the doctor was telling the truth. "I think you're lying."

"There's one way to find out."

"Yeah? How?"

Mack smiled thinly. "Get on the elevator and see what happens when the door opens."

Cook started to say something but decided against it. He slowly unclenched his fists. "That pill really helps, huh?"

"A lot," Mack assured him.

Cook hesitated a moment before saying, "I'll give it a try."

Joanna waited for the pair to leave. When they were well out of earshot, she asked quietly, "Are there really cops on the platform with orders to shoot?"

Mack nodded. "With stun guns."

"And what if that doesn't work?"

"Then they'll use real bullets."

The phone on Mack's desk rang. He picked it up and spoke briefly to another doctor. Mack's expression turned grim. "Please describe the skin lesions."

He pressed the phone against his ear, listening carefully to every word. "And where are the lesions located?

"I see, I see," Mack muttered, reaching for a pencil and legal pad. He drew a large outline of a human body and began placing dots on the figure's face and arms. "And when was the first time you examined the patient?

"Five days ago," Mack repeated. He took a deep breath, the strain showing on his face. "All right. Here's what I want you to do. Close all the windows and doors and lock them. And don't let anybody—and I mean anybody—in or out of that house until you hear from me."

Mack listened again, then nodded. "Exactly. You'll hear from me in a matter of hours."

Joanna watched Mack slowly place the phone down. "What is it?"

"Another case of smallpox."

"Oh, Jesus! Who?"

"The doctor in Mojave who examined our patient."

14

Jake sensed something was wrong the moment he walked into the forensics laboratory at Memorial. Lori McKay was pacing the floor in front of Joanna's desk. She was lost in thought, with a worried expression on her face.

"Where's Joanna?" Jake asked.

Lori looked over and hesitated before she answered. "She's, ah, she's away."

"Where'd she go?"

"To San Diego," Lori lied. "She had to do a stat consult."

"I need a number where she can be reached."

Lori hesitated again. "I can't give out that information."

Now Jake was convinced that something was amiss. "Why not?"

"I just can't," Lori said firmly. "She'll call you when she returns."

"I want that number," Jake demanded.

"Forget it."

Jake gave her a hard stare and continued to stare until she looked away. "We can do this the hard way or the easy way."

"You're not getting that number."

Jake picked up the petite pathologist by her arms and sat her atop Joanna's desk. He gave Lori another long stare, his pale blue eyes cold as ice. "Listen carefully, because I'm only going to go through this once. Joanna and I are working a very important case for the FBI, and they need her help right now. If I have to, I'll call the FBI and they'll be down here in a flash with a handful of subpoenas. They'll go through every inch of this place and question you until your eyeballs drop out. And believe me, they'll get the phone number. Now, that's the hard way. I think you know the easy way."

"Goddamn it!" Lori bristled, coming off the desktop. "I hate it when people bully me."

"Stop wasting time."

Lori glanced over at the door, making sure it was closed, then spoke in a low voice. "There's been an accident."

"Is Joanna hurt?" Jake asked, alarmed.

Lori shook her head. "Not that type of accident. It was a medical mishap."

Lori repeated the story Joanna had told her word for word. Joanna had been with Mack Brown when a critically ill patient arrived at Memorial's Viral Research Center. The patient, who was infected with a nasty, highly contagious virus, had vomited, and some of the spray had landed on Joanna and Mack and several others. Although everyone was wearing protective garb, they still might have been exposed to the viral agent.

Jake swallowed hard. "Are they going to get sick?"

"Probably not," Lori said. "But to be safe, they're all being immunized against the virus. It takes about ten days to build up full immunity."

"What kind of virus is it?"

Lori shrugged. "It's got a name a mile long. Apparently it's one of those viruses that lives in the tropics."

"So they're quarantined down there, huh?"

Lori nodded. "For the next ten days or so."

Jake lit a cigarette and puffed on it nervously. "It sounds dangerous as hell to me."

"It could be," Lori had to admit. "But Mack Brown thinks they're going to be fine, and he's the best there is."

Jake took a final drag from his cigarette and doused it under a faucet. "Get Joanna on the phone for me."

"Oh, Lord!" Lori groaned. "They're going to have my scalp for this."

"Make the call."

Lori picked up the phone, but before dialing said to Jake, "You keep the information I just gave you to yourself. The last thing we need is for word to leak out that we've got a dangerous virus on the loose at Memorial."

"Make the damn call!"

Lori punched in the numbers to Mack Brown's office and talked briefly, then handed the phone to Jake. "I guess you'd like me to leave?"

"Stick around," Jake told her. "You might have to do some of Joanna's work while she's locked up.

"Joanna?" Jake asked, holding the phone close.

"I'm here, Jake."

"How are you doing?"

"All right, so far," she said.

"Lori says you've been exposed to some virus."

There was a pause. Then Joanna asked, "How did you get the information from her?"

"I threatened her."

"Very nice," Joanna said sarcastically, then let a few seconds tick by. "You're not to mention a word of this to anybody. Understood?"

"Understood," Jake replied. "Now tell me, are you in any real danger down there?"

There was another pause, longer this time.

"Some," Joanna finally said.

"How much is some?"

"Just leave it at some."

A streak of fear shot through Jake. He had a bad feeling it was something much more than some damn virus. "Are you going to be okay?"

"I don't want you to worry, Jake."

"Goddamn it! How do you expect me not to worry when the woman who means more to me than anything else in the world is facing real danger and I can't do a damn thing about it?"

Joanna sighed. "Oh, Jake, why do you always wait until it's too late to say the right things?"

"We'll talk about whether it's too late another time."

"Next you'll tell me I'm your whole world."

"And some," Jake added.

"Of course, I'll want to hear that face-to-face."

"That's where I do my best work." Jake heard her chuckle softly and he felt better. But her exposure to some contagious virus was still bothering the hell out of him. "Is there anything I can do for you?"

"Not really," Joanna said, her voice becoming more businesslike. "But I have the feeling I can do something for you. This isn't just a social call, is it?"

"The Feds need a little help." Jake took out his notepad and began flipping pages. "Do you feel up to it?"

"Fire away."

Jake came to the page he was looking for and quickly reviewed his notes. "The FBI just received some new information on Khalil Mahmoud. Before he became a terrorist he was a master electrician, working primarily in the aerospace and aviation industries. So the bits of copper wire and insulation you found under his nails go along with that. The FBI is assuming he worked while he was in the Northwest. That area is filled with aerospace and aviation companies, and our guy could have easily gotten a job in any of them."

"There must be a hundred companies like that," Joanna thought aloud.

"Closer to a thousand, if you count subcontractors," Jake corrected her. "And they have a workforce of at least a hundred thousand."

"The FBI has a rough road in front of them."

"Made rougher by the fact that Khalil Mahmoud sometimes wore a mustache and beard, sometimes a mustache or a beard, and sometimes he was clean shaven," Jake went on. "Now add that to the mix and try to track him down."

"Impossible."

"Just about. But they're going to try anyhow."

Jake cleared his throat and turned to another page in his notepad. "The FBI did pick up something new, and they'd like your opinion on it. On the sleeve of his coat they found a few flecks of lightweight plastic. The FBI says the automobile and aviation industries use tons of it because it allows them to reduce the weight of cars and planes, which increases their gas mileage substantially. But they can't track it to a single product. They want to know if you have any ideas."

"Not offhand," Joanna had a flash image of the copper wiring and insulation under the terrorist's fingernails. Those, together with the lightweight plastic, could indicate that Khalil Mahmoud had made a bomb and placed it in a plastic container. But there were a dozen other possibilities as well. "Let me think about it for a while."

"I'll give you a call tomorrow."

"You'd better let me call you," Joanna told him. "We have a rotating work schedule down here, and I'm sleeping at odd hours."

"What sort of work?" Jake asked.

"Looking after a very sick patient."

"You be careful!" Jake said, concerned.

"I always am."

"And stay well."

"That's my plan."

Jake slowly put the phone down and looked over to Lori. "They're in real danger down there, aren't they?"

Lori nodded. "Big-time."

"Are they going to get out alive?"

"With a little luck."

Jake tried to think of ways he could help Joanna. In a fight or interrogation or stakeout, he was gangbusters. In a hospital he was useless. "If there's any change, you call me right away."

"Will do."

Jake headed for the door. "And the conversation you heard about the terrorist never occurred. Forget every word of it."

"Lieutenant," Lori called after him, "is this guy really a terrorist?"

"Oh, yeah," Jake answered. "He was a strap-on-the-dynamite-blow-yourself-up-and-go-to-paradise type."

Lori gulped. "Was? You mean he's no longer here?"

"He's dead," Jake said darkly, reaching for the door. "But he's got some friends here who aren't."

Mack Brown had overheard Joanna's phone conversation with Jake. He looked across the desk at her and shook his head, obviously displeased. "So now Jake knows, huh?"

Joanna nodded. "He thinks it's a virus, but he doesn't know which one."

"The word is going to leak out for sure," Mack predicted. "As a rule of thumb, the more people in on the secret, the faster the leak."

"Maybe not," Joanna said. "Jake can be very tight-lipped. He'll keep his mouth shut."

"That's what you said about Lori."

"She was at a disadvantage," Joanna told him. "Jake is an expert at breaking people down and getting information. He does that for a living."

"I suspect Jake scares the hell out of people," Mack commented. "He's big as a tree, and he's got that scar across his chin. That gets your attention, doesn't it?"

"He has other qualities that get your attention, too," Joanna said softly.

Mack noticed that Joanna's voice became lower and more seductive when she mentioned Jake's other qualities. "You two are still a pair, eh?"

"I guess."

"What the hell does that mean?"

"It means we're fighting more and more, or at least finding more reasons to fight."

"Sounds like you're already married."

Joanna squinted an eye at Mack. "Are you telling me the fighting continues after you're married?"

"Hell, it gets worse. Marriage doesn't stop the fights. It just makes them louder and longer." Mack paused and smiled at her. "Now, I don't know why this happens, but an esteemed psychiatric colleague once told me the reason marital fights are so bitter is that the parties are no longer pretending to be nice to each other. There's no more camouflage, you see."

Joanna grinned back. "You're impossible."

"You sound like my wife."

Mack rocked back gently in his swivel chair, thinking about Martha Ann, his wife of twenty years, and their two teenage sons. They were off in Colorado on a hiking trip and not due back for another week. He had tried repeatedly to reach them by cell phone, but wherever they were, the signal wasn't getting through to them. He desperately wanted to talk with them one last time.

"Maybe I should call Lori," Joanna broke into his thoughts, "and remind her how important it is not to say a word to anyone."

Mack waved away the suggestion. "We aren't going to be able to keep this under wraps much longer, no matter how hard we try. There are too many suspicious events happening in full view of the public."

He held up a hand and began to tick them off on his fingers. "One: The loading dock and elevator to the Viral Research Center are now under police guard. Two: The ambulance and platform had to be roped off while a HAZ-MAT team disinfected everything. Three: The ambulance company and the families of their workers had to be notified of the mishap at Memorial. Four: The old doctor's home out in Mojave is now under quarantine and guarded by the Highway Patrol."

Mack dropped his hand disgustedly and said, "Somebody is going to put all this together—and soon. And then we'll have panic, and all hell will break loose."

"Do you think there's any chance we'll be able to control this smallpox outbreak?"

"Only if the virus has an incubation period long enough for the vaccine to take effect."

"So there's a little hope?"

"Not much," Mack said discouragingly. "The old doctor in Mojave came down with smallpox five days after first examining our patient. That means the incubation period for the virus is five days—and it takes the vaccine ten days to be effective. This means exposed people will get the disease regardless of when we vaccinate them."

"But maybe the short incubation period in the doctor was

due to the fact that he received such a huge dose of the virus," Joanna hypothesized.

"Or maybe the incubation period is so short because the virus is so virulent," Mack countered.

Joanna sighed. "If that's true, we're all dead."

"Like I said, there's not much hope."

Joanna thought about Jake and her sister, Kate, and the very real possibility that she'd never see them again. "Maybe we'll get lucky."

"Every time I've ever said that," Mack said glumly, "I've ended up losing."

Joanna stood up and stretched her back, then went over to the coffee machine and refilled her cup. She noticed a big calendar above the machine with two consecutive days crossed off in red ink. *Two days,* she thought, wondering if that was how long they'd been in the Viral Research Center. Her eyes went to the wall clock. It read eight o'clock. She wasn't sure if it was A.M. or P.M. "I'm disoriented as to time. Is it morning or night?"

"Night."

"And we've been down here two days. Right?"

"A little over."

"It feels like we've been down here a month."

"This place will do that to you," Mack said. "A week will seem like a year."

"What's the longest you've been cooped up here?"

"A week."

"What happened?"

"You don't want to know."

"What?" Joanna persisted.

"An Ebola-like virus got loose," Mack said somberly. "One of our technicians became ill and died a gruesome death. Don't ask me to describe it, because I won't."

"Was it as bad as our patient?"

"Just about."

Joanna stared off into space for a few moments, then came back to Mack. "I want you to make me a promise, and I want you to follow it to the letter," she began. "If I come down with the blackpox and I'm suffering the way our patient is suffering, I want you to start a morphine drip on me and keep it going until I stop breathing. There are to be no tubes or catheters or heroic measures. I don't want my agony prolonged. Understood?"

Mack nodded gravely. "And I'll expect the same from you."

"Done."

Their eyes locked from across the desk, each wondering if they could really carry out the promise they'd just made.

The phone rang loudly.

Mack picked it up, spoke briefly, then quickly got to his feet. "That was Marshall Wolinsky from the CDC. He needs to talk with me."

"He's here?"

"He's at a military base on the edge of the Mojave Desert," Mack replied. "Would you like to meet him?"

"I guess," Joanna said, wondering how the meeting would take place.

They hurried down a deserted corridor, dimly lit because it was nighttime outside. Everything was quiet, with no signs of life. The only sound they heard was their own footsteps. They came to a large metal door with a red light over it. Next to the door was a wall panel that had numbered buttons. Mack punched in the code 888 and waited for the light to turn green. The door opened noiselessly onto another corridor.

"We're entering the research section," Mack informed her. "This is where the bad bugs are."

Joanna nodded, remembering that the Viral Research

Center studied some of the world's most virulent viruses. It had several high-containment biosafety level three laboratories and one maximum containment biosafety level four suite for work on lethal viruses for which there was no treatment or vaccine. The research center was restricted to employees and patients only. No one was allowed in the research section unless he had been vaccinated against yellow fever, Rift Valley fever, Q fever, and a complex of horse brain virus.

"Should we put on protective garb?" Joanna asked.

"Naw," Mack said easily. "We're all right in this area."

They stopped in front of a door halfway down the corridor. There was no doorknob or handle, or any panel on the wall. Mack inserted a plastic card into an overhead slot. The door slid open and the lights in the room came on automatically.

"This is our telecommunications center." Mack took Joanna's arm and guided her in. "From here we can hook up with anybody we want to."

Joanna glanced around the medium-sized room. Four cockpit-type chairs faced a large television screen built into the wall. The side walls were filled with consoles and smaller television screens, each with a name above it to indicate what world city the picture was originating from.

"Have a seat," Mack said, gesturing. "The show is about to start. And remember, they can see us as well as we can see them."

They sat in comfortable cockpit seats that could be tilted back or rotated a full 360 degrees. Mack lifted up a lid that concealed a console in the armrest. He pushed a button.

The large television screen suddenly came to life, turning white, then blue. A warning appeared on the screen.

THIS IS A RESTRICTED CHANNEL. ANY
UNAUTHORIZED USE IS PROHIBITED BY
FEDERAL LAW AND IS PUNISHABLE BY FINES
AND IMPRISONMENT.

The warning gradually faded, replaced by a picture of two men.

"That's Wolinsky on the left," Mack said quietly to Joanna. "That bushy beard makes him look like a mountain man, doesn't it?"

Joanna nodded as she eyed the other man, who was obviously the junior member of the team. He was young and good-looking and fidgety. He was repeatedly straightening his tie.

"Good evening, Mack," Wolinsky began. "I'm with Elliot Durr, whom you've spoken with several times."

"And I'm here with Joanna Blalock," Mack said to the screen. "She's a forensic pathologist at Memorial Hospital and, like the rest of us down here, was unfortunately puked on by our smallpox patient."

"Bad luck," Wolinsky sympathized. "But hopefully your vaccination will take effect soon enough for you to avoid the disease."

"The odds are against us," Mack said. "The old doctor developed smallpox five days after seeing the patient. A five-day incubation period gives us no chance at all."

"You'll be interested to know that the doctor has prostate cancer and was on chemotherapy," Wolinsky told them. "Thus, his immune system may have been suppressed, and this could have shortened the incubation period in him."

Joanna and Mack exchanged looks and nodded, both thinking the same thing. At least there was some hope now. Not very much, but some.

"As you requested," Wolinsky went on, "I'm having

some vaccinia immune globulin flown out to you from Atlanta. Now, you've already received one injection of the immune globulin. Correct?"

"Y-yeah," Mack said hesitantly. "But we didn't have enough to give everybody the maximum recommended dose."

"How much did you give?" Wolinsky asked.

"Point three milligrams per kilogram."

"Mmmm," Wolinsky hummed to himself. "That's a borderline dose."

"Which is why everybody needs a second injection," Mack said.

Joanna recalled reading an article about vaccinia immune globulin years ago. The globulin preparation consisted of antibodies against the smallpox virus, which had been isolated from the plasma of patients immunized with the virus. "How potent are these antibodies?"

"We can't be sure," Wolinsky admitted. "They may be weak because they've been sitting on the shelf for a while."

"Damn," Joanna muttered softly. "So the injections may not help us very much?"

"But the vaccinations still could," Mack said hopefully. "If the old doctor was on chemotherapy, that could have really shortened the incubation period in him. So there still may be time for the vaccine to work in us."

" 'Was on chemotherapy' is the key phrase here," Wolinsky said. "The doctor stopped his chemotherapy over a month ago, so it's not possible to predict the status of his immune system."

Joanna groaned to herself. The head of virology at the CDC had just minimized the scant bit of hope he'd given them a moment earlier. "What about the large dose of virus he received?" she asked. "That would have shortened the incubation period, wouldn't it?"

"I would think so," Wolinsky replied, with little encouragement. "But only time will give us the real answer. We're going to have to wait it out."

We! Joanna wanted to yell at the screen. *We, hell! You're not down here waiting for the first signs of smallpox to appear on your skin.*

Mack asked, "Does the doctor have blackpox?"

"Yes," Wolinsky said. "With plenty of garden-variety pustules as well."

"And there have been no other cases?" Mack inquired.

"None so far."

Wolinsky glanced down at an index card and quickly reviewed it. "I've put out discreet feelers to our colleagues in the World Health Organization, and none has heard of any proven or suspected cases of smallpox."

"Did you focus on India or Pakistan?"

"We did, but again nothing." Wolinsky tilted back in his chair and seemed to be looking beyond the camera. "But if I had to guess, I'd guess we'll find the source of the smallpox somewhere in India. Before the eradication of the disease, they had numerous outbreaks of smallpox, some of which occurred as late as the nineteen seventies. They still have more than a few isolated villages in India where the people are poor and never see a doctor or health official."

"But surely the villagers would report an outbreak of a vicious disease like smallpox," Joanna argued.

Wolinsky shrugged. "To villagers with no education and never enough to eat, it's just another way to die. Their biggest concern is where their next meal is coming from."

"We're doing a lot of assuming," Mack commented. "Even isolated villages in India have people passing through them—visitors, relatives, salesmen, and the like. Eventually the word gets out."

"That's what we're waiting for while we try to contain the disease here in America."

Wolinsky took out a pipe and slowly lit it, then began to rock in his chair. "But you are right, Mack. At this point in time we have no choice but to do a lot of assuming and guesswork. But here's what we know for a fact. A young man, most likely Indian or Pakistani by appearance, comes down with smallpox in a small desert town outside Los Angeles. We don't know who he is or where he's been recently. He's seen by an elderly physician who is retired and has prostate cancer. The doctor develops smallpox five days after seeing the patient. There have been no other cases reported anywhere in the world. That's all we know for certain. Now, what do you make of that, Mack?"

"I'd be guessing."

"That's what we did, because that's all anyone can do for the moment. But sometimes guesses can be very helpful, particularly when they are made by knowledgeable people. So I presented our problem to the epidemiologists at the CDC, and this is their best-fit scenario." Wolinsky turned to Elliot Durr. "Elliot, would you read the pertinent parts of the report to our colleagues?"

Durr straightened up stiffly and cleared his throat, his eyes glued to the folder he was holding. " 'Our conclusion, based on the facts presented to us, is that the initial patient with smallpox, thought to be Indian or Pakistani, was exposed to the virus within the past twenty-one days. Since there have been no other reported cases in the United States, except for the treating physician, we believe the most likely probability is that the exposure occurred outside our continental borders. Assuming the initial patient is Pakistani or Indian, one scenario envisions the patient traveling to one of the countries recently, being exposed in some isolated region or village, then returning to the United States while the disease was still in the incubation period. We recommend careful surveillance in these areas. It might also be helpful if the smallpox virus present in the initial patient was analyzed and its DNA sequence determined. The virus could then be compared, using DNA makeup, to the smallpox isolates that were obtained from the Indian subcontinent during the outbreaks of the nineteen seventies.'"

Durr paused to clear his throat again. "And this part of the report is in capital letters. 'Nevertheless, we cannot exclude the possibility, however unlikely, that the patient's initial exposure to the smallpox virus occurred within the United States. The probability that this represents bioterrorism seems remote in view of the very limited number of cases and the remote location where they occurred.'"

"Thank you, Elliot." Wolinsky relighted his pipe and sent up a dense plume of smoke. "So the key here is finding out who our initial patient is and where he's been. I've of course notified a few select people in the California Department of Health, as well as certain federal agencies. Only those who need to know have been informed. I'm also having two investigators flown in from the CDC so we can track the patient's trail as quickly as possible. If we had a picture of him, it would be very helpful."

Joanna shook her head. "That won't be possible. His face is a mass of pus and black hemorrhages. All of his features are hideously distorted."

"Have you uncovered any clue that indicates his nationality?"

Joanna pondered the question at length. "Nothing you could bank on."

"Too bad," Wolinsky said. "That could have—"

"Hold on!" Joanna interrupted him. "Most of the time the patient babbled incoherently. And now he barely talks at all.

But there was one word he kept saying over and over. It sounded like he was saying *nacbar.*"

"Spell it."

"N-A-C-B-A-R."

Wolinsky hurriedly scribbled a note. "We'll try to trace it and see if it's Indian or Pakistani."

"And there may be another way to get an accurate picture of this patient," Joanna continued on. "Have a police artist talk with the doctor and get a description of the patient."

Wolinsky exhaled wearily. "The old guy's got bad cataracts. I don't know how much help he'll be."

"Then talk with Maria, the doctor's housekeeper," Joanna suggested.

Wolinsky's eyes suddenly widened. "He has a house-keeper? He didn't mention that. And we asked him specifically about others in the house."

Durr nodded his agreement. "I asked him twice about maids and gardeners and others he might have come in contact with. He denied any such contacts."

"He may have been trying to protect the housekeeper," Joanna guessed. "We think she's an illegal alien."

"And she definitely had close contact with the doctor?" Wolinsky asked quickly.

"And with the initial patient," Joanna added. "She's his girlfriend and looked after him during the initial stages of his illness."

"Was his rash hemorrhagic at the time?"

"Yes."

"Son of a bitch!" The pipe dropped from Wolinsky's mouth, ashes going everywhere. "She's infected and she's out there on the loose somewhere."

15

Haj Ragoub and Yusef Malik were having a late lunch at Arabia. They sat in a corner booth, enjoying a stew of lamb and rice and vegetables. Although the tables around them were vacant, they still spoke in subdued voices.

"Our brothers managed to slip through the Israeli defenses again," Ragoub said, leaning closer to Malik. "It was a marketplace just north of Tel Aviv this time."

Yusef smiled thinly. "How many?"

"Four killed by the explosion," Ragoub reported. "Dozens wounded."

"And the brave martyr?"

"That's the best part," Ragoub said between mouthfuls of stew. "He placed the bomb under a vegetable stall and walked away. Minutes later he detonated the device by remote control."

"A thousand blessings on him."

"That makes two successful missions in the past week."

"Too bad it's not a dozen," Yusef said disappointedly.

Ragoub laughed. It was a hollow laugh without humor. "Patience, my young friend. Patience."

"We need another nine-eleven," Yusef persisted. "Except this time in Israel."

Ragoub ignored the remark and reached for the steaming bowl of stew. "More lamb?"

"Please."

Ragoub ladled more stew onto Yusef's plate, then took another large helping for himself.

A waiter came over and filled their glasses with water. But Ragoub didn't know him and thus didn't trust him.

"You are new here?" Ragoub inquired.

"Yes, sir," the waiter said respectfully.

"You are from America?"

"I am French," the waiter replied, bowing slightly. "Can I get you anything else?"

Ragoub shook his head and watched the waiter walk away. He made no attempt to hide his scorn for the waiter. *French, my ass! You are Algerian, an Arab, whose family suffered under French occupation until they gained their freedom. And then the French, out of guilt for their past deeds, allowed your family to immigrate to France, where they made you citizens. Yet they still treat you like shit because in their eyes you are only an Arab.*

Ragoub shoveled more stew into his mouth as he turned his attention back to Yusef Malik. Now there was a real Arab. Although born in America, Yusef had remained true to his heritage. Ragoub had become aware of Yusef over two years ago and had watched him closely. The young man wasn't just a so-called activist who would yell and scream at rallies, then run at the first sign of danger. He was a true revolutionary, full of hate and waiting to take revenge on those who had hurt his people the most. Ragoub smiled inwardly, recalling the report of Yusef disrupting a pro-Israel rally by taking a sign with the star of David on it and bashing a Zionist supporter with it. The boy had courage and zeal, and would someday become a useful member of the Holy Land League.

"And how is your beautiful girlfriend, Rawan?" Ragoub asked, making conversation.

"More lovely than ever," Yusef replied, warming at the sound of her name. "She is very precious to me."

"You must make certain she does not become American-ized," Ragoub warned. "This country has a natural talent for corrupting people."

"But not Rawan," Yusef said at once. "During the day she works at the mosque under the careful watch of my father, the imam. I take up her evenings."

"But I saw the way she dressed the other night, with tight-fitting clothes and, well, you know . . ." Ragoub let his words trail off.

Yusef's voice dropped to a cold monotone. "We fit right in, don't we?"

Sweet Allah in heaven, Ragoub was thinking. *This boy will someday make a wonderful terrorist.* His English and Arabic were perfect, and with his dark good looks he could easily pass for being Italian or Spanish. "I did notice that she correctly walked a step behind you, as Muslim women should."

"Two steps would be more appropriate," Yusef said, warmth returning to his voice. "But here in America one must make allowances."

"I would not let it become a habit," Ragoub advised. "Women are women everywhere. If you give them an inch, they will take a foot."

Yusef shook his head. "Not my Rawan. When we were back home last year, she adapted easily to all the customs of Muslim women."

"Will you return there soon?"

Yusef hesitated. "Sometime this summer, perhaps. My father, the imam, is not well and would like to see his broth-ers one last time. It, of course, will be very expensive, but a good son must follow his father's wishes." He took a deep breath and exhaled resignedly. "Yes, sometime this summer, I think."

"Perhaps you could go sooner."

"That's not possible."

Ragoub debated how much of a warning he should give Yusef. The boy was so valuable it would be a shame for him to die with the others. *Get him out of harm's way,* Ragoub decided, *but tell him nothing.* "I would like you to go back in the month of May."

"Impossible."

"The month of May," Ragoub insisted.

Yusef looked at Ragoub quizzically. "What is so important—"

"I will not say it again," Ragoub cut him off. "Go before the fifteenth of May."

Yusef's brow went up. *"Naqba?"* he whispered.

"Naqba." Ragoub nodded and glanced around, making sure no one was within earshot. "Take Rawan with you."

Yusef leaned in closer and spoke in a barely audible voice. "Should I buy a one-way or round-trip ticket?"

"Round-trip," Ragoub said, then explained. "Arabs who buy one-way tickets are quickly brought to the attention of the authorities."

"Give me a moment to think it through." Yusef slowly drummed his fingers on the tabletop as he considered all aspects of the upcoming trip. "We can't just leave abruptly. That might arouse suspicion."

"To whom?"

"Some idiot at the mosque who might talk too much." Yusef stopped drumming the table and nodded to himself. "We need an excuse for an emergency trip."

Ragoub nodded back. The boy was a natural. He knew

how to cover himself and those around him. "Would a sick relative do?"

"Perfect."

"The imam will be notified by telegram that one of his brothers has become very ill."

"Jibril is the sickly one."

"Then it is Jibril who will become sick."

Yusef looked at Ragoub, his eyes filled with fire. *"Naqba."*

"Naqba," Ragoub repeated, and reached for the pot of stew. "More lamb?"

Jake and Lou Farelli entered Arabia and walked over to the bar. A short bartender with a ferret face and slick black hair was drying glasses with a small towel.

"Where's the maître d'?" Jake asked.

The bartender glanced up. "Who wants to know?"

Jake flashed his shield. "Where is he?"

"In the kitchen."

"Get him."

Jake waited for the bartender to disappear behind swinging doors, then asked Farelli, "Are you sure the maître d' is okay?"

"He's a solid citizen." Farelli reached for his notepad and opened it. "His name is Jerry Jabeer and he's got no record of any kind. He's worked here for eight years, and before that at another Arab restaurant downtown. Married. Two kids. Lives in the Valley in a middle-class neighborhood."

"Does he belong to any radical groups?"

"Nope."

"And he's really been sick the past few days?"

"With the flu, according to his wife and neighbors."

This was going to be another blind alley, Jake was thinking. They had returned to Arabia the day after seeing Yusef

Malik and his girlfriend at the club-restaurant, hoping to question the maître d'. But he was out sick, and that set off alarm bells in Jake's mind. Maybe the guy decided to split because word was getting around the Arab community that the police were looking for people who might know the terrorist. Maybe the maître d' had gotten scared. But no such luck. He had the flu.

The maître d' came out of the kitchen and hurried over. "Is there some problem?"

"No problem," Jake assured him. "We just need a little help."

Jake showed the maître d' the photograph of Khalil Mahmoud and explained how the man was apparently robbed and murdered in the men's room at LAX. "So far we've had no luck identifying him. That's why we're showing his picture around."

Jerry Jabeer studied the photograph carefully. He looked at it for at least ten seconds, then shook his head. "He's not a customer here."

"So you've never seen him before?"

"Never."

Jake glanced around the almost empty restaurant. No one was at the bar or manning the cash register up front. He eyed the two men sitting in a corner booth. He studied them for a moment, then quickly looked away. "Who handles the cash register?"

"Shirley," Jabeer said. "She's having a little lunch in the kitchen."

"Could you get her for us?"

"Sure."   •

Jake waited for the maître d' to enter the kitchen, then nudged Farelli with his elbow. "Let about ten seconds pass, then look at the corner booth and tell me what you see."

Farelli examined his fingernails while counting to ten,

then glanced over at the booth, then back at his nails. "Well, if it ain't old Yusef."

"And he's got a friend with him."

"And the way they're huddled together, I'd say they were close friends," Farelli observed.

"Ah-huh."

"And you know something else?" Farelli asked under his breath.

"What?"

"The maître d' looked at the picture of the terrorist too long."

Jake nodded. "Way too long."

The maître d' returned with the middle-aged, chubby cashier. She was shown the picture of Khalil Mahmoud but couldn't identify him.

"Thanks for your time," Jake said appreciatively, and turned for the door.

"Sorry we couldn't help," Jabeer called after them.

He waited for the detectives to leave, then rushed over to the table where Haj Ragoub and Yusef Malik were sitting.

16

"Doc, I think something is wrong with my vaccination," Charlie Cook said.

"I'll check it in a minute," Mack told him as he tried to move Ahmed Hassan onto his side. But the patient was like deadweight and barely budged. "Give me a hand here, Charlie. I want to turn him so we can clean up the bed a bit."

Cook hesitated, not wanting to get any nearer to the patient than he absolutely had to. Just being in the same room with a guy who looked like a heap of pus was bad enough. "Hell, Doc, he's already breathing his last. Why bother?"

"Get your ass over here!" Mack barked.

"All right," Cook said reluctantly, and pushed his mop and bucket aside. He walked over slowly, frightened despite the protective garb he wore. "Which way you want to move him?"

"Onto his left side."

With effort the men lifted the patient and placed him on his side. Black feces were everywhere, the stench overwhelming. Mack cleaned up the mess with a handheld vacuum device, then called to Joanna, "We need one of those big cotton pads."

Joanna came over with the pad and put it under the patient. Mack and Cook slowly lowered Hassan onto his back, while Joanna sprayed the air with a deodorizer that had a sickly sweet aroma.

"I don't think that's going to help much," Mack said.

Hassan began to cough weakly. His chest was the only part of his body that moved. He coughed a little harder and phlegm rattled in his throat. Then he lay perfectly still.

Mack watched the dying man, his respirations so shallow now they were difficult to detect. "I don't know how he's managed to live for five days."

"Jesus," Joanna hissed softly. "Have we been down here five days?"

"A little more," Mack replied. "It feels like a month, doesn't it?"

"More."

"Just another five days," Mack said wistfully. "That'll make ten days since our vaccinations. And that's enough time for us to become fully immunized against smallpox."

Joanna prayed silently for a moment before saying, "I never thought ten days would be so important."

"Me neither."

And me neither, Charlie Cook was thinking. He hated every second he was cooped up in the dungeonlike research center. But he had to admit the pills had helped his claustrophobia. Too bad they didn't get rid of the pain in his arm where he had been vaccinated. It hurt like hell, and he thought it was giving him some fever too. "You want to look at my vaccination now, Doc?"

"When we get outside the unit," Mack said.

Cook's arm seemed to be aching more with each passing second. And it was itching like the devil too. He used the back of his hand to scratch it vigorously.

Hassan groaned loudly, startling everyone. Then he

started babbling in some foreign language. The only word he spoke distinctly was *nacbar.*

"I wonder what the word means," Joanna mused.

Mack shrugged. "Wolinsky says they're having trouble tracking it down. It's not Indian or Pakistani. They're now trying to determine if it comes from some Afghan dialect."

"Why Afghan?" Joanna asked.

"Because the Afghans and Pakistanis have common facial features, according to Wolinsky's experts."

Joanna nodded slowly. "And Lord knows, there are a lot of isolated villages in Afghanistan where the smallpox outbreak could have started."

Mack nodded back. "That's another reason to see if *nacbar* is an Afghan word."

"And if the source is in Afghanistan," Joanna went on, "all of our troops stationed there will have to be vaccinated."

It was a disaster in the making, Mack thought. Somewhere, someplace, there was a pocket of smallpox just waiting to explode and cover the Earth. They had been lucky so far, but Mack knew their luck couldn't hold up much longer.

Joanna broke into his thoughts. "Do you talk with Wolinsky often?"

"Daily."

"And there have been no other reported cases. Right?"

"None so far."

"So maybe this minioutbreak is contained," Joanna said.

"Not as long as Maria Rodriguez is out there wandering around," Mack told her. "Hell, she could be back in some Mexican village, sick as a dog, and spreading the disease to anyone who comes close."

"Naw," Cook opined. "She ain't back in Mexico. Them illegals, like her, come to stay. And if she wants to hide, that's not a problem. The San Joaquin is nearby and has plenty of towns that are filled with Mexicans. She could disappear in a flash."

"Yeah, I guess," Mack had to admit, watching Cook scratch his left upper arm. "Don't scratch your vaccination site or you'll spread it."

"Hell, it's already spread," Cook said, unconcerned.

Mack's jaw dropped. "What!"

"Yeah," Cook continued, still unconcerned. "There are little pimples all around it."

"How many pimples?"

"A lot," Cook said, and started to remove his gown. "Here, I'll show you."

Mack hurried over to Cook and pushed him against a metal door that led to the adjacent isolation unit. Quickly Mack stepped on a floor pedal and the door opened with a hiss. He shoved Cook into the vacant unit, then waited for Joanna to enter before securing the door.

"What the hell is wrong?" Cook demanded.

"Let's see your vaccination site," Mack said, hoping against hope that his diagnosis was wrong.

Cook jerked off his gown and lifted up the sleeve of his scrub suit, exposing the vaccination area. On the upper deltoid was a black lesion the size of a silver dollar. It was surrounded by pustules that extended up his arm and onto his neck and chest.

Mack stared at the characteristic skin lesions and tried to keep his expression even. "You've had a bad reaction to the vaccination."

"That's what I thought," Cook said, remembering a severe reaction he'd had to a typhoid shot while he was in the military. His whole arm had swollen up. "So I shouldn't scratch it, huh?"

Mack ignored the question. "You're going to get sick with fever and chills, and the rash could spread."

"I can stand it," Cook said bravely. "I've been sick before."

"Well, you're going to feel real sick again, so we'll treat you like a patient."

Cook's eyes narrowed suspiciously. "What do you mean, 'like a patient'?"

"You've been sleeping in one of the isolation units. Right?"

"Right."

"You'll continue to sleep in this one because you'll be sick," Mack explained. "That way, if you need a doctor or nurse, there'll always be one next door, looking after our foreign patient."

"Like, if I needed pain medication or something for the itch?"

"Exactly," Mack lied.

"And I'll get my meals and everything brought to me?"

"Of course."

Cook grinned widely. "That sounds good to me."

Mack didn't smile back. Instead he pointed to a supply closet. "I think you'll be more comfortable in a hospital gown."

"I'm going to keep my shorts on. Okay?" Cook asked modestly.

"No problem," Mack said. "I'll be back to see you in a little while."

Mack and Joanna walked out and through the adjacent isolation unit, then entered the decontamination area, where they discarded their protective garb and went through three separate procedures that destroyed any virus still clinging to them.

Moments later they stood in the observation room looking in on Charlie Cook. The ambulance driver was lying on the bed, hands folded across his chest. He was already asleep.

"That's not just a reaction to the smallpox vaccine, is it?" Joanna asked quietly.

"It's much more than that." Mack took a deep breath and exhaled heavily. "He's got vaccination-induced smallpox."

Joanna looked at Mack quizzically. "I've never heard of that. How often does it occur?"

"Rarely," Mack replied, "very rarely. And only under special circumstances."

Mack described how vaccination with the virus could lead to full-blown disease if the vaccine was administered to someone with a crippled immune system. "The person's body can't mount an immune response to the injected virus, so it spreads all over."

"And there have been documented cases of this in America?"

Mack nodded gravely. "In 1984 in a military recruit with subclinical HIV infection."

"So you think Charlie Cook has subclinical AIDS?"

"That would be my best guess," Mack said. "We'll do a blood test and find out."

Joanna gazed through the Plexiglas window and studied the ambulance driver who had just been given a death sentence. "With a crippled immune system, he's not going to last long."

"He'll have a malignant course," Mack predicted. "He'll be dead in days."

"Are you going to tell him?"

"Not now," Mack said promptly. "It's already taking thirty milligrams of Paxil a day to control his anxiety and claustrophobia. Can you imagine what he'd be like if I told him he had smallpox?"

"He'd probably bounce off the walls," Joanna conjectured. "He'd turn into a wild man."

Mack nodded. "That's why I'm not telling him."

"Sooner or later you'll have to."

"Then it'll have to be later."

Joanna nodded back. The patient would be told when he was sick and weak and unable to throw a major tantrum. Then he would be unable to hurt himself or any of the others. It sounded cold, but it was the best way to deal with the situation.

The door behind them opened and Kathy Wells slowly walked in. Her hair was disheveled, her eyes red and puffy. She had a stunned expression on her face.

"What's wrong?" Mack asked.

Kathy nervously wet her lips. "A few days after my vaccination I had some fever and body aches. I thought it was caused by the vaccination."

Oh, Lord! Joanna thought, shuddering. Not another case of vaccine-induced smallpox.

"And?" Mack pressed the nurse.

"And now I've got a rash," Kathy said, her voice just above a whisper.

"On your arm?" Mack asked at once.

Kathy shook her head, then pulled down the front of her scrub suit. "It's on my neck and shoulders."

Mack moved in closer and, without touching Kathy, he carefully examined her skin lesions. They were raised red papules that were turning into pustules. They were characteristic for smallpox.

"Please tell me it isn't," Kathy pleaded.

Mack quickly covered his nose and mouth, hoping to stop any more smallpox virus from entering his body. "Get into the third isolation unit," he ordered. "And do it now."

"Oh, God!" Kathy cried out.

17

The assassins left the last of the physicians' offices and walked to a nearby parking lot. The afternoon sun was blazing hot, the temperature over a hundred degrees. In the distance was a vast stretch of desert that reminded both men of home.

"It is as if Maria Rodriguez never existed," the shorter assassin said.

"Oh, she exists," the taller one assured him. "And wherever she is, that is where we will find Hassan."

"If we had a picture of the whore, it would make things easy for us."

"Life is not meant to be easy, my friend."

The assassins were drawing a blank, trying to track down Maria Rodriguez, the Mexican housekeeper. They had gotten a list of doctors in the area from a phone book and visited twenty offices, posing as investigators for a big Los Angeles law firm. Maria Rodriguez, they had explained, was the beneficiary of a $25,000 bequest in her late uncle's will, but she was no longer at her last known address and had told a friend she was going to work as a housekeeper in Mojave. Every office manager wanted to be helpful, licking their lips at the idea of a $25,000 windfall and wishing they were on the receiving end. But the assassins couldn't find anybody who knew Maria. No one had ever heard of her.

The assassins climbed into their car and, turning on the air-conditioning, drove away. The shorter man lit a cigarette and began to hum an Arabic tune. The taller assassin was still thinking about Maria. A picture of her would have really been helpful, because the description they had was flimsy and would have fit almost any Mexican: young, thin, dark, black hair. But she must be a real pig, he decided, if she was sharing her bed with an ugly Pakistani. No matter, he thought, because soon Hassan would be dead, and so would his Mexican whore, Maria. Ragoub wanted the girl killed too, just in case Hassan had told her things he shouldn't have.

The assassins turned onto the main street. Traffic was light, the sidewalks deserted. Up ahead they saw the only pharmacy in town.

The taller assassin looked over to his companion. "If we are unsuccessful here, Ragoub wants us to extend our search to Tehachapi."

"We should have killed the little shit first," the companion grumbled.

"Who was to know he would run?"

"And who was to know he would hide so well?"

They pulled over to the curb and entered the pharmacy. The store was small and cramped, with shelves that were lined with bottles of vitamins and supplements and home remedies. One long, narrow counter was devoted to perfumes, lipsticks, and other makeup items. A druggist was at the rear, busily filling prescriptions.

The taller assassin approached the elderly druggist, who had reading glasses on the very end of his nose. "Excuse me, sir. I wonder if you could help us."

"I'll try," the druggist said pleasantly as he secured the top on a plastic vial. "What do you need?"

The tall assassin told the druggist about Maria Rodriguez, who had inherited $25,000 and whom they couldn't find. "It's as if she just disappeared."

The druggist whistled softly. "Twenty-five grand—just like that!"

"If we can locate her."

"Well, she doesn't work here."

I know that, you idiot, the assassin thought, bristling. *I told you she was a housekeeper for a doctor.* He nodded and kept his voice friendly. "We thought she might pick up goods here for her doctor."

"Nah," the druggist said. "Doctors want their orders delivered."

"Even to their homes?"

"Especially to their homes."

The old druggist took off his reading glasses and rubbed the indentation on his nose. "You'd probably have better luck talking with Jimmy, our delivery boy. He might know this Maria."

"Where is Jimmy?"

The druggist motioned with his thumb to a rear door. "He might still be out back."

"Might?" the tall assassin pressed, his voice harder.

The druggist nodded. "He's not feeling so well, so I told him to go home."

The assassins hurried out into the bright sunlight. A bespectacled young man was standing in the shade, leaning against the back of the building. He was smoking a crinkled cigarette that gave off the sweet, distinctive aroma of marijuana. The front of his T-shirt was soaked with perspiration.

"Are you Jimmy?" the taller assassin asked.

"Yeah." Jimmy sucked on the joint, holding the smoke down as long as he could. "Why?"

"We're looking for a woman named Maria Rodriguez, who is about to inherit twenty-five thousand dollars—if we can find her."

Jimmy blinked rapidly. "Shee-it! Twenty-five large."

"If we can find her," the assassin said once more. "We thought maybe you could help us, since she works for a doctor and you deliver to most of the doctors around here."

"So Maria is going to get twenty-five big, huh?"

The assassin smiled humorlessly. "Do you know her?"

Jimmy Vash gazed out into the sunlight, thinking about the nice Mexican woman who always gave him a soft drink when he delivered stuff. The last time he was there she tipped him five dollars for helping her carry a badly stained mattress from the guesthouse. It had black stuff all over it and smelled terrible.

"Well?" the tall assassin demanded. "Do you know her?"

"Maybe," Jimmy finally answered as a chill went through his body and caused him to shiver. Then he coughed and sent a spray of fine droplets into the air. The damn flu was getting worse, he thought, and the spots on his arms were starting to look funny. "Yeah, maybe I do. But my memory is not so good."

The assassin reached in his pocket for a twenty-dollar bill and held it up. "Does this help your memory?"

Jimmy snatched the bill from the assassin's hand. "She works for Dr. Bishop."

"Spell it."

"B-I-S-H-O-P."

The assassin went into his coat pocket and extracted a sheet he'd torn from the yellow pages. It contained the names of all the doctors in the area. There was no Bishop listed. "Where is this Dr. Bishop's office?"

"He doesn't have an office," Jimmy replied. "He's re-tired."

"Where does he live?"

Jimmy hesitated, wrinkling his brow as if he were con-centrating. "I'm trying to think."

The assassin produced another twenty-dollar bill.

Jimmy coughed hard again, sending up another spray in the direction of the assassins. "Ten-ten Arroyo Drive," he said, grabbing the money. "It's the last house on the right."

Maria Rodriguez knew they would never find her. No matter how hard they looked, they would never find her. She had carefully picked and stocked the hiding place, certain the day would come when she would need it.

She had learned to hide well in Mexico, in order to avoid the man who would come to their house and force himself on her. Twice it had happened, both times so painful that Maria could feel the searing pain between her legs. And when Maria's mother had tried to intervene, the man beat her and broke her ribs and laughed while he did it. So she learned the art of hiding, and the man never found her again. The cruel man was still alive, according to Maria's mother, but old and sick and withering slowly away. Maria hoped the man would have a bad death. That would be just. Yes, she thought vengefully, a horrible death in which he cried out for mercy every day but none came. Maria spat at the man's cruelty, wishing him an eternity in hell, where he would receive the full measure of pain he had caused others. With effort she pushed the awful memory from her mind.

Maria stood and stretched and then peered out into the darkness of her hiding place. It was cool and surprisingly damp where she was, and the temperature seemed to stay comfortable despite the outside heat. And there was plenty of room to walk about, very similar to her hideout in the Mexican village where she was raised.

Her mind drifted back to the house she was born in and where her mother still lived. A nice little house with a small garden and a deep well, and soon it would be entirely paid for, thanks to the money she had been sending home since her arrival in America ten years ago. And with the extra money Ahmed had given her, her mother could now afford the stronger medicine that eased the asthma that afflicted Maria's younger brother. A picture of Maria's mother and brother flashed before her eyes, and she felt a wave of sadness wash over her. Oh, how much she missed them! If she could only see them and—

A noise from somewhere in the darkness.

Maria froze, instantly on guard, with all of her senses alert. She concentrated her hearing in the direction of the sound and waited for it to happen again. But everything stayed quiet. Maria remained motionless, holding her breath and wondering if the sound could have been made by a person entering her hideout. No, she quickly decided. There was only one way in and out, and the door was old and creaky and couldn't be opened without making a high-pitched squeal. And besides, the noise wasn't made by a footstep.

Then the sound came again. It had a soft, rustling quality. A rat, Maria guessed, or some other small creature looking for a cool, safe place.

She eased herself back down on the ground and sipped water from a plastic bottle. She hoped she wouldn't have to stay in the basement of the doctor's house much longer. The doctor would need her. He was old and sick and dying of cancer, which had spread to his bones. But he had improved a little recently, Maria remembered, and seemed to be moving about more easily. Then the disease struck, the one with the black marks on the skin, the same one that had affected poor Ahmed. But the American doctors would get them all well. American doctors were so wonderful, so much better than those in Mexico.

Yes, she thought determinedly, Ahmed and the old doctor would be made well, and the newly arrived doctors would depart, and then she could leave the basement of the house. She could not go back upstairs with the new doctors and other government officials there. They would demand to see her papers and discover that she was an illegal alien and send her back to Mexico. And then her mother's house would never be paid off and her brother's asthma would grow worse.

Maria decided to stay put and wait for the sickness upstairs to pass, confident that she herself would never become ill. She was healthy and strong, and her resistance was so good she never even had a cold. Yet for the past day she had felt feverish and her body ached and the skin on her arms itched. But she attributed this to the dampness of her hiding place and the hard surface she slept on. She was certain it was not the illness the others had. If it were, she would be much sicker. But if by chance the illness struck her, Maria had a plan in mind. She would slip out and go to the barrios of East Los Angeles with their dense Mexican population. There she would be treated for the illness with no questions asked.

Yes, Maria nodded to herself, Los Angeles would be the place to go.

18

"I don't think he can hear you," Joanna said to Mack. "You'd better try again."

"Charlie!" Mack yelled, leaning over the patient. "Things are not going well. I think you've got smallpox and it's getting worse."

Charlie Cook grunted and then moved his head away from the loud noise.

Mack was about to try again but decided not to. "Maybe it's better this way."

Joanna nodded sadly, transfixed by the horrible appearance of the patient. The mass of pustules on his face made him unrecognizable. "His disease is so malignant. It's like it devoured him in thirty-six hours."

"That's what happens when you vaccinate somebody who has clinical or subclinical AIDS," Mack explained. "The person has no immune defenses, so the virus literally eats him alive. Now you can see why we have to be so careful with mass vaccination programs. If you vaccinate a person with AIDS, not only will they get smallpox but they'll spread it to a bunch of others."

"And there are ten million people in America who are HIV positive," Joanna recalled.

"At least."

Joanna looked away from the man dying right before her eyes. Mack had warned her that the disease in Charlie would follow a malignant course, but she had had no idea it would be this vicious and aggressive. And Kathy Wells in the adjacent unit wasn't much better off. Kathy had the blackpox and it was rapidly consuming her, although she was still lucid.

"Have you noticed that all the naturally occurring cases of smallpox we've seen have the blackpox?" Joanna asked. "Isn't that kind of unusual?"

"It's very unusual," Mack told her. "The blackpox is said to occur in three to five percent of cases. In this outbreak everyone seems to have it."

"Is there a reason for this?"

Mack shrugged. "If there is, nobody has defined it yet. The textbooks say that it occurs in a random fashion, although it's seen much more commonly in pregnant women. Again, nobody knows why."

"You are aware that Kathy is two months pregnant?"

"Yeah," Mack said somberly.

Charlie Cook began tossing around in his bed, mumbling loudly. It sounded like he was calling for Dolly.

"Who is Dolly?" Joanna asked.

"His wife."

Joanna squinted an eye. "How did he get HIV?"

"By spending Friday afternoons with prostitutes, having unprotected sex."

Charlie Cook started to gag, with phlegm rattling in his throat. He was too weak to cough and clear it. Mack grabbed a suction tube and slid it into Cook's pharynx, sucking out a glob of blood-tinged mucus. The gagging stopped.

"Have you told Charlie's wife about his diagnosis?" Joanna asked.

"Not yet," Mack replied. "And I don't plan to for now, although she'll eventually have to be told and tested for HIV. Except for a few select individuals, nobody knows about this outbreak of smallpox, and I want to keep it that way."

Joanna looked at him oddly. "Surely the news is out now that the doctor in Mojave came down with the disease. He would have told someone."

"He thinks it's Ebola, and we left it that way," Mack elucidated. "And Wolinsky arranged for the house to be cordoned off and guarded by the California Highway Patrol. All the neighbors think the doctor caught some strange contagious virus that's now in the process of being identified. With that in mind, people keep their distance."

"And still no Maria?"

"Still no Maria," Mack replied. "She's a walking time bomb."

Joanna gazed up at a bank of monitors above Charlie Cook's bed. Next to the EKG screen, Mack had taped a calendar that now had seven days crossed out in red ink. "Three more days," she said wistfully. "Three more days and we'll be protected."

Charlie Cook started gagging again, and Mack went about the business of clearing the patient's airway.

"I'll go check on Kathy," Joanna said, and headed for isolation unit number one. She stopped at the door as she remembered that the room belonged to the Middle Eastern patient who had died the day before and was still in there, sealed in a plastic bag. She turned back to Mack. "When are you going to put the dead patient in your morgue?"

"I've already told Hughes to do it twice," Mack groused. "The guy just won't get off his ass."

"Maybe he's frightened."

"Hell, we're all frightened."

Joanna made a mental note to talk with Melvin Hughes,

whom she had gotten to know a little over the past week. Hughes was brighter than his partner, Charlie Cook, and had taken the ambulance job to support himself while he went to night school. He planned to become a medical technologist and work in a big laboratory or clinic. He had carried out his duties in the Viral Research Center without complaint, until Charlie Cook became ill and broke out in pustules all over. When Melvin saw those hideous lesions, he freaked out. It took twenty milligrams of Paxil a day to keep him calm.

"Let me chat with him," she said.

"Be my guest."

Joanna walked across the room and pressed down on a floor pedal. The door opened with a hiss, and Joanna entered isolation unit number three. The pungent odor of rotting flesh permeated everything. It was the smell of smallpox.

"Hi," Kathy said weakly.

"Hey," Joanna greeted her back, trying to sound upbeat despite Kathy's gruesome appearance. Her entire face was so densely covered with blackpox that no white skin was observable. "Do you feel any better?"

"A little worse, I think."

"I've got a feeling you're going to pull through," Joanna lied.

"No, I'm not." Kathy turned her face away and began sobbing. Her whole body seemed to shake. "I want to see my little girl again. I want to hold her close once more."

"I know." Joanna reached out and gently patted Kathy's shoulder. "I know."

"And who is going to look after my daughter?" Kathy went on, sniffing back her tears. "My husband is an airline pilot who spends half his time away from home. Who will be there for her?"

Joanna had no answer. No one had an answer for that. "Maybe the drug Dr. Brown gave you will help."

"It hasn't helped so far," Kathy responded. "If anything, my skin lesions are worse."

"The drug takes time to work," Joanna said, again trying to be optimistic.

But Joanna knew that the chances of the experimental drug slowing the disease were very small. Mack had managed to obtain samples of the drug Cidofovir, which was reportedly effective against the smallpox virus in vitro and shown to have some effectiveness in experimental animals. But it had never been used in humans.

Mack came into the unit and walked over to the bed. He took Kathy's hand and gave it a squeeze. "Any improvement?"

"I think my skin is worse," Kathy reported, sounding braver than she felt. "Some of the lesions on my arms are bigger."

"Don't worry about the skin lesions," Mack instructed her. "Those were when we started the drug. What counts is how you feel."

"Maybe a little better," Kathy replied, then decided to be totally candid. "About the same. If anything, a little worse."

"What about your cough?" Mack asked.

Kathy shook her head. "No change."

"I'm going to push the dose of the drug way up," Mack said. "We'll double it."

"Won't that cause a lot of side effects?"

"We'll have to take that chance, unless you say no."

Kathy considered the new idea, then slowly nodded. "Double it."

Joanna and Mack left the isolation rooms and went through the decontamination procedures. After changing into fresh scrub suits, they met in the observation area that looked into all four isolation units. In unit one the bed held a body bag containing the corpse of the Middle Eastern patient. In unit two Charlie Cook was vomiting up copious amounts of dark blood. In unit three Kathy Wells was crying herself to sleep.

Joanna asked, "That drug isn't going to help her, is it?"

"Probably not," Mack admitted.

"Then why double the dose?"

"Because there's a one in a million chance the drug will work," Mack answered. "And if it saves Kathy it just might save our asses too."

"How do you mean?"

"I mean that if we came down with smallpox, Cidofovir would be our only chance to survive."

"Come on, Kathy!" Joanna yelled out, sounding like a high school cheerleader. She shook her head, embarrassed, and looked over at Mack. "Do I sound like an idiot?"

"Hell, no."

They left the observation area and walked down a long corridor that was brightly lit. That signified it was daytime. Joanna glanced at her watch. It was two P.M.

"Want to get a bite?" Joanna suggested.

"After I talk with Melvin Hughes," Mack said hoarsely.

"Don't be too tough on him, Mack. Remember, he's not much more than a kid, and he's looking death right in the face."

"He's still got to pull his weight."

"He's trying, Mack."

They turned into another corridor and came to the recreation room. It had a regular door with a large frosted-glass pane. Inside there was the sound of music.

"Christ!" Mack growled under his breath. "He's listening to music."

"Or to his favorite soap opera."

Mack pointed to the shadow coming through the frosted pane. It was moving to and fro, swaying as if caught by a breeze. "People don't dance to soap operas. He's listening to the radio."

Mack pushed the door open for Joanna. She stepped into the recreation room, then stopped in her tracks, stunned by what she saw.

"Oh, my God!"

Melvin Hughes was swinging back and forth, hanging by his neck from the end of a rope.

19

The coded message on Ragoub's answering machine was the one he had been waiting for. It contained the number six, which meant all six jumbo jets were now in service. Ragoub pushed a button on the answering machine and listened to the message once again.

"This is Joe. I must cancel our dinner appointment for tonight. Let's make it for six o'clock tomorrow."

Ragoub erased the message and reached into his desk for the remote control. Moments later he was studying a large television screen that had a blue background and an outline of the United States in white. He focused in on the six flashing white dots. Two were stationary, one in New York and one in Atlanta. The other four dots were moving across middle America.

Ragoub picked up his phone and began making coded calls to his six lieutenants who were located in New York, Atlanta, Chicago, and Los Angeles. They were instructed to start tracking the jumbo jets and to obtain the flight schedules of the planes as far in advance as possible. Each lieutenant, along with his backup, was to make two practice runs aboard the planes, carefully rehearsing every move.

Ragoub tilted back in his swivel chair as he made the

third phone call. The plan was so simple. And so deadly. The flight schedules of the six jumbo jets would be known in advance, giving the lieutenants and their backups plenty of time to buy their tickets for May 15. Each of the six teams would board separate jets and sit in coach class on opposite sides of the plane, preferably between seat numbers thirty and forty. Each man would carry a laptop computer that would activate the aerosol devices that had been connected to the ventilation system. Once activated, the device would spew out the smallpox virus into the plane's cabin. And since the air inside the plane was continually recirculated, everyone on board would receive a massive dose of the virus. Everyone would come down with the disease, except for the twelve agents who had all been immunized against smallpox. The vaccines were provided by rogue Russian scientists who worked for the Holy Land League at a secret laboratory in the Sudan.

The scientists had been controlled by the KGB and had once worked at Vector, the supersecret facility in Siberia where the smallpox virus and other microorganisms were studied for their use in germ warfare. When the Soviet Union broke up, their top scientists scrambled for jobs in other parts of the world. The league had hired two of them whose particular expertise was genetically converting the smallpox virus into an even more virulent form. They also knew how to construct devices to deliver the deadly virus. Each scientist was paid $5,000 a month. A bargain by anybody's standards.

One more call, Ragoub told himself as he punched in the phone number of a rented apartment on the outskirts of Los Angeles. The phone rang five times before it was answered. Ragoub and his lieutenant exchanged coded greetings that indicated it was safe to talk. But Ragoub sensed trouble. The agent's voice sounded strained.

"What is wrong?" Ragoub asked.

There was a pause. In the background Ragoub could hear music and somebody singing.

"Is someone there?" Ragoub asked sternly.

"No one is here."

"Then what?"

The agent took a deep breath. "I have broken my ankle."

"What!"

"It was an accident."

"What kind of accident?" Ragoub demanded.

The agent paused again, then said quietly, "I broke it playing soccer."

Ragoub gritted his teeth, furious with the agent. *The idiot! We are so close to success, so close to destroying America, and this buffoon goes out and breaks an ankle.*

Ragoub calmed himself before asking, "How bad is the break?"

"It is in a cast."

"Can you walk?"

"With crutches."

Ragoub tried to hold his anger in check. An Arab with a broken ankle on crutches would draw attention and close inspection. They would search every square inch of his body and go through his belongings with a fine-tooth comb. And what if something went wrong and the agent had to move quickly?

"I can still do it," the agent said earnestly.

"Yes," Ragoub muttered. "I'm certain you can."

"Have faith in me, brother."

Ragoub gave a coded message and hung up.

Ragoub grabbed a box of candy from his desk and flung it across the room. It hit the television screen with a loud crack, sending pieces of candy flying everywhere.

The idiot! The moron! The most important mission of his

*life and he plays soccer and breaks an ankle. And he jeop-
ardizes everything.* An Arab with a cast on his leg would be
searched from top to bottom. They would double-check his
ID and discover that he was in America with an expired
visa and wanted by the INS for deportation. And they might
double-check the other Arab on board, the backup, and
learn that he, too, was wanted for deportation.

Ragoub shook his head angrily, trying to find a way out
of his dilemma. He considered a number of different op-
tions. He could let things go ahead as planned, but that
would be very risky. Or he could allow only the backup to
board that particular plane. But he would hate to do that.
Things could go wrong with only one man aboard. Maybe
the single device would foul up and not be properly activated. And that would waste a planeload of potential carriers.

Ragoub suddenly clapped his hands as a solution came to
him. *Get a replacement. Of course! But not someone from
abroad. Someone here. Someone bright who could learn
quickly and perform flawlessly. Someone like Yusef Malik.*

Ragoub began to pace the floor, deliberating the pros and
cons of bringing in someone new so late. It would increase
the chances of a mistake, regardless of the individual cho-
sen. But Yusef was smart enough to pull it off. Yes, he could
do it. He would be the perfect replacement. But there was
another matter to consider. Yusef had not been vaccinated
against smallpox, so he, too, would get the disease and die.
A good soldier lost forever.

Ragoub shrugged his shoulders indifferently. There were
casualties in every war.

The assassins, dressed in business suits, rang the bell of
the ranch-style house located a block away from the home
of Dr. Paul Bishop. A moment later a chubby middle-aged

woman with her hair up in curlers opened the door. She was wearing a faded bathrobe and was chewing gum. In the background a television set was playing loudly.

"Sorry to bother you, ma'am," the taller assassin said, flashing his phony badge. "We're with the sheriff's department and would like to ask you some questions."

"Jesus," the woman said irritably. "I've already talked with a dozen of you guys."

"We know." The assassin nodded to his companion, who nodded back. "And you've been very helpful, too."

The housewife's eyes widened. "I have?"

"Yes, ma'am," the assassin went on. "We just need to check a few things."

"Sure." The woman opened the door and stepped aside. "Would you like to come inside?"

"Yes, ma'am."

The assassins were glad to be off the porch, where they might be seen by passersby or nosy neighbors or by the Highway Patrol officers cordoning off the doctor's house.

The woman turned off the television set in the living room and came back to the assassins. "Like I told the other guys, I didn't know Dr. Bishop that well."

"But you did know him," the taller assassin said.

"Enough to wave and say hello," the woman answered. "But I was never in his house. And now I'm glad I wasn't. You know, with that awful disease in there."

"Did they tell you anything about the disease?"

"Only that it was something catching."

"Did you have contact with anyone in the house?"

"Oh, no," the woman said at once, then decided to alter her answer. "I mean, I never really touched anybody. On occasion I'd pass his Mexican housekeeper in the street and we'd say hello. But nothing more than that."

"Maria," the tall assassin said knowingly. "Has she worked for the doctor long?"

"At least five years." The woman moved in closer and lowered her voice. "I hear he pays her very, very well. And he lets her live in the guesthouse behind the mansion."

The assassins said nothing and let the woman ramble on.

"But I don't think there was any funny business between them," the woman added. "He's a sick old man, after all. I doubt that he'd be interested in . . ." She allowed her voice to trail off.

The assassins remained silent as the woman reached in her robe for a cigarette and lit it. She was obviously enjoying the interview.

"I hope she's not sick," the woman continued on. "Poor little thing. She's not sick, too, is she?" The woman stared up at the tall man, hoping he'd answer her question.

"We can't talk about that."

"I hope she's all right."

The assassin nodded slightly, as if he were taking her into his confidence. "Did Maria spend most of her time alone?"

The woman thought about that. "She was usually alone. But she has a foreign-looking boyfriend who comes around a lot and stays with her. That's according to my neighbor, Rose."

"When was the last time you or Rose saw Maria?"

"Three or four days ago, when Dr. Bishop got sick." The woman took a deep drag off her cigarette and exhaled a lungful of blue smoke. "She was out on the front lawn. But now, with that catchy disease and all, she probably spends most of her time in that guesthouse."

The assassins thanked the woman and left.

20

Jake remembered William Kitt from a case of domestic terrorism they'd worked on together five years ago. A nutty, far-right paramilitary group had tried to blow up the president of the United States and had almost succeeded. At the time, Kitt was section chief of the FBI's domestic terrorism unit. Now he headed a special counterterrorism unit that, together with a similar unit from the CIA, kept track of aliens from the Middle East who were suspected of having terrorist ties.

"We think our terrorist spent a lot of his time in Seattle," Kitt said. "In all likelihood, that was his base of operations."

"Is that solid?" Jake asked.

"It is."

"Based on what?"

"This."

Kitt opened a folder and placed it on the conference table in front of Jake and Lou Farelli. It contained a large black-and-white photograph of an open suitcase.

Jake studied the photograph, then slid it over to Farelli. "Where was this suitcase found?"

"In the unclaimed luggage section at Charles de Gaulle Airport outside Paris."

Kitt walked over to a large window in the Federal Building in West Los Angeles and looked out. The day was gray and gloomy, with a thick fog rolling in from the ocean. "We played a hunch and asked the French police to check the unclaimed luggage from planes arriving in Paris from Los Angeles on the day our terrorist was murdered. We knew his wife and children still lived in Paris and thought he might stop there first. The police found four pieces of unclaimed luggage. With three they were able to track down the owners. The fourth suitcase came off an Air France flight from Los Angeles. Khalil Mahmoud's fingerprints were all over it."

"Don't tell me you've got an American address," Jake said hopefully.

"I wish," Kitt told him. "What we've got are two gift-wrapped packages. One contained toys and a doll for his children, we assume. The other had a sweater for his wife. The children's package was of particular interest, because it still had a sales receipt inside it. The toys were purchased from a big department store in Seattle on April fourth."

"And no doubt paid for in cash," Jake added.

"Of course."

"Shit," Jake said slowly, thinking that a credit card number would have revealed the guy's whole life to them. He studied the photograph of the opened piece of luggage again and focused in on a neatly folded shirt. "Does the shirt in the suitcase have the same label as the one he had on when he got whacked?"

"The same," Kitt replied. "But the shirt in the suitcase is new and still in its wrapping. If we get lucky we may be able to narrow its origin down to one store."

Jake closed the folder. "Well, you've still got your hands full. Seattle is a big city."

"A very big city." Kitt was a tall man, in his early fifties, well built, with sharp features and his hair cut very short. "And it's ethnically diverse, just like Los Angeles. It's a perfect place for terrorists to fit in."

"They got a lot of Arabs up there?" Farelli inquired.

Kitt nodded as he came back from the window. "If you count only the ones with student visas, there's over forty of them we're keeping tabs on."

"We ought to kick the bastards out," Jake growled.

"A lot of them come from friendly countries," Kitt commented.

"Yeah," Jake said sharply. "Just like those assholes who flew those planes into the World Trade Center and into the Pentagon."

Kitt took a deep breath and refocused on the immediate problem they were facing. "We've got to find Khalil Mahmoud's trail and locate his fellow terrorists because time is running out. We now believe an attack is imminent, almost certain to occur in a matter of days."

Jake's brow went up. "Did you learn something new?"

"Two things," Kitt answered. "First, the number of intercepted communications between terrorist groups has increased substantially in the past week. Almost without exception, whenever there is a dramatic increase in the volume of intercepts, a major terrorist event soon follows. Second, the Italian intelligence service recently listened in on a phone conversation between two men who were known to have strong ties to a radical Islamic group. From the tone of their conversation, whatever is about to happen will happen very soon, and it will be awful, almost unimaginable. It'll be worse than nine-eleven."

"Did they give any clues about what they're planning?"

"No clues whatsoever."

"Then how do you know it's going to be so awful?"

Kitt hesitated, wondering if he should let them in on the

highly classified intercept. It was so chilling, yet it revealed
nothing about who, what, or where. Maybe it wasn't even
meant for America, Kitt hoped. But he knew that it was. "I'll
read you part of the intercept. I know that you'll make certain that its contents stay in this room."

Jake and Farelli leaned forward, ears pricked.

"This is it, word for word." Kitt reached for his glasses
and began reading from a sheet in another folder. " 'This will
be one of those strikes that will never be forgotten. This is a
terrifying thing, far worse than nine-eleven. This is a thing
that will spread from south to north, from east to west. The
person who came up with this program is a madman from a
madhouse, but he is a genius. He is fixated on this program;
it will leave everyone turned to ice.' "

There was a long, hushed silence in the room.

Farelli finally murmured, "Holy shit."

"Any ideas?" Kitt asked.

Jake rubbed his chin as he went over the key parts of the
intercept. "It talks about spreading in all directions and
everyone turning to ice. It's like a huge atomic explosion
that blots out the sun and causes things to freeze over."

Kitt nodded, thinking Jake Sinclair would have been a
good FBI agent. "That's what our analysts think, too. But
it's only a guess, of course."

"Fuck me," Farelli mumbled, more to himself than to the
others. "Could they manufacture a bomb like that?"

"They don't have to make one," Kitt informed them.
"They could simply buy one ready-made from some rogue
state and put it on a ship that's about to dock in Los Angeles or Seattle or New York. Or maybe they'd place bombs in
all three ports. With their simultaneous detonation, you'd
see a true nuclear winter in America."

"Son of a bitch!" Jake cursed angrily. "And we're just sitting here waiting for it to happen."

"Now you can see why we're so rushed for time," Kitt continued. "And every minute that passes brings us a minute closer to disaster."

"Why not flood the entire Seattle area with agents?" Jake suggested.

"We have, and so far we've come up with a big zilch."

Kitt took off his reading glasses and put them away. "To crack this one we're going to need more than legwork. We need good, solid information to lead us in the right direction. Otherwise our investigation will be slow and plodding, and take up time we no longer have."

"Are you talking about an informer?" Jake asked.

"That would be nice, but we can't just wait for one to come forward, because chances are one won't."

"What about bribes?"

Kitt shook his head. "That never works with the fundamentalist groups. That's why no one has pointed out bin Laden despite a twenty-five-million-dollar reward."

Jake considered the matter further, then threw up his hands. "I'm out of ideas."

"So are we," Kitt went on. "And when we run into a blank wall, the Bureau always retraces its steps to see if we've missed anything. Our analysts in Washington are restudying all of Khalil Mahmoud's belongings and remains, looking for any clue we may have overlooked. They'd like Dr. Joanna Blalock to do the same."

Jake hesitated briefly, then said, "She's, ah, she's ill."

"Too ill to think?" Kitt prodded.

"I'll see," Jake replied, reflecting on Joanna and the dangerous situation at Memorial. Now everybody in the Viral Research Center was sick with the contagious disease, except for Joanna and Mack Brown. No one had died, according to Joanna. But Jake wasn't sure she was telling the truth. When he had talked to Joanna late yesterday, her voice sounded strained, yet even, as if she were trying to cover up her feelings. Deep in his bones, Jake was certain something awful was going on down there.

"Please stress how important this is," Kitt urged.

"I will."

Kitt sat down and drew his chair close to the conference table. Outside, a light rain was falling, the sky darkening more. "You've been following a man named Haj Ragoub. He's small potatoes. You're wasting your time."

Jake gave Kitt a long look and asked, "You're sure of that, huh?"

"Positive," Kitt said without hesitation. "He's been checked fifty ways from Sunday, and he's clean. He can't lead you to anyone important."

"Why did you check him out so thoroughly?"

"He was contributing heavily to a Muslim charity that was suspected of funneling money to Hamas," Kitt explained.

"And?"

"We were wrong," Kitt said. "All the money was going for true humanitarian causes."

Jake gave Kitt another long look. "Haj Ragoub keeps some interesting company."

"Like who?"

"Like Yusef Malik."

Kitt flicked his hand disdainfully. "He's a bit player. He goes to rallies, yells 'Free Palestine' a dozen times, then ends up at some nightclub on Sunset Strip."

Jake nodded. "That pretty much sums up our take on him, too."

"Like I said, he's a bit player."

"And Ragoub's not a player at all, eh?"

"He runs an electronics store and pays taxes."

"Sounds like a solid citizen."

"Very solid."

Jake pushed himself up from his seat and said, "I'll try to reach Dr. Blalock tonight."

"Get back to me as soon as possible."

Outside, the rain was falling harder. A bad accident at the intersection of Wilshire and Veteran had snarled traffic in all directions. Jake and Farelli stood under a roof on the patio of the Federal Building, watching the traffic back up as they waited for the rain to ease.

Jake asked, "What do you make of Kitt wanting us to drop our tail on Ragoub?"

"Something's wrong," Farelli said. "Something doesn't smell right."

"How do you figure?"

Farelli coughed up some phlegm and spat it out into the rain. "Because there are only two ways the FBI could know we were following Ragoub. Either he noticed we were watching him and bitched to someone big, or the FBI was following him and we got in the way of their tail."

Jake nodded slowly. "And either way, the FBI was lying to us."

"Those bastards never learn to play straight, do they?"

"Not with the outside world."

"So what are we going to do about Ragoub?"

"We're going to keep following him."

The rain let up and they ran for their car.

21

With effort Joanna and Mack lifted the bagged body of Kathy Wells and placed it on a shelf in the small refrigerated morgue next to the corpse of Charlie Cook, who had died the night before. The morgue had no beds or gurneys, just shelves built into the walls, and now all four were filled.

Joanna was still stunned by the way Kathy had died. She had literally bled to death right in front of their eyes, with black blood pouring out of every orifice in her body. "I've never seen anything like that."

"Me neither," Mack said, pausing to catch his breath. "And I hope to God I never see it again."

They had been at Kathy's bedside, talking with her, when the young nurse started to retch and heave. At first nothing came up. Then all hell broke loose. Black blood suddenly gushed out of her mouth and nose and rectum. It came out in torrents and flooded onto the floor, covering everything in black gook. Kathy Wells bled out in less than two minutes, and died with her eyes wide open.

"Think we should decontaminate ourselves?" Joanna asked, closing the door to the morgue.

Mack shook his head. "Twice should be enough."

"I've never seen blood go over everything like that before."

"That's what happens when you pump out six quarts real fast."

Kathy's blood had splashed over everything in the unit, including the bed, floor, machines, and supplies. It had also soaked into Mack's and Joanna's gowns, gloves, and shoes. Only the ceiling was spared. They had decontaminated themselves twice after placing Kathy Wells in a sealed plastic bag. But still Joanna worried. They had again been doused with blood that contained tons of the smallpox virus.

"Two more days," Joanna hoped out loud, "and we'll be immunized against smallpox."

"Two more days," Mack repeated, taking her arm and guiding her away from the morgue. "Let's go talk with Marshall Wolinsky."

They left the restricted area and walked down a long corridor. The lighting was dim, indicating it was night outside. There was an eerie silence in the hall, a reminder of all those who had died.

Mack glanced at the frosted pane in the door to the recreation room, remembering the shadow of Melvin Hughes's body as it swung back and forth. "I didn't see any signs that the kid was thinking about suicide."

"Nobody did."

"Hell, he might have survived the disease."

"No, he wouldn't have," Joanna said. "He would have died a miserable death from smallpox, just like the others."

They had examined Melvin Hughes's body after cutting it down. He had clusters of the telltale lesions of smallpox on his chest and shoulders, and a few on his face. Melvin was a walking dead man and he knew it. Joanna wondered if she would have the courage to kill herself if the smallpox virus began to ravage her body.

They entered the telecommunications center and sat in the comfortable cockpit chairs. Joanna tilted back and stretched out her legs, still thinking about Melvin Hughes, a nice kid who was working for an ambulance service so he could pay his way through school. And he walked right into a cesspool of smallpox. Like everyone else, he believed he was helping and had no idea it would cost him his life.

"Ready?" Mack asked.

"Ready."

Mack lifted the lid on the armrest and fiddled with the buttons on the console. Moments later Marshall Wolinsky appeared on the big television screen. He wasn't in a studio this time, but rather in a hospital ward of some sort.

"Have you changed locations, Marshall?" Mack asked.

"Same place, different area," Wolinsky replied, and moved aside to give the viewers a better look. In the background were beds and monitors, and doctors and nurses who were dressed in white. "As you know, we're at a military base on the edge of the Mojave Desert. The base was recently downsized to a skeleton crew until final closure next year. Fortunately they left the dispensary and small hospital behind it open, and we've taken it over."

"Where's the staff from?"

"We flew in a special infectious-disease unit from Walter Reed."

Joanna leaned over to Mack and whispered, "Why not get a team from the CDC or USAMRIID?"

Wolinsky heard the question and answered for Mack. "Because the CDC and USAMRIID are wonderful research facilities but don't look after sick patients. The team from Walter Reed may well be the best in the world at caring for people who have rare infectious diseases."

The rapid response to the smallpox outbreak had to be part of some rehearsed plan, Joanna was thinking. No one could put all this together so quickly on the spur of the moment. "How many teams do you have?"

"Enough for now," Wolinsky said vaguely. "But then, we only have two cases of smallpox to deal with."

Joanna came forward in her seat. "You have a second case?"

Wolinsky nodded. "A delivery boy who helped the housekeeper, Maria, carry out the blood-soaked mattress that your Middle Eastern patient slept on. The boy must have inhaled a tremendous load of the smallpox virus. He's now covered with blackpox and is terribly ill."

"Christ." Mack groaned loudly. "I wonder how many people he infected with the virus?"

"Very few, we think." Wolinsky motioned to Elliot Durr to come over and have a seat. "Dr. Durr has done an excellent job tracking the boy during the time he was contagious. We may have gotten a little lucky here. Tell them why, Elliot."

Durr stared directly at them, not showing any signs of his earlier nervousness. "The boy first noticed a red rash Saturday evening while watching television. He stayed home, thinking it was an allergy, but the rash worsened and the next day began to show discoloration. That night it turned black, and for the first time he noticed distinct pustules. The next day he was quite ill, but still went to his job as delivery boy for the pharmacy. The pharmacist saw the boy was sick and sent him home to recuperate. The boy made no deliveries. Thus, when he was actively spewing virus, he was either alone or with the pharmacist, who has now been vaccinated and quarantined."

Mack thought carefully about the delivery boy's history, knowing instinctively that the boy would have had plenty of opportunity to spread the virus. "When he carried that blood-soaked mattress out, he must have gotten blood all over himself and his clothing. His clothing had to be saturated with the smallpox virus, so wherever he went he must have contaminated everything around him."

"That's where the luck comes in." Wolinsky picked up the story. "Apparently the black vomitus and what have you did badly stain the delivery boy's clothing. So the housekeeper had him strip and take a long, hot shower while she put his clothes in the washer. The stains wouldn't come out, so she gave him some of the old doctor's freshly laundered clothes to wear. The boy's contaminated clothing was left in the doctor's house. However, to be on the safe side we've cultured the boy's room, car, and clothes for the virus. And thus far everything is negative. A nice bit of luck, wouldn't you say?"

"I wish we had some down here," Mack mumbled to himself.

"What's that?" Wolinsky asked, holding a hand to his ear.

"I said, who made the diagnosis in the delivery boy?"

Wolinsky smiled weakly. "The California Highway Patrol."

"What!" Joanna and Mack said almost simultaneously.

Wolinsky nodded. "When the boy saw the black lesions spreading over his body, he rushed over to Dr. Bishop's house. The old doctor used to treat the boy for free. Anyhow, the patrolmen guarding the gate noticed the black lesions, hustled the boy into the house, and called us."

"Well," Mack concluded, "half the world must know about the smallpox outbreak by now."

"Not really," Wolinsky said, showing little concern. "Even with the new cases, very few people know what it is. That's because very few people, including physicians, have heard of the blackpox form of smallpox. It's given a line or two in most medical textbooks."

"So what do people think it is?"

"A strange, poorly identified virus from Central America," Wolinsky replied.

"Eventually news of smallpox has to leak out," Mack warned.

"We'll deal with it if and when it does," Wolinsky said. "As of now, the local people think the doctor caught the jungle virus from Maria's boyfriend."

Joanna inquired, "And still no Maria?"

"Still no Maria."

Mack rocked back and forth in his chair, trying to fit the pieces of the infectious disease puzzle together. *How the hell does someone come down with smallpox in the Mojave Desert?* he kept asking himself. He looked up at the giant television screen. "And there have been no other reported cases of smallpox anywhere else in the world. Right?"

Wolinsky hesitated before saying, "It's possible there have been other cases."

"Where?" Mack asked at once.

"According to the CIA, there may have been an outbreak in the Sudan three months ago. The report has not been confirmed," Wolinsky emphasized, "but this is what the agency was told by a recent Sudanese defector. In early February of this year there was an outbreak of smallpox in a village north of Khartoum. Approximately twenty cases of smallpox occurred before the outbreak was controlled with ring containment and vaccination."

For Joanna's benefit, Wolinsky explained that ring containment consisted of encircling and totally sealing off any village with known cases of smallpox. Those patients already ill would either die or recover, while those exposed to the virus were vaccinated. The ring containment–vaccination program had been instrumental in eradicating smallpox during the 1970s.

"But that doesn't help us very much," Wolinsky went on, "because your patient was exposed to the smallpox virus within the past three to four weeks. Even if he had been in the Sudan, he wouldn't have carried the virus around for over a month before becoming ill."

Mack asked, "Does the CIA think this report is valid?"

"So far they do," Wolinsky replied. "The CIA tested the defector's blood and found a high concentration of antibodies to smallpox, which means he's been recently vaccinated. That certainly adds credibility to his story."

"How large was their vaccination program?" Mack pondered, wondering if the Sudanese were concealing the size of the outbreak, as many third-world countries tended to do.

"They're checking into that now." Wolinsky turned away to give instructions to a nurse, then came back to Mack and Joanna. "But the CIA's biggest concern is the location of the village where the outbreak reportedly took place. It's located near a big drug-manufacturing facility, which has frequent visitors with ties to known radical Islamic groups. And the latter fact has been documented by photographs from orbiting spy satellites."

"Jesus," Mack hissed disgustedly. "Are they thinking bioterrorism? Do they think those bastards are growing the smallpox virus there?"

Wolinsky chose his words carefully. "It's possible. In this world gone mad, anything is possible."

"Maybe our patient was Sudanese," Joanna thought aloud. "Maybe that's the source of his disease."

Wolinsky shook his head. "The time sequence doesn't fit. The outbreak in the Sudan occurred three months ago. If he was there, his disease wouldn't have waited over two months to make its appearance."

"Maybe a package from that village was mailed to him

months ago," Joanna countered. "Maybe it came by ship and just got here."

Wolinsky nodded in admiration. "I hadn't thought of that," he admitted.

"Would you ask your friends at the CIA if the Sudanese people have any special markers in their blood that might identify them?" Joanna requested.

"Will do."

Wolinsky reached into the pocket of his white laboratory coat and extracted a large index card. "While we're talking about your Middle Eastern patient, I think we've finally tracked down the word he kept uttering. The problem was that you spelled it phonetically. It's not *N-A-C-B-A-R*. Rather, its *N-A-Q-B-A*. It's an Arabic word that means 'catastrophe.' The Palestinians use the word *naqba* in reference to the day Israel declared its independence. *Naqba* to them means the day of catastrophe. So it seems your patient is probably Arab and not Pakistani."

Joanna squinted an eye, puzzled. "But why did he keep repeating the word? I mean, the state of Israel is a fact. It's not going to suddenly disappear."

"Maybe he was thinking of another catastrophe," Mack suggested.

"Like what?" Joanna asked.

Mack shrugged and said nothing.

Wolinsky placed the index card back in his coat pocket. "Well, whatever catastrophe he was referring to, it's unlikely to occur out on the sands of the Mojave Desert. There's nothing out there but—"

Joanna's jaw dropped. "Oh, my God!"

Mack spun around to look at her. "What?"

"It's bioterrorism," Joanna said, taking a moment to gather herself. "We're looking at bioterrorism."

"Based on what?" Wolinsky asked quickly.

"Based on the fact that a known Arab terrorist spent time in the Mojave Desert approximately two weeks ago," Joanna said. "And that was just about the time our patient got infected with the smallpox virus."

"How do you know these facts about a terrorist?" Wolinsky asked.

"Because I did his autopsy."

Wolinsky hurriedly reached for a pen and legal pad. "I need details."

Joanna described how Khalil Mahmoud had been assassinated at LAX, with no identification items on him, and how the police had discovered multiple false passports hidden in his coat, and how, with the help of the French, the terrorist's true identity was established. Then she gave Wolinsky the autopsy findings, emphasizing the type of sand found on the terrorist's shoes. "The most likely source of the sand was the Mojave Desert."

Wolinsky exhaled noisily, rapidly tapping his pen on the tabletop. "And you think the paths of these two men crossed?"

"What are the chances of two Arabs with false IDs being out in the Mojave at the same time?" Joanna retorted. "And of the two, one is a known terrorist and the other a could-be terrorist."

Wolinsky raised an eyebrow. "What makes you believe your patient was a could-be terrorist?"

"Because he was an Arab with an alias who was running around the Mojave Desert for no apparent reason," Joanna explained. "Then he starts babbling about some catastrophe. And on top of that, he was the first case of smallpox in America over the past forty years. I'd say that made him suspicious."

"You've got a point," Wolinsky conceded, rapidly scribbling down the new information. "Too bad there's no way to definitely tie the known terrorist into this smallpox outbreak."

"Maybe there is," Joanna said thoughtfully. "We have a good photograph of Khalil Mahmoud. I suggest you give it to the CIA and see if they can match his face with any of those coming out of that drug-manufacturing plant in Sudan."

"Excellent idea," Wolinsky said, head down as he continued to write. "I take it you've had some experience in intelligence work, Dr. Blalock?"

"Some," Joanna told him. Other ways to connect the terrorist to the smallpox virus quickly came to her. "We should also review all the slides and tissues we have from Khalil Mahmoud. We saw no evidence of smallpox the first time around, but we should look again."

"And the tissues should be cultured for the virus as well," Wolinsky added.

"I'll have my associate, Lori McKay, review all the slides and tissues from the terrorist. We'll need one of your people to do the viral studies."

"Elliot can handle that for us," Wolinsky said, nodding to his assistant, who nodded back. "He'll also need any frozen plasma or blood samples you might have."

"Those will be made available," Joanna assured him. "Please call Dr. McKay tomorrow and set up a schedule for the work to be done."

"Elliot will see to it." Wolinsky tilted back in his chair and rubbed his eyes with his palms, fatigue showing on his face. "Bioterrorism right here in our own backyard," he muttered. "It's just a matter of time before they start killing Americans this way."

"They've already started killing us," Joanna reminded him.

Wolinsky nodded gloomily. "Has there been any change where you are?"

"For the worse," Mack informed him. "Our nurse just died. She bled out in front of our eyes."

"Sad," Wolinsky said softly. "But that's the usual course with blackpox. You get it and you die."

"The room Kathy Wells was in is a mess," Joanna told him. "There's blood and goo over everything. We figured there was an ocean of virus in there, so we just sealed it off."

"Leave it that way," Wolinsky advised. "We can clean it up later."

The giant television screen went blank.

Joanna and Mack stood and stretched their backs, then left the room, closing the door behind them. The light in the corridor was so dim they could barely see the walls.

"You've got to brighten these damn halls," Joanna said irritably. Despite the light system in the corridor, she had no sense of day or night. The absence of sunlight had thrown her body clock off completely.

"I'll change their intensity tomorrow," Mack promised, stretching his back again. "How about some dinner?"

"I think I'll settle for coffee."

They walked down the quiet corridor, past the recreation area, and entered a small, darkened dining room. Bright lights came on automatically, and they had to shield their eyes against the glare.

Mack waited for his eyes to adjust to the light, then stepped over to the coffee machine. As he reached for cups, he glanced down at the upper part of his chest. His face suddenly went pale.

Joanna started to walk over, saying, "I'd like mine black with—"

Mack spun around and held his hands up. "Stay back!"

Joanna was momentarily startled by his outburst. "What's wrong?"

Mack pulled down the top of his scrub shirt, exposing his chest and shoulders. They were covered with red papules.

"Oh, God! No!"

22

Maria Rodriguez waited patiently in the darkness of her hiding place. It had been almost an hour since she had last heard the sound of footsteps overhead and the slamming of the front door. But still she waited to make sure no one remained in the great house of the doctor she worked for. A nice man, she thought, a good man. But even he couldn't protect her if the police discovered she was an illegal immigrant.

Maria felt a chill go through her body and wondered if she, too, would come down with the awful illness. For the past twenty-four hours she had not been well, with fever and body aches. And she thought she had a rash on her arms, too, but it was difficult to see by candlelight. It probably was the sickness, she had to admit, and for that reason she had no choice but to leave her hiding place in the cellar of the great house. She would seek out friends who would give her a ride to Los Angeles, where she would be looked after by other friends and by a Mexican doctor if necessary. Then the sickness would pass and Maria could find new work.

Another chill came. Maria wrapped herself up in a thick woolen blanket. She had never felt this bad, but she had a strong constitution and knew she would survive. But first she had to get out of the dampness of the cellar, which no doubt was making her illness worse.

Holding up a candle, Maria glanced around her secret hiding place. It was nothing more than a corner in the cellar that had been sealed off with plywood. Yet it had served her well. The police had come down the creaking steps into the cellar and looked around and seen nothing. They never came back. And now they were gone from the great house, at least for the night. Maria knew it was nighttime because the cellar had become much damper and colder, like the outside air. She deliberated whether she should wait a little longer in the cellar, but another chill came and told her it was time to go.

Maria reached for her purse and pushed the plywood aside. Wrapping the woolen blanket around her shoulders, she walked over to the stairs and started up, making as little noise as possible. But the wooden stairs still creaked. At the top she blew out the candle and slowly opened the door. The house was black and still, the air musty from lack of ventilation. With careful steps she made her way down the hall and into the living room of the great house. The darkness was almost overwhelming, but she knew the floor plan by heart and inched slowly toward the large window.

Maria cracked the drapes slightly and peered out. The front gate was lighted, with a police car guarding it. She quickly backed away, wondering if the rear of the house was also guarded.

Maria went back to the hallway and walked down to the kitchen at the very rear of the house. The blinds on the window were open. Outside, it was pitch-black, with a moonless sky. Maria opened the back door and quietly crossed the garden, passing the guesthouse she had lived in for five years. She was tempted to go inside and get her things, but then she saw the yellow tape sealing the door and decided not to.

Maria followed the path to the street behind the great house, the same path she had used to sneak Ahmed into her bedroom. *Poor Ahmed,* she thought sadly, remembering how ill he was. But the American doctors were so good they would make him well.

Maria stopped abruptly and leaned against a tree as a giant chill swept through her body. She wrapped her blanket tightly around her, but it gave her little warmth and the chill continued. She sank to the ground, still shaking, her legs so weak she couldn't go on. Her eyelids became heavy and started to close. Desperately she tried to keep them open, but couldn't. She dozed off in the cool night air.

Maria slept for only minutes before she was suddenly awakened. A bright light came closer and closer, then whizzed by. She rapidly blinked her eyes, realizing that it was a passing car. Slowly she got to her feet and continued on, feeling better but still weak. It had been this way with Ahmed, she recalled. He would have chills and fever, and afterward would sleep. When he awoke he was better. But not for long.

Maria trudged on, passing big, expensive homes most with their lights off. Every half block she had to stop and rest. There was no way she could make it to Rosa's restaurant. It was a mile away and she was so very tired.

Up ahead on a corner lawn she saw a bicycle. The house behind the lawn was dark, and the lights were off in the adjacent homes as well. Maria hesitated, still eyeing the bicycle. She had never stolen anything in her life, but she knew the bike was her only chance to reach Rosa's.

Maria saw the lights of a car approaching and waited for it to go by. When its taillights disappeared in the distance, she climbed on the bicycle and rode away.

She still had to stop every few blocks to gather her strength. But the thought of getting well and paying off her mother's house pushed her on. When the house was at last paid for, Maria daydreamed, they would have a party and she would kiss her mother's cheeks and never leave her side again. They would plant a garden and grow their own vegetables and live simply. But she would be home, and that was what counted most.

Maria finally came to the commercial district and abandoned the bicycle in an alley a block from Rosa's. She took a poorly lighted street so she could reach the parking lot of Rosa's without being seen. Once again the chills and fever came, and her legs began to wobble. Maria rested against the side of a building and waited for the weakness to pass. In the dim light she could see the black blotches on her arms. They had gotten much larger. She rearranged her blanket so that it hid the skin lesions, then headed for the parking lot. She saw a dozen cars, none of which she recognized.

"Hola, Maria!" the attendant greeted her warmly.

"Buenas noches, Miguel!"

Miguel studied her face and saw that it was pale and drawn. "Are you all right?"

"I have the flu," Maria lied.

"So do half the people in town," Miguel said. "But why are you out in the cold night air?"

"A relative in Los Angeles has become ill and I must go there," Maria lied again. "Do you know of anyone driving there tonight?"

Miguel rubbed his chin as he surveyed the cars in the parking lot. "Let me see." Again he went over the lot, then pointed to a late-model Chevrolet. "Mr. Garcia often drives to Los Angeles after dinner. He has a good construction job there and must be on-site very early."

"Would he give me a ride?"

"I'm certain he would," Miguel said, once more struck by how ill Maria looked. "I could ask him for you."

"Please do."

Miguel motioned to the Chevrolet. "Why don't you lie down in the backseat while I speak with Mr. Garcia?"

"Thank you, Miguel."

Maria was so weak and tired she could barely make it to the car. She lay down in the backseat and sank into a deep sleep, again dreaming about her mother's house in Mexico and the garden they would grow.

Ragoub and Yusef Malik sat at a corner table in Arabia and spoke in low voices. The dinner crowd was gone, the restaurant empty except for the Algerian-French waiter, who was sitting on a bar stool thirty feet away. Ragoub eyed the waiter suspiciously, still not trusting him. Any Arab who claimed to be French wasn't really an Arab at all.

Ragoub lowered his voice even further. "I have heard of an upcoming mission."

Yusef stared at his water glass and said nothing.

"And the mission may include you," Ragoub went on. He waited for a reaction from Yusef, but there was none. "A very delicate mission."

Yusef showed no expression and remained silent.

Ragoub studied the young man's face, thinking Yusef was a born leader. He was smart and disciplined, showed no emotion, and talked only when he had to. Too bad he had to die. "Are you interested?"

"If it serves the cause of my people," Yusef replied.

There was a long silence. The only sound was made by traffic passing by outside. A siren wailed somewhere in the distance.

Ragoub asked, "Aren't you curious about the type of mission?"

Yusef shrugged. "You will tell me when I need to know."

The perfect answer, Ragoub thought. *Damn, the boy is*

good. Almost too good to be sacrificed. "It will occur here in America, and those who take part in it will be honored a thousand times over."

Yusef said nothing, but his eyes seemed to narrow ever so slightly.

Yes, Ragoub thought, *he is eager, but he knows how to hold it in check.* "Have you bought the plane tickets to return home?"

Yusef nodded. "For my father, Rawan, and myself. As you instructed."

"Reschedule your flight for June one," Ragoub told him. "Tell your father and Rawan you'll be joining them later."

"I need a reason."

"You're smart," Ragoub said, smiling thinly. "Think of one."

Yusef was about to say something, but decided not to.

"You can speak freely," Ragoub coaxed. "I can see you have something on your mind."

Yusef shook his head. "It is nothing."

"Speak!" Ragoub commanded.

There was another moment of silence; then Yusef said, "I want to do whatever is required perfectly. And a perfect performance requires rehearsal."

Ragoub nodded. "You make a good point."

"With that in mind, I have a question."

"Ask it."

Yusef lowered his voice to a whisper. "Is there anything in particular I should practice?"

"You will be told more later." Ragoub pushed his chair back and stood up, thinking Yusef would be told much, much later, when there was no chance for him to talk to others. "After all is accomplished, you will be honored a thousand times."

"Thank you, my friend."

Ragoub waved away the gratitude. He headed for the door, wondering if he should go against his instincts and have Yusef vaccinated against smallpox. That would save the young man's life, but it would also be a tip-off as to what was about to happen. It would definitely raise questions and maybe rumors, which could spread like wildfire.

No, Ragoub decided, it was better to sacrifice Yusef Malik. He could be replaced. The opportunity to kill millions of Americans couldn't.

23

"I'm dead," Mack said, showing little emotion. He was sitting on the edge of the bed in isolation unit four.

"Maybe you've built up enough immunity to ward it off," Joanna told him, trying to offer some hope.

"Forget it." Mack pulled up his green scrub shirt, exposing his chest and upper arms. They were covered with black lesions. "The disease is moving too fast. I can already see big pustules forming."

Joanna could see them too. Although she was standing behind a Plexiglas window in the observation area, she could clearly discern the awful skin lesions of smallpox. Now they appeared to be black bumps filled with fluid, but soon they would rupture and exude pus and blood.

"I think we should give you more hyperimmune globulin," Joanna proposed.

"There *is* no more," Mack said. "And even if there was, it's too late. The globulin would have no effect now."

"I'm not just going to let you die," Joanna argued.

"You're not going to have any choice."

"I'm going to call Wolinsky and discuss the—"

"You'd be wasting your time," Mack cut her off. "He'll

tell you the same thing I just told you. And remember, I've seen more cases of smallpox than he has."

"Don't . . . don't a few people survive the disease?"

"Not when it's the blackpox," Mack said with equanimity. "I'm a goner. I've accepted it. You may as well do the same."

Joanna sighed despondently. "Is there anything I can do for you?"

"In the top drawer of my desk is a letter to my wife and children. See that they get it."

Mack looked away briefly, thinking about his wife and two boys, whom he'd never see again. The boys would do fine, just as he had when he lost his father early. But his wife was another matter. She was so dependent on him. "Anyhow"—he brought his mind back to the letter—"I wrote it before I got sick, so it's not contaminated and won't hurt my family."

Oh, yes, it will, Joanna thought. *It will hurt them terribly. And they'll read it over and over again, and each time they read it, it will bring more pain and tears.* A lump came into Joanna's throat. She tried to swallow it away.

"You'll be down here for another two and a half days," Mack went on with his instructions. "That will make twelve days, which should give you complete immunity to the smallpox virus."

"I thought you were protected against the virus *ten* days after vaccination?"

Mack shrugged. "A few people take as long as twelve days. But don't worry. You'll make it."

"No, I won't," Joanna said honestly. "I'm next and I know it."

Mack shook his head. "The hyperimmune globulin injection you were given will protect you."

Joanna shook her head back at him. "It sure as hell didn't protect you."

"That's because I didn't receive the initial injection."

"What?"

Mack got off the bed and started walking around the unit. He involuntarily scratched the lesions on his chest. "I had only one vial of the hyperimmune globulin, which was barely enough to protect one patient, let alone five. The only fair way to decide who would receive the immune globulin was to draw lots. You won."

"But everybody received a shot," Joanna recalled. "Within hours of being exposed, we all got an injection."

"But only you got the immune globulin," Mack explained. "The others received injections of saline. The reason I did it that way was because I knew you'd refuse the globulin injection and insist it be given to someone else— like our pregnant nurse."

"Couldn't you have gotten more of the hyperimmune globulin right away?" Joanna asked, feeling a mixture of guilt and relief that she had received the globulin injection.

"We tried," Mack said. "But some bureaucratic asshole held things up, and it took three days to reach us. By then the virus had already taken hold."

"So that's why we received a second injection so late?"

Mack nodded, then went over to a pitcher and poured water into a glass. He sipped it slowly and tried to ignore the burning sensation it caused. In his mind's eye he could envision the pus-filled vesicles forming in the back of his throat. "So you should have enough of the immune globulin to be protected."

"I feel guilty as hell about this," Joanna admitted.

"Don't," Mack said at once. "You won it fair and square."

And besides, Mack thought, *you're not home safe yet.* The first injection Joanna received contained only the minimum recommended dose of hyperimmune globulin, and that might not be enough to protect her against a virulent strain of smallpox. And to complicate matters, the initial batch of immune globulin had been sitting on a shelf somewhere for six years and might have lost some of its potency.

"There are some things you have to know." Mack broke the silence. "So listen up."

He gave her instructions on how to use the telecommunications system that connected the Viral Research Center to Marshall Wolinsky's command center, and waited for her to write them down. Then he told her about the keys in his desk drawer that would bring the elevator car down, and finally about a secret emergency escape route that was to be used only under the direst circumstances.

"Got it?" Mack asked.

"Got it."

Mack began to cough. It was a dry, hacking cough, but he knew that would change soon. It would become wet and uncontrollable, and finally suffocating. He glanced over at the Plexiglas window. "Do you remember our promise?"

"Which promise?"

"The one about starting a morphine drip," Mack said evenly.

Joanna nodded slowly, wondering if she were capable of performing euthanasia. "I remember."

"I'll tell you when."

Joanna walked away, then recalled another question she wanted to ask and came back to the Plexiglas window. Mack was lying on his bed, his chest heaving up and down. Joanna couldn't tell if he was coughing or sobbing. She quietly crept away.

Joanna went down the empty corridor, gathering herself and listing the things she had to do while she waited to see if her fate would be the same as the others'. The first order of business was to contact Marshall Wolinsky and let him guide her through this nightmare. Maybe there were some things she could do to help Mack. But deep down she knew there weren't any. *What a shitty way to die,* she kept thinking.

She entered Mack's office and sat at his cluttered desk. In the top drawer was a sealed envelope addressed to Mack's wife, Martha Ann. It contained a letter and a small, round metallic object. Joanna resisted the urge to hold the envelope up to the light to see what the metallic object was. At the very rear of the drawer was the key that would bring the elevator down to the Viral Research Center. And beside that was a plastic card, which, when inserted into the appropriate slot, would open the door to a secret passageway.

Closing the drawer, Joanna tilted back in the swivel chair and again thought about Mack and whether she could really kill him. That was what a morphine drip did. It put the patient to sleep and eventually paralyzed the respiratory center in the brain, stopping all breathing. It killed—and the person who performed it was technically a killer. But she would do it if she had to. Better to go out peacefully than to suffocate in agony on your own blood.

And if the blackpox struck Joanna, she would do the same thing to herself. But she wouldn't use an IV drip. She'd put a tourniquet on her arm and inject herself with a big bolus of morphine. She'd be dead in seconds. They'd probably find her with the needle still in her vein.

Joanna wondered if Mack were telling her the truth, if she were really the only one who had received the initial injection of immune globulin. Maybe he was telling her that only to give her some hope. *Stop being paranoid,* she berated herself. *If he said he gave you the damn immune globulin, he gave it.* But that still didn't guarantee her protection, and she knew it. Mack had told Wolinsky that the initial injection of immune globulin contained only the *minimum recommended dose*. And that was unlikely to protect her against a massive exposure to the smallpox virus.

The phone rang loudly.

Joanna took a deep breath and picked it up.

"How are you doing down there?" Jake asked.

"It's bad," Joanna replied, making no attempt to conceal her fear. "Real bad."

"What happened?" Jake asked, alarmed.

"Everybody has the disease," she told him. "Everybody but me."

"You've got to get the hell out of there," Jake urged.

"That won't help."

"Why not?"

"Because I may already be infected with the virus but not having any symptoms yet," she explained. "And if I am infected, there's no effective treatment."

"When will you know for sure?"

"In a few more days."

"Goddamn it!" Jake fumed. "How did you get into this mess? Somebody must have screwed up."

"It's nobody's fault," Joanna said. "It just happened. And I might get out of here yet."

"You talking about the shots they gave you?"

"Yeah."

"Well, they sure didn't work worth a damn on anybody else," Jake cried out before he realized what he was saying. "Maybe it'll work for you, though," he added quickly.

"It's my best chance."

"Anything I can do for you up here?"

"You might consider praying."

"I'm already doing that," Jake said. "And Farelli has been to Mass three times this week. That's an all-time high for him."

"You thank him for me."

"You can thank him yourself when you get your pretty ass out of there."

Joanna felt herself blush. "You'll never let me down, will you, Jake?"

"Never in a million years."

After that he fell silent, and Joanna knew what that meant. "This isn't just a how-are-you-feeling call, is it?"

"We can talk later," Jake said.

"We can talk now," Joanna retorted. "Is it police business?"

"Yup."

"Good," Joanna said as she switched mental gears. "I need to get my mind somewhere else right now."

"How well do you know Seattle?" Jake inquired.

"So-so," Joanna answered. "I've visited there three or four times."

"That's where our terrorist was based." Jake told her about his conversation with William Kitt and the evidence indicating that Khalil Mahmoud had lived for a while in Seattle. "But it's a big city, and so far the FBI hasn't found even a trace of him. They want to know if you have any ideas that might help pinpoint his whereabouts in Seattle."

Joanna considered the matter at length, focusing in on the six positive findings at autopsy. She carefully ticked them off in her mind. One: A stab wound beneath the sternum that ripped the heart open. Two: Bits of copper wiring and insulating plastic under his nails. Three: A chest filled with metallic fragments. Four: Moderately severe bronchial inflammation. Five a high level of Cipro in his blood. And six: desert sand on his shoes. She went over each of the findings individually and then in various combinations. Finally Joanna said, "I can't think of anything that would localize him to a given area."

"Nothing at all?" Jake pressed.

Joanna tried to concentrate, but her eyes drifted over to an opened manual on smallpox and she again started thinking about poor Mack Brown and the awful agony that awaited him. And maybe her.

"You still there?" Jake said.

"Yes." Joanna pushed the morbid pictures from her mind. "But I'm drawing a blank."

"Then think harder."

Once more Joanna listed mentally the positive findings at autopsy and attempted to interconnect them. She focused on the bits of copper wiring and insulation under the terrorist's nails. "Since he was an electrician and previously worked in the aviation and aerospace industry in France, I'd guess he'd do the same here." Joanna shook her head, remembering she had mentioned this to Jake in an earlier conversation. "I think we already talked about this possibility."

"Keep talking," Jake encouraged her. "It might lead us to something new."

"Well, anyhow, that's my best guess."

"That's the FBI's best guess, too," Jake said. "So they're checking all the aviation plants and subcontractors in the Seattle area, but they're not making any headway. The guy probably used an alias, maybe not even Arabic. And then he might have worn a beard or mustache while he was up there. They've got two dozen agents combing the area, and they haven't turned up a trace of that guy. And time is running out."

"How do you mean?"

"I mean, everybody thinks that another nine-eleven is about to happen."

"Oh, Lord!"

"I'll give you the particulars when you get up here."

If I get up there. With an effort, Joanna cleared her mind and came back to the problem at hand. "Are they planning to crash planes into buildings again?"

"Worse, we think," Jake said darkly.

"Does this future event start with the letter A?" Joanna asked.

"Yeah."

"Jesus!" Joanna hissed softly, envisioning a massive atomic explosion in New York City, followed by a giant mushroom-shaped cloud. "Are they sure?"

"Everything points to it."

Joanna refocused her mind and deliberated carefully over each of the positive finds at autopsy. Nothing pointed to a given location or workplace. Nothing. On Jake's end she heard someone coughing loudly in the background. "Who is sick?" she asked.

"Farelli's bronchitis is coming back," Jake replied. "He started on antibiotics yesterday, but they aren't helping much."

Joanna's eyes suddenly widened. In an instant she interconnected four of the six positive findings at autopsy. "I think I know how to track the terrorist down."

"How?" Jake asked quickly.

"There were four findings at autopsy that I can now connect to one another," Joanna began. "He worked in an aviation or aerospace plant, had metallic fragments in his chest, suffered from severe bronchitis, and was taking Cipro."

After a pause, Jake asked, "So?"

"So you need a prescription to get Cipro, which means he saw a doctor for his bronchitis," Joanna went on. "And assuming our terrorist worked for a big aviation company, he had health insurance through that company. Chances are, he saw a doctor for his bronchitis and filled a claim, so the insurance would pay for it."

"How do we track down this claim?"

"Every big corporation has a health-benefits section," Joanna answered. "And all claims will be listed in their computer. You're looking for a middle-aged male, who might have an Arabic name, and who was treated for bronchitis within the past month."

"Will it be listed under bronchitis?"

"Or maybe URI," Joanna said. "That stands for upper respiratory infection. The key feature here is whether the patient was treated with Cipro."

"Will that also be in the computer?"

"Probably not, but the doctor can tell you that."

"So," Jake summarized, "we've got an aviation or aerospace worker with bronchitis and taking the antibiotic Cipro?"

"Right."

"You also mentioned that the metallic fragments in his chest were important," Jake said. "How does that figure in?"

"In patients with severe bronchitis, most physicians will take a chest X ray," Joanna told him. "So when you check with the doctors, you should inquire about an Arab male with bad bronchitis who had metal fragments scattered throughout his chest. If that patient was treated with Cipro, you've got your terrorist."

"Anybody ever tell you that you're smart as hell?"

"On occasion."

"You stay well and get the hell out of there as soon as you can."

"That's my plan."

Joanna placed the phone down and left the office, glad that at least for the moment she had been distracted from smallpox. She was now thinking about Jake's dire prediction that a catastrophe worse than 9/11 was about to happen. And it started with the letter A, as in atomic bomb. She had recently read how easy it would be for a terrorist to set off an atomic explosion in a heavily populated metropolitan area. It would cause destruction and havoc beyond imagination.

She continued down the corridor, wondering if the terrorists had two events planned—an atomic explosion and a smallpox epidemic. But the latter was just a guess, although a damn good one. Two Arabs running around the Mojave Desert and one came down with smallpox. Only an idiot wouldn't be suspicious of that. But it wasn't confirmed. It was still only a guess. She shook her head angrily.

She entered the observation area and peeked into isolation unit four. Mack was leaning over a table, coughing with all of his might, bringing up globs of black sputum. He stopped briefly to catch his breath, then started coughing again. More black phlegm came up and landed on the floor and table.

Joanna backed away from the Plexiglas window. It was the start of Mack Brown's deathwatch.

24

Lori looked up as a handsome stranger walked into the forensics laboratory.

"I'm looking for Dr. McKay," he said.

"I'm Dr. McKay," she replied, getting to her feet.

"Good. I'm Elliot Durr from the CDC." He smiled, exposing even, pearly white teeth, then extended his hand. "Sorry I'm late, but the freeway traffic was awful."

"It usually is."

Lori briefly studied the scientist's handsome features and casual attire. He was wearing tan pants, a white shirt open at the collar, and a blue blazer. He reminded Lori of a model in a Polo advertisement. "This virus is really something," she mumbled awkwardly.

Elliot nodded. "Always has been."

"And you're the expert, huh?"

Elliot shrugged and smiled again. "Just a hired hand."

"The CDC doesn't have hired hands."

"You'd be surprised."

Lori liked Elliot Durr's demeanor almost as much as his looks. He didn't try to impress, because he didn't have to. Not with that gorgeous face, and not with a body that appeared to be sculpted. And he apparently had a brain to go with it. "Joanna told me not to ask too many questions."

"She's really something, isn't she?"

Lori's brow went up. "You met her?"

"In a way," Elliot said vaguely, wondering if all the women in the forensics department at Memorial were knockouts, like the two he'd seen so far. Joanna Blalock was older, with a patrician-type beauty. At least that was how she looked on the television screen. Lori McKay was younger and more petite, with a fresh, pretty face that needed little makeup. His gaze dropped to her fourth left finger. No ring.

Lori couldn't contain her curiosity. "How did you manage to meet Joanna?"

"Via a television hookup," Elliot said, then grinned. "I thought she told you not to ask too many questions."

"I'm not very good at taking orders."

"Me neither."

They smiled at each other. It was instant attraction. They both felt it.

Lori sensed that she was beginning to blush. She brought up a hand to cover it. "Where should we start?"

"With the patient's tissues," Elliot answered. "What have you got?"

"The slides from the autopsy and small sections of organs that were frozen away," Lori said, all business now. "Everything else from the terrorist went back to the FBI."

"Did the FBI take his clothes?"

"Yes."

"But you did keep sections of *every* organ frozen away?"

"Of course, but under the name John Doe."

"Excellent," Elliot said, making a mental note for the CDC to obtain the terrorist's clothes from the FBI. They would have to be cultured for the smallpox virus. Next he turned his attention to how best to transport the organ specimens. "We need to keep the specimens frozen. Do you have any containers with liquid nitrogen?"

"Plenty of them," Lori replied. "But if you just want to move them a short distance, we usually use dry ice."

"They're going back to Atlanta."

"We'll keep them frozen in liquid nitrogen."

Lori quickly calculated the number of tissue specimens that needed to be transported and how many containers would be required. Two large ones, she decided. "Will somebody pick them up?"

Elliot shook his head. "We'll take them to the airport."

Lori hesitated, then said, "Some of the commercial carriers won't carry hazardous materials."

"The CDC has its own planes," Elliot informed her. "And there's one waiting for us right now at LAX."

"Are we going to Atlanta?"

Elliot grinned mischievously. "No, just the specimens. But sometime in the future, that may not be a bad idea."

Lori bit down on her lower lip. "I knew you were trouble the moment you walked in."

Elliot stared down at the pretty auburn-haired pathologist, thinking she had the looks and moves he always fell for. And she was probably smart as hell, too, and that would make her irresistible.

"Are you looking for anything in particular?" Lori asked, keeping a straight face.

Elliot nervously cleared his throat. "I'm afraid my mind drifted."

"So I noticed."

Elliot smiled broadly. "Would you get the damn slides?"

Lori walked into the front laboratory and asked the head technician to gather up all the tissues from the dead terrorist and place them in containers with liquid nitrogen. Then she stepped into Joanna's office and fetched the six boxes of slides from the terrorist's autopsy. Even if they went quickly through the slides, it would still take at least two hours to study them all. *Good,* Lori mused to herself. That would give her time to get better acquainted with Elliot Durr.

For reasons unknown to her, she was always attracted to men from the eastern part of America. They struck her as being so much more sophisticated and worldly than the average guy from California, who wore expensive clothes and lived in an expensive house and had a brain the size of a walnut. She wondered if Elliot Durr were an M.D. or Ph.D. The CDC would have both types. From the way he dressed and talked, he was almost certainly an M.D. But she'd find out for sure. And she'd also find out if he was married.

Lori picked up the boxes of slides and returned to the rear laboratory. Elliot Durr had removed his blue blazer and placed it on the back of a chair. His white shirt was tucked in tightly, accentuating his muscular chest and narrow waist. She glanced down at his ring finger. There was no wedding band.

"Shall we start?" Lori asked.

"By all means."

They sat across from each other, both looking through a specially designed microscope that allowed two people to view the same slide simultaneously. The first slide was from the terrorist's liver. It showed no abnormalities. As they moved the slide their knees touched under the table. They both sensed the instant electricity between them. Reflexively, they jerked their knees back.

"What should we be looking for?" Elliot asked.

"Any evidence of inflammation," Lori replied.

"Did you and Dr. Blalock see any the first time around?"

"Just in the bronchial mucosa."

"What about his skin and mouth and pharynx?"

"All negative."

"Then chances are we're going to be digging a dry hole here."

"We're experts at that."

Elliot looked up from the microscope. "Don't all those dry holes bother you?"

Lori smiled sweetly. "Not when you think there's a gusher waiting for you right around the corner."

Over the next two hours, they studied slide after slide, seeing nothing of real importance. The only positive findings were in the lungs, where there was intense bronchial inflammation.

"Another day or two and the guy would have ended up with pneumonia," Elliot commented as he placed the last slide under the microscope. It contained a section of lung tissue that showed fibrosis and small, irregular metallic fragments. "What are the foreign bodies?"

"Fragments from a hollow-point bullet," Lori answered. "Remember, this guy came from a very bad neighborhood."

"It isn't as bad as the neighborhood he's going to," Elliot quipped.

"Amen."

Elliot pushed his chair away from the microscope and glanced at his watch. "I'm afraid I've got to run."

"I hope I see you again," Lori said, and then couldn't believe she'd actually said that. Her face began to color. "I didn't mean it the way it sounded."

"I was hoping you did," Elliot said smoothly.

Lori slowly shook her head. "It's amazing how awkward one can be at the wrong time."

"Were you awkward?" Elliot asked. "I didn't notice."

"Thanks."

Elliot glanced at his watch again. "Do you have time to go to the airport?"

Lori shrugged. "I guess. Do you need some help?"

"Sure," Elliot said with mock seriousness. "Somebody has to make sure those containers don't tip over."

"Let me get my coat."

Lori hurried over and went into Joanna's office, where she quickly dabbed on lipstick and brushed her hair. *He's gorgeous,* she kept thinking, *and I'm behaving like some high school twit. "I hope I see you again." Jesus! Why not ask him to spend the night while you're at it? Be cool and be calm,* she commanded herself, *and don't push it.* She applied a touch of perfume, checked her face in a hand mirror, and left the office.

Elliot was waiting for her, holding two large plastic containers by their handles.

He briefly sniffed the air and commented, "I like Joy. It's my favorite perfume."

"How did you know I was wearing Joy?"

"I use it myself," Elliot joshed.

"Oh, Lord! Please help me!"

They walked out of the forensics laboratory and into the corridor. A short, stocky man with thinning red hair hurried over to them.

"I'm John Wilkerson from the *Times,*" he introduced himself. "I wonder if I could talk to you for a minute or two, Dr. McKay?"

"Regarding what?" Lori asked, instantly on guard.

"Regarding the disaster that's taking place in the basement at Memorial," Wilkerson said.

"I don't know anything about that," Lori told him.

"Sure you do," the reporter persisted. "You know why the loading dock at the rear of the hospital is cordoned off and guarded by police. And you know why no one can use the elevator that goes from the dock down to the research facility in the basement."

Lori said nothing.

"And you know why an outside ambulance was impounded and sanitized before being released. Correct?"

"No comment."

"But you're not denying it," Wilkerson pressed.

"Look," Lori said evenly, "Memorial has an information and public relations office. That's where you should take your questions."

"You're not going to be able to keep this thing covered up."

"We're not covering up anything," Lori snapped, losing patience.

"Can I quote you?"

"Take your questions elsewhere."

"Oh, I don't think I have to," Wilkerson said, taking out a tape recorder and switching it on. "You just stated that there's no cover-up going on at Memorial. Right?"

Elliot stepped in front of Lori and said to the reporter, "Now would be a good time for you to move along."

"Who are you?" Wilkerson asked.

Elliot stared down at the reporter. "The man who's going to help you move your ass along."

The reporter was about to respond but decided not to. He switched off his tape recorder and walked away, saying, "We're going to run this story. And your name will be mentioned, Dr. McKay."

Lori waited until the reporter was out of earshot, then turned to Elliot. "It looks like the word is out."

"He's just guessing."

"Do you think he'll really run the story?"

"Probably," Elliot said. "That type of reporter is never bothered by lack of facts."

"Shit!"

Ten minutes later they were on the San Diego Freeway heading for the airport. The day was sunny and bright, with a cool breeze coming off the ocean. Although traffic was heavy, Elliot stayed in the diamond lane and cruised along at sixty-five miles per hour. He didn't notice the blue Chevrolet following them.

"It must be exciting to be in the CDC," Lori said as they passed a stretch limousine with darkened windows.

"It's not as exciting as it sounds," Elliot had to admit.

He told her about his duties as an EIS officer and how, for the most part, they involved desk work. In his ten months at the CDC, he'd been out in the field once, to investigate an outbreak of salmonella in a small Texas town on the Mexican border. It turned out that a dishwasher was a carrier of salmonella typhimurium. "And that was my great adventure. After that I went back to my desk—without the Nobel prize, I might add."

Lori chuckled. "It's always rough starting out."

Elliot nodded. "It's just that I expected more after finishing my residency in internal medicine. I guess I daydreamed like everybody else. You know, I'd get to the CDC, discover a new virus, save the world, and become famous. It didn't quite work out that way."

"I went through the same thing," Lori told him. "After I finished my fellowship at Johns Hopkins—"

"You went to Hopkins?" Elliot interrupted.

"Yeah."

"Me, too."

"Get out!"

"I swear," Elliot said, raising his hand and giving the Boy Scout pledge sign. "I did my internship there four years ago. When were you at Hopkins?"

"A little before," Lori lied. She had left Johns Hopkins over eight years ago. For once she was glad she looked so much younger than her thirty-two years.

"So you were saying you left Hopkins and . . . ?"

"And I came out here," Lori continued her story. "I got a position with the Los Angeles Coroner's Office and it turned out awful. All I did was one autopsy after another with damn little forensics. Then I caught a high-profile case and Joanna Blalock was called in as a consultant. We clicked and she offered me a position at Memorial. It was the luckiest break of my life."

"That wasn't luck," Elliot said thoughtfully. "You saw your chance and made the most of it."

"That I got the chance was luck."

Elliot shook his head. "You got the chance because you had the goods. Luck had nothing to do with it."

Lori smiled to herself, thinking that Elliot was too good to be true. *Where is your flaw, Elliot?* she wondered. *It's got to be there. You can't be this perfect.*

They turned off the freeway and followed Century Boulevard into the expanse of Los Angeles International Airport. But rather than drive into the terminal area, they took a side road that led to a guarded gate. Elliot showed the armed guard his papers and ID.

The gate opened and they were waved through. Off to the right was a large hangar that held a Gulfstream jet. Painted white, the plane belonged to the United States Air Force. Without leaving the car, Elliot handed the two large containers to an armed man wearing a blue jumpsuit. The jumpsuit had no insignia.

They drove back to the freeway and headed north. The sun seemed even brighter now, the day so warm that Elliot switched on the air conditioner. Then he turned on the radio. A classical music station came on. They were playing Rachmaninoff's Piano Concerto No. 2. It was one of Lori's all-time favorites.

"You have time for lunch?" Elliot asked.

"I guess," Lori said, trying not to sound too eager.

"How far is the marina from here?"

"We're just a few exits away."

"Is an outdoor lunch okay?"

"Perfect."

"Beats the hell out of a musty old lab, doesn't it?"

Lori nodded, but felt a pang of guilt as she thought about Joanna Blalock, who was quarantined in an underground research facility with some virulent virus on the loose. *And here I am about to enjoy lunch at the marina with a drop-dead-handsome guy, thinking only about myself. Suppose Joanna needs me for something? Suppose something happens down there and they need me pronto?*

Elliot noticed her suddenly somber expression. "Is anything wrong?"

"Nah," Lori lied easily. "I was just thinking about how long it's been since I enjoyed a nice leisurely lunch away from the hospital."

"Long time, huh?"

"Too long."

A cell phone chirped loudly. At first Lori thought it was hers. But it was Elliot's. He reached in his pocket and answered the call.

"Yes, sir . . . Yes, sir . . . Oh, Christ!" Elliot quickly pulled over to the shoulder of the freeway. He motioned for Lori to take notes, then went back to the cell phone. "One-one-eight Alvarado in Boyle Heights . . . Got it. . . . Repeat the doctor's name, please. . . . Dr. Villarosa." Elliot listened intently, oblivious to the cars passing by. "She wouldn't give her name, huh? . . . I'll bet it is, too. . . . Yes, sir . . . I'll call you from the house."

Elliot switched off the cell phone and asked Lori, "Do you know where Boyle Heights is?"

"Sure," she answered. "It's downtown."

"How do we get there?"

"Keep going straight until you reach the Santa Monica Freeway; then get on it and head east."

Elliot pulled away from the shoulder and entered the flow of traffic, still unaware of the blue car following them. He moved over into the fast lane and quickly accelerated to seventy miles per hour. "Where is the turnoff for the Santa Monica Freeway?"

"Three exits ahead," Lori said, now seeing the tension in Elliot Durr's face. He was staring straight ahead, his hands tightly gripping the steering wheel. "You want me to tell you what's going on?"

Elliot pointed to the glove compartment. "There's a thick manual in there. Would you get it out for me? I need to refresh my memory on a particular section."

Lori opened the glove compartment and removed a manual entitled *Control of Communicable Diseases*. "Which section?"

"The one on smallpox."

Lori's jaw dropped. "What?"

"Smallpox," Elliot repeated. "And hold your questions for now. Just read me the part on infection control in the home."

Lori stared at him in disbelief. "Are you saying there's a case of smallpox in Los Angeles?"

"Just read the section," Elliot said tersely.

Lori quickly turned pages until she came to the paragraph on infection control in smallpox. "In the home. Right?"

"In the home."

Lori cleared her throat. " 'Isolation in the home or other nonhospital facilities should be considered where possible, since the risk of transmission is high and few hospitals will have enough negative-pressure rooms for proper isolation. Immediate vaccination should be given to all contacts and all medical personnel. Outside the hospital setting, all patients and household contacts should wear N-ninety-five masks or better. Caregivers should wear disposable gowns and gloves. All linens, clothing, and other exposed articles must be sterilized or incinerated.'"

"Give me a minute to think," Elliot said as he switched lanes and headed for the eastbound Santa Monica Freeway. Knitting his brow, he concentrated on the tasks facing him. Isolating the home would be no problem, although it would probably draw everyone's attention, including the local newspapers and television stations. But listing and locating all possible contacts would be much more difficult. In a crowded urban area, one case of smallpox could easily infect twenty other people. And at any given home, sterilizing and/or incinerating all exposed articles might well be impossible.

Jesus! he groaned to himself, wishing he had at least some experience in dealing with this type of outbreak.

Lori couldn't contain herself any longer. "How do you know it's smallpox?"

"Because there are other cases."

Lori stared at him again. She wet her lips and tried to swallow, but she couldn't. "How many?"

"At least five."

Elliot told her about the Middle Eastern patient and the nurse and the ambulance driver in the Viral Research Center, and about the doctor and the delivery boy at the Mojave facility. "And the case we're going to see is probably the housekeeper of the old doctor I just mentioned."

"Sweet Mary in heaven," Lori muttered, Joanna was stuck down in the Viral Research Center with the goddamn smallpox virus. "Is Joanna all right?"

"As far as I know."

Lori thought quickly, then asked, "Weren't the people in the research center vaccinated?"

Elliot nodded. "Right from the get-go. But the guy had puked on everybody, and that exposed them to a huge amount of the smallpox virus. That shortened the incubation period to days."

"Is Mack Brown okay?"

Elliot shrugged, but he knew that Brown had the disease and was deteriorating rapidly. His chances of surviving were virtually nil. Nobody survived the blackpox.

Elliot brought his mind back to the problem of controlling the spread of the smallpox virus. Too bad he wasn't in Somalia or the Sudan, where villages could be sealed off and the disease controlled by ring containment and vaccination. No, this was downtown Los Angeles, where people lived crowded together and where almost everyone traveled to work in cars and packed buses. And their work took them to every part of Los Angeles. A single case of smallpox in this unvaccinated population could lead to a full-blown epidemic that would spread across southern California like wildfire. And then there was the problem of the illegal immigrants, who would see a doctor only if they were deathly ill. Some of those would go back home to die in Mexico and spread the disease even farther. There were so many problems to deal with, Elliot thought, and so few good answers. He was way out of his depth and he knew it.

"So," Lori interrupted his thoughts, "we were really looking for smallpox lesions in our terrorist earlier today?"

"Right."

"Why do they think he might have them?"

"Because his friend out in Mojave was the first case of smallpox," Elliot explained. "His buddy was the one who infected everybody in the Viral Research Center."

"Was his friend an Arab, too?"

"Yup."

Lori blinked rapidly. "Are you saying this is all bioterrorism?"

"It looks that way."

"Jesus! Jesus!" Lori cried, grasping the scope of the nightmare they were facing. An epidemic of smallpox! A horror from the past about to be revisited.

Elliot said, "I may need your help."

Lori looked over quickly. "I'm not vaccinated, you know."

"I know."

Lori pointed up to an overhead sign on the freeway. "Take the Soto exit and go right."

They left the freeway and, after a series of turns on smaller streets, came to Alvarado Drive. It was a quiet working-class neighborhood. The houses were single-level and plastered with stucco. Most of the windows had iron bars across them. And the houses were very close together, Elliot noted. A gentle breeze could carry a plume of smallpox virus to a half dozen houses or more.

Up ahead, the street was blocked by a black and white patrol car. Beyond that Elliot could see a pink stucco house with yellow tape cordoning off its lawn. Neighbors were standing in their yards, viewing events from a safe distance.

Elliot came to a stop beside a uniformed police officer and showed his ID. "I'm Dr. Durr from the CDC."

The policeman studied the ID, matching the photograph to the driver, then waved the car through. "Go right in, Doc."

As Elliot drove in, he noticed a blue car behind him in the rearview mirror. It was being stopped by the cop. Elliot paid no further attention and turned to Lori. "You stay put until I tell you otherwise."

"This is scary as hell," Lori had to admit.

"Tell me about it!"

Elliot pulled over to the curb and turned off the ignition. "If this patient really has smallpox, you won't see me again—at least not for a while."

"What do you want me to do?"

"Just stay put for now."

Lori watched Elliot climb out of the car. She noticed that he left the key in the ignition.

Elliot ducked under the yellow tape and hurried across the small, well-kept lawn. As he entered the house, everyone in the living room stood. There were three middle-aged men, a middle-aged woman, and a shy-looking teenage girl who clung to the woman's arm. All were Hispanic.

One of the men came over to Elliot. He was thin and well-groomed and wore a dark suit and tie. "Are you Dr. Durr?"

"Yes."

"Good," the man said, shaking Elliot's hand warmly. "I am Dr. Villarosa. Allow me to introduce you to Mr. and Mrs. Gonzalez, their daughter, Juanita, and a family friend, Mr. Garcia."

Villarosa waited for everyone to exchange nods, then continued. "Perhaps, Dr. Durr, it would be best if I gave you the medical history."

"Please do."

"Late last night Mr. Garcia drove into Los Angeles from Mojave," Villarosa began. "He kindly gave a ride to a sick woman who needed to come here urgently. During the drive down, the woman slept in the back of his car. They arrived in the early hours and did not wish to awaken the Gonzalez family, so they spent the night in the car. At about seven this morning, Mr. Garcia brought the sick woman into the house. It was obvious she was very, very ill, and so I was called."

"She wished to go to a friend's house, but I thought it was best to bring her here," Garcia volunteered, then nodded deferentially to Dr. Villarosa. "Here I knew she would be well looked after."

Villarosa nodded back, then went on with the medical history. "Once I saw the sick woman, I was certain of the diagnosis. She has meningococcemia. Her rash is characteristic."

"Well done," Elliot said, knowing that most doctors would have made that diagnosis. Meningococcemia was a form of septicemia caused by the meningococcal microorganism. It induced cutaneous hemorrhages but never vesicles or pustules or pox. "And then you must have contacted the state health department?"

"Correct," Villarosa said. "I talked with several people and was finally connected to your Dr. Wolinsky. He gave me specific instructions that I have carefully carried out."

Elliot pointed to the Gonzalez family and their friend, Garcia. "Are these the only people the patient came in contact with?"

"Only these," Villarosa assured him. "There were no others. Even the dog was kept outside at my insistence."

"Well done," Elliot said again, reaching into the inner pocket of his coat for a mask and gloves. "Could I see the patient now?"

"Of course."

Villarosa led the way back into a small bedroom, where a woman was moaning and twisting around in bed. The sheet was pulled up to her chin. "Maria," Villarosa said softly, "there is another doctor here to see you."

Maria either didn't hear or ignored what she'd just been told. She turned away from the doctors.

Elliot leaned over and slowly pulled the sheet down, exposing the lesions on Maria's chest and arms and face. Black pustules were everywhere, some covered with scabs, others extruding pus.

"The diagnosis is straightforward. Yes?" Villarosa asked.

"Let's talk outside."

Pulling down his face mask, Elliot walked out of the sickroom and back into the living room. He motioned for Villarosa to stay there, then stepped out onto the lawn. Quickly he reached for his cell phone and called Marshall Wolinsky. He answered on the first ring.

"It's Maria Rodriguez," Elliot told his chief. "And she's got the blackpox."

"So we figured," Wolinsky said without emotion.

"How should I handle it?"

"By following my instructions word for word."

Elliot took out a notepad and pen and carefully jotted down the things that needed to be done. There were eight specific instructions to be followed.

"Got it?" Wolinsky asked.

"Got it."

"Your helicopter will be there in fifteen minutes."

Elliot switched off the cell phone and called over to a uniformed policeman. "Please tell Dr. McKay, who came with me, to drive back to Memorial now. I'll contact her later."

"Yes, sir."

The policeman hurried over to Lori and leaned down into the car window.

"Ma'am, you've got to drive back to Memorial now. The doctor said he'll call you later."

"Anything else?"

"That's it, ma'am."

Lori stepped out of the car on the passenger's side and waved to Elliot.

He waved back and made the gesture of zipping his lips shut. When Elliot was certain she understood, he disappeared back into the house.

Lori got behind the wheel and switched on the ignition. She drove slowly toward the black-and-white unit, where a policeman waved her through. On the other side of the blockade, she noticed a blue car with a man leaning against it. It was the reporter from the *Times*.

"You want to tell me about the cover-up now?" Wilkerson yelled out as she passed him.

25

William Buck, director of a sensitive intelligence unit in the Los Angeles Police Department, sat at the window in his office watching raindrops splatter against the pane. It rarely rained in May anymore, he was thinking, but it did a lot when he was a boy growing up in Orange County. But that was a long time ago, when Orange County really had orange groves and the air was so fresh and sweet you could almost taste it. Now the land was covered with asphalt and concrete, and the air smelled like car exhaust. Everything had changed for the worse. Just as it had for the rest of America.

A streak of lightning flashed in the night sky and brought Buck out of his reverie. Slowly he turned his wheelchair around and faced Jake Sinclair and Lou Farelli. "What makes you two think that Haj Ragoub is a bad guy?"

"A lot of things," Jake replied. "First, it's the company he keeps. He's big buddies with Yusef Malik, who is tied in with some radical groups."

"How radical?"

Jake thought briefly, then said, "He's the type who thinks it's great to get an education in America, but after that it's okay to blow up buildings and kill people whose beliefs don't match yours."

"Any terrorist acts?"

"None so far."

Buck flicked his wrist, unimpressed. "Go on."

"We went to a restaurant where a bunch of Arabs hang out," Jake continued. "We showed a picture of our dead terrorist to the maître d'. He told us he'd never seen him."

"So?"

"So the guy was lying."

Farelli nodded firmly. "You could tell that by the way the maître d' looked at the picture of the terrorist. He studied it way too long. A few seconds is the average. He stared at it for at least ten."

"So you think it was an act, huh?" Buck asked.

"By a bad actor," Jake went on. "As we left the restaurant, I glanced over my shoulder and saw the lying prick run over to a table in the far corner. Want to guess who was at that table?"

Buck smiled unevenly. "Ragoub and Yusef Malik."

"And the maître d' didn't go over there to pour water, either," Farelli chimed in. "They were talking serious business."

"So," Jake concluded, "Ragoub hangs out with radicals and is familiar with a known terrorist who gets himself iced at LAX. And the FBI tells us he's a solid citizen."

"My ass," Farelli sneered.

Buck wheeled himself over to his desk. His thighs were covered with a thick woolen blanket. Both of his legs had been blown off by a Viet Cong mine in 1972. "And you don't believe the FBI, eh?"

"Would you?"

Buck ignored the question. "What else have you got?"

"The most important thing," Jake told him. "There's only one way the FBI could have known we were following

Ragoub: They spotted our tail because they were tailing him too."

Farelli grumbled irritably. "And those jerks at the FBI told us he was a solid citizen *twice*."

With an effort Buck shifted his large frame around in the wheelchair. He was built like a tank, with broad shoulders, a thick neck, and a square chin. "Are you going to continue following Ragoub?"

"Unless you give us a reason not to," Jake replied.

Buck hesitated, picking his next words carefully. "Jake, every time you ask me for a favor, it costs me. People all over the intelligence community now have my markers, thanks to you."

"I didn't have any choice, sir," Jake said, wishing he could have gotten the information elsewhere. But only William Buck had connections to every major intelligence agency in America, and to some abroad. It was rumored that he had once been offered a position in the National Security Agency but had turned it down because of an ailing wife. "I really need your help here."

"Mr. Haj Ragoub is not a nice person," Buck said diplomatically. "According to the Company, he associates with some very unpleasant people."

Jake and Farelli leaned forward simultaneously, their ears pricked. *The Company* was the insiders' name for the CIA.

"On the surface he appears to be nothing more than a pain-in-the-ass Arab who thinks the Middle East would be magically transformed into paradise if they could only get rid of Israel. He donates heavily to Arab charities in America, which for the most part are fronts for Hamas and Hezbollah."

Jake squinted an eye. "I thought those were all shut down."

"Most were. But a few remain."

"Shit." Jake reached for a cigarette and lit it, ignoring the law against smoking in municipal buildings. In his mind's eye he could see the pizzeria in Jerusalem filled with mothers and young children who had been blown up by terrorists. He wondered if the money for the explosives had come from America.

Buck opened a desk drawer, took out an ashtray, and slid it across the desk to Jake. "Anyhow, this is Haj Ragoub on the surface. But the Company thinks he goes a lot deeper. A few years ago Al Qaeda had a summit meeting in Malaysia. It seems our Mr. Ragoub was in Malaysia at the same time. Although there was no evidence he actually attended the meeting, he was seen associating with some very unsavory characters."

"Terrorists?" Jake asked at once.

"Of the first order."

"Son of a bitch!" Jake fumed. "I knew it. I knew that guy was bad news."

"A real solid citizen," Farelli droned.

"Is he on the terror watch list?" Jake inquired.

"No," Buck said simply.

"Un-goddamn-believable!" Jake angrily mashed his cigarette in the ashtray. "Why the hell isn't he on that list?"

"Because he hasn't committed any acts of terror—at least none that we know about."

"But he's a prime candidate, and the CIA damn well knows—" Jake stopped in midsentence and gave Buck a long, hard stare. "Don't tell me the CIA and the FBI aren't sharing information on Haj Ragoub."

"That's a distinct possibility."

Jake's face colored. A vein bulged out over his temple. "Those bastards are still fighting a turf war to see who gets to do what, while the average American sits around and waits for another nine-eleven."

"Oh, I think they're communicating better than before," Buck said. "But there are still big gaps, and everybody knows it."

"Terrific," Jake muttered sarcastically. "Now we can all sleep better at night."

"Nobody in intelligence is sleeping very well these days."

"Why the hell don't they get their acts together?" Jake asked acidly.

Buck turned his wheelchair around and looked out at the rainy night. "They're trying, Jake. But they have big problems to overcome. To begin with, let me tell you that the CIA is pretty good at tracking and finding terrorists. But they function primarily outside of our country. We don't like them to spy on people inside America. And that's a big drawback. The FBI, on the other hand, does have jurisdiction in America, but they are inexperienced when it comes to terrorists. They're accustomed to chasing bank robbers and kidnappers. They're new to the game of terror, and it shows."

"Jesus Christ!" Farelli exploded, disgusted with the boondoggle he was hearing about. "Can't one of those assholes pick up a phone and call the other?"

"On occasion they have," Buck told them. "But it usually results in one organization leaking the news about the other organization's fuckups."

Jake scratched the back of his neck. "Haven't they paid any attention to the president's orders?"

"You're dreaming," Buck said. "One organization is always trying to screw the other."

Outside, lightning cracked loudly, momentarily turning the night sky blue. The lights in the room dimmed momentarily, then came back. Again the lightning cracked, bringing more rain with it.

"Why is the FBI lying to us?" Jake asked. "Why tell us Ragoub's a solid citizen when they know he's not?"

Buck shrugged. "They may not know about Mr. Ragoub. Remember, the information I just gave you came from the CIA."

"But they're tailing Ragoub," Jake argued. "The FBI must know something is amiss."

"Maybe it's Yusef Malik they're following," Buck suggested. "And you just happened to bump into their tail."

"So why not tell us to back off from Yusef Malik? Why lie?"

Buck shrugged again. "Welcome to the world of deceit, Jake, where nothing is ever what it appears to be."

Jake studied William Buck's face, sensing that the intelligence director wasn't telling him everything. The old man was holding back information, but Jake decided not to press him. Yet there were still questions unanswered, things he needed to know, things that only Buck could tell him.

Jake stood and stretched his back. "If you were me, sir, how would you handle Ragoub?"

"I'd back off."

"Why?"

"Because you could end up muddying the waters," Buck said, then added, "and in the process obscure everybody's view."

"I'm not sure I follow you."

"Just keep in mind what I told you a moment ago," Buck advised. "In the world of deceit, nothing is ever what it appears to be."

Jake was about to ask one last question. But Buck was wheeling himself over to the window for another look at the rainy night.

Their conversation was over.

26

Joanna closed Mack Brown's eyes and stepped away from the bed. In death Mack looked much smaller than in life. Thin and lean, with deep lines in his face, he seemed older as well. His entire body was covered with blackpox and gave off the sharp odor of rotting flesh. Death was everywhere, Joanna thought. It had come to five of them and would soon come to her. So silly to think she would escape the disease while the others hadn't. She had hoped and prayed, but now she, too, had the rash of smallpox. Red pustules on her chest. The beginning of the end.

Joanna pulled a sheet up over Mack's body and left the isolation unit. She went through the decontamination procedure, although she wasn't sure why. What difference would it make now? The smallpox virus was already multiplying inside her. A few more viruses on her skin or scrub suit wouldn't matter.

Walking into the observation area, she felt for the rash on her chest again. The pustules were still there and seemed even more plentiful now. Joanna moved over to the Plexiglas window. She lifted up her scrub suit and peered at the angry red lesions in her reflection. It had to be smallpox. She never had a rash, never, not even acne as a teenager. When she first discovered the lesions she had cried and cursed and shaken her fist at God. But her fear and anger had passed, and now she accepted her fate. She was a condemned woman, awaiting death. So silly to think she could escape the disease.

Joanna walked down the corridor, which was empty and silent as a tomb. She passed the recreation room, wondering if she would have the guts to hang herself when the disease became full-blown. Probably not. Better to rely on the morphine.

She entered the telecommunications center and sat in a cockpit chair, then pushed the buttons that would connect her to Marshall Wolinsky. Glancing at the empty chair where Mack should have been sitting, she felt the tears welling up. Quickly she sniffed them back and gathered herself.

The television screen lit up and Marshall Wolinsky's image appeared.

"Mack Brown just passed away," Joanna told him.

"Did he die peacefully?" Wolinsky asked.

"I think so," Joanna replied.

"I'll inform his wife as soon as she returns to Los Angeles."

"There's a letter to her and the boys in the top drawer of Mack's desk."

"I'll see that she gets it."

Joanna tilted back in her chair and looked beyond Wolinsky's image on the screen. In the background behind him there was a flurry of activity. Doctors and nurses were hurrying about. A large X-ray unit rolled by.

"Is there anything I need to know about Mack's death?" Wolinsky asked.

Before Joanna could answer, Wolinsky turned away as a nurse approached. He spoke briefly with her, then, reaching for the phone, looked back at Joanna. "Excuse me for a moment. It's an urgent call from Washington."

Joanna nodded to the screen, then glanced again at the empty chair where Mack usually sat. She thought about Wolinsky's last question regarding Mack's death. No, there was nothing special about his passing. Mack became toxic and delirious and called out for his wife and children. As he bled into his throat and lungs he grew more and more agitated, so Joanna gave him a large intravenous injection of Valium. After Mack had calmed down, Joanna had taken a coffee break. When she returned, he was dead. She would never know if the Valium had contributed to Mack's rapid demise. Maybe. Maybe not. Either way he had been spared the agony of slow suffocation.

"So," Wolinsky said, breaking into her thoughts, "I take it there was nothing I need to know about Mack's passing?"

"There was nothing special."

"Pulmonary death, eh?"

"Most likely."

"A good man, a very good man," Wolinsky eulogized, then stared out into space for a few moments. Sighing deeply to himself, he came back to Joanna. "Are you doing all right?"

After a pause, Joanna said, "I don't think so."

"Oh?" Wolinsky leaned forward. "Do you have any symptoms?"

"No, not really," Joanna said, sounding a thousand times braver than she felt. "But I've got a rash."

"Where?"

"On my upper chest."

"Describe it."

Joanna hesitated. "It's difficult to see. The lighting down here is poor, particularly in the rooms that have mirrors."

"Upper chest, you say?" Wolinsky questioned.

"Right."

"Let's see it."

Joanna looked at him strangely. "Here?"

Wolinsky nodded. "First I'll brighten up your room."

He pressed a button and held it down. The telecommunications room was suddenly flooded with light. Joanna shielded her eyes until they acclimated to the glare.

"Now show me those skin lesions," Wolinsky said.

Joanna pulled down the front of her scrub suit, exposing a bra strap on the left side of her chest. "The rash is medial to the strap."

Wolinsky pressed another button and an overhead camera silently focused in on Joanna's chest. The room seemed to become even brighter. Wolinsky studied the lesions at length before saying, "I think we should have Elliot Durr take a look. He did a year of dermatology residency prior to switching over to internal medicine."

Elliot stepped in and peered down at Joanna's upper chest. The lesions were circular and erythematous, with raised borders and pale centers. "Does it itch?"

"A lot."

"You've got urticaria," Elliot said definitely. "Plain old garden-variety hives."

"Are you sure?"

"Positive."

Joanna breathed a long sigh of relief and thanked God for answering her prayers. "So it's due to an allergy?"

"Or nerves."

Joanna nodded gratefully. "Thanks for the quick diagnosis."

"My pleasure."

Wolinsky came back onto the screen, motioning for Elliot Durr to stay put. "Sixteen more hours," he said to

Joanna, "and your worries will be over. You'll be fully protected against smallpox."

"Sixteen more hours," Joanna said wistfully, wondering if she were really going to make it or whether she'd be struck down at the last moment. She had a big syringe filled with morphine, just in case.

"You've been very brave, young lady," Wolinsky told her. "Everyone here has admired your courage."

"I didn't have much choice," Joanna said modestly.

"Oh, you had a choice," Wolinsky said. "You just chose to be brave." He let his words sink in, then flicked a wrist to indicate he was moving on to another topic. "Let me give you an update on what's happening in the outside world. First and foremost, we found Maria, the doctor's housekeeper, in Los Angeles."

"Is she sick?" Joanna asked at once.

Wolinsky nodded gravely. "And dying of blackpox."

"You've got an epidemic about to break loose," Joanna predicted.

"Maybe. Maybe not." Wolinsky described in detail how Maria Rodriguez had traveled from Mojave to Los Angeles and the circumstances under which she was discovered. "Only five people, including the family doctor, were primary contacts. The house they were in is now under quarantine and is currently being sanitized."

"Well, at least there's *some* good news," Joanna commented.

"There is also some bad," Wolinsky went on. "Maria had a purse with her in the backseat of the car, and now we can't find it. Nobody remembered her bringing it into the house or even seeing it—which means it was probably stolen from the car. Needless to say, it's loaded with the smallpox virus, so the thief is certain to come down with the disease."

"Jesus," Joanna hissed softly. "Everything she touches is contaminated with the virus. She's like a walking disaster."

"And she touched a whole lot of things before she arrived in Los Angeles." Wolinsky gestured to Elliot Durr and moved over to give his younger associate more room. "Elliot got a fairly detailed history from Maria while they were waiting for the helicopter to arrive. I'll let him tell you about it."

Elliot cleared his throat and spoke without referring to any notes. "Maria hid in the cellar of the old doctor's house, and that's why we were unable to find her. When she became ill, she left the house and traveled to a Mexican restaurant on a stolen bicycle. She talked to and was in close contact with the parking lot attendant, who was arranging for her ride to Los Angeles. We haven't been able to locate the stolen bike or the parking lot attendant, both of which are undoubtedly carrying the virus."

"Two more mobile sources of the smallpox virus," Joanna said dejectedly. "Controlling this outbreak is like trying to dodge bullets from a machine gun."

"Worse," Wolinsky interjected. "At least a machine gun makes noise and gives you a little warning."

"Well, there'll be plenty of warning now," Joanna said, her expression somber. "Because this will be the lead story in every newspaper in America."

"Oh, I think we can keep this quiet a bit longer," Wolinsky said, unconcerned.

Joanna looked at Wolinsky oddly. "You've got five people quarantined in a house in the middle of Los Angeles, and you think the news media won't get hold of this? If you do, you must be dreaming."

"The house is under quarantine, but the five people were flown by helicopter to our Mojave facility," Wolinsky explained. "We'll do our best for Maria Rodriguez and vaccinate the others. And of course they'll have no contact with the press or with the outside world."

"But the neighbors know," Joanna argued.

Wolinsky shook his head. "The family doctor made the diagnosis of meningococcemia, and this is the word that has spread through the neighborhood. We've done nothing to dispel this rumor. We've even arranged for the neighbors to receive sulfa pills for prophylaxis, which of course will do them no harm."

"Don't lies bother you?"

"Not when they're in the national interest."

Wolinsky reached for a stack of index cards and began thumbing through them. "Let me give you the answers to the questions you asked the last time we talked. First, the Sudanese do not have any specific markers in their blood. Nothing in their blood distinguishes them from the rest of the Arab world. Second, the CIA was very interested in your suggestion that they attempt to match your dead terrorist's face to those entering or leaving the big pharmaceutical plant in the Sudan. They are in the process of looking at all pictures taken by the spy satellite over the past year. But this obviously will take time."

"How much time?"

"Too much," Wolinsky replied. "But I convinced them to put extra men on this project and work around the clock."

Joanna stared up at the screen, thinking about the incredibly powerful connections Wolinsky must have. But then again, the CIA really needed him in this matter. He was their expert on smallpox. "Matching those photographs is still a long shot."

"Maybe not as long as you think," Wolinsky continued. "The CIA was able to track down another defector from the Sudan who lived in the same area as the first defector. He, too, had been recently vaccinated against smallpox. So there's no doubt an outbreak occurred in that region."

Joanna asked, "Do they know what type of smallpox it was?"

"According to the description given by the second defector, it was the blackpox." Wolinsky took a deep breath, as if readying himself. "And here's the really scary part. We've been trying to determine why we're seeing only the blackpox in this outbreak. In all past epidemics, the blackpox form of the disease occurred in less than five percent of patients. Yet all of our patients have it. All of them."

Joanna continued to stare at Wolinsky, knowing there was only one possible answer. "Don't tell me they're manufacturing an altered form of the smallpox virus."

"Where did you get that sharp mind of yours?" Wolinsky asked, shaking his head in admiration. "You're not supposed to know these things."

"Tell me about the altered virus," Joanna pressed.

"I had my colleagues at the CDC do DNA sequencing on the virus that was isolated from your initial patient. As you probably know, the smallpox virus is remarkably stable and does not undergo mutation, as, for example, the influenza virus does. That's why the smallpox vaccine has remained so effective over the years. The vaccine is stable, and so is the virus it attacks."

Wolinsky nervously tapped his fingers on the tabletop, obviously bothered by what he was about to say. "So we compared the DNA sequence of our stock smallpox virus to that of your patients. They're different. Someone has inserted new DNA into your smallpox virus. In all likelihood it's a new gene. We think the new gene induces widespread hemorrhages."

"And probably increases the virulence of the virus," Joanna added.

"That too." Wolinsky took another deep breath. "Have you ever heard of the term *black biology*?"

"No."

"It's the term intelligence agencies use for genetically engineering microorganisms that are to be employed in germ warfare," Wolinsky told her. "With the technique of gene splicing, a fair number of microorganisms can be made far more virulent. The Russians had a huge complex in Siberia called Vector that was dedicated to this purpose."

"But the Sudanese aren't the Russians," Joanna said.

"Here they may be one and the same."

Joanna's brow went up. "Is the CIA saying that the Russians are involved with this nightmare virus?"

"They're saying the Sudanese couldn't do it without outside help."

Joanna thought about altered viruses and bacteria, and the worldwide devastation they could cause. One gene could render bacteria resistant to an entire class of antibiotics. "Have the Russians actually been able to alter viruses?"

"That's a question that remains to be answered," Wolinsky said. "Since the breakup of the Soviet Union, germ warfare has become much less of a priority for them, primarily because of the expense involved. Vector no longer exists, and many of its top scientists have sought employment outside of Russia."

Joanna nodded slowly. "And these Russian scientists may now be in the Sudan."

Wolinsky nodded back. "That's what the CIA thinks."

Joanna stood and began walking around the telecommunications room, mumbling to herself as she considered the worst of all possibilities: an epidemic of smallpox that couldn't be controlled, regardless of the measures used.

"Is something wrong?" Wolinsky inquired.

"Just thinking."

"About what?"

"A smallpox that would be resistant to vaccination."

Wolinsky's eyes narrowed. "Did you read about that somewhere?"

Joanna shook her head. "It just follows that if they can insert a gene for a hemorrhagic factor, they could also insert one that would change the protein coat of the virus. In essence, you would be changing the surface antigens, so our current vaccine would produce antibodies that wouldn't recognize the altered virus. Everybody would get smallpox whether they were vaccinated or not."

Wolinsky stared at her and said nothing.

"Is that possible?" Joanna asked.

"It's possible," Wolinsky said, tight-lipped.

"Have they actually done it?"

"Not to our knowledge," Wolinsky replied carefully. "But after thirty years of research, they probably have the capability."

Joanna squinted an eye as she came back to her seat. "Is there solid evidence they've been at it for thirty years?"

"Probably more," Wolinsky said. "In 1971 there was an accidental release of a weaponized version of the smallpox virus, which had been produced by Russian scientists. An outbreak of smallpox occurred when a boat passed too close to the island where testing of the aerosolized smallpox virus was taking place. There were three known deaths."

"Shit," Joanna cursed loudly at the screen. "So while we were trying to eradicate smallpox from the face of the Earth, the Russians were weaponizing it."

"And probably succeeding," Wolinsky added.

"And the CIA believes our outbreak of smallpox is definitely bioterrorism. Right?"

Wolinsky hesitated, then said, "A lot of things point to it, but there's no concrete evidence yet."

Joanna rocked back and forth in her cockpit seat, trying to think the problem through. Of course it was bioterrorism. Smallpox didn't suddenly crop up on the edge of the Mojave Desert. It was brought there by terrorists. And now it was crucial to pinpoint the origin of the deadly virus, because if the source wasn't wiped out, future outbreaks were a certainty. "You've got to prove that the Sudan is the source of the virus."

"I know," Wolinsky agreed. "And the CIA knows it too. But the problem is that the pharmaceutical plant is owned by radical Islamists who pay the Sudanese officials handsomely to stay out of their way and keep their mouths shut. Our best chance of proving they're involved is to see a photograph of our terrorist walking into that Sudanese plant. And that's a very long shot. But at this point it's the only shot we have."

"Maybe not," Joanna said thoughtfully.

Wolinsky leaned forward. "Tell me what you're thinking."

"First, I've got a question."

"Let's have it."

Joanna asked, "Do we have any defectors from Vector working for our government?"

"Their brightest and best scientists are now in America," Wolinsky answered promptly. "And they work as consultants for the CIA. Why?"

"Because they are the key to our puzzle."

Wolinsky knitted his forehead, concentrating. "I'm not sure I follow you."

"Rapidly go through all the photographs of the Sudanese plant that were taken by the spy satellite," Joanna explained. "Discard all photographs except those of Caucasians. Show these to our defectors from Vector and see if they recognize any of their colleagues—particularly the ones who worked on smallpox."

"Excellent!" Wolinsky said, rubbing his hands together. "If we can connect Vector to that plant in the Sudan, there'll be no doubt where our smallpox virus came from."

Elliot Durr interjected, "And what will we do about that plant?"

Wolinsky ignored the question and turned back to Joanna. "Do you have any ideas that might help the CIA focus in on the former Vector scientists?"

"Just a few things."

"Hold on." Wolinsky hurriedly reached for a pen and legal pad. "What things are you referring to?"

Joanna thought back two years, when she was a visiting professor at the University of Montreal. "First, visiting scientists usually arrive at work early in the morning and don't leave until evening. Photographs from those two time periods should be looked at first. Second, visiting scientists are usually treated very well, so pay close attention to anyone who arrives in a limousine or big government car. Third, zero in on the most restricted area of the plant. Look for armed guards, maybe with dogs. That's where the secret research is being done."

Wolinsky rapidly scribbled down notes, then stared at Joanna and gave her a look of admiration. "You're quite remarkable, Dr. Blalock."

"I do this for a living."

"And you do it very well," Wolinsky said. "Assuming we survive this disaster, would you be willing to serve as a consultant for a very important government agency?"

"No, thanks." Joanna waved away the offer. "My plate is already too full. Let's get back to our outbreak of smallpox.

Do we have any clues as to how the virus got to the Mojave Desert and why it was brought there?"

Wolinsky shrugged. "Nobody knows. Maybe the terrorist who died of smallpox brought it over; maybe he didn't. And as far as the Mojave Desert is concerned, we're in the dark there, too. We sent Elliot to the small town of Mojave to look for any cases that might have been missed. He scouted out the entire area and came up empty."

"There's nothing there," Elliot joined in. "The town is small, with a main street three or four blocks long. There are several residential areas that border the desert, a lot of gasoline stations on the main highway, and no industry of any kind except for a big junkyard that turns old planes into scrap metal."

Joanna asked, "Is there an Arab or Muslim community up there?"

"None," Elliot replied. "I also checked with some of the hookers at the local truck stop. Their customers are all Caucasian. It's as if this guy was never there."

"Oh, he was there," Joanna assured him. "He was there long enough to find a girlfriend and sleep with her on a number of occasions. He wasn't just passing through. Something in that area was important to him."

"Something was important to *them*," Wolinsky corrected her. "According to the CIA, this type of terrorist never works alone. They always come in groups."

"So there's more to come," Joanna thought aloud.

"Much, much more."

"And we have no idea when they'll strike?"

Wolinsky sighed wearily. "The CIA thinks the most likely date is May fifteenth, the day of *naqba*, the day Israel became a country. They want to give us a catastrophe of our very own."

"May fifteenth," Joanna said quietly. "That's only seven days away."

"And we're still in the dark," Wolinsky said glumly.

The television screen went blank.

27

Both assassins were ill. At first they thought their body aches and fevers were caused by a cold. But then things worsened and the black marks appeared. The skin lesions were everywhere now—on their arms and legs and chests and even their faces. And their weakness was so severe they could barely walk.

"Where did we get this awful illness?" the shorter assassin asked, scratching the sores on his arm and ignoring the pus that oozed out.

"Maybe from the small house where the Mexican housekeeper stayed," the taller assassin guessed. "She was described by neighbors as being very ill."

"Did she have the black spots?"

"That I do not know."

The shorter assassin coughed and spat blood out of his mouth. "The Mexican whore!"

They were in the Mojave Motel, on the outskirts of town. It was near the highway, and the big trucks that zoomed by day and night caused the walls to shake constantly. The misery of the assassins was made worse by the sweltering heat. Although the small room had an air conditioner, it was no match for the outside temperature of 105 degrees.

The sweat poured off the shorter man, and it seemed to intensify the terrible odor that was produced by his sores. "Perhaps we should switch to a cooler room," he suggested.

"And allow the manager to see us this way?" the taller man snapped. "Is that what you want, you idiot?"

"No."

"Then remain quiet while I think."

The tall assassin dragged himself over to a chair, kicking aside the empty food cartons and soda cans that littered the floor. A cockroach was nibbling on a piece of pizza, while ants nearby waited their turn. The man paid no attention to the bugs and slumped down in a Naugahyde-bound chair. A fly landed on his nose. It took all of his energy to wave it away.

We are very sick, he thought miserably, *and sure to die unless we receive help.* But no doctor could be called because he would alert the authorities, and questions would be asked and passports examined. The tall assassin cursed under his breath, wondering if they had truly caught the disease while in the small house where the Mexican whore lived. In the darkest part of the night they had crept into the guesthouse from the rear, where no guard was posted. And found nothing except a terrible smell. There was no sign that Ahmed Hassan had ever been there. *The little shit-faced son of a Pakistani bitch,* the assassin fumed. The little turd had caused everyone so much grief. *When I find him,* the assassin vowed, *he will die a very slow death.*

"I think we should call Ragoub." The shorter man broke the silence.

"To tell him of our failure?"

"To tell him of our sickness. He will arrange for treatment so we can continue our hunt."

The taller assassin considered the idea carefully, knowing all the while there was really no other choice. But to admit failure could be dangerous. Very dangerous. In the Holy Land League, one either succeeded or one died.

"Well?" the shorter man persisted.

"Shut up and let me think!"

Ragoub showed Yusef Malik the last of the laptop computers.

"It's a beauty, isn't it?" Ragoub asked.

"It's lovely," Yusef replied, admiring its sleekness and metallic covering.

"I bought fifty of them and could have easily sold that number," Ragoub boasted.

"Then you should have bought a hundred."

Ragoub chuckled, genuinely liking the clever young man who always seemed to know what to say and when to say it. "I want you to have this laptop computer as a gift."

"Oh, I couldn't accept this," Yusef refused politely. "It's too expensive. And besides, it's the last one you have on your shelf."

Ragoub picked up the slim computer and handed it to Yusef. "I insist."

"Really, I couldn't—"

"You must," Ragoub urged. He glanced around his electronics store and made certain no one was within hearing distance, then added, "It will be very useful in the upcoming event."

"Then I accept your magnificent gift," Yusef said graciously.

"Notice the red name tag on its handle."

"It has two red name tags," Yusef observed.

"And that is how you will recognize your associate," Ragoub told him. "His laptop computer will also have two red name tags."

Yusef moved in closer to Ragoub and whispered, "What associate are you referring to?"

"You will be told in good time, Yusef."

"I know you will give me the necessary information when it is appropriate."

Ragoub nodded. "When it is appropriate, my friend."

"Nevertheless, there are two questions I must ask now," Yusef said bluntly.

Ragoub was instantly on guard. He didn't like questions at this stage, regardless of who was asking them. "And what are those questions?"

"First, will my associate know the significance of the two red name tags?"

Ragoub breathed easier. It was a good question, and an important one, too. If your associate didn't know the signal, he couldn't recognize you, and you couldn't depend on him in a crisis. "He will know."

"Second, can I use this computer at home, like I would any other?"

Ragoub's eyes narrowed. "Why do you wish to know that?"

Yusef shrugged indifferently. "So I can become familiar with its keyboard. But if you tell me not to touch it until the great day arrives, I will, of course, follow your instructions."

Ragoub gave the matter thought before saying, "You can use it as much as you like."

"Excellent," Yusef said, picking up the computer by its handle and testing its weight. "Then I have no further questions."

Good, Ragoub thought, *because I will give you no further answers. The less you know, the better.* "Did you change your plane reservations?"

"I did," Yusef said. "I will depart after my father and Rawan."

"And the reason you gave?"

"A final examination at school."

"Well done," Ragoub said, knowing that the boy would never make the trip home. They would have to kill him after the mission. Otherwise he would carry the smallpox virus back to the Middle East and spread it everywhere.

Ragoub's cell phone rang.

He flipped it open and answered. "Yes?"

Ragoub listened intently as his face began to lose color. Beads of perspiration popped out on his forehead. "What? . . . When? . . . Did anyone see you? . . . Where did you eat? . . . Good. Good. Everything was delivered. . . . And what about the cleaning lady? . . . You did exactly right. . . . Stay where you are. I will send someone to help you."

Ragoub put his cell phone away, then mopped the sweat from his brow with a handkerchief. More beads of perspiration popped out.

Yusef had overheard Ragoub's end of the phone conversation and in his peripheral vision could see how distressed Ragoub looked.

His expression was that of a man who had just received terrible news. Yusef was on the verge of asking Ragoub about the phone call and the disturbing message it had obviously brought with it, but he held his tongue. He had asked too many questions already. He kept his eyes on the laptop computer for a few seconds more, then glanced over at Ragoub, who was again mopping his brow. "Are you all right, my friend?"

"A . . . a family member is sick," Ragoub lied.

"I'm so sorry," Yusef said sympathetically. "Is there anything I can do?"

"I will deal with it," Ragoub said curtly, then pointed across the store. "Take the computer to the manager. He will show you how to use it."

"Are you certain I cannot help?"

Ragoub ignored the question and hurried up the stairs to his private office.

After locking the door, he began to angrily pace the floor. *The idiots! The stupid idiots!* Somehow they had managed to come down with the disease. But how? Only Khalil Mahmoud and Hassan had had contact with the vials of smallpox virus. And Mahmoud was dead. So that left only Hassan. But the assassins hadn't yet found Hassan, so they couldn't have caught the disease from him. Unless they had captured Hassan and were waiting for the price to go up on the young Pakistani's head. Yes, that would explain everything. They had found Hassan, who had accidentally infected himself with the virus. The assassins had captured Hassan and caught the disease from him, then killed him. And now they were withholding the news, hoping for a bigger payoff. Or maybe they were still holding Hassan captive. Either way, they had gotten the disease from Hassan, so they must have him or must have already disposed of him.

Ragoub cursed to himself, wondering if the assassins had kept themselves concealed. Maybe someone saw them with their awful, disfiguring disease. If word of smallpox were to leak out, everything would change. The federal authorities would issue a nationwide alert and probably begin a mass vaccination program. They might even track Ahmed back to his former job at the airplane storage facility. Then their entire plan would unravel and everything would be lost.

Ragoub's thoughts returned to Hassan. He again wondered if the assassins were holding the Pakistani captive or had already killed him. *Which is it? Alive or dead? The latter, I would guess. But there is only one way to find out for sure.*

Ragoub reached for the phone.

28

"Dr. Blalock, you're a free woman," Wolinsky proclaimed.

"Are you certain I'm fully protected against smallpox?" Joanna asked the image on the screen.

"As certain as we can be," Wolinsky told her. "We tested your blood sample from this morning, and it's loaded with antibodies against the virus."

"How much is 'loaded'?"

"A liter of one to one thousand."

Joanna nodded at the number. A liter of one to one thousand meant that when her serum was diluted a thousandfold with saline, it still had detectable antibodies against the smallpox virus.

"Thank God," she breathed softly.

"So let's make plans to get you out of there."

Joanna glanced up at the wall clock: four o'clock. She was totally disoriented, having no idea if it was day or night. "Is it afternoon now?"

"A bright, sunny afternoon."

Joanna smiled broadly. "It'll be good to see the sun again."

"Could you wait a few hours more?" Wolinsky requested. "Until it's dark?"

Joanna's smile faded. "Why?"

"Because Memorial has attracted the news media," Wolinsky explained. "They're camped out behind the hospital with long-range lenses, just waiting for someone to step off that freight elevator."

"And I'll be recognized by the local press," Joanna said, nodding. "Then Memorial will be forced to answer all their questions."

Wolinsky nodded back. "Just a few more hours, if you can bear it."

Joanna tapped her finger against the armrest. She didn't want to stay in the Viral Research Center any longer than absolutely necessary. "Did you know that there is a secret passageway out of here?"

"Mack never mentioned it."

"He did to me," Joanna went on. "It opens with a special card and leads up to a big room on the A level, just to the rear of Radiology."

"Do you have a room number?"

"A-two-two-eight."

"Good." Wolinsky quickly jotted down the number. "Wait fifteen minutes; then take the passageway out. When you reach the room, stay put. You'll have to be decontaminated one more time."

"I'd better bring a fresh scrub suit with me."

"Remove all the clothing you're now wearing, including bra and panties, and leave them," Wolinsky advised. "Then change into a fresh scrub suit. Bring nothing up with you."

"Not even Mack's letter to his wife?"

"We'll fetch that later."

The screen went blank.

Joanna pushed herself up out of the cockpit chair and slowly gazed around the telecommunications room with its clocks and electronic switches and multiple television screens. She remembered the first time Mack had led her into the room and showed her its sophisticated equipment. That seemed like months ago, not days. And so did everyone's death. They had all gone so quickly, but Joanna had no time frame for the awful events. Charlie, the ambulance driver, went first. Mack went last. Everything in between was a blur.

Taking one last look, Joanna left the room and hurried down the corridor.

As she passed the recreation room, she tried not to think about Melvin Hughes. But a picture of the pleasant black kid came into her mind. A nice guy trying to work his way through school, and he got killed by a terrorist. It sounded like they were in Tel Aviv, not Los Angeles. Joanna sighed sadly, envisioning Melvin's mother still waiting for her son to call.

Joanna stopped in Mack's office and reached into his desk drawer for the plastic card that would open the secret passageway. Carefully she positioned Mack's letter to his wife so it would be easily seen by anyone opening the drawer. Near the telephone on the desk, Joanna noticed the capped syringe that she had earlier filled with 10 cc's of morphine sulfate. It was a lethal dose of the drug, which she would have injected into herself if she had come down with the disease. *Oh, yes,* she assured herself. *I would have done it.*

Joanna picked up the syringe and after emptying it, threw it into a nearby trash can.

Leaving the office, she moved quickly down the corridor and entered the observation area. She peered through the Plexiglas window and saw Mack's shrouded body. The various monitors were still on, but they showed only flat lines.

Tears came to her eyes as she said a final prayer for him. Deep down Joanna knew that Mack had saved her life, no doubt at the expense of his own. He could have given the immune globulin to himself and nobody would have ever known. But he chose to give it to her instead. Because that was the way it was with men like Mack. Ladies always came first. Johnnie Mack Brown from Del Rio, Texas, she thought sadly. The last of the real cowboys.

She took a final look and hurried away.

In less than five minutes Joanna had stripped down to bare skin and gone through the decontamination procedure. Then she put on a fresh scrub suit and ran down the corridor, thinking only about getting out of the dungeon and away from the smallpox virus.

Joanna turned into a small corridor and raced past the morgue. Ahead she saw a blank wall that was poorly illuminated by an overhead light. Mack had told her that the slot for the plastic card was located above the fire alarm box. But it was difficult to see the alarm box in the dimness.

Finally she found the box and the very thin slot above it. She inserted the card and removed it, then watched as the blank wall slid open automatically.

As she started up the narrow passageway, the door closed behind her. There was no light in the staircase and no railing to hold on to. Joanna had to make her way up by feel alone. The air was musty and still, the darkness pitch-black and disorienting.

She went up slowly, keeping a very tight grip on the plastic card that would also open the door to the room on the A level. The climb seemed to go on and on, straight up, and steeper with each step. Joanna began to tire, but she kept going, thinking about freedom and sunlight and getting back to some semblance of a life. Just to sleep in her own bed would be— Abruptly the staircase came to a dead end. In the deep darkness, Joanna felt for the slot and found it. She inserted the plastic card, which went in and then disappeared completely. The door opened. Blinding light flooded in.

Joanna squeezed her eyes shut against the painful glare. Slowly she opened them. Two technicians dressed in white space suits were waiting for her in the large decontamination room.

A technician handed Joanna a set of dark goggles. "Strip down and put these on, please."

Joanna did as she was told, saying, "I'll need another scrub suit."

"What size?"

"Medium."

"No problem."

The room went dark for a moment. Then deep-blue ultraviolet light poured in, killing any exposed viruses. Joanna stood perfectly still and let the UV light do its work. She had been initially surprised to find a complete decontamination facility at the top of the stairs, but on second thought she realized she shouldn't have been. Of course Mack would have designed a decontamination unit at the end of the passageway, just in case there was an emergency evacuation.

The second technician moved in with a large canister that had a hose attached. "To make double sure," she said, and began spraying Joanna with Enviro Chem. Three powerful sprays later, the technician handed Joanna a towel, canvas shoes, and a fresh scrub suit. "You're clean."

With her hair still dripping, Joanna left the unit and walked out into the world of conventional medicine.

The wide corridor in the radiology department was busy, with doctors and nurses and aides rushing about. Joanna was happy to see normal people who weren't worried about catching some goddamn deadly virus. When the passing people looked back at Joanna strangely, she realized she was gawking. She walked on and picked up the pace, with a lively bounce to her step.

Joanna took the stairs to the B level and walked into the forensics laboratory. Her head technician, Mary Chen, looked up from her microscope and stared, speechless.

"I'm back," Joanna announced.

Mary Chen rushed over and gave Joanna a tight hug. "Oh, Dr. Blalock! It's so good to see you."

Joanna returned the hug. "It's good to see you, too."

Mary stepped back and carefully studied Joanna's face. "Are you well?"

"I'm fine."

"You look tired."

"Maybe just a little."

"Then you must go home and rest."

"I need to talk with Lori briefly. Then I'm out of here."

Mary took Joanna's hand and held it to her cheek. "I'm so glad you are well."

"Thank you," Joanna replied, touched by the technician's warmth and concern. "Now, if you don't stop babbling over me, I'll never get out of here."

Mary smiled and moved aside. "Go like the wind."

Joanna went into her small office and took a hand mirror from her desk, then studied her appearance. Her hair was still dripping wet with Enviro Chem, which gave off a sweetish odor. She quickly combed her hair straight back and held it in place with a simple barrette. Then she again looked into the mirror. Her makeup was entirely gone, and her face did appear tired. And the crow's-feet around her eyes seemed deeper too. Brushing up against death tended to do that, Joanna thought. She dabbed on some lipstick and rouge and headed for the rear laboratory.

Lori McKay jumped up when she saw Joanna. She

rushed over and embraced her, then gave her a kiss on the cheek. "God! We were all so scared."

"So was I," Joanna admitted.

Lori stepped back and carefully inspected Joanna. "You look pretty good."

"Liar."

Lori shrugged. "Okay. Then you look like hell."

Joanna grinned, happy to be back with friends and colleagues, and happier yet to be away from the nightmare in the Viral Research Center.

Lori pointed to Elliot Durr. "I think you've met Elliot."

"Indeed I have," Joanna said, waving to him. "Thanks again for the diagnosis."

"What diagnosis?" Lori asked quickly.

"A touch of urticaria." Elliot reached into his coat pocket and took out a tube of cortisone cream. He placed it on the countertop. "This will ease the itching until the lesions disappear."

Lori looked at Elliot, wide-eyed. "You were in the Viral Research Center?"

"Via television," Elliot explained.

Joanna sat in a swivel chair and glanced around the spacious laboratory, with its microscopes and workbenches and sophisticated equipment. She noticed a large blackboard against the wall that had no writing on it. "I take it you two are still working on the outbreak."

"Day and night," Lori told her.

"Any progress?"

"Nada. Zilch."

Lori walked over and tapped on the empty blackboard. "We haven't written anything on it because there's nothing to write."

"There must be some news," Joanna insisted.

"There is," Elliot said. "And it's all bad."

Joanna looked over at a calendar on her desk. It was May ninth. Only six days until *naqba,* the day of catastrophe.

She exhaled heavily. "Okay, let's have it."

"Remember the delivery boy from the Mojave pharmacy?" Elliot began, and waited for Joanna to nod. "Well, we were under the impression that he had no direct contact with anyone while contagious—other than the old pharmacist. That turns out not to be the case."

"Christ!" Joanna groaned under her breath, wondering how many more people were going to become infected.

"He had direct contact with two Middle Eastern—"

Joanna held up her hand. "Don't be politically correct down here. If they were Arabs, say Arabs."

"They were Arabs."

"Go on."

"Anyhow, two Arab men approached the delivery boy and questioned him regarding the whereabouts of Maria Rodriguez," Elliot continued. "The Arabs were within a few feet of the delivery boy, and he was coughing at the time. Beyond much doubt, he infected them. There's now an all-points bulletin out for the two Arabs, but so far they haven't been found."

And they aren't likely to be, Joanna was about to say, but remained silent. Now four Arabs had been seen in the Mojave over the past few weeks, and the last two were almost certainly connected to the first two. They had to be. Maria Rodriguez interconnected them. She was the girlfriend of the terrorist who died from smallpox, and he was associated with Khalil Mahmoud, the terrorist who was iced at LAX. And now two more Arabs were looking for Maria. Oh, yeah, they were all from the same pod. But why look for Maria Rodriguez? What could she tell them? "Did they say they were looking for Maria?"

"They claimed she was a beneficiary in somebody's will," Elliot answered.

"And they were anxious to locate her, huh?"

"They tipped the delivery boy twenty bucks when he told them where she lived."

"But they obviously didn't find her."

"Obviously."

Joanna tilted back in her swivel chair, still trying to figure out why Maria would be so important to the two Arabs. The young Mexican housekeeper couldn't have been part of the plot. No way. Her only involvement was being the girlfriend of the terrorist who died from smallpox. She had cared for him during the initial stages of his illness, and then had him examined by the retired doctor who arranged for the terrorist to be transported to a hospital, where—

Joanna blinked rapidly as the answer came to her. The two Arabs weren't looking for Maria; they were looking for their fellow terrorist, who was so ill he couldn't contact them. They believed Maria could tell them the whereabouts of their friend. Four Arabs were involved in this smallpox business, Joanna thought sourly, and that was probably just the tip of the iceberg. "Did you get a description of the two?"

Elliot gazed down at an index card and read from it. "Both were middle-aged, with dark skin and black hair."

That narrowed it down to about a billion people, Joanna was thinking. "How tall were these Arabs?"

Elliot studied the index card again. "One was short and one was tall."

"How tall?"

"The delivery boy didn't say."

"Was he asked?"

"I'm not sure."

"Then ask."

"We can't," Elliot told her. "The boy died yesterday."

Joanna grumbled to herself. For every step forward they took, they were going back two. "What else have you got?"

"The people taking pictures from the sky are having problems," Elliot said cryptically. "There are times when their cameras aren't in the right place."

Joanna nodded her understanding of the coded message from Wolinsky. Spy satellites circled the Earth and took pictures as they passed over a given location. There were times every day when no photographs of the plant in the Sudan would be available. Wolinsky had mentioned this possibility to her in an earlier phone conversation. Joanna wondered how big the time gaps were. Big enough for a lot of terrorists to slip through, she guessed.

Lori couldn't hold back her curiosity. "What kind of pictures are you talking about?"

"Pictures of bad places," Joanna said vaguely, glad that Lori hadn't been given all the details. At this point in time, the fewer people who knew, the better.

"Are we talking about another outbreak of smallpox?" Lori probed.

"Yes," Joanna said. And that was the truth. An outbreak had occurred in the Sudan months earlier. She gave Lori a long look. "You know enough not to breathe a word of this, don't you?"

Lori made a face. "I'm not an idiot."

"I know," Joanna said, and smiled at her young associate. But inwardly she was thinking that Lori sometimes had a loose tongue, and that could add more problems to the problems they already had. "Now give me some good news."

"There ain't any," Lori said honestly. "Everything we try runs into a dead end. And I mean everything. You want some examples?"

"Fire away."

Lori held up a hand and began ticking off the failures on her fingers. "First, the terrorist who got whacked at LAX was negative for smallpox. All of his cultures and tissues turned up a big zilch. Second, we compared the black dirt under his nails to dirt samples from all over the Seattle area. He could have been anywhere in the greater metropolitan area. Or he could have been in Oregon or northern California or a dozen other places. In other words, the analysis of the dirt under his nails was of no help. And third and fourth, they still haven't found the parking lot attendant who spoke to Maria and arranged for her ride, or the bicycle she rode to the restaurant."

"We're going to have an epidemic of smallpox on our hands," Joanna said gloomily.

"Tell me about it."

Joanna turned her attention back to the terrorist who was killed at LAX. "Did you retest the terrorist's blood for Cipro?"

Lori nodded and reached for a large legal pad. "His serum level of Cipro was point four micrograms per milliliter, which indicates he had ingested a large dose of the antibiotic within twelve hours of his death. We repeated the drug screen and found nothing but Cipro. So we must have a sick guy with bronchitis, but there's absolutely nothing to suggest he was around smallpox. Every test we—"

"Hold on," Joanna interrupted abruptly, coming forward in her chair. "Did you check his blood for antibodies to smallpox?"

Elliot shook his head. "All of his cultures were negative, and he didn't have any of the lesions of smallpox. So you wouldn't expect him to have antibodies to the virus."

"I would if he'd been vaccinated."

Elliot stared at Joanna as the information sank in. Then he slowly nodded. "The bastards would protect themselves."

"Most likely," Joanna agreed.

Elliot reached for his cell phone and quickly began to punch in numbers.

Joanna rose up out of the swivel chair, feeling very tired. She had tried to do too much too soon and was now paying the price for it. Even her mind was beginning to feel numb. She started for the door, saying, "I think I'll go home."

"By the way," Lori called after her, "how is Mack Brown doing?"

"We'll talk about it later," Joanna said without looking back.

29

Sayed, the trusted man sent by Ragoub to question the assassins, held a handkerchief over his nose and tried to block out the awful smell. He carefully eyed the two assassins, particularly the taller one, who had his weapon nearby.

"Where is the doctor?" the taller assassin asked.

"He will be here in one hour," Sayed replied. "His name is Ibrahim and he practices in Wasco."

"Where is this Wasco?"

"Near Bakersfield," Sayed told him. "That is why it will take him an hour to get here."

The tall assassin licked at the sores on his lips. "Does he know which disease we have?"

"He says it is called valley fever."

"So he has seen it before?" he shorter man asked.

"Many times." Sayed forced himself to look at the badly disfigured men whose faces were oozing pus. He swallowed back his nausea. "He sees at least twenty cases a year."

"How is it treated?"

"With pills," Sayed said vaguely.

"But our throats are so raw," the taller assassin complained. "We may not be able to get the pills down."

"There are injections as well."

The taller man nodded in agreement. "Yes. An injection might be best."

"Now, let us talk about Hassan," Sayed probed gently, watching for a reaction. There was none. "Have you seen him?"

The tall assassin shook his head. "But we were very close."

"How close?"

The tall assassin told Sayed about Hassan's girlfriend, Maria Rodriguez, and how they had searched her small guesthouse and found nothing. "They were both gone. My guess is that they fled to Tehachapi, where they are hiding out."

"And that is where we caught this valley fever disease," the shorter man said. "In the guesthouse."

"How do you know this?" Sayed asked.

"Because of the smell," the shorter man answered. "The terrible stench in the guesthouse was the same as the one you smell in here."

"Very good thinking," Sayed praised him, then looked away as the pieces of the puzzle started to fall into place. Hassan had somehow infected himself with the smallpox virus, and when he became ill, he ran to his girlfriend and infected her. "How do you know they were not in the big house?"

"Because we looked in the windows," the shorter man replied. "It was very dark. No one was there."

"Perhaps they were asleep," Sayed suggested.

The shorter man shook his head. "The house stayed dark all the time. And no one has been allowed in the big house since the ambulance left."

"What ambulance?" Sayed asked at once.

"The neighbors told us that ambulances came to the house before the yellow tapes went up."

Now all the pieces fell into place for Sayed. In all likelihood the ambulances had taken Maria and Hassan to the hospital for treatment. Then the area around the empty house was quarantined. "You've done your work well. Ragoub will be pleased."

The tall assassin checked his watch. "The doctor will be here soon, God willing."

"You must follow his instructions exactly," Sayed said sternly. "Otherwise the disease can linger."

The taller assassin nodded and with an effort lay back in bed. Now his weapon on the night table was out of immediate reach.

"I must return to Los Angeles," Sayed said, and headed for the door. As he reached for the doorknob he glanced back. "Oh, I almost forgot. Do you need any extra money for expenses?"

"Yes! Yes!" the two assassins said almost simultaneously.

Sayed reached inside his coat and came out with a semiautomatic weapon that had a long silencer attached. He squeezed off two head shots—one for each of the assassins. Then, to make sure, he fired a final shot into the left eye of each man.

Sayed hurried out to his car, which was parked directly in front of the unit. He came back with a large can of gasoline and doused both bodies as well as the bed and chair where they lay.

At the door he lit a match and tossed it into the room. Then he ran for his car and sped away.

Ragoub sat on the edge of the desk in his office and watched the white dots on the giant television screen. All six were moving across the outline of the United States. Four were headed east, two west.

"The smell in their room was that of a dead animal,"

Sayed was saying as he, too, watched the moving white dots. "It was like a rotting carcass."

"You are sure they had the disease?" Ragoub asked.

Sayed nodded. "They looked exactly like the pictures you had shown me."

"Large black spots were everywhere?"

"Everywhere."

Ragoub stood and began to pace the floor, wondering again if anyone else had seen the hideous faces of the assassins. "Describe their room for me. I want every detail."

Sayed envisioned the pigsty he had walked into. "It was a simple room with a bed, night table, dresser, and television set. The floor was covered with empty take-out food containers and soda cans."

"How many containers?"

"A dozen or more."

"So," Ragoub concluded, "they did have all their meals delivered."

"Almost certainly," Sayed said, and then added, "They would have never left the room looking as they did. I tell you, their appearance was beyond horror."

Ragoub glanced over at the giant television screen, with its outline of the United States. He wondered how many Americans would soon have the horrible appearance of smallpox. Millions, for sure. And millions upon millions, if things went well.

He returned to the question of whether anyone had seen the sick assassins. "Could you detect the terrible smell from outside the door?"

"No," Sayed answered promptly. "But once in the room, the stench was overpowering."

Ragoub continued to pace, now convinced that no one had seen the disfigured assassins. But someone had seen Hassan and Maria. That was why the ambulances were called. That was why the house was placed under quarantine. "Where do you believe they took Hassan and Maria?"

"To the hospital."

Ragoub shook his head. "Then it would have been reported in the news, and we have heard nothing."

"Maybe they wish to keep it quiet, so as not to panic the people," Sayed proposed.

"Or maybe they don't want us to know *that they know*," Ragoub said suspiciously. "It is much easier to catch prey which is unwary."

Sayed's brow went up. "Are you saying they are on to us?"

"Maybe," Ragoub said, but deep down he knew the Americans had to be aware. America had the best medical professionals in the world. Its doctors would not miss smallpox. He looked over at Sayed, remembering a question he had neglected to ask. "Did you burn your clothes?"

Sayed nodded. "I did exactly as you instructed. I went to a truck stop, showered and changed clothes, then burned the ones I had been wearing."

"And you revaccinated yourself?"

"An hour ago," Sayed replied. "Why all these questions?"

"Because I want you healthy, my friend," Ragoub said. "We have a lot of work in front of us. You see, we are about to change our plans."

"How so?"

"We will strike two days before May the fifteenth."

"But *naqba*," Sayed protested mildly. "The attack was supposed to coincide with *naqba*."

"For America, the day of catastrophe will come two days sooner."

Sayed nodded slowly. "That will give the Americans less time to track us."

"Exactly," Ragoub said. Then he asked, "Do you foresee any difficulty in moving up the time schedule?"

"None whatsoever."

Ragoub picked up the remote control and pressed a button. The outline of the United States and the six moving dots disappeared from the screen.

30

Jake entered Joanna's condominium using his own key. Lights were on everywhere, although it was almost eleven P.M. A log was blazing in the fireplace, giving off a pleasant hickory aroma. From the kitchen Jake heard Joanna humming. He crept in and watched her as she tossed a salad at a large wooden table. She was wearing only a short white terry-cloth robe.

"You're beautiful," Jake said softly.

"You say that to all the girls." Joanna grinned without looking up.

"Nah. Just the pretty ones."

Joanna spun around and flew into his arms. They kissed so hard they drew blood from their lips. In a split second Joanna's robe was open and Jake's trousers were down, and they were atop the wooden table groping for each other. They bounced up and down on the sturdy table, pressing harder and harder, wanting more and more. Both were lost in a swirl of ecstasy that went on and on. Then they seemed to explode at the same time, both groaning and holding on with all their might.

Joanna lifted her head up and kissed Jake's chin. "What am I going to do with you?"

"How about marrying me?" Jake proposed.

Joanna blinked rapidly, caught entirely off guard. Her face began to color.

"Well?"

"Are you serious?" Joanna asked, trying to gather herself.

"About as serious as I can be," Jake told her. "So what do you say?"

"Ma-maybe," Joanna mumbled, wanting to say yes, then no, then yes again, then no.

"Does that mean you want to think about it?"

"I guess."

"Take your time."

"I'll get back to you in a few weeks."

"What!"

Joanna smiled and tied her robe back together. "A girl doesn't want to sound too eager, you know."

"Jesus! Women!" Jake said, as if that explained everything.

He pulled up his trousers and tucked in his shirt, still staring at Joanna. Although she was in her early forties, her body looked ten years younger. And the short white robe she was wearing seemed to accentuate her graceful lines and wonderful curves.

"What are you staring at?" Joanna asked.

"The mess we made." Jake pointed to the sliced lettuce and tomatoes and cucumbers strewn about the floor. "I guess salad is out, huh?"

"I've got some frozen chicken pot pie."

"My all-time favorite."

Joanna reached into the refrigerator for the frozen pies and turned on the oven. She glanced over at Jake and smiled. "You've got a big wet spot on the front of your trousers."

Jake looked down and said, "Shit!"

Joanna watched Jake hurry out of the kitchen. He had to be the neatest person she'd ever known. He couldn't stand anything out of order or unclean, and soiled clothing bothered him the most.

She heard the water go on in the bathroom and thought about how wonderful Jake could be—and how difficult. She loved him, but to live with him all the time, day in and day out, was another matter. She had meant it when she told him she'd have to think about his proposal. She'd really have to think about it. Later. When everything had calmed down.

"Better, huh?" Jake walked back into the kitchen wearing his blue and gold UCLA warm-up outfit. "Lucky I didn't take my things back home."

"Real lucky," Joanna muttered, remembering the awful embarrassment she'd felt when Jake didn't show up for her dinner party of fourteen. He simply forgot, or wanted to forget. And here she was falling for him again and hoping he'd change, but knowing he never would. So stupid to go back. So stupid. But she couldn't help herself.

"What are you thinking about?" Jake asked.

"How smart I am," Joanna replied, then added silently, *And how stupid I can be at the same time.* "Grab a couple of beers while I get the pot pies started."

They went into the living room and sat on a couch in front of the fireplace. The log was blazing and giving off just enough heat to ward off the evening chill.

Joanna quietly said, "We've really got to think about this marriage idea."

"I know," Jake agreed.

"We shouldn't push it."

"I know," Jake said again. "But it sounds like a pretty damn good idea, doesn't it?"

Joanna leaned back and nestled her head against her shoulder. "You bet."

"You tell me when you want to talk about it more."

"That sounds like an open-ended invitation."

"Well," Jake said, hedging a little, "I'd like an answer sometime in the next twenty years."

Joanna chuckled. "That's a long time."

"For a while," Jake said seriously, "I didn't think we'd have any time at all."

Joanna nodded gravely. "It was so goddamn scary down there."

"I can imagine."

"No, you can't."

Jake reached for a cigarette and lit it. "Well, let's not talk about it."

"We've got to," Joanna said. "Everything in our case revolves around it."

"How do you mean?"

Joanna took a deep breath, hating to relive her time in the Viral Research Center. "That wasn't some strange jungle virus we were dealing with."

"What was it?"

"Smallpox."

Jake's jaw dropped. "Holy shit! Smallpox?"

"Smallpox," Joanna repeated. "And it killed five of the six people trapped down there. I was the only one to survive."

Jake shook his head, still taken aback. "Are they sure?"

"Beyond any doubt," Joanna said, trying not to envision the terrible disfigurement caused by the smallpox virus. "And it's every bit as deadly and devastating as the history books say. The patients are covered with boils, head to toe."

"Jesus," Jake hissed to himself. "It sounds like a biblical plague."

"It was worse."

"And you actually saw this, eh?"

"Up close."

"Jesus," Jake said once more, then stared into the fireplace, lost in thought. He turned back to Joanna. "Tell me how all this fits into our case."

"The terrorist who got iced at LAX had a friend," Joanna explained. "That friend was another Arab who was brought to Memorial with a fulminating case of smallpox. He was the patient in the Viral Research Center who infected all the others."

Jake jerked his head around. "Are those bastards planning to attack America with smallpox?"

Joanna nodded. "And soon."

Jake got to his feet and began pacing the floor, nervously puffing on his cigarette. "How do you know they plan to attack us?"

"Why else would a terrorist be carrying around a vial of smallpox, which he probably infected himself with?"

"Yeah, yeah," Jake said hurriedly. "I've got my head up my ass. An Arab in America with smallpox adds up to bioterrorism."

"We're looking at a nightmare about to happen."

"Other than the people in the research center, have any others come down with the disease?"

"A bunch."

Joanna told him about the medical facility on the outskirts of Mojave where the patients and their known contacts were housed. "And there are two more Arabs and a parking lot attendant who were probably infected and are now spreading the disease around. And we have no idea where they are."

"How contagious is this disease?"

"It'll move through this country like wildfire."

Joanna described the ease with which the virus could be transmitted from person to person. "And nobody in America has been vaccinated against smallpox in over thirty years. The virus will literally devour us."

"Why don't they vaccinate everybody right now?" Jake asked.

"We may have to," Joanna replied. "But it might not do much good. This particular smallpox virus is so virulent that it can kill before a vaccinated person builds up any immunity."

"Christ," Jake moaned. "It *is* a nightmare."

"Wait until you see somebody with the disease, and then you'll really know what kind of nightmare smallpox is."

"How many people could this virus kill?"

"Millions in America," Joanna answered. "Millions upon millions worldwide."

Jake angrily threw his cigarette into the fireplace. "We've got to stop these bastards."

"First, we've got to determine how they plan to disseminate the virus," Joanna said. "They won't just open a can and leave it in a shopping mall. They'll use a method that will infect the greatest number of people. Most of our experts think they'll try to infect highly mobile people, because those are the people who are hardest to track and who will spread the disease far and wide in the shortest possible time."

Jake squinted an eye. "What do they mean by highly mobile people?"

"Those on the move," Joanna said. "Like people on subways or in airports. With air travel the way it is today, it would be impossible—"

"Son of a bitch!" Jake cut her off. "Son of a bitch! I know how they're going to do it."

Joanna leaned forward, ears pricked. "How?"

"Using commercial aircraft."

Jake darted back to the couch and sat next to Joanna. He

placed a finger against her lips. "Don't ask a question until I'm finished. Okay?"

"Okay."

Jake lit another cigarette. "This afternoon the FBI informed me that they had tracked down the earlier whereabouts of our dead terrorist, Khalil Mahmoud. They went through the health claims at all the aerospace and aviation companies in Seattle, looking for Arabic names of people who had bronchitis and were treated with Cipro. They found two, but only one had a chest X ray. And it was filled with metal fragments." Jake leaned over and kissed her nose. "The FBI got him because you told them how to track the bastard down. He's not using the same name, of course, but it's him."

"Who does he work for?"

"Boeing."

"Oh, Christ," Joanna groaned. "They're going to disperse the smallpox on planes."

"Planes that son of a bitch worked on, no doubt," Jake added.

Joanna asked, "Do you know how many planes he worked on?"

"More than a few," Jake said sourly. "He worked at Boeing for almost two years."

"Shit."

Jake stood and started pacing again. "You got any idea how many hiding places there are on a big Boeing jet?"

"Too many to count."

"Every plane that bastard worked on will have to be grounded and inspected," Jake thought aloud. "According to the FBI, he worked as an electrician at Boeing, and that could have taken him to every section of a plane."

"See if he had a specialty," Joanna suggested. "You know, whether he worked in the cockpit or some other area."

Jake nodded. "And we should check out the aviation plant he worked at in France. Maybe he was assigned to just one job while he was there." Jake growled to himself, searching for other clues that might help. "We need a road map here. Otherwise we'll never find the damn thing."

"Even with a road map we'd still have problems," Joanna predicted. "There may have been more than one terrorist working at Boeing. Maybe there were two or three of them, which means a lot of planes could be carrying a device that is primed to release the smallpox virus."

"How big would this device be?"

Joanna considered the question briefly. "A Coke bottle filled with the virus could infect a plane ten times over."

"It'll be like looking for a needle in a haystack," Jake said disconsolately. "And I'm talking about a little needle in a big haystack."

"We'll never make it by May fifteenth."

"What's so important about May fifteenth?"

Joanna told him about *naqba*, the Arab day of catastrophe, the day Israel was founded with the support of the United States. "The CIA thinks that's the day they're going to do it. That gives us six days to crack this case. And there's no way we can do it."

Scowling, Jake finished off his beer and wiped the foam from his lips with a finger. "Ready for a refill?"

"Only if you're buying."

Jake walked over to a wet bar in the corner of the living room and reached into a small refrigerator for two beers and frosted mugs. As he opened the bottles, he noticed an opened envelope with an airline ticket protruding from it. "Are you taking a trip?"

"I'm flying to Atlanta for a forensics meeting on May thirteenth," Joanna called over. "I'm giving a paper on a radio-immune essay for the detection of ricin."

As Jake poured beer into the frosted mugs, he recalled the case of Dr. Robert Mariner, a respected director of a giant HMO who was killing off his patients with ricin, one of the most potent toxins known to man. Mariner was currently doing three consecutive life sentences. "How long will you be gone?" Jake asked, handing her a mug.

"Just a day. I'll fly in and fly out." Joanna took a swallow of the ice-cold beer and looked over to Jake. "Maybe I shouldn't leave, with all this craziness going on."

"Go and give your paper," Jake advised. "If we need you, we can always reach you by phone."

"I guess so," Joanna said wearily. "From this point on it's mainly a matter of legwork anyway. And it's going to take a lot of people to search all those planes."

"Well, at least we'll know which planes to tear apart."

"That's assuming only one terrorist—our guy—worked for Boeing in Seattle," Joanna reminded him.

"You really think there's more than one?"

"Could be."

"Shit," Jake said disgustedly, and took out his cell phone. "I'd better call Kitt and get—"

A small television set on the counter of the wet bar came on automatically.

"I've got it set on an automatic timer for the news," Joanna explained.

"Want me to turn it off?"

Joanna shook her head. "I haven't heard the news in almost two weeks."

"You haven't missed a hell of a lot."

A picture of a handsome news anchor with a shock of white hair came on the screen. "From the desert to the sea, to all of southern California, a very pleasant good evening," the anchor began. "Trouble is again brewing in the Middle East as the region braces itself for what could be an outbreak of war. Earlier today Sudanese patrol boats attacked an Israeli freighter in the Red Sea, killing two seamen and injuring a dozen more. The Sudanese government claims that the Israeli ship provoked the incident by entering Sudanese waters. An Israeli spokesman said the ship was clearly in international waters. For more, let's go to our correspondent at the State Department for an update on the crisis."

Jake bristled. "Those bastards shot up an unarmed freighter. They must be out of their minds."

"They'll claim it was a spy ship."

"Who the hell wants to spy on the Sudan, for chrissakes?"

"The CIA," Joanna told him. "They've got pretty good evidence that the smallpox virus was produced at a pharmaceutical plant in northern Sudan."

Jake stared at her, incredulous. "You've got to be kidding."

"That's the source," Joanna went on. "It's apparently owned and operated by a group of Islamic extremists."

"In local news," the anchor continued, "there has been an outbreak of an unusual infectious disease in the East Los Angeles area. The disease, which is caused by the meningococcus organism, can result in meningitis and severe bleeding into the skin. Four cases have now been reported and are now being treated at local hospitals. All are expected to survive. Health officials say that the outbreak is contained and will shortly be eradicated entirely with the use of prophylactic antibiotics."

Joanna turned to Jake and said, "That's CIA misinformation. There was only one case and it wasn't meningococcemia. It was smallpox."

Jake growled, "A goddamn outbreak of smallpox in downtown Los Angeles."

"One case," Joanna repeated. "And she and all of her contacts are now isolated."

"How did this patient get the disease?"

"The patient is Maria Rodriguez, a Mexican housekeeper from the Mojave," Joanna replied. "She was the girlfriend of the terrorist who came down with smallpox."

"Is she going to make it?"

Joanna shook her head. "Unlikely."

"So how many people total are now known to have smallpox?"

"A bunch. And all got it from the same guy."

Jake ran a hand through his hair. How many people, he wondered, could be infected by a plane filled with passengers, all carrying the smallpox virus? "There's going to be an epidemic," he prophesied. "An honest-to-God epidemic."

"And it'll take us back to the Middle Ages," Joanna told him. "There'll be people dying in the streets by the tens of thousands. There won't be enough coffins to bury them."

Jake's cell phone chirped loudly. He picked it up and spoke into it. "Yeah? . . . Yeah . . . What motel?" Jake's eyes suddenly widened. "How many? . . . And you're sure about the phone number? . . . I'll contact Dr. Blalock. . . . Are you in your office? . . . Stay there. We have to talk."

Jake put his cell phone down, then lit another cigarette and inhaled deeply. "That was William Kitt from the FBI. They went through Khalil Mahmoud's phone records in Seattle and discovered he made a bunch of calls to a motel in the Mojave."

"And?"

"And that motel was destroyed by fire tonight."

"Do they know who the calls were made to?"

"To room eight."

"And who was in room eight?"

"Arabs, according to the wife of the motel manager."

Joanna reached for his cigarette and took a puff, then handed it back. "We've got to take a look at that room, Jake."

"And the two bodies in it."

"Do they have the area cordoned off?" Joanna asked quickly.

Jake nodded. "And guarded by the California Highway Patrol. Nobody will get in there. But don't get your hopes up. Kitt says it's little more than a pile of ashes now."

"Sometimes you learn a lot from ashes."

"Well, while you're sifting through those ashes, see if you can find the answer to the single most important question we have—the one that might just crack this case wide open."

"Which question is that?"

"What in the hell were a bunch of Arabs doing in the Mojave Desert?"

31

It was almost nine A.M. when Jake and Joanna approached the fire-ravaged Mojave Motel. The entire structure had burned to the ground. Except for some isolated walls and blackened timbers, nothing was left standing.

"We can forget about any written material," Jake remarked.

"Unless they had a metal lockbox," Joanna said.

"You're dreaming."

"I know."

Jake flashed his shield at a California Highway Patrol officer and was waved into a cement-covered courtyard. They came to a stop near the front wall of a unit that had its windows smashed out. A young FBI agent dressed in a dark suit was waiting for them.

Everyone introduced themselves. The FBI agent's name was Don Bonnerman. He was tall and lean, with very short hair.

"Thank you for coming so promptly, Dr. Blalock," Bonnerman began. "The Bureau appreciates your assistance."

Out of the corner of her eye Joanna noticed a thin stray dog sniffing around. She picked up a pebble and threw it in the direction of the animal. The dog scampered away. "Have you seen other strays around?"

"Just that one," Bonnerman answered.

"Please have the Highway Patrol chase away any stray animals," Joanna requested.

Bonnerman looked at her oddly. "May I ask why?"

"Because they're attracted to cooked meat," Jake said hoarsely.

"I-I see," Bonnerman stammered. "Of course."

He reached into his coat pocket for a sheet of paper and read from it. "I do have some instructions from the Bureau, which I'm to pass on to you. First, please do not remove any items or objects from the search site. Any further study on such items will be performed, at your request, by the FBI laboratory. Second, your investigation is to be limited to unit eight, where—"

Joanna held up a hand, interrupting the agent. "My investigation goes where I think it should go. I'll follow the clues, not your instructions. And we don't have time to send things to the FBI laboratory, because it'll take them a week to process them. And we don't have a week. We've got five days. That's all."

Bonnerman stared at Joanna, perplexed, not understanding the time constraints.

Jake told him, "After we're done here, you call William Kitt. He'll explain it to you."

Bonnerman recognized the director's name and nodded. "Yes, sir."

"Let's see these dead bodies," Jake said.

Bonnerman turned to Joanna. "Ma'am, I should tell you that these people are really fried."

"Bad, huh?" Joanna asked.

"Extra crispy."

"Lead the way."

They walked along the pavement until they came to a unit that had part of a wall still standing. The door, with the metal number eight on it, was lying on the ground. The group entered carefully, each testing the flooring to make certain it wouldn't collapse under the weight.

Bonnerman pointed to a badly charred bed and chair, and the two bodies atop them. "There they are."

Joanna slipped on latex gloves and approached the blackened bodies. Their faces were burned down to bone.

"I think you can smell the gasoline," Bonnerman said. "Our arsonist did sloppy work."

Joanna sniffed the bodies from head to toe, measuring the intensity of the gasoline odor. "Not so sloppy," she announced.

"But he splashed gasoline everywhere," Bonnerman argued mildly. "Like he didn't give a damn."

"Oh, he gave a damn," Joanna assured him.

She started with the taller victim on the bed. His clothes were almost completely burned off, his shoes still on. Both his arms and legs were flexed. There was a small bullet hole in his forehead and two large exit wounds in the back of his skull.

Joanna noticed a handgun on the charred night table near the bed. She picked it up and showed it to Jake.

Jake quickly identified it. "A semiautomatic Beretta."

Joanna put the weapon down and moved over to the shorter victim on a nearby chair. She carefully examined the corpse, using a magnifying glass on his skull. The findings were identical to those seen in the first victim, even down to the head wounds. There was one bullet wound in the forehead, two exit wounds in the occipital bone.

Joanna stripped off her gloves and stepped back. "This job was done by a pro."

"But the smell of gasoline was everywhere," Bonnerman argued again. "A pro wouldn't have made it this obvious."

"That depends," Joanna said. "Professional assassins don't really care about arson. All they're concerned with is killing their target and, in this case, making certain no one could identify the victims."

"What makes you so sure we're dealing with a professional assassin here?" Bonnerman asked.

"The method of killing," Joanna explained. "Both victims had a single bullet hole in their foreheads and two exit wounds in the back of the skull. So we're dealing with one entrance wound and two exit wounds. How do you account for that?"

Bonnerman pondered the unusual findings and tried to come up with a plausible explanation. His eyes suddenly brightened. "Maybe the two bullets entered through the same hole."

"Possible, but not very likely," Joanna told him. "The entrance wound here was too small and too even. Even if you tried to fire two bullets into the same place at point-blank range, you'd still leave a big, irregular entrance wound."

Bonnerman shook his head, puzzled. "Then how do you account for two exit wounds?"

"The second shot probably went through the eye," Joanna explained. "That's how the pros do it. A second shot through the eye to make sure."

Bonnerman nodded admiringly. "I'll remember that."

"And you'll note the faces of the victims are burned so badly that the bones are charred," Joanna continued on. "And the smell of gasoline was strongest around their heads. The assassin wanted his victims to be unidentifiable."

"And the victims knew the pro, too," Jake added.

"Absolutely," Joanna agreed. "The pro didn't surprise the victims. They may have even been waiting for him."

"But they didn't trust him a hundred percent," Jake said knowingly.

"Whoa!" Bonnerman held up his hands, palms out. "How do you know all this?"

"We can assume they weren't surprised, because one victim was lying in bed and the other was sitting in a chair," Joanna elucidated. "This indicates they were resting and probably at ease. That's not how you'd expect to find two people who had been surprised by an intruder."

"Maybe they were asleep," Bonnerman countered.

Joanna shook her head. "They both had their shoes on."

"And the gun on the night table indicates they were expecting trouble," Jake said. "Maybe from the assassin."

Bonnerman was busily scribbling down notes in a notepad, pausing only to underline the important points. He quickly read what he had written, then glanced over to Joanna. "Would it be okay for me to include these findings in my report?"

"Of course," Joanna said generously. "You were part of the investigating team, weren't you?"

"Yes, ma'am," Bonnerman replied gratefully. "And may I say it's a privilege working with you."

You bet your ass it's a privilege, Jake was thinking. *You put ten Joanna Blalocks together in a unit and you could send the entire FBI home.* "Any other bodies?"

"No, sir," Bonnerman said. "They're all we got."

"What about the manager?"

"He's getting treated for burns at the hospital," Bonnerman reported. "But his wife is out back."

"Let's go talk to her."

Joanna and Jake followed the FBI agent out and along a

paved walkway. They stayed back a half dozen steps and spoke in low voices.

"What do you think?" Jake asked quietly.

"One of those Arabs was short, the other tall," Joanna whispered. "I'll bet they are the two who questioned the delivery boy at the pharmacy. You know, the boy who came down with smallpox."

Jake stiffened, remembering how near he had been to the burned bodies. "You think those two caught smallpox from the boy?"

"Maybe. Maybe not."

"But we were so damn close to those bodies in there."

Joanna shrugged. "It doesn't matter. A fire like that will destroy every virus known to man, inside or outside a human body."

"So we're safe, huh?"

"Absolutely."

Jake pulled out the collar of his shirt with an index finger. The sun was beating down, the temperature already near ninety. "Somebody sure wanted those two guys dead and their IDs covered up. I wonder why."

"You got me."

The FBI agent led them to the rear of the property, where a plump middle-aged woman was sitting on a folding chair. She was wearing blue jeans, a checkered red shirt, and a straw hat with a broad brim.

"Mrs. Wallace," Bonnerman said, and pointed to Jake, "this is Detective Sinclair from Los Angeles. He'd like to ask you a few questions."

"Those damned Arabs," Della Wallace blurted out before Jake could say a word. "They burned our place down."

"You sure of that?" Jake asked.

"We were watching television last night when the fire broke out," she recounted. "By the time we got there, unit eight was fully ablaze and spreading to the others. And unit eight was being rented by those two Arabs. Now you tell me, how would you put all that together?"

"Looks like they started it," Jake agreed.

"Damn right," Della Wallace said venomously. "And we've got no insurance. Not a penny's worth."

"Can you describe these two Arabs?"

"One was short and one was tall. And they both smelled bad." The woman shook her head, then cursed loudly. "God-damn it! I told my husband not to rent to those two. I *told* him."

"Would you know their names?" Jake pushed.

She shook her head again. "My husband kept the books and did the registering and all. And our books and office burned right to the ground, just like everything else."

Della Wallace stared out at the desert, her eyes beginning to water. She sniffed the tears back. "Now we've lost every-thing, and there's no way we can recoup."

"Did these Arabs have any friends?" Jake asked.

"Not that I know of," Della answered. "They were like the first Arab we rented to in number eight. They pretty much kept to themselves."

Jake's eyes narrowed. "Who was this first Arab you rented to?"

Della sniffed. "Hussein or Hassin. Something like that. My husband would know."

"Did Mr. Hassin have visitors?"

"Only that Mexican whore who came around once in a while. I never knew her name. She came and she went, and that was her business, I guess."

Jake and Joanna exchanged knowing glances.

"We need the full name of that first Arab," Jake pressed.

"You're going to have to ask my husband."

"What hospital is he in?"

"That big burn center in Valencia." Della looked out at the desert again as tears welled up. "They say he's in bad shape."

32

"Bad burns must be the worst," Jake was saying.

Joanna nodded gravely. "If you're lucky, you end up disfigured with heaps of scar tissue everywhere. But most of the bad burn victims don't survive."

"What determines if the patient lives or dies?"

"The percentage of the body's surface area that has third-degree burns," Joanna answered. "If it's more than fifty percent, you don't survive."

"Is it as painful as it sounds?"

"Worse."

They were standing outside a critical-care unit at the Valencia Burn Center, waiting for the surgeon looking after Cody Wallace. The motel manager was listed in serious but stable condition, with no visitors allowed. It had taken phone calls from two highly placed officials just to set up the interview with the surgeon.

The door to the unit opened. Joanna and Jake stepped aside as a gurney whizzed by. It carried a small child covered with thick white gauze. Only the child's nose and mouth were visible through the maze of bandages. Jake swallowed hard and looked away. As the door closed, Jake peeked into the unit. He saw only doctors and nurses hurrying about.

Jake turned back to Joanna. "Could you imagine working here day in and day out?"

"No," Joanna said honestly. "But then, they couldn't imagine working around smallpox all day long, either."

"Neither of those jobs are picnics, are they?"

"Nor is chasing down terrorists and murderers."

"I guess."

Jake reached into his coat pocket for his notepad and began flipping pages. "While we're talking about terrorists, let me give you the latest on Khalil Mahmoud. The FBI found out that he had a roommate during the first year he lived in Seattle. The roommate was described as a short, slender guy with Arabic features, who moved away to southern California about a year ago."

"Probably the little terrorist with smallpox," Joanna surmised. "Do they have a name?"

Jake shook his head. "Only Mahmoud's name was on the apartment lease."

"Damn," Joanna said. "He's the key to this whole thing."

"Tell me about it."

Joanna stared down the busy corridor, thinking. She wondered if the FBI knew enough to search the Seattle apartment for items that could be related to the smallpox virus. "Does the FBI know about the outbreak of smallpox?"

Jake nodded. "They're aware, whatever the hell that means."

"Did you ask them straight-out?"

"Point-blank," Jake said. "And Kitt's response was, 'We're aware.' They're also aware we're still tailing Haj Ragoub and Yusef Malik, and they're pissed about it."

"Too bad," Joanna said tersely. "They're so busy being

politically correct they don't know if the lights are on or off."

"They know more than they're letting on," Jake told her. "A lot more. They're playing it close to the vest."

"While we sit out here in the dark."

"Not for much longer," Jake went on. "In exchange for me dropping our tails on Ragoub and Malik, they've agreed to disclose everything at a meeting tomorrow morning. They want both of us to attend."

"Why me?"

"You'll have to ask them."

The doors to the critical-care unit swung open and Peter Goodman walked over. He was a tall, heavyset man in his forties, with thick brown hair. The front of his scrub suit was heavily spotted with perspiration. "Lieutenant Sinclair?"

Jake showed his shield and nodded. "And this is Dr. Joanna Blalock."

Goodman nodded back. "What can I do for you?"

"We'd like to talk with Cody Wallace," Jake requested.

"I'm sorry," Goodman said, shaking his head. "He's being prepared for surgery now."

"Has he already been sedated?" Joanna asked quickly.

"If he hasn't, he will be shortly," Goodman replied.

"We need two minutes," Joanna urged. "It's a matter of life and death."

Goodman's eyes narrowed. "Could you be more specific?"

"No, I can't."

"Then again, I'm sorry," Goodman said. "The patient is in a great deal of pain and is on his way to the OR. Perhaps tomorrow you—"

Jake stepped in front of Goodman. They were nose-to-nose, eye-to-eye. "Doctor, I hope you don't make us do this the hard way."

"Which is?" Goodman asked, not backing down.

"Which is we leave and come back in an hour with a bunch of FBI agents and a stack of subpoenas and warrants. Then everybody who had any contact with Cody Wallace will be marched out of here and questioned over and over again until we find out what Cody Wallace may or may not have said to them."

"You can't just—"

"Sure, I can," Jake cut him off. "You've already received two phone calls regarding this matter, haven't you?"

Goodman nodded slowly.

"Well, there won't be any more," Jake said. "The FBI isn't as patient as we are."

"It's that urgent, huh?"

"That urgent."

Goodman sighed reluctantly. "You've got two minutes."

Jake and Joanna followed Goodman into the critical-care unit, passing one open door after another. Some of the patients were moaning in pain. Others were sleeping. The air was filled with the odor of a strong disinfectant. From somewhere a child shrieked in pain, then began sobbing. Again Jake wondered how anyone could stand to work on a ward where human misery never ended.

They stopped in front of room twenty-eight and donned disposable gowns, masks, and caps. A loud groan came from inside the room.

"Two minutes," Goodman reminded them.

Cody Wallace was sitting up in bed, his arms and legs heavily bandaged. His eyebrows were badly singed.

"Doc, that last shot didn't work worth a damn," Wallace complained.

"We'll give you another shot in just a minute," Goodman promised. "But first the police would like to ask you a few questions. Do you feel up to it?"

"Sure," Wallace said, his eyes brightening. "Is this about my motel?"

"Right." Jake stepped forward, careful not to touch the bed, since he wasn't wearing gloves. "Your wife told us that you think two Arabs in unit eight started the fire."

"Damn right they did," Wallace spat angrily. "I knew I shouldn't have rented to those two sons of bitches."

"How do you figure the fire started?" Jake asked.

"From all the trash in there," Wallace said at once, then began to rotate his body without thinking. A sharp stab of pain went through him. He gritted his teeth and waited for the pain to pass. "The trash was piled up in there. Empty soda cans and food boxes were on the floor and stacked up on the dresser. It was like a pigsty."

Joanna asked quickly, "Did you go into the room?"

"No, ma'am. They wouldn't let anybody in there, not even the cleaning woman."

"Then how did you know the condition of the room?"

"Looked in through the window while they were asleep."

Jake inquired, "Did you see anything unusual in there?"

Wallace thought briefly, then remembered something that had caught his attention. "There was one thing funny. The guy asleep in the chair had some big black spots on his arm. I don't know what the hell that was."

Joanna nodded. Now she knew why they wouldn't leave the room. They couldn't. They had smallpox. "Did anybody go into that room? Anybody at all?"

Wallace shook his head firmly. "They wouldn't let anybody in, not even the boys that delivered food. Made them leave the food outside."

"Do you remember the Arabs' names?" Jake asked.

"Long names, like the people from India have," Wallace recalled easily. "Mu-co-do-a-paka, or something like that.

But they weren't from India. They were Arabs. I can tell the difference."

"How did they pay for the room?"

"Cash. Up-front."

"What about the first Arab who lived in there?" Jake pressed gently.

"Mr. Hassan, you mean?"

Jake nodded. "Yeah. Mr. Hassan. Do you remember his first name?"

Wallace shrugged, and that caused him pain. He flinched and waited for it to ease. "Ahmed or Achmed—something like that."

"Did he pay in cash too?"

"Naw. I cashed his paycheck for him."

"Where did he work?" Jake asked at once.

"Out there at Anderson Metal," Wallace said. "They scrap all sorts of things and sell the metal."

"And the check was always good, eh?"

Wallace looked at Jake as if the detective were an idiot. "Are you kidding? Rupert Anderson is a billionaire. A check from him is better than money in the bank."

"Do you know what sort of work Hassan did out there?"

"Worked with scrap, I guess."

Suddenly the terrible pain came back, stabbing through his arms and legs. He shook his head and tried not to scream. "Doc, I need that shot. I need it bad."

Goodman signaled to a nurse standing in the corner of the room, then glanced over to Jake. "Your two minutes are up."

Outside the room, Joanna and Jake peeled off their disposable protective garb and deposited it in a nearby trash bin.

Looking over both shoulders, Joanna made certain no one was within earshot. In a whisper she said, "Those two

Arabs had the skin lesions of smallpox. That's why they wouldn't come out or let anyone in the room."

"Except for the pro who killed them," Jake whispered back. "He was sent to shut them up."

"And make sure they and their disease couldn't be identified."

"That, too."

They walked out of the unit and down a long corridor that led to the front entrance. Outside the sky was darkening as dusk fell.

"So it was Ahmed Hassan who brought smallpox to America," Joanna said. "He brought it here to kill others and he ended up killing himself."

"Kind of poetic justice, isn't it?"

"Nobody deserves to die that way, Jake."

"Well, he'd be at the top of my list," Jake said flatly. "But it's too bad he's dead, because he's the key to this case. And we still know next to nothing about him."

Joanna slowly nodded. "All we know is that he lived in Seattle and Mojave, had a Mexican girlfriend, and died of smallpox. Everything else is a guess."

"And we know he was employed by Rupert Anderson," Jake added, taking her arm as they entered the parking lot. "He worked for Anderson's scrap metal facility outside Mojave. Now tell me, how the hell does that fit into anything?"

Joanna shrugged. "I give up."

Jake pondered the possibilities. "I don't think Anderson could be tied into these terrorists, but you can never be sure in this crazy world."

"No way Anderson is involved," Joanna said firmly. "I know the guy."

"How?"

"His son was killed in the attack on the World Trade Center."

Joanna described how she was able to identify some of the son's body parts using DNA-matching techniques. "So they were able to bury their son. I guess it gave them some closure, although I'm not sure how much that helped."

Jake shook his head sadly. "Can you imagine anything worse than parents burying their child?"

"No, I can't," Joanna said. Rupert Anderson's wife, she recalled, had sunk into a deep depression and committed suicide a few months after her son's funeral. "Anyhow, I can guarantee that Rupert Anderson is not involved with the terrorists in any shape or form."

Jake reached for the car door and opened it for Joanna. "He must hate those bastards."

"With a passion."

33

Haj Ragoub and Yusef Malik were finishing dinner on the outdoor patio of a falafel restaurant in West Hollywood. They sipped black coffee and nibbled on honey-coated dates.

"These are almost as good as the ones back home, eh?" Ragoub commented.

"The dates back home are bigger," Yusef reminisced. "And sweeter, much sweeter."

"Are you certain of that?"

Yusef grinned. "One should never lie about important matters, such as the quality of dates."

Ragoub grinned back, nodding, then looked up at the night sky with its full moon. "And the moon is always bigger and brighter in our homeland. In America the moon seems far away. Along the Mediterranean the moon seems so close you can almost touch it."

"And soon I will have the pleasure of almost touching it," Yusef said longingly.

"Very soon." Ragoub glanced around to make sure no one was near. "You fly the day after tomorrow."

Yusef gazed at Ragoub strangely, then leaned in closer. "But that will be May thirteenth. That is not *naqba*."

"I know," Ragoub said, unconcerned.

"Then why the thirteenth?"

"Because that will be our last practice run," Ragoub explained. "There will be one final rehearsal to assure everything goes smoothly."

"Is this really necessary?"

Ragoub gave Yusef a stern look. "Would I order it if it were not?"

"Of course. Of course." Yusef backed off quickly. "I did not mean it that way."

"Then how did you mean it?"

Yusef waited as a couple strolled by on the sidewalk, then said, "I was thinking we had a practice run only three days ago, and someone at the terminal might recognize me and become aware of my frequent visits. This could cause suspicion."

"You flew National last time. Correct?"

"Correct."

"This time you will fly TransContinental."

Yusef breathed a sigh of relief. "I should have known better than to question your wisdom."

Ragoub waved off the apology. "No, no. It's better to be careful. You'll live longer that way."

Yusef nodded respectfully, but something about Ragoub's tone of voice bothered him. "To be careful is good. To be careful and wise, as you are, is even better."

Ragoub smiled thinly. "Yes. Yes, it is."

A waiter approached to refill their coffee cups, but Ragoub motioned him away. Then he said to Yusef, low, "These are your instructions. On the morning of the thirteenth, you will arrive at the TransContinental terminal in time for the nine-o'clock flight to Atlanta. You have an electronic ticket with seat thirty-six reserved for you. Bring along a carry-on suitcase, as if you're staying a few days. Also bring your cell phone. Any questions?"

Yusef shook his head. "It is the same as we did before."

"There are some changes," Ragoub noted on. "After obtaining your boarding pass at the gate, you will go to the nearest newsstand and wait for your associate to show up. As you know, he will be carrying a laptop computer with two red tags on its handle. Once you make eye contact with him, you must never leave his sight. That way, if he has trouble you will know about it instantly. Make certain that the red tags on the handle can easily be seen by—" Ragoub stopped abruptly in midsentence and stared down at the floor at Yusef's feet. "Where is your computer?"

"In the trunk of my car."

Ragoub's face hardened. "Didn't I tell you to keep it with you at all times?"

"I have." Yusef pointed to a parking lot across the street. "My car is over there."

"And what if somebody steals your car or breaks into your trunk?" Ragoub demanded. "What then?"

"I hadn't thought of that," Yusef had to admit.

Ragoub's eyelids narrowed into slits, his dark eyes cold as ice. "Go get the computer."

Yusef was on his feet in a fraction of a second. "Right away."

Ragoub waited for Yusef to dash off, then nervously strummed his fingers on the tabletop. He would have to watch Yusef carefully. The young man was smart enough to carry out the mission, but he was also inexperienced and unaccustomed to following orders. And that could pose a problem. One error now could endanger the entire operation.

Again, Ragoub wondered if he had made a mistake bringing in Yusef so late in the game. But there was really no other choice. A replacement had been needed quickly.

"More coffee, sir?" the waiter asked.

"Get away!" Ragoub snapped.

"Sorry," the waiter apologized, and disappeared.

Ragoub leaned back, pleased that he had moved up the event from May fifteenth to May thirteenth. Everything was set and ready to go. Why should they wait? The more time that passed, the more chances for mistakes and blunders. Yes, May thirteenth was a perfect day for the big event. With any luck the passengers who sucked in a massive dose of the smallpox virus could be showing symptoms of the disease on May fifteenth. So it could be a *naqba* event after all.

Even though May thirteenth was supposedly a practice flight, everybody would be careful and carry out their orders flawlessly, including Yusef Malik. And after the mission was completed, the unvaccinated Yusef would have to be killed. If he came down with the disease, he might lose his courage and talk. Too bad. Such a bright young man. But sometimes people were more valuable dead than alive.

Yusef hurried back to the table carrying his laptop computer. He paused to catch his breath, then said, "Here's my computer, safe and sound."

"Good," Ragoub said approvingly. "Do not let it out of your sight again."

"I won't," Yusef promised.

Ragoub signaled the waiter and paid the bill, then took Yusef's arm and guided him to the sidewalk. They walked along leisurely, passing teenagers with orange- and blue-dyed hair and pins sticking into their lips and noses. A car went by with its audio system blasting so loudly the pavement shook.

"I would never see this craziness back home," Yusef remarked.

You won't see anything after the thirteenth, Ragoub was

thinking. "Never in a million years. This would never be tolerated."

"It will be good to see home again."

Ragoub nodded, then lowered his voice. "You must tell no one of your upcoming flight. Not even Rawan."

Yusef shrugged. "Why would I tell her? I'll leave in the morning and return that night. I won't be missed."

"What if the date comes up during a conversation?" Ragoub asked. "Suppose someone wants you to do a favor on the thirteenth, for example?"

"Then I will tell them I have an examination at school."

"Good." Ragoub embraced Yusef and pecked him on the cheeks three times. "*Aslam alaikum.*"

"*Aslam alaikum.*"

Yusef crossed the street, keeping Ragoub in his peripheral vision. There was something different about Haj Ragoub tonight, he thought. He'd had a certain urgency in his voice, a stiffness in his manner and body language. Maybe it was the upcoming event that was drawing closer and closer. Yes, that would explain it.

Yusef got into his convertible and put the top down, then drove out of the parking lot and down Sunset Boulevard. In his rearview mirror he saw a car pull away from the curb and move into the lane behind him. Yusef sped up, then slowed down, then sped up again. The car behind him remained four car lengths back. Yusef turned onto Doheny and the car stayed with him. He made a sudden left turn onto a smaller street. The car behind followed, still four car lengths back.

"Goddamn police!" Yusef cursed, and headed back to Sunset Boulevard for his Wednesday-night rendezvous at a nearby motel.

34

Jake went through the metal detector at FBI headquarters and set off the alarm. He placed his shield in a plastic tray and passed through again. The alarm stayed silent. Joanna also set off the detector. She had a large ring of keys in her purse.

They were escorted into a spacious conference room that had a large television screen on its far wall. William Kitt was standing next to another agent who was busily turning knobs on the console. A third agent, with his back to everyone, was pouring coffee at a small wet bar.

"Good morning, Lieutenant Sinclair," Kitt greeted him. "Thanks for being on time."

"No problem."

Kitt looked over to Joanna. "And you must be the famous Dr. Blalock."

"I am," Joanna said, feeling herself blush.

"The Bureau is indebted to you."

"I was glad to help."

Kitt came back to Jake. "I have a beef with you, Lieutenant. I thought we had an agreement. You were to stop your tails on both Ragoub and Malik, and we were to make full disclosure."

"I've kept my end of the bargain," Jake said.

Kitt shook his head. "No, you haven't."

"The hell I haven't," Jake insisted.

"The tail is still there."

"Says who?"

"Says me," the agent at the coffeemaker said, and turned to face them. It was Yusef Malik.

Jake did a double take, not believing his eyes. He moved in for a closer look. "Well, I'll be a son of a bitch."

"Lieutenant Sinclair, meet Special Agent Joseph Malik," Kitt introduced them.

"I'll be a son of a bitch," Jake said again as he gathered himself. "I didn't have the first clue."

"Nor did anyone else," Kitt told him. "We kept everybody in the dark. That way we could be sure there wouldn't be a leak. As a matter of fact, until this moment only five people on the face of the earth knew Joseph was a plant: Joseph and his wife, myself, and the directors of the FBI and the CIA."

"You sure as hell had me fooled," Jake said to Malik. "Nobody would have picked you out as a plant, never in a million years. You fit the profile of a radical to a T."

"That was the idea." Malik poured cream into his coffee and slowly stirred it. "Let's get back to the tail. It wasn't you, huh?"

"Not me."

"What about your partner?" Malik asked.

"No way," Jake replied promptly. "He's too smart for that. And besides, he's out with bronchitis."

Malik considered the matter at length, then said, "It must have been one of Ragoub's men."

"Is he on to you?" Kitt asked quickly.

Malik thought again before saying, "I don't think so.

Otherwise he wouldn't have given me all the instructions for the important flight tomorrow morning."

"We were told the big event was to take place on the fifteenth," Joanna interjected. "You know, the *naqba* thing."

"Tomorrow is the final practice run prior to the big event."

Malik described in detail the instructions he'd received from Ragoub, with particular attention to the laptop computers and their red tags. "And when Ragoub learned that I didn't have the computer next to me last night, he went berserk. I've never seen him get that upset."

"I take it you've checked out that computer?" Joanna inquired.

"A thousand different ways," Malik said. "It's just a simple laptop computer. There's nothing unusual about it."

"They wouldn't use a computer only as a source of recognition," Joanna mused. "It's got some other function."

"We think so, too," Malik agreed. "Perhaps the computer can send a signal that will activate the smallpox device. That wouldn't require anything special."

Kitt stared out the window, wondering again if Joseph Malik had made a mistake. "I'm still worried about Ragoub putting a tail on you. Something must have made him suspicious."

"Not necessarily," Malik said. "With the big event so close, he may have put tails on all of his associates to make sure no one goes astray. Haj Ragoub is a very careful man."

"Maybe you're right," Kitt said with uncertainty. "And maybe not. You'll have to be doubly cautious from here on."

"That's my plan."

Kitt was still bothered by the tail on Joseph Malik. Something must have gone wrong. "Are you sure you weren't followed here today?"

"Positive," Malik assured him. "I spent the night at

Rawan's apartment. When I left this morning I took her car, which was parked in a lot behind the building. The driveway opens onto a narrow one-way street. There was no one following me."

Jake suggested, "If they've got a tail on you, they may have a transmitter in your car and in Rawan's."

"Could be," Malik said, unconcerned. "That's why I parked the car at a hotel in Beverly Hills and took a cab here."

"Maybe Rawan is a plant for them," Jake added. "Maybe she alerted them that you were taking her car."

Malik smiled warmly. "Rawan is my wife, Lieutenant. And she hates terrorists every bit as much as you do."

"Maybe that hooker you see every Wednesday night talks with Ragoub," Jake wondered aloud.

"That hooker is really an undercover FBI agent," Malik told him. "She acts as a courier between me and the director."

Jake shook his head slowly, thinking back to Buck's admonition: *Welcome to the world of deceit, Jake, where nothing is ever what it appears to be.* "Is there anything else I need to know?"

Kitt picked up a folder from the conference table and opened it. "I think you'll be interested to learn that our terrorist worked on ten planes during his stay at Boeing. Four have not been put into service yet. The remaining six will be grounded effective noon today and inspected with a fine-tooth comb. They will be replaced by six other planes, which will have the same serial numbers and be the same model as the original six. The terrorists who board the planes will have no idea that there's been a switch."

Jake asked, "How many agents will you have on each plane?"

"Four," Kitt replied. "And four more at each gate."

"What about Ragoub?"

"He'll be in our sights."

Jake smiled crookedly, hoping that Ragoub and the other terrorists would try to make a run for it and get their heads blown off in the process. It would save the American taxpayers a bunch of money.

"Sir," the agent at the console called over, "your call is ready."

Kitt pointed to the chairs around the conference table. "Everyone, please have a seat. We're about to talk with Dr. Wolinsky from the CDC."

The lights dimmed as a picture came onto the giant television screen. Joanna noticed that Wolinsky was no longer at the medical facility in the Mojave. He was in a telecommunications center somewhere.

"Good morning, Dr. Blalock," Wolinsky greeted her cordially. "It's good to see you in the outside world."

"It's good to be here," Joanna told him.

"And the gentleman next to you is Lieutenant Sinclair?"

"It is," Jake answered.

"You're both no doubt wondering why we've asked you here this morning," Wolinsky said. "The answer is simple. It's because you two are the only people in the world—except for a select group of federal officials—who know about the smallpox outbreak. And we want it to stay that way."

"It's going to be impossible to keep this under wraps much longer," Joanna warned. "Too many people are involved now."

"Not as many as you think," Wolinsky continued. "Let me give you some medical follow-ups, and I think you'll see what I mean. First, I should tell you that the smallpox outbreak is currently under control, and we're in the process of eradicating it altogether. Unfortunately, we've had a number of deaths. In addition to those who died in the Viral Research Center, three more have expired at the Mojave facility. These include the retired doctor, his housekeeper, Maria, and the delivery boy. Mr. Garcia, who gave the housekeeper a ride to Los Angeles, came down with a mild form of the disease. He was protected in large measure by the vaccination and immune globulin he received. We found the bicycle Maria Rodriguez used and tested it for the smallpox virus. Those tests were negative. We also located the parking lot attendant. We've treated him and those around him, and all are now quarantined and under observation. Since there have been no further cases of smallpox reported, I think it's fair to say this outbreak is over."

"Thank God," Joanna said softly.

"So the number of smallpox cases and their primary contacts have been limited to twenty," Wolinsky concluded. "Those who died of the disease took the secret to their graves. The contacts believe they were either exposed to some strange virus or to the meningococcus organism. Thus, the number of people who actually know about the smallpox outbreak is small—so far."

Wolinsky glanced down at a legal pad and made a check mark. "Now, I understand that the terrorists will be apprehended shortly and the planes they planned to use will be grounded indefinitely. That should prevent any further outbreaks in the immediate future. So much for the good news. Let's now get to the bad."

Everyone in the conference room sat up abruptly, eyes glued to the screen, ears pricked.

"Allow me to stress again, word of this smallpox outbreak must not spread to the outside world. You'll understand why in a moment."

The image on the screen became blurred, then disappeared entirely and was replaced by zigzag lines.

"There's no way they can keep this thing quiet much longer," Joanna thought aloud.

"Oh, I think we can," Wolinsky said as his image reappeared on the screen.

"What about Mack's letter to his wife?" Joanna argued. "Surely he mentioned the disease."

"We read the letter before we gave it to her," Wolinsky said unabashedly. "He mentioned a terrible virus but not smallpox by name."

Joanna glared at Wolinsky. "You had no right to read that letter."

"I know," Wolinsky admitted. "But we're not dealing with rights here. We're dealing with national security."

"You're going to have to explain that to me."

"I will shortly. But first, allow me to make a few requests of you, Dr. Blalock." Wolinsky cleared his throat and briefly studied the notes on his legal pad again. "You do plan to attend Mack's funeral on Sunday, do you not?"

"Of course."

"Almost certainly his wife and many of Mack's colleagues at the funeral will ask you about his illness. They will want specifics."

Joanna nodded slowly. Everyone would be curious about what went on at the Viral Research Center. And they would demand clinical details.

"Please make no mention of smallpox. Blame the disease on the Marburg or Ebola virus." Wolinsky sighed deeply, then added, "That will also explain the hermetically sealed coffin."

Joanna asked, "Will the public ever learn of this outbreak?"

"Perhaps sometime in the future," Wolinsky said carefully. "Let me tell you why it's so important to keep this under wraps for now."

Once again everyone at the conference table leaned forward.

"What I say to you stays with you," Wolinsky advised sternly. "One loose word and all could be lost. One person not thinking and the outbreak becomes common knowledge. Let me give you an example. Yesterday Mr. Kitt sent one of his agents to Dr. Blalock's laboratory to speak with her associate, Dr. McKay. She wasn't there, but the agent noticed some notes scribbled in chalk on the blackboard. One of the words was *pox.*"

Joanna cringed and slumped down in her chair.

"Hopefully no one saw the word and, if they did, they weren't smart enough to put it together with what occurred in the Viral Research Center," Wolinsky went on. "Dr. Blalock, please instruct your associate not to use or mention the word *pox* again."

"I will," Joanna said at once. "Did your agent erase the word?"

"He did."

"Good."

"Let's return to the bad news."

Wolinsky briefly glanced into a thin folder, then came back to the group. "The CIA has reviewed the photographs taken by our spy satellites as they passed over the pharmaceutical plant in the Sudan. Two scientists with Caucasian features were photographed entering the facility. The CIA consultant who once worked for Vector immediately identified the two men. They were Russian scientists who worked for Vector in the early nineteen nineties. Both were assigned to the viral biowarfare section. Their primary job was to weaponize the smallpox virus."

"Oh, Jesus!" Joanna groaned.

"It gets worse," Wolinsky said darkly. "Both of the Russian scientists were working on genetically engineering the smallpox virus. One of the scientists was attempting to insert new genes into the virus to make it hemorrhagic and more virulent. As we now can see, he has succeeded."

Joanna asked quickly, "Are you certain the terrorists are using a genetically altered strain of the smallpox virus?"

Wolinsky nodded. "That's why all of our cases had blackpox. And that's why the DNA sequence of our virus was different from the other strains. It had a new gene inserted."

"My God," Joanna moaned. "This is like a horror show."

"It gets even worse," Wolinsky said, his jaw tightening noticeably. "The second scientist was working on developing a strain of smallpox virus that would be resistant to existing vaccines. In essence, the new virus would have surface proteins or antigens that the human immune system could not recognize or defend against."

Joanna gulped. "Don't tell me they've done that, too."

"We don't know," Wolinsky said. "But they are obviously very advanced in the technology of genetically manipulating the smallpox virus. Could you imagine anything more terrifying than a highly virulent form of smallpox that would resist every known vaccine?"

"It would be the end of the world," Joanna predicted gloomily.

A hush fell over the room as everyone tried to think about the unthinkable. They could be facing a nightmare virus that killed and killed and killed, until there was no one left to kill.

"Why not just bomb the bastards?" Jake blurted out.

"That was my suggestion, too," Wolinsky said. "After all, we know where the pharmaceutical plant is located in the Sudan. And there's some pretty fair evidence that points to that plant as being the source of the smallpox virus."

"So what's the holdup?" Jake demanded.

"The CIA says there is no solid evidence to show that the

Sudanese are actually producing the smallpox virus," Wolinsky explained. "We have two former scientists from Vector working at that plant, and there was an unconfirmed outbreak of smallpox in a village near that plant. The evidence is suggestive, but certainly not conclusive."

"But there were antibodies to the smallpox virus in the Sudanese defector's blood," Joanna argued. "So he must have been exposed to the virus."

Wolinsky shrugged. "Ten percent of the Iraqi prisoners captured during the Gulf War had antibodies to smallpox in their blood. They had been vaccinated, and that was how they got their antibodies. So the presence of antibodies to the virus doesn't prove that you've been working with the virus."

Jake waved a hand disgustedly and cursed under his breath. "I didn't know the CIA was so gun-shy."

"Usually they're not, but with the Sudanese they have to be very careful," Wolinsky told him. "You may remember that during the Clinton administration we bombed a plant in the Sudan that we thought was producing chemical weapons. We were wrong. The CIA later learned that the plant was manufacturing veterinary medicines. It turned into a public-relations disaster. It's one they don't wish to repeat, particularly now with our war on terrorism. The last thing they want to do is to alienate our Arab allies, which we'd do if we bombed the Sudan and we were wrong again."

"So America just sits and waits for it to happen, eh?" Jake asked gruffly.

"What we do, Lieutenant, is say nothing about the smallpox outbreak until the CIA figures out a way to deal with the source of the virus. I cannot stress enough how important it is for all of us to keep our lips sealed on the matter."

Wolinsky glanced down at his folder once more and held up three fingers. "There are three reasons why word of this must not be leaked. First, it would obviously panic the American public. Second, a panicked population would demand to be vaccinated, and we'd have to tell them that the vaccine might be worthless because the enemy is developing a vaccine-resistant smallpox virus—and this would cause more panic. Third, and most important, if word leaks out about the smallpox virus and its source, the terrorist group would quickly move their operation out of the Sudan to someplace we'd never find."

Joanna strummed her fingers nervously on the armrest of her chair. "Isn't there some way to deal with the Sudanese government?"

"Our best information says that the Sudanese government isn't directly involved," Wolinsky replied. "That industrial complex is privately owned by a corporation that is registered in Panama. All of its funding comes from the same source that funds most of the radical Islamic groups."

"Which is?" Joanna asked.

"The poppy fields of Afghanistan and Pakistan," Wolinsky answered. "Those fields supply the world with most of its heroin."

Jake squirmed in his seat, knowing that heroin traffic worldwide was worth billions and billions of dollars. And most of that money went right into the terrorists' pockets. *My God!* They had more money than they knew what to do with.

Joanna slowly shook her head. "I can't believe the Sudanese government would want a smallpox virus–producing plant in their country."

"They probably don't, but some high-ranking official— who has been bought off—no doubt does," Wolinsky said. "So if we go to the Sudanese government, the terrorists will learn about it in short order, and they and their scientists will vanish into thin air."

"You've got to destroy that plant now," Joanna urged. "Otherwise you're just delaying the inevitable, no matter how many terrorists you catch in America."

"The pres—" Wolinsky caught himself in midsentence and started again. "The CIA is fully aware of that."

Yeah, Jake thought sourly, *just like the CIA was aware of the names of two of the 9/11 hijackers but didn't provide the information to the INS or FBI so the terrorists could be tracked in America.*

Wolinsky got to his feet and nodded to the group. "I'd like to thank all of you for meeting with me today. I'll of course keep you informed of any progress we make."

Wolinsky's image on the screen faded, and then disappeared altogether.

As Joanna reached for her coat and purse, Jake turned to William Kitt. "I'm sorry I got so pissed at you the other night when I learned you had been holding back information."

"You had every right to be angry," Kitt said graciously. "But we had to play this one very close to the vest. One slipup and the whole operation could have gone up in smoke. And Joe Malik would have been a dead man."

At the door, Jake stopped in front of Joseph Malik. "Out of curiosity, how did you pick up our tail?"

"I didn't," Malik told him. "Rawan did. Outside the restaurant she noticed your car but didn't pay a lot of attention to it, except for the fact that your partner was coughing. The next day your partner was at Rawan's apartment building asking the manager questions, and coughing. Rawan saw him and the cough and made the connection."

"She ought to work for the FBI."

Malik smiled. "She does."

Jake and Joanna walked out into a bright, cool day. The air was crystal-clear and fresh, with a strong breeze coming in from the ocean. Overhead Jake watched a moving cloud that seemed to change shape as it passed by.

"In the world of deceit, nothing is ever what it appears to be," he said, more to himself than to Joanna.

"Where did you get that from?" Joanna asked.

"From a guy who spends a lot of time in the world of deceit."

"You mean someone like Kitt?"

"Hell, they're all the same," Jake grumbled. "They tell you the truth half the time. You figure out which half."

Joanna grinned briefly. "Yeah, I guess. But I really think Marshall Wolinsky is a straight shooter."

Jake took her arm as they crossed the street behind the Federal Building. "Where did that guy get so much power? It's like he's telling the FBI and CIA what to do and when to do it."

"That's exactly what he's doing," Joanna said. "The FBI and CIA know nothing about smallpox, and Wolinsky knows everything. I think it's fair to say he knows more about smallpox than anybody else in America. He's their one and only expert. So the FBI and CIA won't make a move until they check with him first."

Jake pursed his lips, not at all certain that that was the case. "I'll bet there are some things they don't ask his permission for. Like, for example, the FBI's plan to catch the terrorists on those planes."

"Oh, they asked Wolinsky plenty about that," Joanna countered. "They'd want to know such things as, Is it possible that the terrorists could be carrying tiny vials of the smallpox virus and spread it that way? Is it possible that lethal doses of the virus could somehow be hidden in those laptop computers? And on and on and on. I can assure you they won't make a move without Wolinsky's advice and consent."

"The incredible power that guy must have," Jake thought aloud. "He could probably get the president on the phone."

"Anytime, day or night."

"I'll bet he didn't expect to be doing this when he was in medical school."

"None of us did, Jake," Joanna said quietly. "None of us."

At Joanna's car, Jake pecked her on the cheek. "I'll try to reach you later."

"I'm going to be on the move," Joanna told him. "I've got a million things to do before my trip to Atlanta tomorrow."

Jake snapped his fingers. "I forgot about that. Do you need a ride?"

"No, I'm fine," Joanna replied. "I'll only be gone a day, so I'll take my car and park it at the airport."

"If you change your mind, let me know."

Joanna kissed his chin. "I will."

Jake stepped away, then turned back to Joanna. "You know, there's still one question we haven't answered here."

"What's that?"

"What were those Arab terrorists doing in the Mojave Desert?"

Joanna thought for a moment, then shrugged. "Do you think it matters now?"

"I don't know," Jake said as he turned to leave. "But every time I've left a big question in a case unanswered, it always comes back to haunt me."

35

Traffic was snarled on the freeway to Mojave. A big rig had jackknifed and overturned, leaving only one lane open. As Jake drove past the wreckage, he glanced at the clock on his dashboard and cursed under his breath. It was 7:10 A.M. And probably no one would be in the office at Anderson Metal.

Jake reached for a cigarette and lit it, and that set off a paroxysm of coughing. He quickly flipped the cigarette out the window, wondering if he had smoked too much or had caught the bronchitis bug from Farelli. Either way, he felt like hell and wanted to finish things up. Just one more task to do: Check the scrap metal company where Hassan had worked and see if it might explain why a bunch of Arabs were congregating in the Mojave Desert. It was a loose end that needed to be tied up.

Jake drove past the burned-down ruins of the Mojave Motel. That reminded him of the terrorist who had brought smallpox to the Viral Research Center and killed everybody there except for Joanna. Christ; she had been so lucky. He tried to envision being trapped in a dungeonlike facility with a deadly virus for twelve days. It would have driven him

crazy. No way he could have handled that. But Joanna did
and never bitched once.

A picture of Joanna flashed into his mind. He had tried to
reach her earlier, but she was out probably on her way to the
airport for her trip to Atlanta, where she would give a talk in
front of a thousand very bright forensic scientists. Jake had
asked her if she would be intimidated by such a large,
knowledgeable audience. Joanna had shrugged and told him
no. After all, she knew more about lethal toxins than they
did.

Jake reached for his cell phone and punched the redial
button. It connected him with the front office at Anderson
Metal, which he had called thirty minutes earlier. Again an
answering machine clicked on and told the caller to leave a
name, number, and brief message. Jake switched his cell
phone off. He had left the information twice already and
hadn't received a return call.

Jake turned off the main highway onto a narrow paved
road and followed the signs leading to the Anderson Metal
Company. The facility had a high chain-link fence with
barbed wire across the top. In the foggy morning light Jake
couldn't see any guards or patrolling vehicles. Up above, the
sun was beginning to show itself in the gray, misty sky.

Jake came to the front gate and got out of his car. The
gate was locked, but there was a buzzer to ring in case of
emergency. Jake pressed the buzzer twice and waited.

In the distance he heard a vehicle start up and then saw
a pair of headlights coming toward him. It was a Jeep with
no top and no doors. The driver was a balding, barrel-
chested man who was wearing blue jeans and a short-
sleeved shirt.

He came over to the fence and studied Jake briefly.
"What do you want?"

"You the manager?"

The man nodded. "The manager, the night guard, and every goddamn thing else. Now what do you want?"

Jake flashed his shield. "I need some information on Mr. Hassan, who used to work here."

"The dumb little prick," the manager said disgustedly. "We had to fire him because he was taking the motorized lifts for joyrides while he was on duty. Can you think of anything dumber to do?"

"Not really," Jake said. "What was his job here?"

"He was a guard," the manager replied. "An eight-dollar-an-hour guard."

"I'd like to look at his work file."

The manager hesitated, then reached for his keys. "Shit," he grumbled loudly, opening the gate. "I hope this ain't going to take long."

"Just a quick look."

Jake got back in his car and drove into the facility, then stopped and waited for the manager to relock the gate.

So the man had been a guard, Jake was thinking. But why? The job paid next to nothing and offered him no cover. There weren't any other Arabs in Mojave. He'd stick out like a sore thumb. But there was a reason he had been here. Terrorists did things for reasons.

"Follow me and go slow," the manager yelled out. "We've got some bad potholes."

They drove down a bumpy, single-lane road that was covered in places with sand and drifting sagebrush. A cloud passed in front of the sun, turning the misty morning even darker. Now Jake could see nothing except the red taillights of the Jeep in front of him. They slowed down even more as the road became rougher. Then they went around a gentle curve and the road smoothed out. Up ahead, Jake saw a large lighted maintenance shed with a small office next to it.

They stopped in front of the shed. Jake got out and stretched his neck and back. He took a deep breath of fresh air just as the clouds moved away from the sun. He glanced out at the desert floor, which was now colored a mixture of tans and browns. Then he saw the planes.

Rows and rows of commercial jets were parked in the desert like perched birds.

"What the hell are those?" Jake asked breathlessly, pointing.

"Airplanes," the manager said, looking at Jake as if he were a simpleton. "Airplanes that nobody wants."

"What do you do with them?" Jake asked quickly.

"Turn 'em into scrap."

"Are all of them scrapped?"

"For the most part," the manager said. "But some of them are just stored here until the airlines want to put them back into service. You see, the dry desert air keeps them from rust—"

"How many planes were stored here over the past month?" Jake cut in brusquely.

The manager shrugged. "I don't know. Maybe six or eight. Something like that."

"When was the last one flown out?"

"A couple of weeks ago. Why?"

Jake ignored the question. *The sons of bitches,* he was thinking. *The no-good sons of bitches.* They didn't plant the smallpox virus on the planes being made by Boeing in Seattle. They planted the virus on the planes that were parked out on the desert. That way they could take their time out here with little or no chance of getting caught.

Ahmed Hassan hadn't taken the motorized lifts out for joyrides. He was taking his buddy Khalil Mahmoud out to the planes, where the smallpox devices could be planted.

Jake quickly turned to the manager. "I need a list of all commercial jets that were stored here last month."

"That's in the office."

Jake reached for his cell phone.

36

Joanna arrived at gate fifty-four in the TransContinental terminal just after the first call for boarding. The gate area was crowded with business travelers and college students and parents with screaming kids. Joanna disliked the waiting areas in airports, where people stood around and complained, and rudely blocked the way of passengers whose row numbers had already been called. That was why she always tried to fly first-class. But the first-class section on this flight had been sold out, so she had to settle for business class. If she was lucky, the seat next to her would be empty and she could stretch out and rehearse her upcoming talk without being interrupted.

Joanna felt in her purse for the box of slides she would use in her talk. She was still unhappy with the security woman who had opened the box and examined each slide, leaving thumbprints on most of them. And the same woman had gone over Joanna with a handheld metal detector—for no reason. *Maybe she thought I fit the profile of a terrorist,* Joanna said. *Yeah, right. A forty-two-year-old female physician with fair skin and sandy blond hair.* Joanna shook her head. Security at America's airports was still a joke.

She glanced over at gate fifty-four and saw the last of the

first-class passengers walking through it. Joanna thought about hurrying to the newsstand and buying a magazine but decided not to. She'd use the time to review her slides and rehearse her talk. And if there was time left over, she'd watch the movie.

The PA system came on with a loud burst of static. ". . . Now boarding medallion passengers. Medallion passengers only, please."

Joanna picked up her carry-on luggage and headed for the boarding gate.

At a nearby newsstand Joseph Malik was thumbing through the latest issue of *Newsweek*. He held his laptop computer so that the two red tags on its handle were clearly visible. The terrorist by the newspaper rack was holding his computer in a similar way. The two men made eye contact, then looked away quickly.

Malik replaced the magazine and reached for another, keeping the terrorist in his peripheral vision. The terrorist was a tall, thin man, dark-complected, with a wisp of a mustache. If the man was nervous, he didn't show it.

A female voice announced over the PA system, "TransContinental flight fifty-four to Atlanta is now boarding rows forty-eight through forty. Rows forty-eight through forty only, please."

Malik flipped through the pages of *People* magazine, still watching the terrorist out of the corner of his eye. The man had a long neck with a prominent Adam's apple. That was where Malik would go if trouble started. A quick chop to the larynx and there would be one less terrorist on the face of the Earth.

Malik's cell phone rang. It was Haj Ragoub.

"Listen carefully and say nothing," Ragoub instructed. "This is *naqba*, not a rehearsal. This is the day of the big

event. You will board the plane shortly and remain in your
seat throughout the flight. Two and a half hours from now,
at twelve noon, you will join together the two red tags on
your computer's handle. You will see how well they fit into
tiny grooves. After they are joined together, you will not be
able to separate them. Once this is done, turn on the computer and type in the word *naqba*, which will activate a special device we have planted on the aircraft. Make no phone
calls from the plane. If you understand, say *naqba*."

"*Naqba.*"

"Good. When you leave the newsstand, drop your cell
phone on the floor. Someone will pick it up shortly."

The phone line went dead.

Someone would pick up the dropped cell phone, Malik
kept thinking, which meant he was being watched in the terminal—and probably aboard the plane, too. Of course he'd
be watched on the plane. The other terrorist would see his
every move. *If I try to use the plane phone, it will be a sure
tip-off and they'll know exactly what I'm doing. And they'll
know I'm a plant. They've got me boxed in.*

Malik glanced around the crowded terminal and tried to
pick out other terrorists who could fit the FBI's profile. But
he saw none. He wondered if the hidden terrorist were
armed, with orders to kill if Malik failed to follow orders.
That was almost a certainty, Malik decided. Haj Ragoub was
a very careful man. He left nothing to chance.

The terrorist's cell phone chirped loudly and he quickly
answered it.

Malik knew from the timing of the second call that it, too,
was from Ragoub. He watched the terrorist's face light up.
The bastard was happy to be releasing the smallpox virus
and infecting God knew how many thousands. Malik
thought about killing the terrorist here and now. But then he

remembered the hidden terrorist who would be picking up his discarded cell phone.

Malik again rapidly scanned the gate area, looking for anyone who seemed suspicious. But all he saw was nondescript people streaming by.

The terrorist let his cell phone drop from his hand, then gazed over at Malik and waited until he, too, dropped his phone to the floor.

A female voice came over the PA system. "We are now boarding rows thirty-nine through thirty. Rows thirty-nine through thirty only."

Malik and the terrorist headed for the door to gate fifty-four, each watching the other's every move.

37

"Do the airlines understand the gravity of the situation?" Jake asked, pacing the floor at FBI headquarters.

"And some," Kitt told him.

Jake glanced up at the wall clock: 9:50. Two of the six planes had already been located and ordered grounded. The airlines were still trying to locate the remaining four. "We should have guessed that the devices weren't going to be installed at the Boeing plant in Seattle."

Kitt said, "I don't see how. Unless we had a crystal ball."

"We just didn't use our brains," Jake went on. "Of the ten planes that Khalil Mahmoud worked on at Boeing, five were delivered to foreign carriers. The terrorists wanted those devices on American carriers, not on some plane that might go to a Muslim country."

"But five of those planes were American," Kitt argued.

"And then there's the timing," Jake continued. "There was no way of telling when those Seattle planes would all be in the air at the same time. Months and months passed between finishing work on one and starting work on another."

Kitt nodded slowly. "They were aiming for *naqba*. All those planes had to be up in the air on May fifteenth."

"You got it," Jake said. "That's what made the Mojave facility so perfect. All those jumbo jets were American, and the terrorists had their man watching them every day. They knew the moment those planes were ordered back into service."

"And that's when they told Khalil Mahmoud to make his move from Seattle to the Mojave."

"Exactly."

"Clever bastards," Kitt said. "They had the perfect setup and nobody even knew they were there."

The door to the conference room flew open and an agent hurried in, holding a freshly faxed sheet.

Kitt spun around and asked quickly, "Where are those other planes?"

The agent hesitated. "We . . . we're still working on that, sir."

"Then what's that in your hand?"

"A report from Interpol in Paris," the agent replied, giving the sheet to Kitt. "At the French aviation factory where Khalil Mahmoud last worked, his primary job was installing the ventilation systems on commercial jets."

Jake's jaw dropped as the pieces suddenly fell into place. "Son of a bitch! Son of a bitch!" he blurted out. "That's where they planted the smallpox device."

Kitt nodded grimly. "It's the ideal place. You put a little canister in the ventilation system and let it spray out its contents. Since the air on jumbo jets is continually recirculated, everybody on board would inhale an incredibly large dose of the virus."

"And each of those six planes will be carrying at least two hundred and fifty people," Jake calculated darkly. "Which means fifteen hundred innocent people will become infected and spread smallpox to every corner of America. It's a catastrophe about to happen."

Kitt nervously rubbed the back of his neck. "We keep assuming they're going to do it on the fifteenth. But we don't know that for sure."

"They could do it anytime," Jake opined. "Anytime they wanted."

Kitt hurriedly turned to the agent. "I want the locations of those goddamn planes—now!"

38

Joanna stood in the aisle next to her seat and stretched her legs. They had been flying for only an hour, but it seemed like a lot longer. She checked her wristwatch again. It was 10:30 exactly. The flight attendants were already bringing out the drink carts, which meant the awful airline food was not far behind. Joanna decided that now was the time to walk the length of the plane and exercise her calf muscles. She firmly believed that sitting stationary on a plane could lead to venous thrombosis in the lower extremities, and this could result in pulmonary embolism. A walk every hour would prevent that.

Joanna waited for a portly woman to squeeze her way past, then followed her down the aisle through the business section. The tourist section was half-empty, with some of the passengers lying across three seats and dozing peacefully. There were still plenty of vacant seats, and Joanna thought about moving to the rear and grabbing a quick nap. But she decided against it. She wanted to rehearse her talk and go over the slides at least one more time.

The obese lady stopped to chat with a friend sitting in an aisle seat. Joanna eased her way through, saying, "Excuse me." Someone's suitcase was protruding into the aisle, so

Joanna paused and moved it back under the seat with her foot. As she looked up, she found herself staring directly into Joseph Malik's eyes. He shook his head briefly, then went back to the magazine on his lap.

Joanna walked by, straining to keep her gaze straight ahead. Her thoughts flashed back to their meeting at FBI headquarters. She remembered that Joseph Malik had told them he'd be making one more practice run and that there would be another terrorist aboard as well. Malik's quick shake of his head was probably a signal to tell her to stay away. Or did it mean something else? He could have been saying no to a lot of things.

At the rear of the plane a line had formed for the rest rooms. Joanna stopped and waited with the others, then gradually turned and glanced around the back cabin. Most of the passengers were Caucasian, with only a few Asian and African Americans near the front. Other than Joseph Malik, there was only one person with Middle Eastern features. He was sitting in an aisle seat across the way from Malik. He had a computer on his lap.

Malik glanced back and caught Joanna's eye, then rapidly looked away. But he kept his arm dangling down over the armrest. He moved his hand back and forth, as if signaling her to come back. Then he extended his wrist, flattening his palm, and performed a pushing up-and-down motion. It took Joanna several seconds to figure it out. It was a stop signal. He was telling her to come back and stop. Why? she wondered. Why take even the smallest risk of being discovered? It had to be something very important. But how could she get close to Malik without the terrorist seeing and becoming suspicious?

Again Joanna eyed the terrorist sitting on the opposite aisle. The row of seats between Malik and the terrorist was totally vacant. The terrorist had a clear view of the FBI agent. There was no way to get to Malik without being noticed.

How do I do this? There's got to be a way to get to him. But how? I can't just sit down next to him and start talking, although he's handsome as hell. And I can't send a message via the flight attendant. The terrorist would pick that up in a second.

One of the rest-room doors opened and an elderly lady came out, leaning heavily on her cane. Everybody pressed back and made room for her. She nodded appreciatively, then limped down the aisle back to her seat. Joanna watched the woman and smiled to herself. She had a way to get to Joseph Malik.

Joanna saw a pretty blond flight attendant across the way and waved her over. As the flight attendant approached, Joanna put a grimace on her face.

"Is something wrong, ma'am?" the flight attendant asked.

Joanna nodded with effort. "I've got bursitis in my hip and I'm not going to be able to get back to my seat in business class. Would it be possible for me to lie down on some of the empty seats back here?"

"That's no problem at all," the flight attendant said, concerned. "Would you like me to help you to a seat?"

"That's very sweet of you."

Joanna took the flight attendant's arm and leaned on it as she limped along. She guided the flight attendant to the empty row of seats that was adjacent to Joseph Malik.

"Here we are," the flight attendant said.

"Thank you." Joanna sat down carefully and began lifting up the nearby armrests. "Could you get me a small pillow to put under my hip? It really helps."

"I'll have one for you in a second."

Joanna leaned back and sighed deeply. She rubbed her

right hip for the benefit of the terrorist, who was less than a dozen feet away. She stared straight ahead at an overhanging television screen, but she could feel the terrorist's eyes on her.

"Here you are," the flight attendant said, and handed her two small pillows.

"Thanks again."

"You're welcome."

Joanna lay on her side in the seats, with a small pillow atop her right hip. Her head was toward Joseph Malik. She snuggled up like someone about to go to sleep, then briefly opened her eyes. The terrorist was still staring at her. She snuggled up again and appeared to doze off.

Joanna stayed perfectly still for the next few minutes and made no effort to contact Malik. Then she slowly reached into the pocket of her blazer for a pen. Again she waited, counting slowly to a hundred. With feigned annoyance, she repositioned the pillow atop her hip so the terrorist could no longer see her head. With her head now resting on her left arm, Joanna began making a scribbling motion with the pen in her left hand. She repeated the motion a half dozen times.

The PA system came on with a burst of static. "In just a few minutes we'll be showing our in-flight movie, which is entitled *Brainwaves*. The cost of a headset is . . . "

Joanna saw her chance. She pushed herself up and searched her blazer, as if looking for a wallet or small purse. She quickly glanced around the seat, like someone looking for a lost item. Then she stood, making sure her back blocked the terrorist's view of Joseph Malik. Stepping out into the aisle, she felt Malik's hand touch her. The note Malik passed to her was so small it fit under her thumb. Limping noticeably, Joanna made her way back to the business section. She waited a full minute before glancing over her shoulder to make sure the terrorist hadn't followed her. Carefully she unfolded the tiny message. It read:

NAQBA TODAY
CALL KITT

Joanna's pulse started racing. *They're releasing the smallpox virus today! And on this plane! Oh, my God!* Joanna reached for the plane phone in front of her.

39

Jake's cell phone chirped loudly. It was Joanna.

"Hey," Jake said warmly. "Where are you?"

"Halfway across America," Joanna replied hurriedly.

"Well, I've got some interest—"

"You've got to contact the FBI right now," Joanna cut him off. "The bastards are going to do it *today*."

"What?"

"Get the FBI," she demanded.

"I'm at their headquarters now."

"Can you put this call on a speaker?"

Jake snapped his fingers at Kitt. "It's Joanna Blalock. She says *naqba* is going to happen today."

Kitt's face lost color. "How does she know that?"

"She didn't say, but she's on a plane heading for Atlanta," Jake said quickly. "And she wants her call put on a speaker."

Kitt scribbled down a number and handed it to Jake. "Tell her to call back on this line."

Jake gave Joanna instructions and turned his cell phone off. He looked up at the wall clock. It was eleven o'clock and they still didn't know the locations of four planes that had been stored in the Mojave Desert.

Kitt asked, "Was she *sure* of her information?"

"She sounded sure."

The phone on the conference table rang. Kitt picked it up on the first ring and put the call on a speaker.

"Kitt here," he said, his voice sounding a hundred times calmer than he felt.

"Are we on a speaker?" Joanna asked.

"Yes."

"Then listen carefully," Joanna urged, "because we're in big, big trouble."

"Be specific," Kitt said.

"Don't interrupt," Joanna snapped at him. "Interruptions will cost us time, which we may not have."

In the conference room they heard another female voice come over the speaker. "Would you like to purchase a headset?"

"No, thanks," Joanna told the flight attendant, and waited for her to go by. Then she continued in a hushed voice. "I'm on TransContinental flight fifty-four to Atlanta. Joseph Malik is also on this plane. He was able to pass me a note without anyone seeing it. The note read, 'Naqba today—call Kitt.'"

Dead silence fell over the conference room.

"Did he give you a definite time?" Kitt asked.

"No."

"Or how the device would be activated?"

"No," Joanna said again, then added, "but in all likelihood it's going to be done with those laptop computers."

"But you're only guessing. Right?"

After hesitating, Joanna said, "It's a damn good guess. The other terrorist aboard also has a laptop computer."

"How do you know the other person is a terrorist?"

"Because he's an Arab who's holding on to his laptop computer as if his life depended on it."

Another agent asked, "Are you saying he has definite Middle Eastern features?"

"I'm saying he's an Arab," Joanna bristled. "Save your political correctness for the Kiwanis Club!"

The agent's face reddened.

Kitt moved in closer to the speaker. "Dr. Blalock, can you get back to Joseph Malik?"

"Not without making the terrorist suspicious," Joanna answered.

"Somehow you've got to do it," Kitt implored, hurriedly telling her about the device in the ventilation system. "There are two pieces of information we need desperately. We need to know how the device is activated and whether it's already been activated. The latter question is particularly important because, if the virus has already been released, we'll have to make special arrangements. Do you follow?"

"Yes."

"You must get that information for us."

Joanna sighed wearily, wondering how in the world she could do it. If she went back there now, the terrorist would know something was wrong. "I'll try."

"Be very careful, kiddo," Jake interjected. "They might have another terrorist on board as a backup."

"Yeah, I know."

Kitt thought ahead quickly. "I'd better call Dr. Wolinsky and put him on alert."

"Ask him one question for me," Joanna requested. "Ask him if vaccination protects a person against a massive dose of the smallpox virus."

The phone clicked off.

Kitt looked at Jake quizzically. "Is she talking about some sort of preventive action?"

Jake's throat went dry as he shook his head. "She's talking about herself."

"I don't follow you."

"She's been vaccinated, and she's about to receive a big blast of the smallpox virus."

The door to the conference room opened and an agent stuck his head in. "Sir, we've located another one of the planes. It was scheduled to leave San Francisco at eleven-ten. We've arranged for it to be delayed because of mechanical difficulties."

"What about the locations of the others?" Kitt asked at once.

"Still no luck."

40

Joanna hastily scribbled down the questions Kitt wanted answered and folded the note into a small square. She got to her feet, still not knowing what she was going to do. Getting the message to Malik would be no problem. All she had to do was drop the note from her hand as she passed his seat. Obtaining the answers was another matter. She would be up and walking. The terrorist would remember her and watch her every move. Seeing her a second time would arouse his suspicions for sure. He might even move in closer, so as not to miss anything. She would have to be very, very careful. One false step and the terrorist would probably set off the device—if he hadn't done it already.

Again she wondered if her recent vaccination would protect her against a massive dose of the smallpox virus. Probably not. Too many viruses, she thought grimly, and not enough antibodies. Joanna took a deep breath, gathering herself, then glanced at her watch: 11:20. She headed for the rear cabin, reminding herself to limp.

Joanna walked at a slow pace, looking ahead at the long line waiting outside the rest rooms. A passenger carrying a small child came down the aisle. Joanna moved aside for them. She smiled up at the little girl and, at the same time, caught a glimpse of the terrorist. He was standing by his seat, his eyes glued on her. She limped on, using the backs of the seats as partial supports. As she approached Joseph Malik, she let the folded message slip from her hand. It landed on his lap and stayed there. Malik swiftly covered the note with his forearm.

Joanna reached the line of people waiting for the rest rooms. She stopped and rubbed her hip, resisting the urge to look back. In front of her was a young college student with a book bag slung over his shoulder. He grinned at Joanna and she grinned back.

"Long wait, huh?" Joanna asked.

"It's taking forever," the young man said grimly.

Out of the corner of her eye Joanna saw the terrorist still standing by his seat. His head was moving back and forth between her and Joseph Malik. The terrorist had become doubly suspicious. Something must have tipped him off. She couldn't get anywhere near Malik now. And there might even be another terrorist aboard, watching everything. *Christ, how do I get Malik's answers?*

The line began to advance, and the college student in front of her said, "At last."

An idea came to her. Joanna glanced at the book bag on the student's shoulder and smiled at him. "Want to make twenty bucks?"

The young man studied Joanna's face for a moment. "Doing what?"

"Doing exactly what I tell you," Joanna replied, keeping her voice low. "I want you to go to seat thirty-six B on the aisle and open the compartment above it. Then put your book bag in the compartment and close it. Then tell the man sitting in thirty-six B that you've come for Joanna's note. Whisper it without looking directly at him."

The college student looked at Joanna strangely. "What the hell is this all about?"

"It's about his wife, who is sitting on the other side of the plane," Joanna lied easily. "She's spying on him."

"Ah-huh," the student said knowingly.

Joanna reached into her purse and handed him a twenty-dollar bill. "I don't want her to see the note being passed."

"She won't."

Joanna stared straight ahead, but kept her hearing concentrated. Somewhere nearby a baby started crying, and its mother shushed it back to sleep. Behind her Joanna heard an overhead compartment being opened, then slammed shut. Then a second overhead compartment was opened and shut. Joanna forced herself not to look back. The line started to move.

The college student came back without his book bag and spoke in a quiet voice. "Done."

Joanna continued to look ahead so that the terrorist couldn't tell that a conversation was taking place between her and the student. "Put the note in my hand, then tell me why you had to open two compartments."

The student passed her a folded note and said, "The first compartment was packed full. But don't worry. Nobody saw anything."

Oh, yes, they did, Joanna was thinking. *The terrorist watched you open and close the two overhead compartments near Joseph Malik. The only question was whether he saw you receive the note.* There was one way to find out. The line of people began to move.

Joanna washed her hands in a vacant rest room, then headed for the aisle where the terrorist was seated. A flight attendant pushing a drink cart was blocking the way. Joanna squeezed around the cart and for a moment came face-to-face with the terrorist. She smiled at him briefly and saw confusion come to his face. *Good,* she thought. Now he was really uncertain about what was happening. She continued down the aisle, limping badly.

Entering the business-class section, Joanna noticed a heavyset, dark-complected man sitting by a window. He was well dressed in a dark blue suit and a yellow tie. Joanna studied the man, wondering if he had just moved into the business section or if she had simply overlooked him earlier. Either way, he could be the hidden terrorist. She quickly checked her watch again: 11:36. Once more she considered the possibility that the virus had already been released and that she and the other passengers were inhaling millions of viral particles with each breath.

"Excuse me," said a dark-complected woman wearing a brightly colored dress.

"Of course," Joanna said, and stepped aside.

The woman sat down next to the heavyset man and they began speaking in a clipped British accent so characteristic of people from India. Joanna breathed a sigh of relief, reminding herself not to be so quick with racial profiling.

She hurried to her seat and unfolded the note from Joseph Malik. It read:

> PUT RED TAGS TOGETHER
> TYPE IN NAQBA
> AT NOON

Joanna reached for the phone and punched in the FBI's number.

Kitt answered on the second ring. "Kitt here."

"The big event happens at noon," Joanna told him quietly, rechecking her watch. "Which leaves us exactly twenty-one minutes."

"How is it activated?"

"The red tags on the handle of the computer are placed together," Joanna said quickly. "Then the word *naqba* is typed in."

"Stay in your seat. We'll get back to you."

Kitt switched off the speaker and glanced rapidly around the conference room. He snapped his fingers at Special Agent Alex Monroe, a computer expert. "Is there any way to block the signal from that computer?"

"Not from here," Monroe said.

"What about the red tags?"

Monroe shrugged. "We X-rayed those tags and saw nothing."

"Well, there sure as hell is *something* in those red tags," Kitt pressed on. "What do you think it might be?"

"I'd have to guess."

"Then guess."

"They probably contain some highly miniaturized circuitry that's necessary for the correct signal to be sent."

"Can that circuitry be interrupted?"

"Only by destroying the tags."

Kitt stomped around the conference table, head down, hands behind his back. "We'd better come up with an answer or a lot of people are going to die."

Everyone's eyes went to the wall clock. The big hand moved. It was 11:42 A.M. They all knew there wasn't enough time. The hush of defeat fell across the room. Another minute ticked off the clock.

"Maybe Malik could rush the guy?" a young agent mused.

Jake waved away the idea. "The terrorist would see him coming a block away. Chances are that computer is already on, which means the guy could send the signal in the blink of an eye."

"Maybe we could enlist the help of a flight attendant or somebody on the flight crew," the young agent suggested.

Jake shook his head. "You're dealing with a cold-blooded terrorist who's rehearsed this a hundred times. He could send the signal and slit the flight attendant's throat while he did it."

"Slit her throat with what?"

Jake sneered. "With a knife that any idiot could get past airport security."

The door to the conference room swung open. A special agent rushed in and hurried over to Kitt.

"Sir, we've located all the planes," the agent said, catching his breath. "Four are on the ground and will stay there. Of the two remaining, you already know about TransContinental's flight fifty-four to Atlanta. The final 747 is en route to Miami and is now crossing the Texas-Louisiana border." A half smile came across the agent's face. "We may be a little lucky here, sir."

"How's that?"

"The flight has a sky marshal aboard."

It took Kitt less than twenty seconds to devise a plan. "Get the captain of that plane on the line."

In college Maurice Wolf played tight end for Florida State. He was a big African-American man, well over six feet tall, with broad shoulders and hands the size of hams. Althought a knee injury ended his football career, he remained in excellent shape, keeping his weight at two hundred forty pounds. On his numerous flights he always wore dark suits that were carefully tailored to conceal the weapon he carried.

Wolf strolled down the aisle of National's flight 68 to Miami, smiling to the passengers who smiled back. He had a warm, friendly face that told people he was easy to like. Little kids thought he looked like Shaquille O'Neal.

As he approached row thirty-six, he grinned at the Arab sitting in the aisle seat.

"Good morning," Wolf said cheerfully.

The Arab almost had a chance to reply.

"Now!" Wolf cried out and slammed a huge fist in the man's face, knocking him senseless.

Across the way a flight attendant threw a cup of steaming hot coffee into the other terrorist's face and swept the computer off his lap.

Wolf had the semiconscious Arab handcuffed in an instant. Then he hurdled over a row of seats to reach the second terrorist, who was screaming and trying to rub the pain from his eyes. He too was quickly handcuffed and dragged over to where the other terrorist was sprawled out.

"You did good," Wolf told the flight attendant.

"I'm still shaking," the flight attendant admitted.

"You've got every right to," Wolf said soothingly. "Now why don't you tell the captain to put this plane down in New Orleans so we can unload this garbage?"

41

Joanna sat in the darkened business section, paying scant attention to the movie being shown. She kept checking her watch as her anxiety level rose higher and higher. There were only eight minutes left and she still hadn't heard from Jake or the FBI. And how were they going to reach her, anyway? They couldn't call in on the passenger phones.

The person seated in front of Joanna tilted his seat back as far as it would go and pushed a button on the armrest. Cool air blew in through the ventilation vents above, hitting Joanna's face and ears. She shuddered, envisioning billions of smallpox viruses flooding into the cabin. This was a thousand times worse than the predicament she had faced in the Viral Research Center. On the plane there were no safe zones.

In the darkness Joanna felt someone touch her arm. It was the pretty blond flight attendant. "Dr. Blalock, would you come with me, please?"

Joanna followed the flight attendant through the first-class cabin and into the cockpit. The flight attendant waited until Joanna was well inside, then closed the door behind her.

The captain of the plane turned in his seat and handed Joanna a headset. "Doc, what in the world is going on here?"

"We've got a terrorist aboard and he's about to release a nasty toxin," Joanna said, putting the headset on.

"Oh, shit," the captain cried. "What kind of toxin?"

Joanna ignored the question and spoke into the microphone of the headset. "Who am I talking to?"

"Jake," he replied. "Kitt says to remind you that this is not a secure line."

"Nothing is secure right now," Joanna said darkly. "And in five minutes it's going to get a hell of a lot worse."

"We've got an idea that might help you out of this mess."

"I'm listening."

"Have one of the flight crew go to the back of the plane and bust out a window," Jake instructed in an even voice. "The pressure in the cabin will rapidly drop and air will be sucked out through the window. During that time the yellow masks will drop down from overhead. Everyone is to put a mask on tightly. That way they'll be breathing fresh air that's enriched with oxygen."

Joanna rapidly thought through the plan, looking for flaws. She checked her watch: 11:56. Only four minutes left. "What do you use to break out the window?"

"Something that you can swing," Jake said. "Maybe a fire extinguisher."

The captain looked over quickly. "Those windows are made out of thick plastic. It'll take a lot of whacks to break one open."

Joanna asked him, "How many hits are you talking about?"

The captain shrugged. "Four or five. Maybe more."

Joanna went back to Jake. "The terrorist will hear the banging, Jake. He'll guess what's happening and set off the device."

"It's your best chance," Jake urged, his voice rising. "Even if the terrorist activates the device early, a lot of the stuff will be sucked out through the window."

But everybody will still get a big, whopping dose of the smallpox virus, Joanna was thinking. A dose big enough to kill a person ten times over.

Joanna's throat went dry as her fear heightened. "What does Wolinsky say?"

"That you'll decrease the load substantially by breaking the window."

"And?"

"That's all he said."

Joanna checked her watch again. "The passengers will still get a massive dose, and a lot of people will die."

"There's no other way."

There's got to be a way out, Joanna thought. *But where is it? Where? We have to do something without giving the terrorist a chance to release the smallpox virus. But what? And how?*

"Joanna, you've only got two—"

"Hold on!" Joanna cut in, and quickly turned to the captain. "Can you drop the cabin pressure and make those yellow masks come down without breaking a window?"

"We don't need a drop in pressure for those masks to drop down," the captain told her. "I can push a button and they'll come down pronto."

Joanna's eyes brightened. She went back to her headset. "All right, everybody, I think I know a way out."

"Wait just a moment," Kitt interceded. "The plan we gave you has been carefully—"

"It's my ass on the line, not yours," Joanna said sharply, then turned back to the captain and glanced once more at her watch: 11:57. "Now listen and listen closely, because our lives *are* going to depend on it."

42

Joanna hurried back to her seat and quickly buckled herself in. The alarm bell on the plane suddenly went off. Lights began to flash.

The PA system came on.

"Ladies and gentlemen, this is Captain Wiley from the flight deck. We've got double trouble up here," he said urgently. "We're rapidly losing cabin pressure, and smoke is coming from one of our engines. Do exactly as I tell you and we'll get this plane down safe and sound."

The movie was turned off. The overhead lights came on. The fear flooding through the passengers was palpable. Nobody moved.

"The cabin pressure is still dropping," the captain reported. "In just a moment the panels above you will open and yellow masks will come down."

On cue the overhead panels opened and yellow masks descended. They dangled on the ends of slender tubes.

"Place the mask firmly over your face and hold it tightly. This will ensure that you get maximum oxygen."

Another alarm bell went off.

Somebody screamed loudly, and others joined in. All the lights began flashing again.

"Please turn off all electronic devices," the captain urged. "Everything from computers to DVD players must be turned off. Otherwise they will interfere with our navigational systems. We've got to get this plane down—now!"

The jumbo jet abruptly went into a nosedive. The entire plane began to shake violently. Overhead compartments opened, and pieces of luggage and packages flew out. People screamed at the top of their lungs. The tray table in front of Joanna broke loose and scraped against her legs, abrading them. The woman next to her began throwing up.

Joanna held the yellow mask to her face so tightly it left indentation marks. The pressure within her ears kept building and caused a deep, stabbing pain. She tried to swallow, knowing that would relieve the discomfort, but she couldn't swallow because her throat was so dry.

The plane lurched, then seemed to veer to the left. Again the screams came.

"Somebody has an electronic device turned on and it's distorting our navigational signals. Turn the damn thing off!" the captain demanded.

The plane continued to shake and rattle, with more overhead compartments opening and spilling out their contents. A shoebox landed on Joanna's lap and she swept it away. She was now wondering if the captain's admonition about someone having a computer on was true. If it was, it could mean that the terrorist had pushed his fear aside and had activated the smallpox device. Joanna held the yellow mask against her face even more tightly than before.

The plane hit an air pocket and dropped precipitously. All passengers felt their bodies being lifted up, then being restrained by their seat belts. The dark-complected woman wearing the brightly colored dress didn't have herself buckled in securely. She flew up and struck her head on the panel above. Blood gushed from her scalp wound.

"My wife is bleeding badly," the Indian man cried out.

Joanna yelled over, "Is she conscious?"

The man spoke to his wife hurriedly. "Yes, yes. But her head hurts very greatly."

"Fold up your handkerchief and press it against the wound," Joanna instructed.

"But my handkerchief is not clean."

"Then use your necktie. Take it off, wind it up into a ball, and use it as a compress."

"Thank you, madam."

Joanna suddenly realized her mask was off. Quickly she returned it to her mouth and nose. *Too late,* she thought glumly. If the smallpox virus had been released, she had already sucked in more than enough to kill her.

"Folks, we're now passing through ten thousand feet," the captain announced over the PA system. "We're still having big trouble with one of our engines, so we're going straight into Memphis International Airport. Please keep your masks securely on. And remember, don't use any electronic devices whatsoever. It's going to be difficult enough as it is to get this baby down."

The steep descent continued. A service cart broke loose from its restraints and started banging against a forward bulkhead. The pretty flight attendant stood up, and with the help of a male flight attendant hastily secured the cart. They returned to their seats just as the plane hit an area of turbulence and again shook violently. Small bottles of whiskey flew into the air, where they stayed suspended before dropping to the floor. The person behind Joanna began to retch.

"Look!" a passenger seated in front of Joanna shouted, and pointed to the ceiling.

"Oh, my God!" another shrieked.

All eyes went to the panels above. White smoke was

seeping through, clouding the air. The pretty flight attendant quickly reached for a phone to contact the cockpit.

The PA system crackled loudly. "Folks, we'll be on the ground shortly. They are foaming the runway now to give us some extra protection. Because of the fire hazard, we're going to deplane by chute. Just follow the flight attendants' instructions and you'll be fine."

The white smoke grew denser in the cabin, making it difficult to see. Everyone held their masks on as tightly as possible. The passengers by the windows looked out and tried to see the ground below. The others sat stiffly and silently, some praying, some crying, all trying to hold their fear in check.

Joseph Malik gazed across at the terrorist but couldn't even make out his outline in the white, dense smoke. In an instant Malik unbuckled his seat belt and dropped to his knees, then quickly crawled on all fours to the rest rooms at the rear of the plane. Silently he got to his feet and tiptoed down the aisle toward the terrorist. A baby nearby cried out, and somewhere in the smoky fog a woman was praying. The plane hit a small pocket of turbulence and rocked back and forth, but Malik was able to maintain his balance.

Then he saw the terrorist glancing back over his shoulder, staring at him. Malik lunged for the man and wrapped his powerful arms around the terrorist's head and neck. With a sudden violent twist, Malik snapped the man's spinal cord. Quickly he picked up the laptop computer and hurried down the aisle, heading for the cockpit.

Moments later the plane landed with a loud thump, tilting to one side, then the other, before leveling off. The pilot applied the brakes and reversed the thrust of the engines, then came on the PA system. "Folks, our gauges up here in the cockpit show that the white stuff you see is really coming from a busted water hose, so we're just going to go right into the terminal and deplane in the usual fashion."

There was a collective sigh of relief before the cabin broke into loud applause.

Joanna saw Joseph Malik walking toward her, two laptop computers under his arm. He stopped and showed her the handles.

The red tags were still apart.

The smallpox device had not been activated.

The nightmare was over.

43

Haj Ragoub knew something had gone badly wrong. He stared at the six blinking dots on the giant television screen in his office. None of the planes were where they should have been. Four of the commercial jets had not left their West Coast points of origin, although it was hours after their scheduled times of departure. And the two planes that had taken off had landed prematurely.

"There has been a leak," Ragoub said sourly. "They found out about the planes."

"But who would have talked?" Sayed asked. "Only Khalil and Hassan knew about the planes at the Mojave facility. Khalil could not have betrayed us, because he is dead. And Hassan became ill and—" Sayed stopped in midsentence and spat at the floor. "Hassan! It had to be him."

Ragoub nodded. "They somehow got to Hassan. But there was also somebody else, somebody on the inside."

Sayed furrowed his brow, puzzled. "Why somebody else?"

"Because Hassan knew the planes but not the day of the big event," Ragoub explained. "The day of *naqba* was changed at the very last moment. Only the twelve brothers aboard the planes knew, and one of them talked."

Sayed thought about the twelve and tried to pick out the traitor. "Which one do you think?"

"Yusef Malik," Ragoub said with disgust. "He was the only American, the only one native-born. And he asked too many questions, now that I think about it. He asked far too many questions."

Sayed asked, "But how could he do it? He wasn't told about the change in our plan until he was at the airport. And I watched his every move while he was there. He dropped his cell phone, exactly as instructed."

"Maybe he had an extra cell phone with him and somehow managed to use it." Ragoub shook his head, angry at himself. "I should have been more suspicious of him, particularly when he kept pressing me for more details. It was an important clue, which I missed."

"And there was another clue that we both overlooked."

"Which was?"

"Malik's girlfriend," Sayed said. "The one who dressed like a Muslim during the day and behaved like a whore at night."

Ragoub nodded. "Malik needs to be killed."

"And the whore?"

"Her, too."

"You want it done now?"

"We'll attend to it later."

Ragoub turned off the television set, then placed the remote control on the floor and stomped on it repeatedly, smashing it into a hundred pieces. "And remember, my friend, if they know about the planes, they surely know about us."

"So what do we do next?"

"We run."

Ragoub hurried over to a wall safe and opened it. He removed fake passports and thick stacks of twenty-dollar bills, then stuffed them into his coat pockets. Quickly he scanned the office, searching for anything else of value that he needed to take. There was nothing. "Come, my friend!"

They left the office and went down the stairs, which led to the back of the electronics store. At the bottom Ragoub took a final, wistful look around. The shop had served him well. He had made well over a million dollars, all of it safely deposited in Middle Eastern banks. Too bad he couldn't stay longer and make another million.

The bell on the front door tinkled and more customers entered. *A gold mine,* Ragoub was thinking, *a virtual gold mine.* And he had to leave it behind. His eyes suddenly widened as he glanced at the last customers to enter. Two tall men wearing dark suits were showing their IDs to the Pakistani store manager.

Ragoub swiftly turned away and took Sayed's arm. "Federal agents are at the front."

Keeping their heads down, they walked out the back door and into a small parking area. Both men quickly surveyed the alleyway, looking for more federal agents but not seeing any. A delivery truck slowly approached. Sayed reached inside his coat and placed his hand on a semiautomatic weapon. Then he waited. The truck passed by.

"Quick!" Ragoub said urgently. "We'll use your car. They will have my license number."

They drove out of the alleyway and turned onto Brand Boulevard, where one of the lanes was closed for repairs. The afternoon traffic was heavy and creeping along at a snail's pace.

Sayed moved in and out of lanes, trying to make better time.

"Be patient," Ragoub advised. "Drive safely and obey all the laws. Now would not be a good time to be stopped by the police."

Sayed nodded. "The less attention we draw, the better."

"Exactly."

Sayed came to a busy intersection and waited for the light to turn green. "Should we go by your house?"

Ragoub shook his head. "The federal agents are sure to be there as well."

"But what about your wife and children?"

"They flew out last week," Ragoub said, and thought about his wife and daughters, who were now at their home on the Mediterranean. Soon Ragoub would join them. He would leave behind nothing of value. Everything he had here was leased—his car, his store, even the house he lived in.

Traffic began to move. Ahead were the entrances to the Glendale Freeway.

"Take the freeway," Ragoub instructed.

"Which way?"

"East to the Four-oh-five, then south to San Diego."

"What is in San Diego?"

"The Mexican border."

Sayed nodded, pleased. "And then home."

"Then home," Ragoub repeated. "But first we must stop briefly in the Sudan."

"Why the Sudan?"

"Because I have another surprise in store for America." Ragoub closed his eyes and rested his head on the back of the seat. "An even bigger surprise this time."

44

Joanna sat on the edge of her bed and dabbed Neosporin ointment on her abraded knees.

"We were lucky, Jake," she said somberly. "Very, very lucky."

"And you were very, very smart," Jake told her. "How did you think of that plan to fake an emergency landing?"

"It was the airline captain who gave me the idea," Joanna explained. "The moment he mentioned that he could make the yellow masks drop down by just pushing a button, I knew what we had to do. When I described the plan to the pilot, he didn't hesitate a second. And he put on one hell of a show."

"Was it as scary as it sounded?"

"Even more so," Joanna said. "Everybody froze in their seats when those masks came down. Then they did exactly as they were told. And that included turning off all computers, which was the main thing we wanted to accomplish."

Joanna stared across the bedroom, remembering back to the terrifying plane ride and the terrorist she had outsmarted. "You should have seen the eyes of that terrorist, Jake. They were cold as ice. They looked like black marbles."

Jake nodded. He had seen eyes like that before. Stone-cold, lifeless eyes that saw everything and felt nothing. Psychopaths had them. So did hit men. And so did terrorists.

"It was really frightening up there," Joanna said. "We were in deep descent and hitting air pockets and bouncing all over the place. The overhead compartments broke open and stuff was flying out and landing on people. It was like a nightmare."

Joanna placed bandages on her abraded knees, then stood and pulled up her blue jeans. Jake watched her tuck in a white, tight-fitting T-shirt. "But you were aware it was all a sham. Right?"

"Except when white smoke started filling up the cabin," Joanna said quietly. "That scared the daylights out of me."

"Where did the smoke come from?"

Joanna headed for the living room, Jake a step behind. "It wasn't smoke. The captain kept alternating the air-conditioning with the heating system, and that produced a dense mist. But to everyone on the plane, including me, it was smoke. We thought the plane was on fire." Joanna shivered. "Christ, it was so real."

"That pilot did one hell of a job, didn't he?"

Joanna nodded. "I'll fly with him any day of the week and twice on Sunday."

She thought back to the captain, who was the last one to come off the plane. He still had his airline cap on. His tie was centered; his shirt had barely a wrinkle. He was one cool customer. "You want a beer?"

"Oh, yeah."

Joanna went to the wet bar and came back with ice-cold bottles of beer and frosted mugs. She sat on the sofa next to Jake and expertly poured the beer into mugs, making sure there was minimal foam.

"Jake, I've got to get away," she said softly.

"I know."

"I mean really away," Joanna went on. "This last case really took it out of me. I don't have anything left in my tank. It's on empty."

"You'll snap back."

Joanna sipped her beer absently. "It's going to take time, Jake. A lot of time."

"How much?"

"Months."

"Jesus," Jake hissed under his breath. He took her hand. "What really happened up there?"

"Not just up there, but down here as well," Joanna said, her voice barely above a whisper. "I was trapped twice with one of the deadliest viruses known to man, and I had no way out. It was like your worst nightmare, except you didn't awake from this."

"It was kind of like dodging a bullet, wasn't it?"

Joanna smiled, but it quickly faded. "I guess."

"It'll pass."

"I guess," Joanna said again. But she knew those were just words. In her mind's eye she kept seeing Mack and the others with their faces hideously disfigured by smallpox. She took a deep breath and sighed. "We lost some good people, but we saved a lot of others."

Jake nodded. "For once the FBI did its job right."

"They got all the terrorists, huh?"

"All eleven, before they could activate their devices."

"Lucky," Joanna said, more to herself than to Jake. "So lucky."

"Lucky for now, but not for later."

"How do you mean?"

"I mean we only caught the little guys." Jake lit an unfiltered cigarette and inhaled deeply. "The terrorists in charge are still out there. They're still making their goddamn smallpox virus somewhere in the Sudan, and we're not going to do a damn thing about it. We'll just sit here and wait and hope nothing happens."

Joanna reached for the cigarette and puffed on it, then handed it back. "Hopefully they'll think of some way to get them."

"Don't bet on it."

The telephone rang loudly. Joanna ignored it and stared at the embers blazing in the fireplace. On the fifth ring the answering machine clicked on. It was Marshall Wolinsky from the CDC. He needed to talk with Joanna at her earliest convenience.

"What does he want?" Jake asked.

"He's going to ask me again to attend a conference in Atlanta," Joanna replied. "They're convening all the people involved in the smallpox outbreak. They want to document every aspect of it."

"Is this for the history books?"

Joanna shook her head. "They think it'll happen again, and they want to develop better techniques to respond to it."

"Are you going?"

"No way!" Joanna blurted out. "I've answered all of Wolinsky's questions by phone, and that's enough. I don't want to hear anything more about smallpox or blackpox or any other damn virus. I just want to get aboard that Air France plane tomorrow and start my year's leave of absence."

Jake's eyes widened. "A year!"

Joanna nodded. "I'll spend the first few months in France with my sister, Kate. We'll travel the countryside and eat cheese and drink wine and get fat. Then I'll float around the Greek islands for a while, maybe for a long while."

Jake smiled, remembering the Greek isles, where he and Elena had spent their honeymoon a thousand years ago. He tried to envision her face, but her features were blurred.

Again he wished he had been able to see her one last time, but the casket was sealed because she'd been so badly mangled in the car accident outside Athens. It all seemed like a lifetime ago.

He brought his mind back to the present. "Do you know anything about the Greek islands?"

"Only what I've read."

"Go to Rhodes," Jake suggested, putting his arm around her shoulder and drawing her close. "It's a special place."

"What makes it so special?"

"The flowers," Jake told her. "And the cool evening breezes and the wonderful outdoor restaurants. And then there's Lindos."

Joanna rested her head on his chest. "What's Lindos?"

"It's an ancient Greek temple that was built way up on top of a mountain," Jake described. "You've got to climb hundreds of steps to get to it. From there you can watch the sun rise into the sky, then melt into the blue sea. And that's when you see it."

Joanna gazed up at Jake. "See what?"

"An old Greek fisherman once told me that from there you can see the beginning and the end, and that's when you realize how lucky you are to be in the middle."

Joanna grinned. "I like that. What else did he say about Lindos?"

"He said that people who propose there are never refused."

Joanna looked up at Jake skeptically. "Did you just make that up?"

Jake gave her a wink and a smile.

"You're impossible."

Joanna rested her head back on his chest and stared at the fireplace. A blazing log cracked and split, sending up a plume of sparks and ashes that gradually settled down. Then the flame returned even brighter. "It's going to take time for me to put myself together again, Jake."

"I know."

"I'm talking about months and months."

"I know that, too."

"When things are right again, I'll call you from Europe."

"Is that a promise?"

Joanna snuggled up to him. "Keep your passport handy."

45

Haj Ragoub and Sayed sat in the backseat of the air-conditioned limousine, puffing on Cuban cigars and watching the countryside pass by. Outside, the afternoon temperature was 120 degrees. The heat in the Sudanese desert was so intense it reflected off the sand in waves.

"I don't understand how anyone can work in these conditions," Sayed commented. "It is like being in hell."

"Not really," Ragoub said. "Like our car, the plant is air-conditioned, and the Russian scientists have very comfortable living quarters. They are well paid and take frequent holidays in Europe."

"I hope they are carefully watched while they are away," Sayed said suspiciously. "You cannot trust Russians."

"Particularly these Russians," Ragoub agreed. "If they are willing to betray their own country, they will have no difficulty betraying us."

Up ahead they could see the large industrial complex. It seemed to jut up out of the flat desert. There were no villages to be seen, no other cars on the road. The limousine slowed as it passed a checkpoint guarded by a military vehicle. Then it speeded up again.

"I hope the new plan of yours does not include planes,"

Sayed broke the silence. "The Americans will be very watchful now."

"Not planes, my friend," Ragoub told him, pausing to examine the ash on the end of his cigar. "Not planes, but ships."

Sayed looked at Ragoub oddly. "Ships? How can you do it with ships?"

"Very easily," Ragoub replied. "Let me begin by asking you how many people in America take vacations on cruise ships."

Sayed shrugged. "I don't know."

"During peak season there are ten thousand people at a minimum on those ships," Ragoub went on. "These great ships leave the ports of Los Angeles and New York and Miami, sail for ten days, then return to port. Suppose—just suppose—we placed canisters of smallpox virus in the air-conditioning systems of these cruise ships and released them a day or two before they reached home port. At least ten thousand people would become infected and not even know it. Then they would travel to their homes all over America by plane or train or car. A thousand outbreaks of smallpox would occur at the same time. Imagine the fear and panic and chaos that would follow. America would collapse overnight."

"And that which did remain could easily be destroyed by other means," Sayed thought aloud. "A coordinated attack could wipe out the White House and the Pentagon in a single stroke."

"Now, given what we now know, would you prefer planes or ships to spread the virus?"

"Ships," Sayed said at once. "But how do we get our men aboard?"

"As we did with Khalil," Ragoub replied. "We have them

trained to work on air-conditioning and heating systems, then have them apply for jobs aboard the cruise ships."

Sayed licked his lips. "Can it really be done so easily?"

"All we have to do is pick a time, my friend."

The limousine stopped at the gate to the industrial complex. Ragoub pushed a button, and the darkened window next to him came down. An armed guard looked in and, recognizing Ragoub, gave him a half salute and waved the limousine inside.

"Who will be at this meeting?" Sayed asked.

"Our leader and his top two lieutenants," Ragoub answered. "The head Russian scientist will also attend and inform us of the progress he is making with his new research."

"What research is that?"

"He is trying to produce a smallpox virus that will be resistant to all known vaccines."

Sayed smiled malevolently. "A deadly virus that cannot be treated or prevented. A doomsday weapon."

"Yes, my friend. A doomsday weapon."

The limousine came to a halt in front of the main entrance to the plant. The two men got out of the car and immediately felt the oppressive heat bearing down on them. It was like being in an oven. They hurried up the steps and entered a large, well-appointed lobby, where the temperature was maintained at a comfortable seventy-two degrees. To the left was a cafeteria, to the right a string of small offices.

"Which way?" Sayed asked.

"Follow me."

As they approached a set of swinging glass doors, the entire building began to vibrate. Heavy furniture shook and rattled around. Framed pictures flew off the wall and crashed to the floor.

At first Ragoub thought it was an earthquake, but then he heard the swoosh of fighter jets overhead. He ran for the front door, but incendiary bombs were already exploding, one after another.

Ragoub and Sayed were knocked to the floor by the violent blasts. They managed to get to their feet just as another bomb detonated. Again they were thrown to the floor. Now the air was filled with smoke and dust, and everything darkened. For a moment there was quiet and they believed the attack was over. But another bomb landed near the front entrance and exploded with a loud roar.

Through the dimness, Ragoub and Sayed saw something bright and orange coming at them. They barely had time to scream before a giant ball of fire engulfed them.

46

As the Air France 777 leveled off at thirty-five thousand feet, Joanna leaned back in her first-class seat and tried to relax. Hours earlier she had given the eulogy at the graveside funeral for Mack Brown. Everything she had said about Mack was true, except for the way he died. The mourners believed her story that Mack had been killed by a virulent Ebola-type virus, although she could tell by the looks on certain faces that a few thought otherwise. But the matter had been hushed up and would stay that way. Nor would anyone learn about the terrorists' plans to release the smallpox virus in America. The public was told that the planes made emergency landings after it was discovered that there were terrorists aboard who were carrying lethal toxins.

The tale was being played up big by the news media, which credited the FBI with averting a disaster. Joanna shook her head, thinking about all the people and groups involved who were never mentioned. Marshall Wolinsky, the CDC, the CIA, Jake Sinclair. Maybe Jake most of all. Because if he hadn't gone out to the Mojave facility to tie up a loose end . . .

"Dr. Blalock?" A flight attendant holding a tray interrupted her thoughts.

"Yes?"

The flight attendant handed her a glass of wine. "Dom Perignon, 'seventy-eight."

"A good year?"

"The best."

"What's the occasion?"

"You are celebrating."

"What?"

"That I do not know." The flight attendant gave Joanna a square white envelope. "I was asked to give you this."

Joanna glanced at the envelope and saw that it was from Marshall Wolinsky. She sipped the delicious wine, feeling a twinge of guilt over her refusal to attend Wolinsky's conference in Atlanta. But enough was enough. Wolinsky would have to make do with her detailed typed report on everything that went on in the Viral Research Center.

Lori McKay would carry the report to Atlanta and sit in for Joanna. Lori was excited over that, but she was even more excited about the time she would be spending with Elliot Durr. Joanna wondered again if Lori had the insight and savvy required to run the large forensics department at Memorial. Probably. But only time would tell.

Joanna took another sip of wine and opened the envelope from Marshall Wolinsky. It contained a newspaper clipping.

Khartoum, Sudan—In retaliation for the attack on one of its merchant ships, Israeli warplanes today bombed a military-industrial complex in the northern Sudan, setting off an intense fire that destroyed the entire facility. The Sudanese government claims that the complex manufactured only pharmaceuticals and is calling for the United Nations to strongly condemn the attack. The United States is urging Israel to show restraint and not overreact.

Joanna smiled. Now there was one less loose end to worry about. She started to crumple the news clipping, then decided not to. She would show it to Jake while he was showing her Lindos—the place where proposals were never refused.

Author's Note

This novel is not science fiction. The threat of smallpox reemerging is very, very real. With the eradication of the disease in the late 1970s, the smallpox virus disappeared and was no longer present in nature. However, for the purposes of medical research, small stockpiles of the virus were kept frozen in two secure vaults, one located at the Centers for Disease Control and Prevention in Atlanta, the other at a Soviet research facility in Siberia. These were thought to be the only two places on earth where the virus existed. Unfortunately, this turned out not to be true. Secretly the Soviets were producing the smallpox virus in huge quantities and had an extensive, ongoing program to weaponize the virus. Intelligence experts estimated that the Soviet Union had the industrial capacity to produce the smallpox virus at a rate of a hundred metric tons per year. *That's 220,400 pounds of the virus annually by dry weight!* Although much of this immense stockpile was eventually destroyed, some of the smallpox virus remained unaccounted for. And with the dissolution of the Soviet Union and the defection of many of its top scientists, cultures of the virus were believed to have found their way into countries such as North Korea, Iraq, and Iran, all known to have ties to terrorism. Indeed, the

New York Times reported in December 1988 that at least five former Soviet bioweapons experts were working in Iran, which was paying them $5,000 per month rather than their previous $100 monthly salaries. Any of these scientists could have transported a freeze-dried culture of smallpox virus out of Russia in a vial that would fit easily in a shirt pocket.

The nightmare of all nightmares would be for a terrorist group to unleash the smallpox virus on an unprotected, unvaccinated population. In the United States the vaccination program was discontinued in 1972. Since the vaccine provides immunity for only ten years, virtually none of our citizens have any resistance to this virus, which is a superb bioweapon in that it is readily mass produced, is highly contagious, and has a kill rate of 30 percent. In fact, some strains, like the blackpox described in this novel, are universally fatal. The threat of a terrorist-induced outbreak of smallpox is of such great concern that the government has ordered 300 million doses of the smallpox vaccine to have on hand to protect the entire population and limit the number of cases if an outbreak were to occur. This preventive program is based on past experience in which smallpox was successfully eradicated by the process of vaccination and ring containment. Unfortunately, a similar program may be far less effective today for a number of reasons. First, there is a substantial segment of the population that cannot be vaccinated against smallpox because they have weakened immune systems and vaccinating them with a live virus would lead to a generalized disease simulating smallpox. People in this group would include those with HIV/AIDS, those receiving chemotherapy, and those with organ transplants who are taking immunosuppressive agents. In the United States alone, there would be millions of people who could not be vaccinated and thus would serve as reservoirs and transmitters of the virus. Second, an outbreak of smallpox would be impossible to control if it was caused by a new form of the smallpox virus. For example, the virus could be genetically engineered so that it contained new proteins on its surface that would not be recognized by the patient's immune system and thus be resistant to existing vaccines. In addition, genetic engineering could render the smallpox virus far more lethal by inserting genes that make it hemorrhagic and capable of causing the invariably fatal blackpox form of the disease. And finally, there is the horrendous scenario of combining the smallpox virus with the Ebola virus, producing a chimera that had the transmissibility of smallpox with the lethality of Ebola—an absolute doomsday virus that would kill more than 90 percent of its victims. The Russians were actually working on these terrifying projects under the code name Okhotnik ("hunter").

But Russia wasn't the only country performing research on weaponizing smallpox. As documented in Jonathan B. Tucker's *Scourge: The Once and Future Threat of Smallpox* (Atlantic Monthly Press, 2001), there is strong circumstantial evidence to indicate that both North Korea and Iraq have retained clandestine stocks of the smallpox virus for the purpose of military-biologic research. It is particularly chilling to note that the British Secret Intelligence Service reportedly spotted a Russian bioweapons expert in Baghdad in 1991; this scientist was known to work at Vector, the top-secret facility in Siberia that specialized in developing the smallpox virus for biological warfare. Now that Saddam Hussein has been ousted from power, one cannot help but wonder what has happened to the stockpile of smallpox virus Iraq was believed to have.

Thus the threat of weaponized smallpox is frighteningly real. This risk is succinctly summed up by a quote attributed to Dr. Kanatjan Alibekov, a senior Russian scientist at Vector who defected to the United States in 1992. Regarding the Soviet scientists who were involved with weaponizing smallpox, he said, "Thousands of people know how to work with the smallpox virus. Where these people are and what they're doing nobody knows. It makes me very nervous."

Leonard S. Goldberg, M.D.